# Eastward to Zion

OTHER BOOKS AND AUDIO BOOKS
BY SUSAN AYLWORTH

*Right Click*

*Zucchini Pie*

# Eastward to Zion

*a novel*

## Susan Aylworth

Covenant Communications, Inc.

Covenant

Cover image: *She Is Not Gone* © Daniel Gerhartz. For more information please visit www.danielgerhartz.com; *Storm Tossed Ship* © C. Wallace, courtesy of Hope Gallery

Cover design copyright © 2014 by Covenant Communications, Inc.

Published by Covenant Communications, Inc.
American Fork, Utah

Printed in the United States of America
Printing: June 2014

18 17 16 15 14    10 9 8 7 6 5 4 3 2 1

78-1-62108-376-4

For Henry Gale and Sarah Wills,
my ancestors whose story
inspired this one;


For Elizabeth Gale Kartchner,
their daughter and
my mother's mother's mother;


For my children and grandchildren,
whose love inspires me;


For Emma and Vaughn,
Adelaide, Sadie,
and Corbridge;


And always,
for Roger.

# Acknowledgments

DEEP APPRECIATION AND MANY THANKS are in order for my marvelous readers: professor colleagues Dr. Lynn Houston and Dr. Anne D'Arcy; authors and artists Heather B. Moore, Deborah Talmadge, Stacy Whetten Johnson, and Sue C. Lucas; readers extraordinaire Hugh and Anonna Hubbard and Patricia Kimsey; as well as Valus and Mariana White, Beth Larson, Jeanne Sparks, and all of you who read every word or just a little here and there. Thank you for your unselfish sharing and invaluable insights.

Thanks also to my friends in LDStorymakers and ANWA who have encouraged the writing of this book.

The section on the transpacific journey would not have been possible without the invaluable assistance of Gina Bardi, reference librarian at the J. Porter Shaw Library of the San Francisco Maritime National Historical Park. I also learned much about sailing from *Two Years Before the Mast*, the memoir of Richard Henry Dana Jr. The details of the desert crossing came from the wonderful docents at Sutter's Fort State Historic Park in Sacramento, California, and some excellent online sources.

I am deeply indebted to my cousin Kathleen Perkins Mitton; to Mildred Rhoten and Michael A. Karl; and to Carie Mae Gale Wilkins McGrath—all relatives whose records of the lives of Henry and Sarah Gale and their daughter Elizabeth gave me the impetus to write. I especially acknowledge my debt to Great-Uncle James Gale for his careful history of his parents and of his own desert crossing. I also gratefully acknowledge my husband, Roger, and also Paul, Carly, and Adelaide, who have shared my living space and changing moods during the creation of this tale. My deepest thanks to you all.

47. Ibid., 208.

48. See Metcalf, "Two Fatwas"; Sanyal, "Are Wahhābis Kafirs?"; Masud, "Apostasy and Judicial Separation."

49. The Urdu language grew and developed into a written language in the twelfth century. As such, it is one of the youngest languages of the Indian subcontinent and was greatly shaped by the language and culture of the Muslim conquerors of India. The Muslim conquerors initially introduced Arabic, Persian, and Turkish vocabulary into the standard spoken language of the northwest region of India. The dialect that evolved was called Urdu (language of the military camp). Not surprisingly, they used the Arabic script to write down this spoken language. The structure of Urdu is Indo-Aryan and is virtually identical to that of Hindi (Schimmel, *Islamic Literatures*, 126).

Arabic literary influence was predominantly filtered through the creative expression of Muslim art and court culture via Persian, which was greatly influenced by Arabic. In India, Persian, the language of court culture, held greater appeal than Arabic. Indeed, the most direct and obvious Arabic literary influences occurred with the adoption of Arabic words and expressions and the adoption of the Arabic script. This is not surprising because the overwhelming majority of Muslims who settled in India from points west were Persian and Afghani, although others were Turco-Mongolian and Arab. Urdu remained closely connected with Persian language and literary tradition. As such, it has always been closely associated with Muslim art and culture.

While the Urdu language may have originated out of the military camp, it quickly evolved into the language of poets, scholars, and Sufis. The rise of Islam throughout India can generally be attributed to the Sufis, who introduced religious teachings to the people. The Sufis used this spoken language as early as the thirteenth century in their sermons and religious tracts. Some of the first Sufis to do so were Mu'inuddin Chisti and Baha'uddin Zakariya. Biographers of the Ghaznavid court poet, Mas'ud-i Sa'd-i Salman (d. 1121), have asserted that he composed poetry in Arabic, Persian, and an early dialect of Urdu called Hindawī.

While Urdu was developing in the north, a separate and distinct development of Urdu literature occurred in the southern Indian region of the Deccan. From the thirteenth century, northern Muslim rulers made successful military campaigns in the south. As a result, Muslims began to settle in the south, and by the end of the fourteenth century, Urdu literature began to flourish in the court of the Bahmanid sultans. One of the first to write Urdu prose was 'Ainuddin Ganj al-'ilm, who focused on Sufi themes. See Schimmel, *Islamic Literatures*.

50. Metcalf, "Two Fatwas," 188.

51. For a similar response to Christian translations of the Qur'an into Swahili, see Lacunza-Balda, "Translations of the Qur'an into Swahili."

52. Metcalf, *Islamic Revival*, 210.

53. Rafiuddin Ahmed, *Bengal Muslims*, 30.

54. Ibid., 74–75.

# PART ONE:
## Meeting

## Chapter 1

*October 1852*

JAMES MARTIN SIGHED AND STOOD straight. His back ached fiercely. He tried to stretch some of the tautness from his muscles but quickly returned to his task of unpacking boxes. Working in Hogan's General Store had its challenges, but it was a grand improvement over the work that had brought him to this fair land, the work that caused his back such misery in the first place.

News of a gold strike in the Australian colonies had reached his family when James was a lad of only sixteen years. Work was hard to come by in their small village in Wiltshire County, England, and he had begged his father to consider all that the gold nuggets might buy. In a few weeks, the gold fever had overtaken even his practical father, who helped him gather the money for passage. James had bidden his family farewell and started for the port in Liverpool with just enough hard cash to book his voyage to Melbourne in Victoria Colony. He wouldn't need more—the gold was practically lying about, just waiting for him to pocket it.

How green he'd been! And how foolish. His only comfort was that a number of other fools were taken in just as he was. The foreman was at the dock when they disembarked, looking for the young ones and bragging about easy digs and rich pay. Neither James nor his companions realized they would be working for weekly wages on a rich man's claim, searched every evening before they left the mine, and watched over by armed guards while they slept in a bug-infested tent village along Burra Creek, allegedly to protect them from robbers and claim jumpers.

Nor had he spent his time picking up nuggets. Ah, no. This had been down-and-dirty hard-rock mining with a pick, a shovel, and a strong back, and most of what they'd mined was copper, not gold—a promising vein, though it all belonged to the wealthy owner of the mining company, and James had not so much as a fraction of an ounce for himself.

His wages were decent despite the back-breaking labor and the bitter disappointment. In something over a year, he had saved enough to pay back his travel to the mine and his purchases from the company. With what was left, he sailed to Sydney. He'd stepped off that second ship, walked into Hogan's, and met the kindly man who had given him work, renewed purpose, and his second family. James owed much to Elmer Hogan.

Just then Hogan entered the room. Still in his middle thirties but already portly and balding, Hogan, at a younger age, might have looked a bit like James, with bright blue eyes and brown curls. He announced himself with "Afternoon, Jimmy-boy."

"G'day, sir," James answered as he separated the tins of coffee from the tins of black powder with several small bottles. *Best not to confuse those.*

"I see the sewing things are gone from the counter. Did Mrs. Pembroke come by?"

"Aye, she did. I rang it up, and the ticket's there, by the cashbox. She's having a new dress made for Miss Celeste."

Hogan's face crinkled in a grin. "That red-haired daughter of hers will look smashing in the green calico, don't ya think, lad?"

"Aye." James grinned back, enjoying Hogan's joke. "But ya know I won't be looking for a spoiled and pampered filly like Miss Celeste Pembroke."

"No, I don't s'pose ya will. So, what do ya s'pose ye'll be lookin' for? A fine lad like ya, now turned twenty . . ."

"Ye sound like my dear mother, God rest her soul." James felt tears threatening. "She was always pestering my brother, Sam, to be about finding someone and settling down."

Hogan cocked an eyebrow. "So did Sam settle down?"

"Aye, sir, the year before I left Box, in Wiltshire. He married the vicar's daughter, who gave him a strong son straightaway."

"He did well for himself then."

"Aye. They seemed happy enough when I last saw them, and their recent letter tells me young Sam has a sister. They're calling her Eliza."

"A pleasing name, Eliza."

"Aye, I s'pose it is," James answered, choosing not to tell Hogan that a neighbor back in Box had called his fractious mare Eliza. James always imagined a girl with a horseface whenever he heard it. He lifted another box of baking soda and then remembered. "Ah, sir? That gentleman from Ballarat came in again. He bought a cravat, suspenders, and gloves to go with the breeches and shirt ya sold him yesterday. The ticket's there beside the register."

Hogan patted his expanding waistline. "A fine thing, that. If he keeps coming back, we'll soon have everything he made in the gold fields without breaking our backs to get it."

"Aye, that's the truth," James said, moving to straighten the farming tools leaning against the wall.

"Was there anyone else in while I was away?"

"No, sir. Just those two, but then ye weren't away long."

"No, I was not, and this is hardly our busiest time of the day. We had plenty of traffic this morning, and there'll be more when folks get off the ship that's just in from Southampton."

"A ship is in? I hadn't heard."

"Aye. It docked a few minutes ago. Why don't ya run on down to Farnham's? Ya can see if the nails and coffee mills I ordered have arrived. There should be a few papers of them tiny needles as well, the kind Mrs. Pembroke's ladies like for their sewing."

"Aye, sir. I'll check right away." James untied the front of his clerk's apron and then reached behind to loosen it. "Is there anything else I should take care of?"

"Nah. I think that'll do it. Go ahead and check out the disembarking passengers while you're there. Just get back in time to help me with the crowd when those passengers begin arriving." He winked, and they shared a smile.

Both knew it was unlikely they'd be crowded with patrons.

"See ya soon, sir." James left his apron behind the counter and waved as he left, taking long, purposeful strides.

"Have a good walk."

Spring had brought pleasant, warm temperatures to Sydney. The cold breeze that blew down from the Blue Mountains had finally let up, and it was too early yet for the blast-furnace heat that would come with the summer sun, tempered—thank goodness—by Sydney's proximity to the sea. James could taste the pleasant tang of the salt-sea air.

A light rain had fallen the night before and washed away the dust of the city, leaving the air clean enough that he could smell the fresh, sweet bloom of boronia flowers. Just then a flock of cockatoos flew overhead, squawking, and James grinned. This was not Wiltshire County.

It had taken some time to understand how the Southern Hemisphere's backward seasons worked, and to grow accustomed to trees and flowers and wildlife so different, but James had come to love his adopted country. These weeks in late October as the spring warmed were among the loveliest of the year.

"G'day, Martin."

James turned at the sound of a familiar voice.

"G'day, Welsh," he answered, smiling in spite of himself.

"I see ye're still playin' at being a merchant." Big Edmund Welsh caught up to him on the boardwalk and threw a beefy arm around his shoulders.

"Aye, I s'pose I am. And ye? What're ye up to these days, Edmund? Another gold strike in the Blues?"

"Ye heard, then!" Welsh boomed, and James shrank inside, anticipating the recitation of all Edmund was doing and seeing and buying.

Several minutes later as Ed's recitation wound down, James said, "Good for ya. If ye'll excuse me now, I need to stop at the warehouse to see if our order's in."

"Go, then, and be a merchant. When ye decide ye want to do a real man's work in the ore, I'll have a place for ye."

"Thank ya. I'll remember that, but the gold has never loved me as it loves ya."

"Ye just need to give it more of a chance."

James grinned and clapped his friend on the shoulder. "I'll let ya take yer chances. God be with ya."

"And with ye, James." Ed walked a few steps and then called back, "Perhaps ye'll be lucky in love, mate."

James chuckled. "Aye. Perhaps I will."

James turned the corner, sending a spiny echidna scurrying. *The poor thing looks like a large leather work glove with spikes.* He smirked at the thought. He came out beside the docks. In the distance, he could see the three-masted clipper that had been tied up and whose cargo was now being unloaded. Amidships, a plank had been run out, and the passengers were gathering on deck, preparing to debark.

James quickened his step, knowing Hogan wouldn't mind if he took extra time to watch the new immigrants come ashore. In fact, his employer often arranged James's trips to the shipping warehouses at around debarkation time. He knew James's affinity for the new people—especially the young ladies—and he trusted him to make up any missed work time. James smiled, once again whispering thanks for the blessing of Elmer Hogan. The man had changed his life.

As he came alongside the clipper, he couldn't help noticing an unusual number of unaccompanied women. Just then, he saw Matthew Sutton coming from the colonial shipping office. Employed by the colonial secretary of New South Wales himself, Sutton met each passenger ship, checking in each immigrant by name.

"G'day," Sutton said as James approached.

"G'day, mate," James answered happily. "I can't help noticing an unusual mix of pastel colors today."

"Aye. Seems we've a shipment of mail-order brides for the miners in the Blues."

James's expression fell. "Don't tell me they're all spoken for?"

"Not all. Some poor girls have come looking for work, and a few others were recruited to work for the Pembrokes."

"The Pembrokes, y'say?"

"Aye. I heard Mrs. P. sent one of her mister's business stewards to Southampton. She needed new servants after dismissing the last bunch all at once. He hired them on contract and paid their way here. Seems Mrs. P. didn't think the local riffraff were good enough."

"Doesn't surprise me."

"I've been thinking I might talk her out of one of them," Sutton said.

"Why? Haven't ya enough mouths to feed?" He thought of the wife and five small children who filled his friend's pew at church.

"That's just it, mate. There's going to be another this year, and the wife is having a hard time. If I can afford it, I'd like to get her some help."

"And here I was, just looking for someone to pay court to," James said, hoping to lighten the mood.

"Honestly, James, I don't see why ye're in such a hurry." Matthew dropped his voice in a conspiratorial whisper. "Ye've only twenty years, man. Have a little fun. Sow some wild oats. Ye'll settle soon enough, and once ye're settled, ye're done. Take it from someone who knows."

"Aye, friend. I know," James answered. He looked long and hard at Sutton, who had only recently passed his thirtieth birthday. Matthew, though still handsome, was already graying at the temples and crinkles were beginning to show around his eyes. No doubt the strain of providing for a rapidly growing household had taken a toll, even on this educated man who worked with his mind, not his back. It was a lesson James could scarcely avoid. Still it was not his answer.

"I appreciate yer advice," James said, still whispering, "but ya have to know I'm not the kind for sowing wild oats. I long to find a proper companion, someone to love and cherish who can be my partner and helpmeet. I hope to raise a family like yers."

Matthew slapped his shoulder. "I feared ye'd say that. Very well. Have a look as they come ashore. I'll be checking the new brides in first, and I'll give you a sign when those who are unspoken for start debarking. Ye might find some bawdy women among them." He grinned.

"My thanks, Matthew." James took a place a little away from the gangplank and leaned against a piling to watch.

Most of the debarking passengers, as usual, were men. James found himself watching, sizing them up, as they queued on the deck behind the departing women. A would-be miner hoping for a strike? A banker coming to take advantage of the miners' wealth? A baker, perhaps, come to feed the hungry colonists and perform the old alchemy of turning wheat into gold? Certainly there were many of them, and as polyglot a group as ever he'd seen.

James turned his attention back to the brides as they came down the gangplank one by one. Each stated her name and showed her papers, eyeing the wagons waiting nearby to haul them out to the gold fields. A minister in clerical collar stood at the first wagon, prepared to do his duty as soon as husband and wife met in person.

As James watched the women wind their way to the plank and down to the deck, he realized that many among them may well have been England's bawdy women, talked into this long trip in the hope of finding stability and something better for the future as their youth faded. He shrugged. At least they weren't convicted bawds. It had been twelve years since the last prison transport landed in Sydney, though other ships still brought convicts to the colony in Western Australia.

Some of the younger girls looked like half-starved waifs; they probably hoped a miner was good for three square meals a day. He hoped that all of them—bawds, young widows, or starving girls—would be content as miners' wives, but it was clear there was nothing here for him. Briefly, he wondered if he shouldn't be moving on to the warehouse.

As he turned away, he noticed a young woman still on the deck. He turned back to get a good look at her. A second glance revealed nothing exceptional. She was of average height and average-to-slim build, and she wore a simple, tailored dress of dove gray. Her hair was shoulder length, styled up on the sides in the current fashion—a medium mousey brown color, although it shone like spun honey when she moved into the sunlight. Her face was a delicate oval, and her features were even and soft, not the prettiest but neither was she plain. Then she caught his eye, smiled like the radiant sun bursting over the sea at dawn, blushed, and dropped her gaze.

James was smitten.

Just what it was that caught him, he couldn't rightly say. Maybe it was her softness, surrounded by all that brassy female harshness and desperation. Maybe it was the fact she had instantly smiled at him or perhaps the flush that followed. Maybe it was the way the soft gray of her dress brought out the pink in her blushing cheeks. Whatever had woven the spell, James was well and surely caught.

He stepped back into the shadows along the wharf, impatiently tapping his foot while he waited for the girl to work her way toward the gangplank. Was she already promised to some burly miner in the Blues? If not, who was she and where was she going? He couldn't imagine her here all alone, unescorted, without some kind of promise of work or show of commitment. She didn't seem that kind.

The line wound on interminably, and James was beginning to wonder how much time he would have to make up to Mr. Hogan when the girl finally came to the top of the gangplank. Six, then five more women to go . . .

He worked his way through the crowd until he stood behind Sutton's elbow. Three to go . . . just two now . . .

"Well, then, that's the end of the brides for the Blue Mountains," Sutton declared, and James released a breath he didn't know he'd been holding. "Reverend, that's your full count."

"Thank you, sir," the reverend responded. "Ladies, if you'll load up, please, we'll be on our way." There was a bit of shuffling and scurrying, but James missed it. He had already turned his full attention to the young lady just one away from approaching Matthew. He could tell from her heightened color and lowered eyes that she was keenly aware of him and fighting not to look up. James couldn't help grinning, knowing he had affected her. He hoped it was nearly as much as she had affected him.

The girl before her finished her paperwork and walked off. The one in gray stepped up and presented her papers.

"Name?" Sutton asked.

"Eliza Wells," she answered, her voice strong and clear.

"Full name?" Sutton repeated.

"It's Mary Elizabeth, sir, but I'm called Eliza." James thought she must be making a studied effort to look so intently at Matthew without ever once glancing toward him.

"Where d'ya come from, Miss Wells?"

"In the countryside, sir, a couple o' leagues outside of Castlebar in County Mayo."

"Ah, you're Irish, then," Matthew observed.

"Aye, sir. Is that a problem?" A flash sparked in the girl's eyes.

"Not at all. We've plenty of Irish here." Sutton gave the girl a fatherly smile and made a quick perusal of her papers. "Ye're here to work for the Pembrokes, then?"

"Aye."

"Very well. Welcome to Australia," he said and then called, "Next!" The girl moved on, still determinedly looking away from James.

"Miss? May I help ya with yer satchel?" James asked, approaching her.

She refused to meet his eyes, looking determinedly at his collar. "I do not speak with strange men, sir." The color was rising in her cheeks.

He chuckled. "I'm a strange one, I'll grant ya, but I'm also a friend of the official who checked ya in. If ya want to walk back a step, he can perform a proper introduction."

"No, thank ye," the girl said, rather more stiffly than James thought necessary. She took a long, deep breath and turned away.

Impatience sneaked up on James. "Look, miss, I'm not tryin' to give ya trouble. I thought from the way ya smiled at me—"

"I . . . I didn't smile at ye." She looked up at him and then quickly back down at her feet, blushing furiously. "I just smiled, and ye . . . ye happened to be there."

James nodded. "Ah, I see." He let his tone tell her how little he believed her protests. "So, since I just happen to be here now, is there somethin' I can help ya find?"

"Aye," the girl said. She seemed relieved to have something to talk about. "Ye could do me a service if ye—What's that sound? Is someone ringing bells?"

"No, miss. Those are bell birds. They sing that two-toned pitch."

She shook her head. "Birds that chime like bells. What a strange place this is."

"Aye, miss. It's surely that, but ye'll find ya rather like it after a time. Now, what was it ya wanted help with?"

"I'd be obliged if ye can point out Mrs. Pembroke."

"Aye, Mrs. P.," James said, looking around for that august presence. Finally, he spotted her coach. "There she is. That's the carriage from Pembroke House arriving now."

"Very well. Thank ye." Eliza straightened and looked pointedly away.

James couldn't keep from grinning. If she was working this hard to avoid him, Miss Eliza Wells must be as attracted as he was.

The coach pulled up, and James stepped ahead, opening its door. He recognized Cooper, who sometimes picked up Mrs. Pembroke's orders. "Cooper," he said, trying to sound as formal as possible, "this is Miss Eliza Wells, just arrived from Southampton. Miss Wells, this is Cooper, from Pembroke House."

The two nodded to one another, but Eliza stayed back a step, and James could see fear edging about her eyes. It seemed odd, but then he suddenly understood. The girl was in a strange place and didn't recognize anyone. If the area she came from was even smaller than his village, she must have little experience with strangers. How could she even be certain that he and Cooper were who they said they were? Just then the Pembrokes' steward came up behind her with three other young women. Eliza relaxed, taking her place among the group as they climbed inside the coach.

As Cooper closed the door, James asked, "Cooper, d'ya think I might call on these ladies? Just to welcome the newcomers, of course. See if they have any special needs we might fulfill from the store 'n all?"

Cooper shook his head. "Mrs. Pembroke won't be wantin' ye to distract her help."

"Oh, I won't be a distraction. Is there a time when I might come by?"

"The household servants who aren't cooking are free Sunday after morning services, but Mrs. Pembroke prefers they spend their time studying the good book." Cooper, out of view of the women, wrinkled his nose whenever he discussed Mrs. Pembroke's preferences, and James fought to keep a straight face.

"I understand. Is there another time, then?"

"The girls are off on Thursday evenings after tea, say half past six?"

"That sounds good. I'll call then." He looked back to the carriage window, where he could barely see Eliza stuffed in among the others. "Is that all right with ya, Miss Wells?"

The coachman released the brake. Just before the coach pulled out, Eliza looked James in the eye and nodded.

"Glory!" James slapped his thigh.

"I take it the lady said yes?"

James turned to see Big Ed. "At least she said I can call."

"That's a start then, isn't it?"

James grinned. "Aye, mate, it just may be."

Big Edmund Welsh clapped him on the back. "Let's get to the warehouse and pick up that order so ye'll have a job to support yer courtin' habit."

"Aye, let's be goin' then."

"It's as I said," Ed spoke as they walked. "Ye'll be lucky in love."

"I hope ye're right, mate." As James walked, he murmured, "Eliza Wells." He found it was a pleasing name after all.

# Chapter 2

ELIZA CAREFULLY PLACED EACH DISH in Mrs. Pembroke's extensive cupboards. Then she washed her hands, drying them on a kitchen towel instead of her apron. This was one of several dozen rules she had learned in the past three weeks, each gained from a mistake she had vowed never to make twice. Mrs. Pembroke demanded a great deal from those who served her, but she seemed evenhanded in passing out both reprimands and compliments. Though Eliza had earned both, her ledger tipped toward the positive.

Her duties finished for the day, she removed her apron and prepared to retire to the top floor, where she lived with the other unmarried women. She was beginning to settle in.

At first she'd been grateful merely that the earth beneath her didn't lurch and pitch. She'd known she might be sick at the beginning of their travel, but she'd never expected to be violently ill throughout the trip. She doubted she'd kept down more than one meal a day, and if it hadn't been for her constant prayers to Mother Mary and Saint Elizabeth, she may not have managed even that. When she arrived safely on the dock in Sydney Harbor, she vowed never to step foot on a ship again.

She had left Ireland knowing she would never return. Having never found her sea legs in all her weeks of travel, she thought it would be easy to get used to being on land, yet that was an adjustment as well. Mrs. Pembroke wasn't patient when she or one of the other new girls stumbled because they thought they felt the ground heave.

Then there had been the adjustment to the work. Sarah, who had made the trip from Southampton with her, had very nearly been dismissed after forgetting a second time to put the lid back on the sourdough starter. Neither Mrs. Pembroke nor her housekeeper, Mrs. Biel, had any patience for a mistake made twice. Eliza had struggled to learn from every mistake made by anyone at Pembroke House.

And such a house! She had never seen anything like it. Some of the women back home had talked about mansion houses in Castlebar, but she had never seen one. All this space and elaborate furniture for five people? Mrs. Pembroke lived here with her mister, who actually spent most of his time at his mines; then there was their son, Michael, and their spoiled daughters, young Augusta and marriageable Celeste. It seemed a shame that one small family should have so much when Eliza had seen families of ten and twelve living in two-room soddies. She thought she could probably stuff her whole parish back home into just the first floor of Pembroke House with room left over for guests and cousins from the city.

During the first week, Mrs. Biel had tried each of the girls at multiple tasks until she came to an arrangement she found most fitting. Now each had a daily list of chores. Molly, the other Irish girl who had traveled from Dublin, was the upstairs maid. Pretty English Sarah, who had cooking experience, worked in the kitchen alongside Elsie, the cook. Eliza and Dolly divided up the daily chores of washing and drying the family's fine china, keeping the multiple fireplaces going (although, thank heaven, they had young Will and Charlie to bring in the wood and carry away the ashes), and keeping the downstairs common rooms clean and ready to receive visitors.

Eliza's favorite job was polishing the grand piano. She tried to be working nearby whenever the younger daughter, the one the family called Gussie, had a lesson, and she found she was slowly learning to read music just by watching and listening. Sometimes, in her few private moments, she even placed her fingers in the positions that Augusta had been taught. Had the good Lord given her a different life, Eliza would have loved to play that beautiful instrument. She sighed.

"Welcome, Eliza," Molly called as she reached their room. "Is Dolly with ye?"

"Not yet. She was still finishing when I came up the stairs. She'll be along soon, though."

"Sarah's not here, either. Perhaps we can have a word?"

Eliza sat on the edge of the bed she shared with Molly. "Aye, go ahead then."

Molly looked around uncomfortably and lowered her voice. "It's about Mass."

"Oh. Aye," Eliza answered. Of the flies in her ointment, this was one of the most vexing. Mrs. Pembroke called their faith "heathen idol worship" but considered herself broad-minded enough to allow Catholic servants to attend Mass if they were willing to give up their evening meal on Thursdays and if someone was willing to clean up after the family meal alone. Once the kitchen was cleaned, no one was allowed in it again until Elsie came in the next day to start the family's breakfast. No one, save the mister himself, ate anything outside of the scheduled meals.

Dolly had agreed to do the wash-up on Thursday in exchange for Eliza taking over the disgusting twice-daily job of cleaning the downstairs privy chamber—which only the members of the family were permitted to use—and carrying the waste to the outhouse. So the past three weeks, Eliza and Molly had made the weekly Thursday trek up the hill to St. Patrick's. Though they were hungry in body, they were eager for the spiritual nourishment they didn't find at Mrs. Pembroke's Presbyterian Church, where they were made to sit through services each Sunday. Of course, Eliza always got a glimpse of James Martin beside the Hogans, but James was another of the flies in her ointment. She sighed. "What about Mass, Molly?"

"It's just . . . I get so hungry, y'know?" Molly rubbed her substantial stomach.

Eliza sighed. "Aye, I know."

"It seems wrong that she makes us go hungry—"

"Sure 'n 'tis our own choice, Molly, not hers. We knew what the hours were. If we leave an hour early on Thursdays, it's our choice to give up evenin' tea."

"But every place that sells food—at least, every one near us—is closed by the time we leave Mass, and we really ought to be able to eat somethin'."

"Aye, I think we ought, but giving up a single meal won't kill either of us." She refrained from mentioning that Molly might do well to go without a meal or two.

Molly looked around and dropped her voice still further. "I've been thinkin', maybe if we're careful, we could sneak into the kitchen after Mass, and—"

"Don't even think it. Ye'd be caught for certain, and Mrs. Pembroke would have ye out the door before ye could finish swallowin'. Ye know how she feels about servants who steal—"

"Why is it stealin' to take what we'd eat if we were here?"

"*Because the mistress forbade it.* Really, Molly, if ye can't skip yer tea on Thursday, see if Cook will let ye pocket a biscuit after lunch. If ye've permission —"

"I've tried that." Molly spoke too loudly then looked around and dropped her voice. "Elsie says the missus is very particular about people not carryin' food about or stowing it anywhere but the kitchen. She's fearing the pests, y'know? There's really no option but—"

"Well hello, girls. What's going on in here?" Dolly entered with Sarah just behind her.

"We were just talkin'," Molly said.

"We were speakin' of a girl we know," Eliza said. "She's a servant in a rich house, like us, and she's on the verge of gettin' herself into serious trouble."

"Is she in a family way?" Dolly asked with a show of eagerness. It seemed she was glad of the gossip.

"No!" Molly cried.

"Nothing like that," Eliza assured them, "but we'll have to warn her she'd best be *very careful.* Jobs this good aren't easy to come by, and if she is dismissed from a respectable house, no one else will risk taking her on. She could find herself on the street." Eliza spoke the words quite pointedly as she looked at Molly, who flushed and dropped her eyes.

With the other women now present, there would be no more talk of this tonight. Eliza dressed for bed. The girls chatted for a time, but soon the lights were out and all quieted. To avoid drawing the scorn of the other girls, Eliza lay in her bed murmuring her prayers to Mary the mother of God, asking her and dear Saint Elizabeth to please bless Molly to avoid anything foolish. Then she begged them once again to help her, please, to know what to do about James.

Ah, James. She wished she could ask her mother's advice, for James was surely a bug in her butter. He wasn't the most handsome man she'd ever met, but his brilliant blue eyes and sharply etched dimples made her catch her breath every time he smiled. He wasn't the strongest either, though she had no doubt of it when he told her of the hard work he'd done in the mines. He certainly had the muscle. It was what he *was*, not what he wasn't, that was causing her grief. He was kind and caring and fully respectful of the distance she had set between them—and he was a Protestant—a committed, serious Protestant with nothing to be done about it.

She should send him away, but it was difficult not to smile when she caught his eye in church or to very nearly run home from Mass on Thursdays to find him sitting near the servants' entrance in the Pembrokes' side yard, waiting just for her. For three Thursdays in a row, he had come to visit with the household ladies. Then, shortly after arriving last week, he'd asked permission to court Eliza. From then until Mrs. P.'s curfew, Eliza sat with James on the side porch swing as they chatted and learned more of one another's lives.

She smiled to herself, recalling their first visit. He had come pretending to be a one-man welcoming committee, but no one was fooled. He had eyes only for Eliza, and it was only minutes before Molly started talking about "Eliza's beau" and asking him the questions Eliza herself should have been asking—if she'd been able to form a sentence.

She had been no more comfortable with him that first Thursday than when they'd met at the docks. She was stumbling and foolish, tongue-tied and blushing, and yet he seemed unwilling to let her withdraw into herself. He had teased her out of her shyness with Molly and Sarah and Dolly all looking on, and then he had returned specifically to call on her, all pretense gone. He was kind and charming, and he kept coming back. And now, if he kept coming . . .

But she couldn't allow that. Could she? At the same time, how could she send him away when he'd never done anything except be kind? The problem was in what the two of them could never be together—a Catholic and a Protestant unequally yoked, just as the Gospels warned. She shuddered. She was weaving a sticky web just by seeing him.

*  *  *  *

Two evenings later, Eliza and Molly were walking home from Mass when Molly's stomach growled loudly. "Law!" she declared. "My stomach thinks my throat's been cut."

"Sure, 'n I'm hungry too," Eliza said, "but we can't forget—"

"Stop yer preachin'. I hear ye plain enough." A walleroo scurried out of the bushes beside them and bounced across the street like a miniature kangaroo.

"Ye shouldn't be so loud, Molly. Ye scared the little fella."

"Aye, and he scared me too," Molly grumbled.

They came around the corner above Pembroke House to find James waiting. Eliza had to contain herself to keep from breaking into a run. "Come on. Let's go a little faster. Ye'll stay with us, won't ye?"

Molly pouted but nodded. "It'd be easier if I had a beau of my own, but aye. I'll stay."

Mrs. Pembroke's rule said the help could only receive callers on the porch or in the side yard and only if chaperoned. "I'll have no illicit behavior at this house," she had declared, and the girls never questioned she'd follow through with the implied threat.

They soon reached the porch. James said a quick hello to Molly and greeted Eliza by solemnly shaking her hand.

Molly said, "I think I'll just look at the stars awhile."

James grinned gratefully and sat next to Eliza on the porch swing. Then he produced a small package wrapped in paper. "I've a small gift for ya, Eliza."

"Ye know I can't accept—"

"Ya can accept this one," he said. He untied the string; a pair of warm meat pies sat between in the wrapper, so fragrant Eliza thought she could almost eat the scent.

"Oh, they smell delicious! James, how did ye—?"

"When we sat here together last week, I heard yer stomach growl."

Eliza blushed. "I'm sorry. I—"

"After I left, I got to thinkin' about what time ye leave for Mass and when Mrs. Pembroke serves tea. When Elsie came to pick up the grocery order, I asked if what I suspected was true, and she told me the two of ya go hungry every Thursday. Is that true?"

"Aye, sure it is, but I can't have ye feeding me, James."

"I brought two meat pies. I thought we could share a meal."

Eliza saw Molly a few yards away. "James, if ye don't mind, I'd like to share mine with Molly. She is powerful hungry. She went without dinner too."

James's expression fell. "How foolish of me. I never thought." He called out, "Molly girl, come here. I've food for ya."

When Molly arrived, smiling brightly, James handed one pie to Eliza and the other to Molly. "I already ate a full dinner," he said. "Missus Hogan fed me well. I thought we could share, but I can't let ya go hungry, Molly."

"We can't eat in front of ye," said Eliza.

"I can!" Molly made the sign of the cross and began eating greedily.

"I s'pose we can." Eliza chuckled as she ducked her head and gave thanks. Then she turned to her benefactor. "Thank ye, James. This is a kindness."

James's lips twitched. "It seemed the Christian thing to do."

Eliza smiled in turn. "Aye, but we can't have ye doin' it again . . ."

"Aye, we can," Molly interrupted. "What if we each gave James a coin when he comes on a Thursday? He can use them to buy a pie for us the Thursday following. It will be just like askin' him to deliver the groceries from his store."

"I'd be happy to do that for ya," James said. "Eliza?"

She couldn't think of any reason why it wouldn't work—beyond the fact that she ought not to see him at all. "Aye," she said. "Thank ye."

An hour later the couple still sat on the swing while Molly, no longer fearing starvation, waited patiently in the yard.

"And that's when ya promised yerself ya'd never go to sea again," James said, surmising the end of Eliza's tale as she recounted her long and miserable voyage.

"Aye, that was when I promised. Of course, the sea has been a major part of my life from the beginning. I told ye that part, didn't I?"

"I don't think ya did."

"I was born on the sea, or at least, aboard a seagoing vessel."

"No. Truly?"

"Aye. My parents were a young couple—I'm their firstborn—and they were traveling to where Da had work on a farm. I was born on the vessel in Mayo Harbor just about an hour or so before the ship reached port."

"It must have been very difficult for yer ma, giving birth on a rockin' ship like that."

"Aye, sure'n it was. She always said—" Eliza stopped, her eyes full of tears, her voice choked with emotion.

James cleared his throat and tried changing the subject. "When was that, exactly?"

Eliza smiled through tears. "Are ye tryin' to divine my birthday, James Martin?"

He smiled. "Aye, that I am."

"It was nineteen years ago tomorrow, since ye asked. I was named for Saint Elizabeth because I was born on her saint's day, November 5, in 1833."

"Well then, happy birthday, Eliza Wells."

"Thank ye. And when is yer birthday?"

"I turned twenty last summer, July 15."

"So ye're just a year and a half older."

"Approximately so."

"My ma always said—" Eliza stopped, blinking hard.

"Ah, Eliza, I'm so sorry. I should have known when ya didn't speak of her." James laid his hand atop Eliza's. "If it helps, I understand. My mother passed just a year before I left home. She took a fever and was gone within days."

"Mine . . ." Eliza gulped and started again. "Mine went almost as I left," she said, "and I still haven't forgiven myself for leavin' her."

James patted her hand. "Tell me?"

"She took ill the day I was to leave. I wanted to delay, but she said no, it was minor and I should go ahead as planned. Da's letter caught up to me in Southampton. He told me she died suddenly the day after I left, and she was askin' for me at the end."

"He shouldn't have told ya that," James said, solemnly shaking his head. "Ya couldn't do a thing about it then, and knowing it didn't help ya any."

"Da probably thought it would be a comfort to know that Ma was thinkin' of me." Eliza wiped tears.

"I didn't mean to speak ill of yer father. It's just . . . well, ya don't seem comforted."

"No, I don't s'pose it was a comfort, after all." They sat together while Eliza wiped more tears. "I miss her so."

"I know," he answered. "I miss mine too."

That evening as she lay in bed saying her prayers, Eliza said her thanks for James's kindness and compassion. Then she asked once again what she should do about his place in her life. She was becoming closer to James Martin, the Protestant. She had even confessed these feelings to Father Michael, who warned her what it would mean to marry out of the faith. "If he wants to be commit to the true faith, I'd like to meet this beau of yours," her priest said, "but if he remains stubborn, ye could be consigning your soul to hell."

Eliza sighed and turned tear-filled eyes into her pillow. One way or the other, this could only end in sadness.

# Chapter 3

"So it's another typical Thursday evening for ya?" Hogan asked as James hung out the Shut sign. "Ye'll buy three meat pies or Cornish pasties and be headin' out to see yer girl."

"I don't think I can call her 'my girl.' Wouldn't I have to do something . . . formal?"

"Tell me this, is she seeing anyone else?"

"Not that I know of. She only has Sunday afternoons and Thursday evenings off—"

"But she's not allowed visitors on Sundays, and she spends every Thursday evening with ya, right? Just as she's been doing for months now?"

"Aye, that's right."

Elmer grinned. "She's yer girl, sure and certain, whether ye've done anything formal or not." The two men grinned foolishly at each other. "So tell me, are ya thinkin' of something more formal? A proposal, maybe?"

James sobered. "It's odd ya should ask. I've been going over my records, asking myself if I can afford a wife. I'll be reaching twenty-one years in July, and well . . ." He reached into his pants pocket and drew out a folded paper. "Here's my budget."

Elmer read through it silently. "So ye're thinking of taking a couple of rooms with a kitchen at Mrs. Slattery's?"

"Aye. It's a good enough place, not too far a walk from here, and the rent is right."

"Would ye consider our little cottage?"

James's eyes widened. "Primrose Cottage? Where yer late mum-in-law lived?"

"Aye, God rest her soul. There was some legal trouble when she passed last spring, but it's free and clear now, and we'd be thrilled to have ya and yer missus in it. Of course, the rent would be a wee bit higher than this," he said, indicating James's budget sheet, "but ye'll be able to afford it since Abby says it's time I increase yer pay."

When he said how much he planned to raise it, James's eyes filled with tears. "Are ya sure, sir?"

"Aye. Abby's been at me to raise it for a while now, and I figure that much is fair given our income has nearly doubled since ya came."

James felt himself blush. "Ya know that's not all me. It's the gold mines and the immigrants comin' and the growth of the wool industry . . ."

"Nonetheless, I can afford to raise yer pay, and I intend to, starting this week."

"I . . . I don't know what to say."

"Then don't say anything. When d'ya think ya and yer girl might be gettin' hitched?"

"I can't guess. There are a few problems we'll have to overcome . . ."

"Aye, aren't there always?" Elmer nodded sagely. "Well, lad, if ye'd like to move into the cottage right away, it's yers. Best to get it before I rent it to someone else. It's fully furnished, but I can't guarantee all the furnishings are in good condition. Ye'll have to do some cleaning, but the first month's rent is free if ya whitewash the outside and fix the place where the fence has broken down."

"I'll be happy to do that, sir."

"Then, if Mrs. Pembroke will let yer girl stay on for a time after the wedding, ya two can maybe save enough to buy the place yourself. It's small, but it would accommodate a small family, and ya might be able to add on in time." Elmer cocked an eyebrow.

James could scarcely believe it. He and Eliza together, in a home of their own? "I . . . I'm stuck for words. I can't think of anything to say except thank ya so much." He solemnly held out his hand.

Elmer took it and pulled James into a rough embrace. "Abby and I have come to love ya as the son we've never had, and our girls love ya like a brother. We'll be happy to have ya and yer lady in the cottage."

"Then ya've made up my mind," James said. "Sell me three meat pies, and I'll ask her this very night."

"This will be my favorite sale of the year," Elmer said as he rang it up.

*  *  *  *

"There's somethin' I have to say to ye, James Martin." Eliza stood sternly facing James on the porch swing. Molly sat in the garden, pretending fascination with the stars.

It was late February, and the weather was cooling after the summer's heat. Eliza tried to hide the fact she'd been crying. It didn't help a bit that James looked so happy, as if he was about to burst with some great news. But she couldn't lose her nerve now that her decision was finally made. She plunged ahead. "I . . . I don't think we should see each other anymore."

"What?" James sat wide-eyed, stunned.

"I know it may come as a shock, but—"

"Shock? Eliza, I came here tonight to propose to ya. I want ya to be my wife."

Eliza paled. "Oh no! Oh, James, no. I'm so sorry, but we can't . . ." She broke down in hopeless sobbing. She had waited too long—far too long. *Oh, Mother Mary!* She prayed silently. *I should have known. What can I do?*

She only felt worse when James's arms came around her, comforting her as she wept. He had never held her like this before, and despite misgivings, Eliza enjoyed his closeness. No one had held her at all since she left home, and she needed the comfort so much.

Molly noisily cleared her throat to let them know she saw, but James drew Eliza nearer, stroking her hair, ignoring Molly. Eliza stammered, "P-please don't be kind. Not now. I've led ye on all this time . . . I didn't mean to. Oh, please be angry! That would make this so much easier." She broke down again, distressed that he held her so closely and that she liked it so much. She ought to pull away, especially since she had to reject him, yet she couldn't help clinging instead. How could he be so kind when she was breaking both their hearts?

"Shhh, darlin' girl. Shhh." He brushed the hair out of her eyes and lovingly wiped her tears. "Will ya tell me one thing?"

She took a deep breath. "Aye. Ye deserve that much."

"Why *can't* we be married?"

She hiccuped hysterically and couldn't seem to stop the tears. "Don't ye see how impossible it is, the two of us?"

"No, I don't. Maybe ya should explain."

Eliza stomped one small foot. "It's plain as daylight. Will ye please see reason?" But when James simply waited, she went on. "For one thing, ye're English. I'm Irish."

James shrugged. "Here we're both Australian."

"Well then, there's the other difference. Oh, James, don't ye see? It's so plain!"

"Maybe it's not as plain as ye think, lass. Go on."

She tried, she really tried. She blurted out things like *Catholic*, *Protestant*, *unequally yoked*, and her fear of hellfire. "Don't ye see?" she finished, the tears running freely. "It's impossible."

"I don't see at all," he said. "I think it's been working well. Besides, I know something of religiously mixed marriages, and I think we'll do grandly."

"Ye do?" Surprise broke through Eliza's tears.

"Aye, lass. I do. My father was strictly Anglican—Church of England all the way. My mother's kin had come from Scotland, so her folk were considered 'dissenters' back when that could still get a body killed. They were Presbyterian, and they'd raised my mum that way. When my parents married, it was the first time there'd been a Presbyterian in his family, and he was the first Anglican in hers."

"And . . . how did they work it out?"

"They agreed to disagree. Papa took us to Anglican services one week, and Mum took us to the Presbyterians the next. When we got old enough to make a choice, each of us followed our own paths. Mum had the upper hand, since she was teachin' us at home. Most of us were baptized Presbyterian."

"And yer parents? They've been happy?"

"They've had their off moments, but overall they've been as happy as most and happier than some." He took out a clean handkerchief and began to dry her tears. "If this concerned ya so much, why haven't ya mentioned it before?" He paused, letting Eliza absorb that last comment, then he went on. "Ye'll want to keep working for Mrs. Pembroke for a time, if only to fill yer contract, and she'll expect ya at Sunday services as usual. Only now ye'll sit with me, instead of just stealing glances when ya get the chance." His teasing smile gave her pause.

"And what about Mass?"

"Ye can go with Molly on Thursday evenings, just as ye've been doin'," he answered. "Only when ya walk home together, she can drop ya off at Primrose Cottage instead of walking ya all the way to Pembroke House."

"P-p-p-primrose Cottage?" Eliza stared.

James shared his news, and Eliza couldn't help feeling the excitement of possibility. But the impossible hope caused her to cry even harder. She thought her heart might shatter when James said, "I love ya, Eliza. I think I've loved ya since ye smiled at me from the deck of that awful ship ya hated so. I've never imagined making a life with any other woman, and I can't imagine it with anyone else now that I've seen ya in it."

Eliza struggled to catch her breath. Couldn't the man see reason? "Oh, but James, be serious. Think of all ye're askin'. D'ye really want *all* of me?"

"All. Every bit," he answered, gently kissing her forehead. It was their first kiss. In fact, if she chose not to count the time Raleigh O'Hare had kissed her cheek the year they were both six, it was her first kiss ever. She felt joy and elation—and sadness.

Then she thought of the sticking point. "What about my faith, James? What about my religious things?" She mentioned her small statuette of Mother Mary and the tiny painted icon of Saint Elizabeth, as well as her rosary. "My prayers to Mary and my patron saint were all that kept me alive on the sea," she concluded. "I can't give them up. Ye can't ask me to."

James's face hardened. "You're right that it would be difficult for me, seein' my wife worshipping graven images," he said, his voice stern.

Eliza gasped. "Graven images?"

"I didn't mean—"

"Yes, ye did. Don't ye see?"

His face slowly softened. "It wouldn't be easy for me to have . . . um, yer religious things around, but if ya kept 'em in a corner of a back room . . ."

"And why should I be the one to hide?" Her anger must have sparked in her eyes because she saw him flinch. "Why don't ye convert and come back to the true faith? If ye do, Father Michael can marry us. If ye don't and I marry ye as ye're asking, I'll be committing my soul to eternal damnation. Would ye ask me to give up heaven for ye?"

She had deliberately chosen hard words, and she knew she'd hit a tender spot when James's jaw tightened. He barely kept his anger in check when he said, "I will *not* change my faith. Why don't *ye* convert and save us both a heap o' trouble?"

The air between them sizzled.

"Well?" James pressed. "Why don't ya convert and give up yer idols? Then we won't have to worry where to put them."

Eliza let her anger drain, remembering her resolve. She had made her decision and had confirmed it in her heart during Mass today. Leaving James was the right thing to do.

She slowly stepped back from the man she had come to love. "D'ye see now? D'ye think this argument would be any easier in our own home? Oh, James, what would we do when children came? As much as I want a different answer, someone has to be sensible." She took another step away. "Ye're not changing yer faith, and I'm not changing mine. We need to put an end to this before we hurt each other even more."

She watched James pull himself up straight. He took one deep, calming breath. "Perhaps ye're right," he said. "Perhaps I hadn't thought this through completely." He stepped away. "Forgive the intrusion, Miss Wells," he said. "I shan't be troubling ya again."

"Good-bye then, Mr. Martin," Eliza said, forcibly holding her emotions in check. "Thank ye for yer many kindnesses. I . . ." Her voice broke. "I wish ye every ha-happiness."

His voice softening, James whispered, "And I wish ya the same. Good-bye, Eliza." He turned and strode toward the gate. He reached it and pushed it open, looked sadly over his shoulder, and walked down the street. Eliza watched as the tears ran freely.

\* \* \* \*

"Well, son, how did it go?" Elmer slapped James on the back. "When're ya getting married?"

"We're not." James looked up through weary eyes.

"Yer not? What happened?"

James started explaining about religious differences.

Hogan cut him off. "Ya mean she's a Catholic? An idol worshipper? But I saw ya watching her in Presbyterian services Sunday—"

"Mrs. Pembroke insisted."

"Ah. She goes to Mass?"

"Every Thursday before I see her. I expect it's what all her family did back in Ireland."

"She's Irish too? Good heavens, boy. Count yerself lucky. Ye're better off without her."

James turned to Hogan, his eyes filled with pain. "I don't feel better off. I love her."

"But have ya thought it through? Ya marry her, yer children will be Irish. Ya know how those people are. She'll have a passle of half-Irish brats and teach 'em to pray to idols." He shook his head. "Nah, ye're better off without her."

James stood, his face glowing. "What if I could convert her, Elmer? She's a good person and a hard worker. What if marriage to me is all she needs to recognize how corrupt the old church has become? What if I could persuade her to keep coming to Presbyterian services and to bring all our children along? Don't ya think it would grow on her in time?" Not finding the answer he looked for in Elmer, James sank down onto a nail keg. "I feel I have to try. I love her."

"Ye'd be smart to leave well enough alone, but maybe she's not past saving. If she's willing to be married by the minister, she might be worth yer trouble."

James nodded in response, but he knew how the idea would go over with Eliza. Still, he had to try. He couldn't imagine his life without her.

\*   \*   \*   \*

Eliza left the confessional feeling dismal. Pleading a headache, she had sneaked from Presbyterian services to confess. Now she almost wished she hadn't. Instead of sympathizing with her pain and sacrifice, the priest had lectured about how foolish she had been to allow a Protestant near her heart. He had warned of eternal damnation for those who chose not to marry in the church, thus living in a state of sin, becoming ex-communicant and unworthy to partake in the Holy Sacraments. She had done the right thing—hadn't she?—yet now she felt dirty, soiled.

Before going to Southampton, she had never met a Protestant, never known anyone who wasn't Catholic. Her mother had raised her on the rosary, the missal, and the Mass, and she had never questioned them. But she questioned now, and she feared she might not like the answers.

* * * *

"Ye seem so sad. I wish there was something I could do." Molly turned worried eyes to Eliza as they walked home from Mass.

"Ye're just sad for yerself," Eliza said, trying to lighten their mood. "Ye know there'll be no meat pie waiting."

"True, but I'm worried about ye. I know ye care about him."

Eliza sighed. "I love him. More than I ever imagined I could. I can't help wondering what would make it such a sin to marry a good man like James."

"Ye know the answer—"

"I know the priest's answer, but can it be so wrong to marry a Protestant? It's not as if he's a heathen, ye know. I keep thinking that if I showed him a good example—"

"Ye'd be risking yer eternal soul on the hope that he'd come 'round."

"Maybe it would be worth it," Eliza mumbled, the words barely audible.

"Well, whatever ye're thinking, ye'd best make up yer mind," Molly said, looking ahead. "James is here."

"What?" But there he was. There were stiff greetings while Molly took her meat pie and went to the garden. Then Eliza asked, "What're ye doin', James? I thought I was clear—"

"Ye were plenty clear, but there's one more thing I need to ask ya, and I need for ya to be fully honest with me and with yerself. Can ya do that?"

Eliza swallowed hard. "Aye, James. I can. I will."

"Think about it now," he said. "If ya've known it couldn't work between us, and ya've known it for a good while, why have ya waited so long to say something?"

"Because . . ." Eliza's voice quavered, and she had to force the words. "Because . . . I couldn't bear . . . to give ye up, James." She sucked in a shaky breath. "I c-c-couldn't b-b-bear to give ye . . ." She broke into sobs.

The next thing she was aware of was James's strong arms wrapped warmly about her, his lips on her cheek. "I love ya, Eliza, and ya love me. Don't ya think that if we try, we might work out our differences—live peaceably under the same roof and raise happy, healthy children?"

Despite her tears, Eliza's heart filled with joy. "D'ye really think we can do it?"

"Aye, Eliza. I do."

"Oh, James," she whispered. Whether she moved her lips toward his or he toward hers, she could not have said, but the kiss was real, filled with joy and passion and love and hope and longing, and Eliza allowed herself a spark of faith.

When James asked again, "Will ya marry me, Eliza?" she allowed herself a moment to ponder heaven and hell, the risk of eternal damnation against the chance of saving a soul she loved. Then she answered, "Aye, James, I will." Then they were holding each other again and kissing and crying, and good things seemed real and possible.

"Exactly *what* is going on here?" Mrs. Pembroke announced her arrival with the crash of the door against the wall. "Miss Wells, I will not have my help—"

"Mrs. Pembroke?" James interrupted.

"Mr. Martin, what have you to say for yourself?"

"Mrs. Pembroke," James said, carefully stepping between Eliza and her employer. "I have just asked Eliza to marry me."

Mrs. Pembroke visibly calmed as she looked from one happy face to the other. "Well then, perhaps that's different." She paused. "And I gather she said yes, did she?"

"Aye, ma'am. She did."

"She has a contract with me, you know."

"Aye, ma'am, and we plan for her to work out the contract as agreed."

"Surely you understand there will be problems," Mrs. Pembroke said, her voice and mien imperious, "you being Protestant and her a Catholic."

Eliza watched James struggle to compose his face, but he managed to avoid a smirk. "Aye, ma'am. We were just discussing that." Beside him, Eliza choked down a giggle.

"And there will be arrangements to be made, about where she will live and her work hours and so forth."

"Aye, ma'am. We know there will be."

"Well then, if you both think you can handle this . . . I suppose I shall agree."

"Thank ya, ma'am," James said, and Eliza suspected he had refrained from telling her just where her business ended.

Mrs. Pembroke took a deep breath. "Then perhaps this is a moment for celebration. Come inside, please. I'll have Elsie bring some tea and cookies."

Molly gasped. "Tea and cookies?"

"That's what I said, Molly." Mrs. Pembroke lifted her chin and marched into the house.

"See, Eliza?" James whispered. "Miracles can happen."

Eliza smiled as they followed Mrs. Pembroke into the kitchen.

\* \* \* \*

On an evening in mid-March, Eliza sat upon her bed in the attic room with Molly at her side, carefully sewing alterations into the dress she would wear for her wedding. Celeste had gone through her armoire, noisily weeding out the gowns she considered no longer fashionable and passing them on to the help. In the end, there were four—one for each girl—and Celeste had given Eliza first pick.

Eliza knew from the moment she saw it what her pick would be, and she suspected Celeste may have included it on purpose.

Made of tightly woven silk taffeta, the skirt had three expanding tiers, stiffened with horsehair braid. Wide pagoda sleeves—almost a new fashion—ballooned over false undersleeves of white linen, trimmed in lace. The gown was finished in pink bows at the neck and sleeves. Best of all, it was in soft dove gray, the color James had declared his favorite. She carefully took in the full bodice for her smaller figure while Molly let out the hem.

"I still don't see how ye talked him into it," Molly was saying. She lifted a hand to brush the hair from her eyes.

"I s'pose ye could say it was a type of blackmail," Eliza answered with a twinkle. "I told him I could not behave like a married woman until our union had been blessed by the church."

Molly tried to clarify. "Ye . . . um, ye wanted the priest's blessing before yer wedding was . . . uh, concentrated."

Eliza blushed. "I think ye mean consummated?"

"Aye. That too."

"Anyway, James agreed we could be blessed by Father Michael, but the good father refused." Eliza sighed. "James's minister said he could marry us in their faith if I'd declare my commitment to Our Savior. It was all affirming what I believe, no renouncing of anything and no promises, so I had no trouble with that. Of course that doesn't solve the problem for me. So far as the church is concerned, we'll still be living in sin."

Molly's face fell. "I'm sorry, Eliza." She put on a false brightness. "And then . . . ?"

"After the ceremony the Hogans and the Pembrokes are givin' us a little party. It'll be well into autumn, but if the rains haven't started yet, we can mingle on the lawn outside. Elsie will serve tea and cakes near the rectory."

"I know. I've been volunteered to help."

Eliza touched her hand. "I'm sorry, Molly, but I promise I'll be there to serve for ye when yer time comes."

"And who knows if it ever will?"

"It will." Eliza carefully clipped her thread and rolled a knot. "I comfort myself that James was willing to see it through—the blessing from Father Michael, I mean. If the good father hadn't said no, James would have gone through with it. Maybe that means he'll come 'round and marry me in the church someday."

"With God's blessing, it may happen."

Eliza hugged her. "Ye've been a great friend to us, Molly. I'm grateful."

"Are ye teasin' me? If it hadn't been for yer beau, I might have starved to death months ago—or gotten myself dismissed and put out on the street."

They were interrupted when Sarah came to the door, her expression somber. "Eliza, if ye've a minute, the missus wants to speak to you in the library."

"Oh no. Am I in trouble? Not this close to the wedding."

"Ye're not in trouble," Sarah said, swallowing hard, "but ye may wish ye were when ye hear what Mrs. P. has in mind."

Eliza straightened. "Tell me."

"She says since ye've no mother, someone needs to teach ye the facts o' life and how things are between women and their men. She reckons it's her job."

Eliza groaned. "I wish I were in trouble." Molly and Sarah crooned sympathetically as she started for the stairs.

* * * *

Item, *The Australian Banner*, Society Section

*James William Martin and Mary Elizabeth "Eliza" Wells were married in the Presbyterian Church of Eastern Australia on the ninth day of April, 1853. It was a crisp autumn Saturday with clear skies.*

*The bride wore a gown of dove gray silk taffeta that—to some—seemed far above her rank and station as a housemaid, although she does work for the prestigious Pembroke House. Her groom, a prospering mercantile clerk, wore a simple black suit. The bride's family of County Mayo, Ireland, was represented by the family of prominent society locals, Mr. and Mrs. Augustus Pembroke. The groom's family—of Box, Wiltshire, England— was represented by Mr. and Mrs. Elmer Hogan and their three young daughters. A large number of guests attended.*

*Following the ceremony, tea and cakes were served on the lawn between the church and the rectory.*

* * * *

The newspaper account didn't capture everything. It didn't note how James's face lit up when he saw his bride enter on Cooper's arm, or how he watched as she walked down the aisle—as if she were the dearest and most beautiful of women. It didn't mention the strong, clear way Eliza repeated her vows or the smile that lit her face. It didn't comment on the almost reverent way James kissed his new bride, and it didn't mention the way Elmer Hogan forced himself to speak kindly to her. Nor did it mention the happy friends who walked the couple back to Primrose Cottage where they were finally and blessedly alone.

# PART TWO:
## Growing

# Chapter 4

*March 1857*

ELIZA SNAPPED HER HUSBAND'S SHIRT into the late-summer breeze and affixed it to her clothesline with wooden pegs. She worked at a steady pace, enjoying the hint of cooling in the air, while Little Jimmy played in the family's garden. He was a blessing, her precious son, and she thanked the Blessed Virgin for him every day.

Nearly four years had passed since she had bound herself to a Protestant, but Eliza felt she had done the right thing. On the day she married James Martin, she had thought it impossible for anyone to love as much as she did. Today, she loved him more.

He was a good man, her James— a wholesome, faithful husband, and a kind and caring Christian who treated everyone with dignity and respect. He worked hard to make her happy every day of their life together. She had never met anyone who showed greater tenderness toward a child than James did with their Jimmy. He loved that child to distraction! If it had not been for the few small hillocks in their path, their journey together might almost be ideal.

There were hillocks, though, some smaller and some that loomed like mountains, even shadowing their sunny days. Though Eliza was making a home for herself and her family, she knew she hadn't found her true home, not yet. Their differences over religion were always before them. While Eliza worked out her contract with Pembroke House, she had faithfully attended services with the Presbyterians every Sunday. When her contract was up, she continued to attend to keep up appearances for James's sake and for his career at Hogan's store, but she also prayed the rosary as she sat there, and she heard Mass at least twice weekly, including once each Thursday evening when she attended with Molly, who was still in Mrs. Pembroke's employ and still single after discovering her most serious suitor was also pursuing two other women.

The many hours of exposure to Protestant doctrine had only deepened her resolve to stay faithful to her saints although she couldn't partake in the Holy Sacraments. Though James said little and never mentioned the statues of the Virgin and St. Elizabeth near their bed, she sometimes saw him cringe when she made the sign of the cross. He worshipped the same Trinity she did, but her Catholic way of showing it underscored their differences. He also found reasons for her to leave three-year-old Jimmy behind when she went to Mass, a point she might have to argue should things continue in this vein.

Yet she had questions she dared not ask. At Jimmy's birth, she had to wonder why a loving God would consign innocent children to eternal punishment simply because they died before baptism. She wondered why the church could not recognize her marriage when it had obviously been such a blessing, and now that she was a happily wedded woman, she wondered what was so sinful about the act the priests called the original sin. Worse still, she wondered what it would hurt to ask these questions—since Father Michael assured her she was already condemned. Yet he refused to discuss any "why" questions and referred to the mysteries of God.

She paused briefly, then reached for a pair of James's work trousers, snapped them in the breeze, and hung them out.

Until recently they'd had few money problems. In fact, things had gone surprisingly well. James had a good mind for business, and Elmer Hogan made fair use of it, expanding into a second store and putting James in charge. As store manager, he was bringing home a better salary than ever. Two years ago, he and Eliza had begun the process of purchasing Primrose Cottage. Since the birth of Little Jimmy, Eliza had left Pembroke House, but she now made curtains and braided rugs, working to beautify their home, and occasionally sold a rug to help the family budget. They'd kept up with their payments, and their family prospered.

Then just over a year ago, her Aunt Kate wrote to tell Eliza of her father's illness. He was sick with the consumption, and although her brother Teddy knew of a sanitorium that helped those with lung ailments, the family didn't have enough cash to get him admitted. James did not hesitate, selling what few things they could part with in the hope of sending her father what he needed. When that was not enough, he arranged with the Hogans to fall several months behind in house payments, sending the money to Ireland instead.

In the end, their sacrifices had done no good. The sanitorium accepted all their money, but her father died anyway, and these three months later, Eliza still found herself in tears at odd moments as she realized that now she was truly orphaned, with neither a mother nor father and no home but the one she made here.

"Don't play with the bugs, Jimmy," she said, wiping stray tears. She gently lifted her son to his feet and held him with one arm as she brushed the ants off his hands and legs. She tucked him against her side. It was then that she saw the distinctive, sticky web of the redback spider. She carried Jimmy to the porch and told him to stay there, then she took a stick and beat the web down. When the little spider showed itself, she stepped on it, crushing it with her shoe. Rather than risking the bite of the mildly venomous redback or trying to explain the hazards of ant encounters, she simply moved Jimmy's toys to another part of the garden.

She shook the wrinkles from the apron she had just washed and added it to the clothes on the line. Although she was pleased with both her money-saving efforts and James's ability to see a good opportunity, they had made up only one house payment so far. She sometimes couldn't help worrying over that.

And then there was her other, more private, worry.

"Come on, little drover," she said to her son as she lifted him up onto one hip. "Let's get ye some lunch. Then we'll put ye down for yer nap."

Some forty minutes later, with her child fed and sleeping, Eliza knelt in the corner of her room, made a meticulous sign of the cross, and began her prayers to the Blessed Virgin. She thanked her as she always did for interceding with her Son and giving Eliza a beloved husband, her start in a new land, and her Little Jimmy, the crowning glory of her life. With tears in her eyes, she begged Holy Mary to seek her Son's forgiveness for marrying out of the faith. Then, if she was so inclined, could she please ask Him to take the curse from her body, open her womb, and let her bear a second child?

*   *   *   *

James was in his element today, striding among the men at the docks and haggling for the purchase of goods that had been shipped from England. In the pair of years since the battle at the Eureka Stockade, a new form of democracy had come to the land Down Under. They now had a degree of autonomy from Mother England, and with it, James had seen a burgeoning in both the population and the business. Both branches of Hogan's General Store were doing well, but the one he managed, nearer to the prosperous part of town, was growing by the day. With a bit of good luck, James thought he might scrape together another back house payment in only a few more weeks.

He didn't regret his choice—not for a minute. Though he'd never met his late father-in-law, he was family, father to the woman he loved and grandfather to the sweetest little boy on earth. He'd have given up any material thing he had to try to spare his family this loss. The only point that sorrowed him was his efforts had come too late.

"Is that ye, Martin?" a large voice boomed behind him.

James turned just in time to be wrapped in a smothering hug. "Good to see ya too, Edmund," he said as he put his feet on the dock again and straightened his creased shirt. "So what brings ya down to Sydney?"

"I've moved here, mate. I've got crew chiefs and managers running one mining operation, and I've sold the other, so I've come down to the city to set up shop with a partner." He grinned. "I find I rather like working with wealthy men and not havin' to hurt my back. So I'm a prosperous banker now."

James's face lit with excitement. "Will wonders never cease! Ye constantly amaze me, Ed. So can ya come to the house? Maybe have tea with the wife and me, meet my little boy?"

"Aye, I heard ye married that girl ye saw on the docks."

"Aye. That's the one. Her name's Eliza, and she is the best woman I've ever known. So how about ya? Ya must surely have gathered a wife by now, and maybe a child or two?" The two fell into an easy stride as they walked back toward James's store.

"Ye'd think so, wouldn't ye? But that story's for another time. If the offer for tea is good for tonight, I'll come by around six or so. We can talk more then."

"Half past six is our usual tea time," James answered. "I'll stop by the house on the way to the store to let Eliza know ye're coming."

James explained to his friend how to find Primrose Cottage. Then Ed said, "See ye at half past six." He turned up a side street and strode away.

"See ya then," James happily answered. He walked homeward beside the harbor, watching the mice fight for scraps in the rushes along the path, stretching out his strides and enjoying the touch of autumn in the air, eager to share his news with Eliza.

A few minutes later, he arrived at their house. Knowing this was the time when Little Jimmy often napped, he quietly opened the door and crept into the front room. "Eliza?" he whispered. Hearing no answer, he walked to the door of their bedroom.

There was the woman he loved on her knees in the corner of the bedroom, praying to her idols. He eased forward a little, and that was when he realized Eliza was crying, tears muddying her lovely voice. He was there just in time to hear her say, "Please, Holy Mother, please ask God to forgive me for the dread sin of marrying outside the true faith. Please take the curse of barrenness from my body, open my womb, and let me conceive again."

Stricken, James bit his lip to keep from crying out and quickly stepped back into the living room, out of sight. He felt the emotions as a sharp physical pain, squarely in the center of his chest. His darling Eliza considered herself barren? Heavens, no. It was clear enough that Jimmy was past his third birthday without a younger sibling, but barrenness had simply never crossed his mind. He only wondered why it was taking so long the second time when the first came in just eleven months.

He staggered as he realized the full import of what he had just heard. His sweet wife thought she'd been cursed *because she'd married him*. Hearing her beg that statue in the corner to forgive her for their marriage—he thought that might be the worst pain of his life, worse even than watching his mother die.

James eased back away from the door, slowly working his way back to the front door as if he'd never been here, as if he hadn't come home at all. But the words were seared into his mind and heart. Now the question was what to do. He stood on his porch with his back against the front wall of his home, sucking in deep breaths. The first step was to regain some calm. Through the open window, he could still hear Eliza murmuring to her statue, so he still had time. He would gain some calm and say a few prayers of his own. Then, well, then he'd just have to play out the scene to see what happened.

Minutes passed as James waited on the porch, trying to get past the shock. It was duty that finally moved him, duty to Elmer Hogan and a realization that it had been some time since he concluded his business for the store. Eliza's mumbled prayers had ceased, and he decided he needed to move forward no matter how painful it might be.

And then an idea occurred: maybe it would be better to avoid the pain. After all, if he'd come home now instead of then, he would never have heard her prayers, and he wouldn't know how she felt about their marriage. He wasn't sure he could pull it off, and he wasn't even certain it was the right thing to do, but this plan had the virtue of being the only one he could manage. He straightened, opened the front door, and called out, "Eliza, my love, are ye home?"

She stepped out of the bedroom looking as lovely as ever, her face not even showing the traces of her recent ordeal. "Shhh, James! Ye'll wake the boy."

"Ah, yes," he said, softer now. "I'd clean forgotten he sleeps at this hour."

"And speakin' o' this hour, what are ye doing here? Is there a problem at the store?"

"No, nothing like that. I just had a message to deliver, and I wanted to hug my wife."

"Well then," Eliza said with a smile. She stepped toward him.

James stepped forward and swept her off her feet, holding her as tightly as if he feared she was slipping away—and wondering if perhaps she was. With dread in his heart but a light tone in his voice, he delivered his message about company coming to tea. Then, pretending that all was well with his world, he turned back toward the mercantile. Outside, a kookaburra chattered from a neighbor's red gum tree, its song of laughter mocking his pain.

* * * *

"So, there's my problem," Big Edmund Welsh concluded. "If they don't know about the gold, women shy away just because . . . well, because I look like a wombat—or some sort of hairy man-mountain. If they know I have money, I have no way of knowin' which among them might be interested in me for *me* and which just want to get their delicate little hands on me bankroll. I didn't know striking it rich could have such interesting consequences." He sighed and put down his fork, adding, "Excellent meal, Mrs. Martin."

She shook her head. "Please, call me Eliza. We're practically kin, what with all ye did for my James when ye were at the Burra-Burra together. He's talked about ye often."

"I promise James did at least as much for me and probably even more. If he hadn't nursed me through that poisoning bout, I'd've died before I had a chance to find gold." Ed lifted his glass to his friend.

The Martins both spoke at once. James said, "Pah. Ye're overdoin' it already," while Eliza looked at him, wide-eyed, and said, "Ed, ye were poisoned?"

James said, "Not exactly," at the same moment Ed said, "Aye, I was." Then Ed asked James, "Haven't ye ever told her that story?"

"Mum, can I play by my bed?" Little Jimmy asked, interrupting them.

Eliza looked to James, who nodded. Then she answered, "Aye, ye may, Jimmy. Say good night to Mr. Welsh before ye leave."

"Good night, Mr. Welsh," Jimmy said. Then he bounced out of the room with a half skip, his shock of white-blond hair bouncing along with him.

"Ye've a bonzer boy there, bouncin' like a 'roo," Ed said, staring after the child. "Makes me wonder if I'll ever have a young'un of me own."

"Bonzer? Ye're soundin' like a real Aussie," James said.

"Aye, I've learned the hard way, just like ye. Which reminds me about the poison."

"Good. I want to hear," Eliza answered while James sighed.

Ed described a day on the Burra-Burra when he'd been sent to search out additional sources of ore. "I was down on my knees, rooting around the bank of a creek with both hands, when I accidentally turned up a platypus. A big, healthy male, it was—nigh on to a foot long, and I'm guessin' it didn't want its nest disturbed, so it grabbed onto me with its forepaws and stung me with both hind legs right on my bare arm. I dropped it, of course, but the damage was done. Turns out those little critters can carry a whoppin' load of poison."

"I had no idea," Eliza answered. "I've heard about the platypus, of course. Everybody wants to tell ye about the strange creatures when ye first arrive in Australia, but I've never seen one, and I'd never have guessed they've poison in their legs."

"Oh, aye," Ed said, nodding sagely. "Most of the critters here carry poison in little sacs on their hind legs—at least the males do. They sting ye with their dew claws."

"Most, ye say? Like the 'roos?"

"Aye, all the different kinds of 'em—grays, reds, walleroos, potteroos. Koalas too and wombats. Everything with a pouch, mar-something—What's that word, James?"

"Marsupial," James supplied.

"Aye, that."

"Amazing. They seem like such peaceful creatures," Eliza said. "So how long did it take ye to get well?"

"I never would have without yer James."

"Ye're overdoin' it again," James protested. "He was sick, but he recovered quickly."

"Not so quickly," Ed countered. "James stayed up with me that whole first night, mopping my brow when I sweated and keepin' me from going into shock. He skipped work the next day—so he didn't get paid, neither—just to stay beside me. By that second night, I was better, but James still woke up to check on me every time he heard me groan—and I fear I was groaning a fair lot." He paused, and his face sobered as he said, "Honest, I don't know if I'd have made it if he hadn't'a been there. It's rare that a man dies of the platypus sting, but it's also rare for anyone to take that much poison in a single sting, and men do die sometimes. I was startin' to think I was a goner."

"I'd no idea such stings even existed," Eliza answered. Then she looked at the expressions on both men's faces. "Ye're not teasin' me, are ye?"

"No, 'Liza. Honest!" Ed said.

And James confirmed, "Male marsupials really do carry poison, and Ed took a bad platypus sting."

"My goodness," Eliza said. "Ye've had quite the adventures together. It's obvious ye two have been close for some time."

"Aye, I s'pose we have," James answered, "though we've not seen each other much lately."

"I know ye've been a good friend to us, Ed. It makes me wish all the more that I had a good woman for ye to court," Eliza said, and then the light went on. "Wait a minute." Her voice brightened. "I think maybe I do; that is, if ye don't mind meetin' a plain girl."

"Plain?" Ed asked, his brow wrinkled in suspicion. "Do ye mean homely as a mountain mud bog or just . . . well, plain?"

"Plain," Eliza repeated firmly. "And plump. In fact, quite plump." She looked at James, hoping he'd catch her thought, but the confusion on his face said her idea wasn't nearly as contagious as she'd hoped.

"Well then, let me ask a couple of straight questions. Is she bigger than me?"

"Oh no. Not by half." The idea seemed to amuse Eliza.

"Is she homelier than me?"

"Not at all," Eliza said, then added, "Uh, not that I'm sayin' yer homely, Ed."

He waved a hand dismissively. "Ah, don't worry about that, dear lady. Ye can't hurt a boar hog's feelings by sayin' he looks like a boar hog. If this gal ye know isn't bigger or uglier than me, then why hasn't somebody else snapped her up?"

"I've wondered that for some time now," Eliza answered. "She's a dear and would make someone a wonderful wife. James and I have talked about it often."

"We have?" James said, still mired in confusion.

"Aye, we have," Eliza said pointedly. Then, with a disgusted huff, she gave up on her husband and turned back to her guest. "She's a housemaid, Ed, just as I was. In fact, she works where I used to work, and her circumstances are very . . . let's say, limited."

"Ah," James said, and Eliza sighed, grateful he was finally catching on. "It's tough for a girl who works for the Pembrokes," he explained. "She only has Thursday evenings free, and she uses a part of that time to attend Mass. Then if she wants to socialize . . . Wait. Eliza, d'ya think we could talk Mrs. P. into letting her come here for tea and to stay for the evening? We'd be actin' as chaperones."

"I don't see why not," Eliza answered. "She already stops by to eat."

"I'm sure Mrs. P. would approve her comin' to tea, especially if ya ask her, Eliza. Ye're in a favored position since ya gave birth to that little darlin' of ours."

"That's true," Eliza grinned. Mrs. Pembroke, whose two eligible children had yet to marry, was enamored with Little Jimmy, called him her borrowed grandchild, and invited Eliza to visit often, so long as she brought the boy along. "If it's all right with Mrs. Pembroke, and if our friend decides to join us next Thursday after Mass, would ye like to come to tea again next week? Maybe meet an eligible lady?"

"She's a good person, this one?" Ed asked.

"Aye, the best," James said. "Men don't look to her immediately because . . . well, because she's not as beautiful as my Eliza." He nodded to his wife, whose answering nod acknowledged the compliment. "But she's a good woman, and she's been a wonderful friend to Eliza and me. In fact, she's helped us in many ways."

"Sure'n 'tis true," Eliza added succinctly.

"I couldn't ask for a better recommendation than that," Ed said. "Very well. Let's try for tea next Thursday. But how do we keep her from knowin' about the money?"

"I won't lie to her," Eliza said.

"Nor will I," James assured, "but I don't think we have to. We can just tell her that Ed and I sailed down here on the same ship and took our first job together on the Burra-Burra. We can just say he's still in mining. Ed, if ye come to the point that ye want to tell her about ya *owning* the mines and the bank and whatever else it is that ye own now, that will be up to you. She would never imagine that a couple like us, from such poor beginnings, actually know a fella worth a million pounds."

Eliza looked shocked. "Really? Ye're worth a million, Ed? I've never heard of such wealth. I mean, I knew ye had money, but a million? Surely James exaggerates."

"Not this time." Ed was somber. "When I bought into the bank, they insisted on appraisin' my whole net worth. Just now it's near two million pounds, give or take a handful."

"And ye came here with nothing, just as I did." James spoke with admiration.

Ed meekly nodded. "I've been lucky with the gold is all."

"Ye've been blessed," James corrected gently.

"Aye," Ed responded. "I've been blessed, and I'll be blessed still further if yer friend turns out to be the companion I've been lookin' for. What's her name?"

"Mary Margaret Mulvaney," Eliza answered, "but she goes by Molly. She's a sweetheart."

"Molly," Ed repeated. "I like it."

"Say, Ed," James began. "What would ye think of comin' to church with us this Sunday? That way we could point her out to ye and ye can decide what ye think."

"In fact," Eliza added, "I won't have an opportunity to speak to Mrs. Pembroke until after Sunday church. Come with us. If ye like the look o' the lady, just give me the nod."

"It sounds like a plan," Ed said. "Eliza, what d'ya think I should wear?"

James laughed heartily when he heard that, imagining Eliza trying to give fashion advice to big Ed Welsh. As he did, something thrummed at his heartstrings, and he realized he'd had little to laugh about during the past few hours. One thing was good about the match they were trying to arrange: Ed wasn't Catholic, but he wasn't a committed Protestant, either. Although he believed in God, he wasn't a church-goin' man. Perhaps that would help those two avoid the problems in his own marriage, the depth of which he was just coming to acknowledge.

An hour later, when James and Eliza had cleaned up the house and put Little Jimmy down for the night, Eliza took a trip to the outhouse and returned, announcing with a smile that she was ready for bed.

Instead of his usual eager response, James stretched. "I think I'll sit out on the porch a while this evenin', maybe see if I can watch the Southern Cross." As he started for the front door, he saw Eliza's face fall and knew he'd hurt her, but he knew he couldn't disguise his own wounds in the intimacy of their bed. Something between them had been damaged today. He hoped it could somehow be repaired.

# Chapter 5

Big Ed Welsh stood at the Hogans' pew in the Presbyterian Church staring heavenward, his face aglow, as if caught in the midst of a transformative experience. The minister looked toward Ed and nodded with a self-satisfied smile as he rose to start the meeting, but Ed was oblivious. James had to tell him to sit down when others had already taken their seats.

"Ye said she was plain," Ed murmured as he finally took his eyes off the pew where Molly sat in the church mezzanine. "She's bee-you-ti-ful!"

James, amused, whispered, "Come on now—"

"I'm serious, mate. Look at that perfect skin, her rosy cheeks, and the sheen of her hair. She has that sweet little nose and those full red lips . . . She's among the most glorious creatures I've ever seen."

James and Eliza exchanged a look of alarm, then Eliza gently whispered, "Ed, are ye looking at the right person?"

Ed's brow furrowed. "The big girl in the rosy red color, right? With the lacy white collar? The girl to the right of her is in brown and the one on the left in green calico."

Eliza seemed disbelieving. "Aye, that's the one." She and James exchanged a look. He shrugged. The minister gave them all a disapproving stare.

Throughout the service, James couldn't help watching his friend. Now that he'd seen her, Ed could hardly look away from Molly. James had to prod him every few minutes to get his attention back on the service.

Molly seemed just as fascinated, and James noticed whenever he looked toward her that she was turned toward them or just looking away, as if embarrassed to be caught.

Secretly James experienced private worry as he watched his dear wife. She seemed to be absorbing the sermon, yet her hand moved inside her dress pocket, where she carried her rosary. Even here, a gulf stretched between them.

In time the service ended, the organist began the postlude, and the congregation rose to leave. By prior arrangement, Eliza started toward the Pembrokes to ask Mrs. P. about the coming Thursday while James went to collect Little Jimmy. Then James saw which way Ed was hurrying and changed his direction.

"I think ye'd better come with me to the nursery," he said, catching his friend's arm. "Ye don't want to mess up everything we've planned."

Ed looked toward Molly, who, with the other serving girls, was working her way toward the staircase to meet the Pembroke family. Then he sighed and looked back at James. "Seems a shame to wait."

"Aye, mate, but it shan't be long—not if we give Eliza the chance to make the introductions all polite and proper-like."

"Aye." Ed sighed and let James lead him toward the nursery. They reached the lawn as Eliza hurried toward them. "Mrs. P. has agreed to Thursday. Now she'd like to meet our friend."

Ed moaned. "Here's the part I'm fearin'."

"It'll be all right, mate. Come. Ya'll see." James took him by the arm. Moments later, Mrs. Pembroke was giving an appraising once-over to "Mr. Ed Welsh, my friend from the Burra-Burra" while Molly stood behind her, looking fit to burst. When he added, "And may I present Miss Molly Mulvaney," James was impressed with the gallant way Ed said, "Miss Mulvaney," and bowed over her hand.

Mrs. Pembroke said, "I understand you want to court our Molly, Mr. Welsh."

Ed looked nervous, but he answered with a firm voice, "Aye, ma'am, with yer permission, o'course."

"And Eliza will serve as your chaperone?" The intensity of her question was diminished by her pausing to stroke Little Jimmy's cheek and by the child's answering giggle.

"Aye, ma'am." Both Ed and Eliza spoke at once.

"And Molly, you want this?" Mrs. P. asked, although James thought the question unnecessary. Couldn't she see Molly's face?

"Aye, ma'am," Molly answered.

"Well then, I suppose it will be acceptable." She smiled at Jimmy, turned, and swept from the churchyard, her staff trailing in her wake. Molly looked back over her shoulder and gave them all a brilliant smile.

Ed let his breath out in a rush. "Oh, me poor heart! Ye ought to feel how it's poundin'. It's a cryin' shame Thursday is so far away."

"I think Cupid has found ye, mate," James said, giving him a solid slap on the back.

"Aye, he has. I fear I'm roped 'n hog-tied. I never knew a man could feel this way without bein' crazy or sick, but I wouldn't feel any way else, either."

James grinned. "Aye. That sounds about right."

For the next two hours, James listened while Ed extolled the virtues of Miss Molly Mulvaney and asked Eliza a hundred questions which she patiently answered. By the time he left their home that Sunday, Ed knew much more about Molly, and he seemed to like it all.

"They seem a good couple," James told Eliza, his arm around her shoulders as they watched Ed leave. "It was a fine thought ye had, bringing 'em together."

"Sure'n it was," Eliza agreed. "Molly seems happy. We'll see how it goes from here."

James leaned down for a kiss.

It was not until the following Thursday that Molly got the chance to quiz Eliza. As they walked to Mass together, Molly waxed poetic on the virtues of "such a big, strong man" and then asked many questions Eliza answered as well as she could, although she found it necessary to equivocate once or twice. Later, as they walked toward home, Molly continued. It was only when she asked, "Is there any more ye can tell me?" that Eliza felt it necessary to speak.

"I'll tell ye the truth, Molly," she said, "because ye're my friend and because I think ye deserve it. There are things about Ed that ye haven't heard yet, things he doesn't want ye to know yet and has asked me to keep secret. I'm honorin' his choice because he's been a good friend to my James and because they are his secrets to tell, not mine. He did promise me, though, that if ye hit it off, he will tell ye his secrets himself—just not straight away."

Molly set her jaw and squared her shoulders. Her eyes were fixed ahead as she said, "So. The man has secrets."

Eliza nodded. "Aye."

"Well, not everyone came here for the gold." She looked Eliza straight in the eye. "Tell me, is he in trouble with the law?"

Briefly it occurred to Eliza that she didn't know Ed well, but remembering the thorough search the bank had done before bringing him in as a partner, she answered, "No, Molly. I'm sure he's not. And he did come here for the gold, same as James. They came from England together and went straight out to the Burra-Burra."

"That's good," Molly answered with conviction. "It must have been a love knot then, perhaps a woman who pursued him to extremes. I can easily picture that, him bein' such a splendid specimen 'n all."

Eliza suppressed a wry smile but kept any comment to herself. They turned the corner near Primrose Cottage to find Ed waiting on the porch. When he saw them, he broke into a wide grin, strode out to open the gate, made an elaborate bow as the two women passed, and bowed again as he presented a huge bouquet. "These flowers are for ye, Miss Mulvaney."

"Thank ye ever so, Mr. Welsh," Molly answered and dipped in a curtsy.

"It's just the four of us for tea," Eliza said. "Well, the four of us and Little Jimmy. I think it will be acceptable for ye to use each other's given names."

"I wouldn't presume—" Ed began.

Molly interrupted him, "Oh please, Mr. Welsh. Ye must call me Molly. I feel we're friends already, ye bein' such a dear friend of the Martins 'n all."

Ed bowed again. "Very well, then, Miss Molly. Please call me Ed." For a moment they all just stood there while he and Molly grinned foolishly.

"Sure'n 'tis a lovely night," Eliza observed, "but if we're to have our tea, I think we should go inside."

Molly blushed, and Ed sputtered. "Of course," he said. "Here, I'll get the door for ye." Then he added, "I brought flowers for ye too, Eliza. James put them in water a'ready."

Eliza answered, "That was thoughtful," and winked at Molly.

As they did on most Thursdays, Eliza had prepared a roasted meal which James had watched over while she was gone. Now James found another container for Molly's flowers—a mixed bouquet made mostly of red roses—while Eliza dished up the food.

James offered a blessing, which both women followed with the sign of the cross. Then began an awkward meal during which James and Eliza tried to maintain conversation while their tongue-tied guests stared and blushed and choked out one- and two-word answers to simple questions. The only comments that seemed to elicit more than the most basic of responses were made by Little Jimmy. Both Molly and Ed seemed able to express themselves when speaking to a three-year-old. By the time the meal was over, Eliza was out of patience.

"Ed, why don't ye carry those two chairs out onto the porch?" she said, making it more an order than a question. "Ye two have little enough time to get to know one another. 'Tis best if ye make good use of it."

To their arguments about cleanup, she turned a deaf ear. "Molly, 'tis yer night off. Ye don't have to wash dishes here. Ed, ye're a dear man and I appreciate the offer, but I'll have no dishes left if I turn them over to ye, ham-handed specimen that ye are. Go on outside then, the both of ye."

With that, Ed made another awkward bow and said, "Miss Molly?" Molly nodded and led the way while Ed lifted the two heavy chairs, one in each hand, and trailed behind.

Once they were out of hearing range, James observed, "I've never seen a man fall any harder. I doubt Ed has ever been in love before. Did ye hear him goin' on about how lovely Molly is?"

"Aye. Ye ought to hear her, callin' him a 'splendid specimen o' manhood' and a 'good-lookin' gentleman.'"

James shook his head. "It just goes to show the old saying is true: there really is someone for everyone."

"Aye," Eliza answered. "And I'm glad we found each other so quickly, James." She gave him a quick, chaste kiss, but there was a sparkle in her eye.

"I'm also glad," he answered. "I love ya, Eliza."

"And I love ye, James Martin."

James warmed. The problems in his marriage were real, but Eliza's sweet smile and kind words gave him hope for their future. He shooed Little Jimmy from the room, picked up the dish towel, and went to work beside the wife he loved.

\* \* \* \*

Over the next several weeks while Ed and Molly courted at their home, James and Eliza enjoyed a peaceful, happy time when it seemed almost as if everything was perfect between them. Eliza still prayed her rosary during each Presbyterian service, but their personal relationship seemed as strong as ever, although James became more discouraged each month she did not conceive. He guessed she still saw it as some sort of curse upon her because of their marriage, but he didn't say a word about it since he didn't want her to know he'd overheard her.

Molly came home with Eliza every Thursday after Mass, and Ed was there to greet them at the gate, always with one bouquet for Molly and another for Eliza. One evening Molly chided, "Ed, ye mustn't be wastin' yer money this way. Ye haven't been up to the mountains fer some time now. Surely yer funds have got to be runnin' thin."

Ed and Eliza exchanged a quick look, but Ed kept a straight face as he answered, "Ye're worth it, Molly. Besides, I have work here in town, and . . . I have a bit extra I can spare."

"I'm just worried about ye, Ed," Molly said, "about yer *future*, I mean."

Ed winked at Eliza, who grinned but kept herself from laughing.

The following day Ed showed up at Primrose Cottage with two big boxes of groceries. "It's not right, ye two payin' fer our dinner ever' week. Molly's talk 'bout the flowers showed me how selfish I was bein'. The least I can do is to bring ye some victuals now an' then."

They protested, but he insisted, and after that he brought a box of food every time he came and sometimes another between visits. He always provided more than he and Molly ate, and with their grocery bill cut so substantially, James and Eliza were able to increase their savings toward another back mortgage payment. They frequently remarked how grateful they were to have Ed as their friend, and each thanked heaven for him in their separate prayers.

It was a golden time for all of them as autumn deepened into winter. Ed learned his new trade at the bank, James caught up with another late payment, and Ed and Molly grew more deeply in love. One day in late June, just past the winter solstice, Ed dropped in at the mercantile and asked, "James, d'ye think ye can walk with me a bit?"

"Surely. Give me a moment to organize things here, and I'll be right with ya." He spoke to Will Carter, the young man who now assisted him as he had once helped Hogan, and soon James and Ed were out walking in the crisp, wintry air.

It took James only a moment to ask, "So what's ailing ya?"

"Ah, James, they say ye can't live a lie, and I'm learnin' it's true." Ed sighed. "I chose not to tell Molly about the money or the bank for reasons that seemed worthwhile at the time. Ye remember."

"Aye. I remember well."

"Yet now . . . I'm in love with 'er, Jimmy. I want to ask her to marry me, but I can't just come clean and tell her I've been leadin' her on this whole time."

James tried not to smirk. "I doubt she'll be unhappy to learn ye're a wealthy man, Ed. Ya know many women seek out men for their money."

"Not my Molly. She talks about in-teg-ri-ty as if it's the most important thing in the world. I fear she'll be plumb crazy if she feels I've lied to her."

"Have ya ever actually lied?"

"No, I've not. Not ever, but I haven't told the whole truth, either."

"And a man isn't allowed a few secrets?"

"Not from the woman he wants to marry."

"She hasn't been the woman ya wanted to marry till now. Really, I don't see the problem. Tell her the truth, and get down on one knee when ya do it. I think it will turn out nicely."

Ed stopped walking, turned to James, and asked, "Will ye pray about it for me?"

James blinked. "What?"

"I asked if ye'll pray about my problem. Ye know, pray. Ask the good Lord to tell ye what I should do."

James cleared his throat. "Ed, don't ya think ya ought to pray about this one yerself?"

"I have been, mate, for more than a month now, but the Almighty isn't used to hearin' from me much, and frankly, I'm not sure I'd know an answer if He sent it to me in the afternoon post. I've never really been the spiritual sort. I just thought if *ye* asked . . . and maybe tell me if ye get an answer?"

"Aye, Ed, I'll pray for ya. Happy to, mate. Was that all ya had to ask me?"

"Aye."

"Then I think we'd better head back to the store. And maybe ya'd better get back to banking as well. Ya wouldn't want Molly to marry a poor man."

"Aye, right y'are, mate," Ed answered, a bit too somberly for the joke.

The conversation faded into the background as the winter wore on through July, but James never failed to say a prayer without asking a blessing on Ed. Nor was that the only outcome. Until then, James had responded to his worry over Eliza mostly with bewildered numbness. Now with Ed's help, he realized he had a resource and an ally he had never turned to before. Throughout those chilly days, James never said, murmured, or thought a prayer that he didn't ask the Father of the universe to please bless his Eliza, to help her convert to the true faith, and to let her conceive again.

\* \* \* \*

Another incident occurred in late July. James was walking back from the docks, where he had just acquired more inventory for the two Hogan stores and a third Elmer planned to open soon. Down the street, a group of young toughs taunted an aboriginal woman and her son, a lighter-skinned child not much bigger than his Jimmy.

James shook his head. Such scenes were common, but they always left him uneasy. It had not been the fault of the aboriginals that Europeans had come with guns, nor had it been the fault of their women that many had fallen into relationships—some willingly, some less so—with the men who had conquered their people. Many aboriginal women now had fatherless "creamy" children who belonged to neither race—half dark, half light, and rejected by both.

As James drew nearer, the taunts grew louder. He heard one boy, his voice still heavy with Liverpool, shout a word no decent man ever used. Another yelled, "Ye heard 'im, sow. You and yer creamy go home!" A third didn't yell at all; he picked up a stone. James broke into a run, but the boys were nearly two blocks away. He watched in horror as the rock hit the child in the arm, tearing his thin shirt and drawing blood.

"No!" James screamed. He was running, trying to get the boys' attention, shouting . . .

The blood seemed to inflame the taunting boys. Another rock missed, and then a third clipped the child in the brow. Like most head wounds, it bled fiercely, which only seemed to egg on the attack. James sickened, fearing he would see the child stoned to death before he could intervene. Heaven knew it had happened before, in circumstances like these. Though the boys hadn't likely begun their taunts with the intention of murder, it sometimes turned out that way. He tried to run faster.

The first boy picked up a large stepping stone, one big enough to kill. James yelled, but the gang ignored him. Then, just as the boy threw it, a tall man ran from the alley, stepped in front of the creamy child, and took the stone squarely in his thigh. It rocked him backward, but he held his ground and put out one arm in a 'stop' gesture. In a deep, calm voice, he said, "That's enough, boys," and the attack stopped.

James, half a block away, slowed his pace as he watched the boys turn, shout some ugly words at the "interferin' foreigner," and leave in the opposite direction. He heard the man say, "Are you all right, son?" The stranger knelt in front of the wounded child and said, "Come, we'll rinse those wounds with some water."

A shorter, thicker man ran puffing from the alleyway as James reached them. "Is he . . ." The second man braced himself, head down, and panted. "Is he all right, Elder Walton?"

James didn't have to ask to know these men weren't local, nor were they English nor Irish. He'd met a few like them on the Burra-Burra. "Ye're Americans?"

"Yes," the first man said. "We are ministers of the gospel come here to teach."

"Well, I'm glad ya taught those young hoodlums," James said. "I feared for this boy."

"As did we," the first man answered while the second—smaller, older, heavier—struggled to catch his breath.

The man named Elder Walton reminded James of the Uncle Sam images that appeared in the Australian press. Although not as old as "Sam," his beard brown instead of white, Walton was very tall, lean, and stern looking until he smiled. He was smiling now as he tenderly knelt in front of the child and cleaned his wounds with a handkerchief. The mother, standing nearby, dropped her face into her hands and wept, her shoulders shaking, though she made no sound. The somber-faced child still hadn't made a sound, not even a whimper.

"There," Elder Walton said, leading the boy back to the arms of his mother, who held him tightly. "The wounds are ugly, ma'am, but they aren't deep. The boy will be fine."

The mother kept her eyes down as she murmured a barely audible, "Ta." Wrapping the boy in her shawl, she led him away.

"You're welcome," Elder Walton called after her.

"I say ta as well," James added. "Thank ya for interruptin' that."

"We've seen it a few times since we've been here," Walton answered.

"Yes," said the second man, panting less now. Not as old as Walton, he was shorter and thicker with a touch of gray in his beard and at his temples. He mopped his brow. "Thank you for trying to get here. I knew I wasn't going to make it."

"I didn't make it, either." He held out his hand. "I'm James Martin."

"Elder Walton," the first man said, firmly shaking his hand.

Gesturing toward Walton's thigh, James said, "Are ya all right?"

"Yes," Walton answered. "It'll raise a nasty bruise and I may limp for a day or two, but it will soon be right as rain."

"I'm glad," James said.

"I'm Elder Yorgasson." The second man offered another firm handshake.

"Ye're both named 'Elder'?"

The taller man chuckled. "It's a title," he said. "We are missionaries of the restored Church of Jesus Christ, here in Australia to bring the good news that God has spoken to a modern prophet. He has revealed His will to the people of earth once more."

"Ye're who?" James said, his brow wrinkling. "What church?"

Elder Walton smiled. "We represent The Church of Jesus Christ of Latter-day Saints."

"Never heard of it."

"Mormons," Elder Yorgasson said. "From America."

James shook his head. "Still never heard of it."

"We'd be happy to teach you," said Elder Walton. "And your family."

"No." James spoke quickly. "My wife and I have our own faith— our own *faiths,* truth be told, and we don't need some new-fangled doctrine from America to muddy things up. But I thank ya for yer assistance to that poor woman and her child," he said. "I'm afraid that happens far too often here."

"We've seen it in America too," Elder Yorgasson answered. "The native people there are going through much of the same."

"Again, my thanks, gentlemen. Ta, and may ya enjoy good health in Australia."

"We thank you for helping, Mr. Martin," Elder Walton said, and the men went their way.

James thought occasionally about that incident over the days that followed. He wondered what would bring two men—family men, if he read them correctly—all the way across the world's biggest ocean to teach people their "gospel." And he wondered why they thought God's gospel had to be restored. Weren't there enough churches already? Some claimed apostolic succession from Peter and Paul; others through the Holy Spirit. Whatever these men taught, James didn't care to hear it. He and Eliza had enough troubles quietly stewing already.

\* \* \* \*

In early August, Ed came to them on a Tuesday evening just before dinner. "I hope ye don't mind me intrudin'," he said. "I brought meat pies for dinner, if that helps."

Eliza opened the door wider. "Ye know ye're always welcome, regardless of the circumstance or the time of day. And ye don't always have to bring food, either. Ye've been more than generous with us. Hurry, come in out o' the cold."

The look on his face warned Eliza that she should probably find something for Little Jimmy to do in the other room. She removed the boy, and the three adults settled down around the table while the food stayed on the stove. James broke the silence. "What is it, mate?"

"I don't know what to do!" Ed blurted, his face showing his distress.

Eliza spoke. "Tell us what's happening."

It took Ed several mixed attempts to get the story out: Mr. Pembroke had come into the bank and had approached him for a business loan. Ed had begun the paperwork when out of the blue, Pembroke asked if he was married.

"I told him no, but I couldn't think of anything more to say," Ed sputtered. "I probably should have told him I was courtin', but I didn't think of it then. Anyway he invited me to dinner at his home, said he has a marriageable daughter he wants me to meet."

Eliza touched his hand. "Oh, Ed."

But Ed suddenly laughed aloud. "I think I've the answer to my prayer."

"What prayer?" asked Eliza.

James explained, and then Ed went on. "All I have to do is accept their dinner invitation, and then show up. Mrs. P. will recognize me as the man who asked to court Molly, and Molly will see me as I am. Wha'd'ya think?"

"I think it's risky, mate." James threw his wife a worried look. "I seriously advise ya against it."

"I don't see why," Ed answered.

Eliza tried to persuade him. "Ye may offend the Pembrokes in front of guests. And what if Molly thinks ye're there to court Celeste?"

"I ain't too worried about the Pembroke's feelings, 'Liza. But I do want to come clean with Molly and I think this may be the way. If she mistakes my purpose at the first, we can work that out. I'll think about what ye're saying, but I'm goin' to accept their invite. I can do that, at least."

"I don't think it's wise, Ed. I fear it sounds like the kind of social manners we'd expect in the mines, not among society folk like the Pembrokes, like ye're trying to be.

"I think it may be my best answer," Ed said.

"Then, we'll pray for ya," James said as he patted his friend's shoulder.

That was when Little Jimmy came into the kitchen. "Mum, isn't it time for food yet? I'm hungry."

"Sure'n 'tis time, Jimmy," Eliza told him. "Come, gentlemen. Let's have our tea. The rest of this situation can work itself out on fuller stomachs." They sat down to eat. Thanks to Ed's pies, the meal easily stretched to feed them all.

\* \* \* \*

On Wednesday, James came home from the mercantile with a weary heart. He tried to pep up before entering the house to greet his wife and child, but he'd had some unpleasant thoughts circulating for the past couple of hours and wondered whether he should share them with Eliza. Just as she was ready to serve, he spoke.

"I've something I'd like to talk with ya about," he said. "Can we sit for a moment while the dinner is cooling?"

"Aye." She dried her hands on her apron. "This looks serious," she said. "Is there a problem? Between us, I mean?"

"No, love. Nothing like that. It's about Ed."

She smiled. "Is he still fussing over what to wear on Friday?"

"No, there's more." He unraveled the story of how he'd been on an errand in the richer part of town when he'd walked past a jeweler's and realized the client inside the shop was Ed. "I thought about popping in, but the shop was small. I paused outside just to wait for him to step out so I could speak, maybe tease him a little about the big dinner, y'know?"

She nodded. "Aye. Go on."

"That's when I realized he was ordering a gift for a woman, custom made."

"A gift?" Eliza's face brightened. "James, he's proposing!"

He patted her arm. "Maybe and maybe not. He asked the jeweler what is the fashion for 'gifts between sweethearts' back in England."

"This all sounds very positive."

"I thought so too. The jeweler explained that ever since Prince Albert gave a ring to Victoria to cement their betrothal, rings are the thing. Ed said, 'I'll have a ring then. Make it in yer finest eighteen-karat gold.'"

"Oh, I knew it!" Eliza was practically bouncing.

"It was the part that came next that vexed me," James continued. "The jeweler said colored gemstones are the fashion and a prospective husband often chooses the stones partly for their color, but also for the first letter in the gem's name, like a pearl for *P*. Then he chooses the order of the stones so the letters spell something, usually the initials or the name of his intended. Ed said he wanted exactly that."

"Ohhhh," Eliza squealed. "I knew it."

"That was when a big cart rumbled by, and I couldn't hear most of the words. The only one I caught was he wanted an emerald for the E."

"What a delightful idea," Eliza said. "Molly will be so excited."

"But sweetheart, there's no E in Molly."

"Oh, no there isn't, nor in Mary . . ." Eliza's face fell. "Oh my. There are three in Celeste. Ye don't suppose—"

"I didn't want to suppose anything. I wanted ya to hear it just as I did."

"Did ye wait to ask Ed about it?"

James shook his head. "By then I was getting pretty uncomfortable, and I remembered what they always say about how eavesdroppers never hear anything good. Ed had more talking to do to finish his order and I needed to get back to the store, so I just went my way. I've been telling myself I shouldn't have been listening in the first place and that I really didn't hear what the whole thing was about. He could be sending it home to his sister for all I know—"

"Not likely. He asked about the fashion between sweethearts."

"Aye, that's true." He patted her hand. "Let's not assume. We've always known Ed to be an honest man. At least he's never been otherwise with us. Let's take him at his word and let it go at that unless we hear something more definite."

"All right," Eliza agreed. She hesitated. "But what if he really is courting—"

"I think it's best we don't consider that."

"But his idea to accept this invitation is harebrained and we as much told him so. That is, unless his real purpose is to— Oh, James! Molly would be so hurt—"

"And so would we. Still, if we're giving Ed the benefit, we have to start here and now."

She paused, but then she nodded. "Aye, ye're right. Still, ye mostly knew Ed when he was a poor man working someone else's mines. We don't really know how being so wealthy may have changed him. They say that happens with some." ·

"That's true enough, and he told me once he enjoys working with wealthy men and having nice things." James paused, his brow knit. "All the same we've never seen him be other than straight, and we know he doesn't always think clearly when it comes to social situations. That could explain why he's not thought this plan through. I think we need to go forward as if we never heard or suspected a thing. Later, if it should turn out we were wrong . . . well, then we will have to deal with it."

"Sure'n that's the way. I'll pretend I've heard nothing, although it won't keep me from fretting." She sighed and rose, brought the food to the table, and called Jimmy. Just before he came she said, "James?"

"Aye, love?"

"One way or t'other, I'm glad ye told me."

He nodded. "I'm glad too. I hope we'll all be glad at how this turns out."

# Chapter 6

"Did he tell ye why he isn't comin'?" Molly asked. Despite Eliza's assurances, she would not stop fretting that Ed would not be at tea. She had been trying to whisper to Eliza all the way through Mass and had even been distracted from going up to receive the Host, something Eliza could no longer do. "I told ye, Molly. I know why he isn't comin', but I can't tell ye."

"He's in trouble, isn't he? He can't come 'cause he's in jail." Molly wrung her hands as they walked toward Primrose Cottage.

"It's nothin' like that, Molly, and ye know it. Ed is not the kind o' man to be in that kind of trouble."

"Then it's another girl," she said. "He realized he's been wastin' his time with the likes o' me, and he's found someone else."

Eliza clamped down her own fear that Molly was right. She had promised herself to trust Ed, at least until he proved untrustworthy. She answered as if she'd never heard about Ed's visit to the jeweler's. "Oh, for heaven's sake. Ye know that man is head-over-heels crazy in love with ye. What would make ye even say that?"

"If I was a man, I'd want somethin' better'n me," Molly said. "Oh, Eliza! I won't see him for another week."

"That isn't necessarily—" Eliza began, but Molly cut her off.

"Mayhap it's just as I've been fearin'. He's too long from his gold claim and outta money. He had to go minin' before he got evicted or run into prison for the debts he's been runnin' up on flowers and such."

Eliza chuckled. "Ye're wrong, Molly, about two million times wrong."

Molly narrowed her gaze. "Now what on earth can ye mean by that?"

"I mean stop fussing and fretting. In the end, ye'll be happy with the answer." She touched her rosary, inwardly praying it was true.

"If ye say so." Molly subsided into pouting.

Feeling mildly dishonest, Eliza decided to help her friend prepare for the coming shock—at least, the one she knew about. "Molly, remember when I told ye Ed had secrets?"

"Aye."

"Sure'n he's getting ready to open up to ye, but the way he's planning to do it is a touch . . . odd. When ye find out, I don't want ye bein' angry with Ed, and I won't have ye bein' angry with me, either."

Molly looked up quickly. "He's not married, is he?"

Eliza laughed. "No, he most definitely is not. Stop frettin'."

They arrived at Primrose Cottage to find no one waiting at the gate though there was a large bouquet on the table. It was when their meal was nearly finished that Molly sighed. "I've been so busy worryin' over Ed that I haven't thought to tell ye the news at Pembroke House."

James and Eliza exchanged a look. James said, "What news?"

Molly spun out the story of how Mr. P. had come home from town with plans for a suitor for Miss Celeste. "He's a wealthy man, I hear," Molly said, "one o' the most eligible men in all Australia, a partner where the Pembrokes do their banking."

"He must have a great deal of money," Eliza said.

"Aye. Someone said he's worth two million pounds. Can ye fathom that? I hardly knew there was so much money in the world."

"It's a fortune," James said, "more than most of the peers in London can claim, more than a prudent man could spend in a lifetime."

Molly went on about how Mr. P. had invited the gentleman to tea, and Mrs. P. was having new linen aprons made for the staff. As she spoke, Eliza thought it a shame she wouldn't be there to see Molly's face when she saw their mystery guest, or to comfort her if . . . Then she had an idea. "Molly, do ye think Mrs. P. could use some extra help?"

James smiled. "That's a splendid idea. Ya can walk Molly home tonight. I'll put Little Jimmy down. Just tell Mrs. Pembroke ye'd like to volunteer."

Eliza agreed.

Somewhat later, as she walked Molly toward Pembroke House, Eliza asked, "Did Mrs. P. tell ye the guest's name?"

"I think she told Mrs. Biel, but I didn' catch it. Somethin' like Filch or Pelch . . ."

Eliza stopped herself from asking, "Maybe Welsh?" She cleared her throat instead.

They arrived at Pembroke House, and Eliza went in to speak to Mrs. P., who offered Eliza nearly twice what she would have expected. They arranged a time for her to arrive the following day.

As she left for the night, Eliza said, "Rest easy, Molly. It'll all come to a head very soon."

"Oh, I wish ye could tell me," Molly moaned.

"Trust, Molly. Remember how Ed looks at ye—like ye're somethin' good to eat and he's starvin'. Say yer prayers and rest easy." She only hoped she could follow her own advice.

"I doubt I'll close my eyes all night." Molly wrung her hands.

"I'll pray that ye sleep like a baby."

A light breeze riffled the leaves of the gum trees as Eliza walked home to Primrose Cottage, fingering the rosary in her pocket, reciting the prayers in her mind, and seeking the blessings of all her saints. If Ed had been leading Molly on this whole time . . . She chose not even to consider that.

\* \* \* \*

That Friday afternoon, James arrived a little early to take over the watch while Eliza went to Pembroke House. He found a pot of soup simmering on the stove and fresh bread cooling in the pie safe. There was a pie too, one Eliza had made using the last of the fall apples. "It seemed only fair," she told him, "seein' as how ye'll be doin' my job this evenin'."

"Ta," he said in thanks, "but ye're doin' my job this evenin', aren't ya? Earnin' bread to feed our family?"

Eliza grinned and kissed him. "Aye, I s'pose I am. It'll give us a little extra to pay back Elmer." She turned to her son. "Now ye be good for yer papa, hear me?"

The boy answered, "Aye, Mum." Then he added, "Come home safe."

"What a grown-up man ye're getting' to be, my wee Jimmy." Eliza kissed his forehead. "I'll check on ye when I come in," she promised.

Then she slipped on her warmest shawl and walked toward Pembroke House.

From the moment she arrived, it was clear this was no ordinary evening. An army of servants had scrubbed and polished until the normally clean home practically shone. They had put out fresh flowers and arranged everything to a *T*. Mrs. Pembroke clearly meant to show their family at its best. Eliza wondered how Mrs. P. would feel when their guest arrived and realized who he was.

A few minutes before the scheduled arrival, Molly found a quiet moment to speak to Eliza as they worked on garnishing plates. "I figured it out," she said, her face somber.

"Ye figured what out?" Eliza asked, not knowing how she'd correct Molly if all her guesses turned out wrong.

"I know Ed's secret," she answered. "He's our dinner guest tonight."

Eliza looked up with a start. "Molly, how did ye—?"

"After ye left last night, I asked Mrs. Biel the name of our important guest. She said he is Mr. Edmund Garrett Welsh, and I thought how strange this wealthy man should have a name so similar to that o' the poor man I've been seein'."

"So ye knew it then," said Eliza, wondering why Molly looked so glum.

"Aye, it was easy to put it together. I recalled ye jokin' I was two million reasons off, and I remembered Mr. P. sayin' the fancy guest was worth two million pounds. Then I understood the whole thing." Molly looked both hurt and angry.

"I hoped ye'd be okay with it when ye understood," Eliza ventured.

"Aye, I understand it all now, him payin' court to one o' the Pembrokes' hired staff afore he came courtin' Miss Celeste, gettin' the inside information . . . It's easy enough to figure now that I know."

"Molly!" Eliza prayed the conclusion was wrong.

"What I can't figure is why ye 'n James went along. Is he givin' ye money? If so, I hope it's enough to make it worth yer while. I thought ye were my friends."

"Molly, ye don't underst—" But the words were interrupted as Mrs. Biel entered the kitchen to say their guest was arriving and Molly was wanted in the dining room.

She left without looking back. Eliza choked back the need to call after her, to assure her of Ed's intentions. But could she really be certain herself? She touched the rosary in her pocket, praying that the rest of the evening would turn out better than it had so far. Then she eased the kitchen door open so she could watch the scene in the hallway.

Cooper opened the door—and there he was. Decked out as a gentleman of quality, Ed looked so refined and sophisticated that Eliza gasped, wondering if this could be the man she knew. He'd had both his hair and his beard trimmed, and he seemed comfortable in formal attire. He looked . . . Eliza searched for a word, and then she realized he looked handsome—large, but handsome and very 'quality.'

The difference was so remarkable that she wasn't surprised when Mrs. P. showed no sign of recognition. Ed was introduced to the Pembroke family, and each made a little bow or curtsy. Celeste outdid herself, sweeping into a deep curtsy and batting her lashes above her silk fan. Eliza suppressed a groan when she saw the extent of the girl's flirting and another as she watched Ed respond, taking Celeste's hand and bowing deeply. Then she thought, *Could Molly be right?* He seemed so at home in this setting. *Oh no,* she thought. *What have we done?*

Just then Mrs. Pembroke asked, "Mr. Welsh, have we met before?"

"I believe we have," Ed answered smoothly, but then he shook Mr. Pembroke's outstretched hand and said, "I hear ye have an excellent library, Augustus. Will ye show it to me before dinner?" Mr. Pembroke seemed flattered, and the two men disappeared into the library.

Eliza had to piece together what happened after that, but every time one of the staff came into the kitchen, they shared quick reports. Apparently, the men had waited in the library, talking about whatever men talked about until it was time for the meal to be served. Cooper had called everyone to tea, and the men had joined the family in the dining room while Molly joined the staff in the kitchen. Eliza kept trying to catch her eye, but Molly refused to look up.

During the first course, Mr. Pembroke regaled their guest with stories of the Pembroke family name—who his people were, what contacts he had in England and the British Empire, what peers were included among his distant relations, and how he had been growing his fortune, seeing to his children's future. When the entrée was served, Mrs. P. had begun discussing the virtues of her eldest daughter and how she had been carefully bred and educated, tutored in French and the pianoforte, and readied to become the wife of a prominent businessman.

It was when Mr. P. ordered the staff to carry out his rare Russian samovar that Eliza got to see what was happening in the dining hall. She helped Dolly with the samovar just in time to hear Mrs. P. ask, "Tell me, Mr. Welsh, isn't she lovely, our Celeste?"

She caught her breath as she heard Ed answer, "Aye, as lovely as a spring morning." He raised his glass to Celeste, and Eliza's heart dropped.

The samovar was heated and the tea prepared for serving. Eliza returned to the kitchen, her stomach in a knot. It was as the dessert was being served that Sarah came running into the kitchen. "Mr. Welsh has an announcement to make," she said as she arrived, breathless. "He wants the whole household staff to be there. Can ye imagine?"

Molly looked up for the first time. "Ye all go on without me."

"No, Molly," Sarah said. "He asked fer ye by name."

"He did?" Molly looked up with a flicker of hope on her face, but her expression fell again. "Oh, aye. I s'pose he may have a thing or two he needs to say to me."

Eliza's heart went out to her. She couldn't imagine how their friendship would recover. She hoped somehow there was still a positive explanation for all that was happening.

Molly put down the spoon she'd been using to stir the hot caramel sauce. "Very well then. Let's go hear it." She squared her shoulders as if marching to the gallows and led the way as the serving staff filed through the house and into the dining room. Eliza, unable to get closer, fell in near the back of the queue.

She found the staff lined up on one side of the room while the family sat at the table with looks of expectation and curiosity. She thought Miss Celeste looked rather like the cat that had eaten the cockatiel, and Eliza murmured a quiet prayer. She feared they'd been horribly misled.

Ed stood from his favored place at the foot of the table and tapped his knife on the edge of his goblet. "I've an announcement to make. I've come here tonight under false pretenses. Although in fairness, Augustus, I never told ye I wanted to court yer daughter. That mistake was of yer own invention."

"But you said she is lovely," Mrs. P. said.

"Aye, lovely as can be, but she is not for me."

Mrs. P. put her hands to her mouth, and Edmund turned toward her. "Harriet," he said, "tonight ye asked if we'd met before. Well, we have—at the Presbyterian Church when I asked if I might court a member of yer household staff."

Now Mrs. P. gasped, her eyes widening in shocked recognition, and she looked from Ed to Molly, who had finally lifted her chin. Ed pushed back his chair and stepped away from the table. "For some months now I've been goin' to tea in the Martin home every Thursday gettin' to know one of the finest women I've ever met in all my days."

Then, as the household held its collective breath, he crossed the room and dropped to one knee in front of Molly, drew out a jewelry box, and opened it to reveal a sparkling ring. Taking Molly's hand, he said, "Molly Mulvaney, I love ye with my whole heart and soul, and I'll be the most honored of all men if ye'll consent to be my wife."

Celeste burst into tears and ran from the room. Her mother ran after her, but the tantrum went otherwise unnoticed as everyone—servants and served alike—watched in fascination. Molly was crying as she said, "Are ye sure, Ed? With all this around ye, are ye sure?"

He took in Pembroke House with a sweep of his hand. "This means nothin', Molly. I can buy it many times over if I ever want it. What I can never buy is the heart of someone like ye. I love ye, Molly. Will ye marry me?"

Molly answered through joyful tears, "Aye, Ed. I will." The family sat with astonished expressions while the staff burst into delighted, if politely suppressed, applause. Eliza looked heavenward, thanking her saints for this blessed reprieve.

\* \* \* \*

"Ye should've seen it!" Eliza said sometime later as she repeated the whole story to her husband. "Ed has never looked more certain of himself, and Molly has never looked happier. Ed suggested she give notice, and Mr. P. got all somber-looking and said, 'No notice will be necessary, Molly. I think it just as well if ye leave tonight.' Molly started to say she had nowhere to go, but Ed told her he had a room waitin' in her name at a quality hotel and she's welcome to stay there until the wedding, though he hopes it shan't be long." Eliza paused to breathe.

James looked pensive. "I didn't know Ed was goin' to take it that far—proposin' in front of everyone. It might not've been a good thing to get on the bad side of the Pembrokes like that."

"Sure'n ye're right about that," Eliza answered. "After the proposal, everything went along so fast. Mrs. P. came out all huffy, paid me in cash, and told me to go and go now."

"That is not good." James shook his head.

"No, 'tis not. Then Ed told Molly to pack her things, and I calmly told Mrs. P. I would help. Molly and I put her few things in her carpet bag while Ed called for the coach he had waitin'. The three of us left together, and they dropped me here on their way into town. As we left there, I heard Ed tell Mr. P. he'd be happy to have his business at the bank, but it didn't matter one way or t'other if the Pembrokes banked with his firm or not. Mr. P. looked glum and said he would consider that carefully.

"Ed and Molly laughed as we drove away, and I'm happy for them, but I can't help thinkin' there was a better way to handle this."

James nodded. "I'm thinkin' ye're right."

"But I'm thrilled for Molly. Ah, can ye imagine it, James? Our Molly is wearing a fancy ring, and soon she'll be the wife of a rich man and the mistress of a rich house. I'm pleased for her."

"As am I," James said. "I'm happy for us too. We have each other and our bonzer boy and good friends, both still speaking to us since Ed did the right thing in the end. Tell me, did ya get the explanation of that emerald and what the ring spells?"

"Aye. There are four cut stones on Molly's ring—lapis lazuli, obsidian, a bright red stone called vanadinite, and the emerald, l-o-v-e. The stones spell *love*."

"Love. That's sweet." James stroked her cheek. "I'd like to give ya something like that."

Eliza returned his touch. "Ye don't need to. God has given me the best husband a woman could have, and if He chooses never to give us another child, we have a bonzer one in Jimmy."

"Aye, we do." He drew her closer.

"I'm grateful for ye, James."

"And I'm grateful for ya, Eliza." He held her tightly against him.

\* \* \* \*

Over the following days, Ed and Molly's plans took shape. Ed explained his appearance at Pembroke House by telling them he had spent his past weeks "studying on how to be a proper gentleman" so he could be a partner at the bank. When Molly went on about what a well-made, handsome man she was marrying, Eliza couldn't help but agree. Ed's transformation had astonished them all. A few days later, Ed also confided that Augustus Pembroke had come to the bank to reaffirm his business dealings—a measure Ed considered prudent for all parties.

Molly often sought Eliza's advice about wedding plans. Too short an engagement would cause tongues to wag, but tongues could be wagging anyway while the prospective bride lived unchaperoned in rooms rented by her prospective bridegroom. Although Ed announced loudly that he didn't give a fig what people thought of him, he was protective of Molly's reputation. Then a friend from St. Patrick's parish volunteered to rent a room at her home to Molly, where the couple would be chaperoned during Ed's visits. Ed complained the widow's house was too plain, but when Molly pointed out she had a ground-floor room to herself and was no longer sharing a bed in the attic of Pembroke House, Ed agreed.

In the meantime, he arranged for Molly to have a new trousseau prepared. He inquired about homes for sale in the richer neighborhoods of Sydney and sent Molly by coach to examine one property or another, giving her the option of choosing where they would set up housekeeping. When Molly complained that he should do the choosing since it was his money, he announced it was *their* money and he'd be happy to live in a canvas tent if Molly was there. Then he added, "And without ye, Molly, even the bloomin' Taj Mahal couldn't please me." Molly blushed and promised she'd choose something nice.

Other days the coach arrived early when Ed sent her out to choose china and silver and all the nice things he wanted her to have. Since Molly had seen lovely things only in places like Pembroke House, she felt uncertain of all her choices. Frequently, she directed the coach to Primrose Cottage so Eliza might accompany and advise her. Little Jimmy usually joined them, but Eliza drew the line when it came to high-quality bone china. On such days, she left him with the Hogans.

On one such expedition, Molly was examining china and wondering if she and Ed couldn't make do with simple crockery. Just as she turned to ask Eliza's opinion, they happened upon Fanny, a serving girl they knew from attending Mrs. Pembroke's church. After appropriate greetings, Fanny asked, "You two worked with Dolly, didn't ye?"

"Aye," Eliza answered. "She left us a couple of years ago to work for the Karl family. Are ye still in touch?"

"Aye," Fanny answered. "We're good friends. She was taken to hospital yesterday with pneumonia. It would be good if ye could stop by to speak to her. Might cheer her a bit."

"We'll do that," Molly said. "Thank ye, Fanny, fer lettin' us know."

As Eliza and Molly rode together to the Hogan home to gather Little Jimmy, they made plans to visit Dolly the following morning. Eliza thanked Abby profusely and asked if she might leave Jimmy the next day while she visited a sick friend. Abby readily agreed, but once mother and son were in the coach together, Little Jimmy complained. "I don't like to stay there, Mum. The girls make me play with their toys, and all they have are dollies 'n girl things."

"I'm sorry ye aren't happy, Jimmy," she said. "I promise I won't leave ye often, but I need ye to stay there tomorrow. The hospital isn't a good place for little boys."

Jimmy pouted but said he'd stay. When they arrived at the cottage, Jimmy wanted to play in the back garden, so Eliza brought chairs out and served lemonade to herself and Molly. She offered Jimmy some, but he wrinkled his nose.

"He's a beautiful boy, 'Liza," Molly said as she watched him dive into the project of turning chunks of sawed wood scraps into a town with buildings, coaches, and carts.

"Aye, sure'n he is," Eliza said. Then she confided to Molly about how she'd almost given up praying for another child. There was a tear in her voice as she said, "I don't know for certain why heaven has withheld the babies, but even if I only have Little Jimmy, I'll consider myself blessed."

"Aye, he's a blessing, even though he doesn't want to stay at the Hogans' again tomorrow," Molly said with a smile, "what with the dollies and all."

"He's all boy. 'Tis true enough," Eliza said. "I don't want to leave him, but I really don't see any other way."

"Ye really don't have a choice," Molly said.

"Aye. Sure'n that's the truth of it," Eliza answered. The women began talking again, sharing opinions about all they'd looked over that day.

*    *    *    *

When James arrived at the block above Primrose Cottage and saw the coach dropping off Molly, Eliza, and Jimmy, he decided to take a quick detour. Although he'd given up stopping by the house since he'd walked in on Eliza's prayers months ago, he knew he would not be interrupting something similar as long as both Molly and Jimmy were there.

He arrived to hear Jimmy playing loudly in the back garden, making the sounds of clopping hooves and coachmen's brakes. He opened the front door and walked through the house. The kitchen window was open, and he could hear the women talking. He stepped toward the back door and was about to open it when he heard his wife confide to her dearest friend, "I don't want to leave him, but I really don't see any other way."

James staggered backward, the pain in his chest as real as if he'd been stabbed. He groped blindly toward the front door, trying to force his chest to move, trying to get air.

She was leaving him. His Eliza had given up on him, had decided their life together had been a mistake, and now she was leaving. He had heard of people who divorced, but he'd never known one, ever, and now . . . James made his way onto the porch, so dizzy and weak he could barely stand.

As he walked toward the mercantile, he hardly knew what his feet were doing. He went to cross the street and stumbled in front of an oncoming cart. The driver stopped his team with a jerk of the reins and shouted, "Watch what ye're doin', mate!" while he veered around him. James stumbled into the store where Will Carter asked, "Are ye all right, man? Ye're white as a sheet."

"Aye, I'm well," James murmured by reflex, but he lurched into the back office and collapsed into a chair. There he sat over his books with his head in his hands, barely able to hold himself upright.

So she told Molly. When did she plan to tell him? Where would she go? What did she plan for Little Jimmy? He would not have her taking his only son. Could she go back home to Ireland? She still had kin there, but James couldn't imagine her willingly getting on another ship. Maybe she planned to work for Ed and Molly. That would explain why she had confided in her friend before telling him. Through it all, he kept hearing the refrain: She was leaving him; she was leaving. How could he live without Eliza?

He felt sick. He felt terrified and foolish and furious. By the time his normal work day ended and he started for home—having gotten no further with the books than he'd been when he entered—he wasn't certain which emotion he felt more, but he knew it was time to end the secrets. He gathered resolve, and a few minutes later he stalked into his home, slammed the door with a bang, and called, "Eliza, come here. Woman, we have to talk."

Eliza, who had been bent over the oven checking her shepherd's pie, straightened and glared at him. "What's the matter with ye, James? Jimmy's in the back garden. Ye keep hollerin' like that and ye're goin' to scare him half to death."

"Better frightened than fatherless, I'd say."

"What?" Eliza looked genuinely confused. "What're talkin' about?"

"I heard ya. I heard it all," he blurted. "Ya were talkin' to Molly . . ."

"Aye. I was talkin' to Molly." She stared, her brow furrowed. "Were ye here, James? Did ye stop in this afternoon?"

"Aye. I was here."

"Then why did ye not come on through? Ye could have had some lemonade—"

"Don't try to pretend. I heard. I heard ye say . . . Fie, woman, ye know what ye said. What I want to know is when were ye gonna tell me? Huh?"

"Tell ye what?" She started toward him. "What's wrong with ye? Ye're scarin' me." She put up a hand as if to touch his forehead, but he brushed it away so violently he rocked her slightly backward. "James, don't—"

"I heard ya!" he cried, grabbing her upper arms. "I heard ya tellin' Molly that . . ." His voice broke. "That ye're leavin' me."

"What?" The confusion was back.

"I heard ya say ye're leavin' me." James could no longer stop the tears. They coursed down his face, but he mumbled right through them. "I was standin' there, by the back door, gettin' ready to come out, and I heard ya say, 'I don't want to leave him, but I really don't see any other way.' Ya said it, Eliza. Ya were tellin' Molly that our ma . . . our marriage is over."

Eliza hurried to clarify. "I never said I was leaving ye." Again she lifted a hand, and this time he moved very slowly as she carefully smoothed the unruly curl from his forehead. "Ye're my one and only love. Why would I leave ye?"

Then the whole story came out: how he had heard her prayers to the Virgin repenting for their marriage and begging for her intercession and another baby, how he had been hoping they'd come to some peace over the past months, how he loved her more than anything and didn't know how he could live without her. "But I did hear ya, Eliza. If ye weren't thinkin' o' leavin' me, why did ya say it?"

"I didn't," Eliza answered, "at least, not about leavin' ye." She explained about Dolly and the hospital, Jimmy staying at the Hogans' and how he didn't like it there because of the girl toys. "Please know this, my darlin' husband: I would never leave ye, never. I love my saints and I love ye. I don't want to have to give up either, but I've already risked damnation for ye. Oh, James, ye're me life!" She put her arms around him, her head against his chest.

"Eliza, Eliza." James wrapped his arms around her, and they held each other and laughed and cried and kissed and held and held. They finally separated when they saw Jimmy, wide-eyed and staring, watching them from the back door.

"Jimmy, my love, come here and cuddle with us," Eliza offered, holding out her hand.

Jimmy just stood. "Ye were yellin'," he said. "Is everythin' a'right?"

"Aye, mate," James said. "It's more than all right. In fact . . ." He looked into Eliza's eyes. "In fact, I'd say it's really all right for the first time in a long while." He too held out a hand to Jimmy, and the boy happily snuggled between them. Then the three of them held and hugged in the kitchen for so long that the shepherd's pie had to be warmed over before they finally ate.

*   *   *   *

Item from *The Australian Banner*, Society Section

*In what is rumored to be the social event of the Sydney season, wealthy miner and acclaimed entrepreneur Edmund Garrett Welsh took Mary Margaret "Molly" Mulvaney as his wife. The pair were wed in a nuptial Mass at St. Patrick's Church on Saturday, September 26. The bride wore white satin with rows of gathered Belgian lace and a multi-tiered skirt with extravagant crinolines in the new continental fashion. The groom was charming in a dove-gray morning coat.*

*It was a lovely spring day as the bride entered the church carrying a bouquet of lilacs and apple blossoms. She wore a coronet of apple blossoms in her hair. Following the ceremony, the couple received guests in the dining hall of the Darling Harbour Hotel, where the groom provided a delightful repast. The newlyweds will make their home in a posh new section of the Balmain neighborhood.*

# PART THREE:
## Changing

# Chapter 7

**February 1858**

"I'm thinkin' Edmund Jr. if it's a boy," Molly was saying, "and if it's a girl, we want to call her Eliza, after ye."

"Ah, Molly," Eliza answered. "Sure'n that would be an honor, but ye can always change yer mind, and it won't hurt my feelings."

"Maybe even as a middle name. Or mayhap we'll give her yer formal name, Mary Elizabeth, and call her Mary."

"That would be lovely. But it's probably a boy."

It was a fair Tuesday afternoon, and they sat sipping lemonade on the back porch of Molly's home, watching over the garden where just a week ago Little Jimmy had celebrated his fourth birthday. The two families had quickly fallen into the habit of Thursday evening tea at the Martin home and Monday evening tea at Welsh House.

Eliza had been there when Molly had chosen a relatively modest house in upper Balmain—"only" six rooms on the main floor with a portion of the second floor taken up by balconies and porches; Ed had argued that it was too small but bowed to Molly's choice. There were no servants' quarters. Although Molly admitted to Eliza that she couldn't keep up this home and garden without plenty of help, she preferred to hire mostly day workers who left to be with their families in the evenings—all except for Ida, the cook's helper, who had nowhere else to go and lived in a spare room in the family part of the home.

Eliza had heard enough talk to know Molly's staff was well compensated. Molly also insisted that each have a voice on any topic that affected their lives, health, and work. More than once Eliza had thought that if she were ever to be in domestic service again, there were few better places to work than Welsh House. Molly's servants obviously loved her.

"When do ye figure ye're due?" she asked. Given her friend's girth, it was difficult to tell if Molly were already well along.

"If my calculations are correct, this little one should arrive just a week or so before our first wedding anniversary."

"I'm happy for ye, Molly." Eliza rose to hug her friend. "And I'll bet Ed is just fit to burst. Such a pleased and proud papa he'll be."

"Aye, ye ought to see him. Ye'd think he's the first human male who ever sired a child. Of course, we're not tellin' most people yet, and I'll thank ye to keep—"

"Oh, don't fret. I understand. Ye don't want people to know at the start—just in case."

"Aye, just in case."

"Have ye written to tell yer family back home?"

"Aye. We'd wait a while if they were here, but since it takes weeks for a letter to go by ship, we decided to write as soon as we were certain. Ed even offered to book passage for Ma if she wants to come, but Ma's never been outside County Cork in her life—and I hear she's not well of late. If I weren't in my current condition, I might be thinkin' of going to her instead—while I still can." Molly's eyes filled with tears.

"I know what ye're sayin'. We both knew when we left Ireland that we might never see it again. I know I won't, considerin' they'd have to get me on a ship again." Eliza set her jaw. "Anyway, it's unlikely we'll ever be back."

"'Tis sad but 'tis so." Molly sighed and rocked. She adopted a lighter tone as she said, "Speakin' of home, I'm wonderin' if any news has come from London of late. D'ye know?"

"James hasn't mentioned anything. Why?"

"The royal wedding was to have been last month, wasn't it? Princess Victoria?"

"Aye, she was to have wed that prince of Prussia—Frederick, I believe."

Molly sighed. "So sweet, a royal wedding."

Eliza gave her a sly look. "So, what's this about? Were ye expectin' an invitation?"

Molly laughed. "I'm just wonderin' what the wedding was like and what she wore. Ye know, just bein' curious."

Eliza grinned. "Well, ye needn't fret. She couldn't have worn anything finer than ye had fer yer own wedding."

Molly chortled. "Now ye're just flatterin'."

"Sure'n ye know I am."

"Well, ye needn't quit anytime soon."

Eliza laughed and added, "The wedding was scheduled for late last month. We probably won't hear for a while yet."

"Aye," Molly answered. They sat in companionable silence until Eliza noticed Jimmy grubbing in the dirt of a flower plot, pulling out the young scarlet ribbon shrubs that Weeks, the gardener, had so meticulously set out moments before.

"Jimmy!" she called. "Come away from there." She got up and darted across the lawn. "I'm sorry, Mr. Weeks. He doesn't mean to be a problem."

"I know it, ma'am," Weeks responded. "He's just an energetic boy is all. I'll have him help me plant the annual flowers come spring. Don't ye be worryin' 'bout him."

"Ta for yer kindness," Eliza said as she pulled her squirming son to the birdbath, where she rinsed his hands. "I think we'd best be goin'," she said as she returned to her friend. "If we don't, Jimmy will tear up yer whole yard. Besides, I've a batch of hand-washing to do before I'm done for the evening."

"I thank ye for comin'," Molly answered. "I fear I don't know how to live the life of leisure. I keep helpin' Jane with the laundry and Ida with the dishes. I do believe I embarrass poor Edmund from time to time."

"Edmund adores ye," Eliza said, "but ye do need to keep learnin' the ways of people of quality. Maybe ye can get into some of those society groups Mrs. P. used to go to."

"Not while Mrs. P. is still in 'em." Molly sighed. "She has nothin' to do with me these days, and she's made certain all her friends know to snub me too. She says I'm pork pretending to be lamb. Can ye fathom it?"

"Sure'n 'tis a shame she can't just let it go, but Mrs. P. always did have a brassy side. I still go with James to the Presbyterian services, on account of the Hogans, and Mrs. P. makes somethin' of a point to brush me by."

"I'm sorry, Eliza. I didn't want any o' this to come back on ye."

"Don't ye be worryin' about it, Molly. James and I have no need of the Pembrokes, and Mr. P. knows better than to snub yer Ed. It's sad they can't be more acceptin', but it isn't hurtin' us any." Through the open window she heard Molly's new grandfather clock chiming the hour. "I really must be goin' now. Thank ye for a lovely afternoon."

Molly asked Smythe to bring the carriage around, and Eliza enjoyed the ride back through the city. She sat near the window pointing out all the sights to Jimmy, who could tell her the names of every kind of carriage, coach, or cart they passed. Her son loved anything with wheels. She snuggled against him, breathing in his little-boy scent.

These few months since their friends' wedding had gone so well for James and Eliza. Eliza hadn't realized that James had been holding back recently, not quite making a full commitment because of his fears. Now he was all hers in ways he had never been, and she couldn't have been happier. With his hard work, James had made up all but two of the back payments they owed to Elmer, and they would soon be thinking about adding on to Primrose Cottage, giving Jimmy a room of his own and not just a space in the loft above the kitchen.

Eliza looked forward to that. Lately she'd had evidence that she might not only be barren but going through the change of life as well— just as her maiden aunt back home had done while still in her twenties. Her monthly courses had continued, but they were becoming spotty and irregular. Was this what had happened to Aunt Tess? And was this some fault in the women of her family? Or was it a punishment from God? She straightened her spine and thought, *So be it then*. If she was only going to have one child, she wanted to give him all the best she could offer.

*  *  *  *

James could not have been happier. Hogan's three stores were prospering, and the one James managed had become their flagship. Each day Hogan trusted him with more and greater responsibility. The Hogans had four daughters, and Elmer was plain about his intention to sell the whole business to James one day—unless perhaps a future son-in-law took an interest.

Even more important was his new understanding with Eliza. Until their catharsis in the kitchen, he'd feared the rift created by their differences; he had pretended with Eliza. He did not realize how much he was holding back, simply because he expected things might go wrong. Now he was astonished by the power of the love that poured forth, both for her and for their growing son.

On this bright summer Tuesday in February, he had just left a meeting with Elmer where they looked at a possible location for a fourth store. He hummed as he walked back to his shop, enjoying the scenery, his mind full of plans and possibilities. He passed by a small park where men were gathering. It wasn't a large group—maybe twenty in all, but he noticed them immediately because of their mood, which was rapidly becoming more hostile as men raised their voices and then their fists. James was beginning to wonder how he might best intervene when a police constable arrived, breaking it up. As those on the outside dispersed, he was surprised to recognize the two at the center. He walked over.

"Elder Walton," he said in acknowledgment. "Constable, is there some kind of problem?"

"Ye know these men?" asked the officer, his face stony.

"Aye, I do, sir." James scrambled to come up with both names. "This is Elder Walton and this is Elder . . . Yorgasson. They are ministers from America."

"Ye're the clerk from the mercantile, ain't ye?"

"Aye, sir. James Martin."

"I've seen ye there. Well, Mr. Martin, can ye vouch for these cobbers?"

James thought carefully. How could he vouch for men he barely knew? Yet he'd seen them resolve a violent situation without violence and care for a defenseless child. "Aye, sir. I can tell ya that I've seen them break up trouble rather than cause it."

The officer hesitated. "Very well, then. You two go your way, but no more of your big gatherings in the park, ye hear? There's too great a risk for 'em to go bad."

"We understand," Elder Walton said. He held out his hand to the officer, who only looked at him.

"Go on, then." The officer waited until James turned to go. When the two Americans followed, the officer left in the other direction.

Elder Walton spoke. "Thank you for coming to our aid, Mr. Martin. We intended no harm, but it seemed harm was about to come of it. We appreciate you speaking for us."

"Happy to help," James answered. "So is there anything else I can do for ya today—besides listenin' to yer teaching?" He said it in a jesting tone, but the answer was more serious.

"We'd be glad of a meal, if you can help us," Elder Walton said.

James stopped walking and gave the men a studied once-over. Elder Walton had seemed thin before, but his features were now almost gaunt, and both men—even the stout Elder Yorgasson—were using their belts to gather up their trousers around shrinking waists. "Don't ye have money from yer church in America?"

Elder Walton answered, "The Savior calls us to travel without purse or scrip. We depend upon the people we teach to give us places to stay and food. Lately . . . well, we haven't seen much success."

James looked squarely at them. "How long has it been since ye've eaten?"

"That's not at issue—" Elder Walton began.

"Two days," said Elder Yorgasson.

James shook his head. "So the good folk here in Sydney consider themselves too Christian to hear yer doctrine but not Christian enough to feed ya?"

Walton managed a weak smile. "We can't blame them for being wary of strangers."

"Come to the mercantile," James said. "I can't do much for ya, but I can come up with a kidney pie and an apple, I think. We may even have hot cross buns left from this morning."

"Thank you," they both responded, and Yorgasson added, "We're grateful."

James led them to the store. He directed them to the outhouse and gave them a place to wash up at the water pump in back. Then he gathered two kidney pies, two apples, and two hot cross buns, along with two glasses of clean pump water. He rang up the sale, paid for the food from his own pocket, and carried it to the hungry men.

He expected to see them set upon the food like hungry wolves, and so he was surprised when they thanked him graciously and bowed their heads. Elder Yorgasson offered a prayer of thanks and a blessing on James and his store. When they had said their amens, they began to eat, carefully savoring each bite.

"I thank ya for yer blessing," James said, impressed, "and I'll invite ya to my home for tea this evenin'—if ye'll not bring up yer doctrines to my family."

"We'd be grateful, Mr. Martin," Elder Walton answered.

As the men finished their meal, James told them how to get to Primrose Cottage, and then he sent Will to tell Eliza he had invited guests for tea. He may not want to hear these men's ideas, but he surely didn't want to see them hungry.

\* \* \* \*

"A grand meal, Mrs. Martin," Elder Walton said as he pushed his chair back from the table. "I don't know when I've ever eaten a better pasty, and the plum pudding is delicious. Aren't you having any, ma'am?"

"No, I think not, but thank ye for asking. I've been thickenin' a bit lately, so I'm tryin' to cut down."

James saw Eliza blush and reached for her hand. "Ya look lovely, sweetheart, and this puddin' is one of yer best. Ya really ought to give it a try."

Eliza's blush only deepened. "No, James. But thank ye."

Elder Walton cleared his throat.

"I'm still not accustomed to seeing summer vegetables in February," Elder Yorgasson said, clearly changing the subject. "They're wonderful."

James smiled. "Aye, the seasons take a bit of getting used to."

"As do the animals," Elder Walton said. "We surprised a little rabbit-eared bandicoot near our cots last evening."

"Ya don't see them often," James said, "them being night hunters and so shy."

"We shall consider it a privilege, then," Walton said with a smile.

Yorgasson said, "Mr. Martin, your wife's a skilled cook and your son's a bright boy. And you, sir, are a decent, Christian man. Your arrival today was an answer to our prayer."

James stood. "It was little enough to do," he said. The missionaries also stood.

Elder Walton said, "We'd like to leave you with a blessing if we may."

James hesitated but remembered the blessing they had left on his store. "Very well," he said. "Thank ya."

Soon he, Eliza, and Jimmy were kneeling with the two Americans. Elder Walton prayed on their behalf, thanking the Lord for the restored gospel of Jesus Christ, for prophets to guide people and reveal His will, for the Savior's great plan of salvation, and for the opportunity of serving in Australia. Then he thanked Him for the Martins and asked a blessing on their home "that they might receive all thy richest blessings and especially those gifts for which they both have prayed." The words caught James's ear, but he tucked them away to consider later.

"I'm glad I came upon ya when I did," James said after the prayer was over.

"So are we," Walton answered. "We've taught in that park often, but we've never had it go that bad. Perhaps being so hungry . . ." He paused, embarrassed. "Well, let's just say we were praying that some Christian soul would see our need."

"Well, don't ya ever get that hungry again," James said. "I can't feed ya ever' day, but Eliza and I are good for a meal now and then—should ya ever find ye're goin' without."

"Aye," Eliza said. "We haven't much, but we're grateful we can share. If ye're hungry, come here and we'll see ye're fed. It may not be splendid fare, but ye'll eat."

"That's kind of you, Mr. Martin, Mrs. Martin. We'll remember it."

James and Eliza stood in the doorway as they left. "They seem like good men," she said, turning to go in.

James answered, "Aye, they do." And James wondered what they had meant in asking for blessings that he and Eliza both had prayed for.

As they turned to go inside, Eliza heard familiar chiming. "Listen, James. It's a bell bird."

"Aye."

"Ye were with me the very first time I ever heard those chimes. Tonight they sound like church bells, don't ye think?"

"Aye, they do," he answered. As he led his wife inside and closed the door, he wondered too if the birds' call this night had a deeper meaning.

\* \* \* \*

James was not the only one who had noticed the missionary's words.

"Really?" Molly asked Eliza the next day. "What *exactly* did he say?"

"He asked that we might have all of the Lord's richest blessings and especially the ones that we both had prayed for."

"That seems an odd thing—unless they just assume everybody's praying for somethin'."

"Sure'n that could be the case." Eliza folded her hands. "I dunno, though. It seemed . . . different, like he knew something. It was . . . odd."

"And these fellas are Yanks?"

"Aye, come all the way across the wide Pacific. Can ye imagine what *that* voyage would be like?" Eliza shuddered.

Molly pursed her lips. "They must be tough fellas. I think I'd like to see 'em for myself. D'ye think James could find 'em again? Maybe invite 'em to tea when we come tomorrow?"

"I dunno. I can ask." Eliza began gathering her things. "Jimmy, we need to be goin'. Let Mr. Weeks do his plantin' without yer help, son."

"He's no bother, missus," Weeks said.

"Thank ye, Weeks. Ye're very kind." Eliza led Jimmy back toward Molly. "I'll check with James about tomorrow. Perhaps I can ask Will Carter to bring ye the message—"

"No need to do that. I'll send Smythe with the carriage in the afternoon. If ye have a message for me, ye can send it back with him."

Eliza smiled broadly. "Sure'n ye're learnin' to be a lady o' leisure, after all."

Molly looked embarrassed. "Aye, I'm catchin' on quickly, if I do say so myself."

"Well enough, then. I'll try to have word for Smythe."

When she told James, he seemed surprised by Molly's interest but said he'd be walking past the same park in the morning. If the men were anywhere around there, he'd invite them. By the time Smythe arrived, Eliza told him Elders Walton and Yorgasson would be joining them at tea.

* * * *

Once again, James had carefully instructed the missionaries on what they could and could not say, and they were respectful of his requests. Introductions to Ed and Molly went well, and James avoided the risk of hearing more unusual doctrine by saying grace himself. He was just reaching for the potatoes when Ed asked, "So what is this about a new prophet?"

The two missionaries looked to James, who pursed his lips, thinking he should have instructed Ed as well. "Ya can answer his question," he said with a curt nod.

"It began in the spring of 1820," Elder Walton began, and over the next few minutes he unfolded an amazing story about an interview between a simple farm boy and the creators of the universe—the Father and the Son. He talked about the restored knowledge that the Father, Son, and Holy Spirit are three separate beings, individuals united in purpose.

This was more than James had bargained for, but just as he was about to change the subject, Ed asked, "And what about this gold Bible?"

Elder Walton looked to James, who reluctantly nodded. He then told of ancient people who left the Old World some six hundred years before Christ and traveled to the Americas. Because of dissension, they became two distinct nations who suffered devastating wars culminating in the annihilation of one group. He talked of how these nations' prophets, inspired by God, had kept records on golden plates.

"The last of those prophets," Elder Yorgasson continued, "a man named Moroni, buried the plates in a stone box on a hill. In 1823, when Joseph was a bit older, that same ancient prophet—now resurrected as an angel—came to him and told him about the golden plates."

Resurrected angels? James drew himself up. He was about to speak when Molly asked, "So how did this farm boy read that record? I don't s'pose it was written in American?"

"No, no English," Elder Walton said, continuing the story without even looking at James. "Over time the Angel Moroni tutored him, and some four years later, Joseph received those plates together with a tool designed for translating. The finished work is called the Book of Mormon because Mormon, Moroni's father, was the editor who abridged all the ancient plates and put them together in one book. The book has now been printed, and we have a copy we can leave with you if you'd like to have a look at it." He held up a copy and looked to James.

But James's patience had run out. Like the others, he had more or less stopped eating while he listened to the men's wild fantasy. As he watched the looks of doubt and disbelief growing on the faces of those around him, he had become steadily more eager to ask these men to stop, yet he had listened out of respect for Ed. Now he saw his chance.

"Gentlemen, with all due respect, that is the silliest bunch of horse feathers anybody ever gathered. I'm glad Ed asked ya the questions so we could all hear what ye're about, and now I think we should have our tea. I'll stick to my Bible, thank ya."

"We use the Bible as well," Elder Yorgasson said eagerly. "We see it and the Book of Mormon as companion volu—"

"Enough!" James's voice was suddenly sharp. The room resounded with the shock. "And now I'll thank ya to keep yer foolishness to yerselves. Let us eat."

A tense silence fell as everyone picked up their forks. It was Little Jimmy who finally broke it. "Did the angel have wings?"

The adults chuckled uneasily, but Elder Walton looked to James before he answered. James reluctantly nodded. "No, Jimmy," Walton said gently. "He did not have wings. Angels are messengers from heaven. Otherwise, they look very much like us."

James cleared his throat, and the silence fell again, broken only by requests to pass the potatoes or the salt.

"D'ye men have families?" The question came from Molly.

"Yes," both men answered, and Elder Walton added, "We both have wives and children."

Molly gasped. "And ye left 'em there alone?"

"For a time," Elder Yorgasson answered.

"Why?"

Elder Walton answered, "God has called his followers to deliver the news of His restored gospel to every nation, kindred, tongue, and people.

The current prophet, Brigham Young, called us to bring the word to Australia."

"I thought ye said his name was Joseph Smith," Ed cut in.

Yorgasson answered. "The first prophet of the new dispensation was Joseph Smith, but he faced severe persecution from the time he spoke of his vision. He was shot to death by a mob a few years ago when the Church was still in Illinois. His successor, Brigham Young, is the prophet and President of the Church now, and the man who led us to the Western territories."

"But it's the frontier," Molly said, "and ye just left yer families there to fend fer themselves?"

"They are not alone," Elder Yorgasson answered. "There are many brothers and sisters in the gospel who are making sure they are cared for."

Elder Walton spoke. "You might say that we left our families for a short time so that other families might be together forever."

"How's that?" Eliza asked.

Elder Walton answered. "The prophets of our day have brought the good news that God's sealing power, given to Peter by the Savior himself, has been restored to the earth. With it, in special buildings called temples, husbands and wives can be sealed together for time and all eternity, and their children sealed to them."

Then Elder Yorgasson added, "The Saints had a beautiful temple in a city called Nauvoo back in Illinois. It was lost when our people were driven out. Now that the Church is in Utah Territory—we call it Deseret—we're building new temples. Someday we will be able to perform sealing ordinances again."

Eliza and James looked quickly at one another. James was gentler when he said, "And now we've heard enough."

Molly helped Eliza clear, and they served a simple dessert. Again, the Americans graciously thanked their hosts and asked if they might leave a blessing. This time James demurred, but he invited them to come again the next Thursday. They let their disappointment show very little as they restated their thanks.

"We so appreciate your kindness," Elder Walton said as they walked to the front gate while James and Eliza watched from the porch, "and please know you will be in our prayers."

"I am always thankful for a good man's prayers," James said, "but please, no more of yer doctrines."

Elder Walton answered, "We promised you, Mr. Martin, and we will comply. Thank you for your patience today while we answered questions." James watched as the men walked away.

"Well, what did ya think of that?" James said as he closed the front door.

Edmund spoke. "It sounded mighty peculiar, but it's also clear those men believe every bit o' their odd story. It may make about as much sense as my great-aunt Martha's scraggly beard, but they are tellin' us the truth as they see it."

"Aye," said Eliza. "'Tis the case. They've given up much to bring their message."

"To leave their families and come here without even any money?" Molly shook her head in wonder. "Aye, they'd have to be believin' it."

"People believe all sorts o' odd things," James said in dismissal. The conversation took a turn, and the couples visited for a time. It was some while later, when Little Jimmy had gone off to bed and James and Eliza watched their friends ride away in their carriage, that Eliza noticed something sitting on the chair near the door. "Look, James." She crossed the room to pick up the book. "The Yanks left their strange Bible. D'ye think they meant to?"

James shook his head. "I don't know what to think. But I don't want that book in our home. Burn it in the stove."

Eliza started to add the book to the wood pile but hesitated. "Sure'n we need to be gettin' rid of it, but I hate to waste good paper. Maybe we can use it in the outhouse?"

James paused, his mouth set in a tight line. Then his face relaxed, and he nodded. "Aye, that's a fair enough purpose for it. Put it in the outhouse. We'll see that it gets its best use there."

# Chapter 8

MIDMORNING THE NEXT DAY, JAMES was unloading a box of horseshoes when Elmer Hogan walked in unannounced. James turned to welcome him. "G'day, Elmer. What're ya doin' on this side o' the street?"

"Is it true ya've been feedin' those Yanks, those Mer-mans?"

"The Mormons, y'mean?"

"Aye. Mer-man, Mormon, makes no difference to me. I don't care what they call themselves; I call 'em deluded tools of the devil. Billy Halstead down the block said he saw 'em leavin' Primrose Cottage last night."

"Aye. They came to tea."

"James Martin, I thought ya were smarter than that. Ya know those two've been causin' trouble all over town. Ye're not listening to their nonsense, are ya?"

James stepped around the counter. "No, sir, I most certainly am not. In fact, I told them I wouldn't have them doin' any of their teachin' in my home."

Elmer relaxed his stance. "Then why did ya have 'em over?"

"They're hungry, Elmer. Giving them a meal seemed the Christian thing to do."

"Aye." Elmer sat on the stool nearest James. "But lettin' 'em get good 'n hungry might be a blessing too. Maybe they'd pack up and leave us all in peace."

James shook his head, but he chose his words carefully. "They seem peaceful enough."

"Then ye've not been payin' attention. I spoke to the police constable yesterday, and he told me about a riot he broke up in the park across town."

James pondered what to say next. He had witnessed that scene and had seen no riot. "Perhaps it's others around 'em causin' the trouble."

"It's *them* causin' the trouble." Elmer's volume increased with the color in his face. "If they weren't teachin' silliness about angels and gold bibles, there'd be no trouble at all."

James kept his voice even. "Perhaps."

"But there's somethin' else I gotta ask ya, Martin. Will Carter said ya fed those fellas here in the store t'other day."

"Aye, sir. They hadn't eaten in two days. It didn't seem decent to leave 'em starvin' in the streets—us being a Christian people and all. Besides, we're here to sell product, aren't we? The money's the same color whether we're feedin' Presbyterians or Catholics or Mor—"

"I won't have it."

"Pardon?"

Elmer stood. "I won't have those Mermans in my store, d'ya hear? I've trained ya better than that. Ya know my policy: no black folk nor riffraff."

James cringed as he heard the familiar words. He had never agreed with Hogan's policy, especially about the aboriginal people. Still, it was Hogan's store. James tried to keep his voice calm. "I didn't see these men as either, sir."

"Well, I do. I can't have my good customers seein' them Yanks here. D'ya understand me? They are not welcome."

James swallowed hard. "Aye, sir. I hear ya."

"And ye'd be wise to make the same policy at the cottage. People see ya entertainin' those Mermans and ye'll lose yer good standin' in this community." He paused. His expression softened as he put one beefy arm around James's shoulder. "Ye've been like a son to me," he said with some feeling. "I don't wanta see ya ruin yer life."

James managed a small smile. "Thank ya, sir."

"See that ya take care."

"I will."

Hogan went his way, but his presence remained throughout the afternoon, both the anger and the implied threats hanging over James as he went about his day. Though the Yanks' story had seemed silly to him, he'd never seen anything to inspire this kind of rage and fear. He couldn't help wondering why so many people were reacting so strongly.

* * *

That Friday afternoon in early March was as pretty a summer day as Eliza had seen. Jimmy was playing in the yard, driving his wood scrap wagons over mounds of heaped earth. James had saved the small coins from his pocket each day to come up with enough cash to buy the cup-and-ball toy Elmer Hogan had been showcasing, and Jimmy was enjoying it thoroughly. Eliza had some time before starting their tea, and she was feeling sick again, so the thought of working with food made her queasy. Perhaps if she rested a bit and took a little time in the outhouse, she'd feel better. She thought it would be safe to leave Jimmy nearby, where she could hear him, while she visited the privy and tried to settle her stomach.

Since there was still paper left in the outdated product catalog James had brought home, she decided not to use the missionaries' book just yet, but because she was curious, she picked it up anyway. It wouldn't hurt just to have a look, would it?

She flipped through the opening material and settled on the first page. The structure and layout seemed familiar, not too different from what she saw in the Bible, but what was a Nephi? She came to "I, Nephi, having been born of goodly parents . . ." and settled in to find out.

* * *

James walked home with a heavy heart. He had never given Elmer Hogan any reason to mistrust him, yet the suspicion and the anger of the morning's visit still hung heavily. He'd been astonished by the missionaries' strange tale and amazed that apparently sensible men could believe such silliness, and yet he had seen nothing in it—and certainly nothing in the men themselves—to stir the emotion that seemed to follow wherever they went. He stopped at the front door and rubbed a crease from between his brows before he stepped inside.

"Eliza, I'm home." He opened the door to the bedroom, but it seemed he was alone in the house. Then he heard Jimmy playing in the backyard. A dark feeling came over him: something was wrong.

He hurried to the back door. "Eliza?"

"She's in the outhouse," Jimmy said. "She's been there a really long time."

Terrible thoughts jumped into his mind. His wife had been ill so often lately. "Eliza!" He ran toward the outbuilding, prepared to break the door down.

That was when he saw her coming out. "Aye, James. I'm here." She looked flustered.

"What's wrong?" he asked, going toward her. "Are ya all right?"

"Y-yes. I'm . . . I'm well enough off. Just embarrassed, I guess." She waved a hand to cool her flame-red face.

"Embarrassed about what?"

She looked around. "What time is it? Are ye home early?"

"Not at all. In fact, I'm a wee bit late." He hesitated. "Are ye sure ye're all right?"

"Aye. I'm sorry, James. I got in there, and the missionaries' book was there, and I started readin' and I guess I lost track o' the time."

"Ye're not . . ." James gulped. "Ye're not actually listening to them, are ya? I thought we agreed to get rid o' that book."

"No, James, I'm not listening. I was just curious, is all. And then I got started reading and it was an interesting story—about a father and his four sons, two faithful and two rebellious . . . I guess it kinda reminded me of my da and my brothers, y'know?"

"It's a story?"

"Aye, kind of an interesting one." She hesitated. "What did ye think it was?"

He shrugged. "Stuff about angels and gold plates, I s'pose." He touched her shoulder. "Ya sure ye're not gettin' . . . involved with this gold Bible?"

She huffed at him. "Sure'n I'm not goin' to give up Mother Mary and all my saints for this. Let me go, husband. I'm late enough gettin' our tea as it is."

James watched as she washed at the outdoor pump and went inside. Then he stood for a long while, watching the door where she had entered, his brow wrinkled in puzzlement.

\*   \*   \*

Before Mass that Saturday morning, Eliza took Molly aside and told her the story of the missionaries' book and the family's late tea. "James asked me if I was actually considering the Americans' stories. Can ye imagine?"

Molly's brow wrinkled in consternation. "Well, are ye?"

"Molly!"

"I can't imagine ye sittin' in there half the afternoon readin' their silly book if ye aren't interested in their message."

"That's not how it is." Several of the other parishioners who were entering the church turned when they heard Eliza's voice rise. She flushed and looked away. "It's not their doctrine that interested me," she said, whispering. "I thought their book would be more stories about this Smith fellow and angels and gold plates and such, but it isn't that at all. It's sort of an adventure story about a father and his sons who left Jerusalem and traveled in the wilderness—" She caught Molly's look. "Please, Molly, don't look at me that way. If I didn't give up my saints for my own husband, ye know I'm not about to give them up for some golden Bible."

"Ye just got caught up in the adventure story, ye say?"

"Aye. It was just so different from what I expected, and I found the story reminded me of my da. The father is called Lehi. He has some sons who are faithful and some who are rebellious . . . I thought of my own brothers. I just found it interesting is all."

Molly let out a long, troubled sigh. "It's almost time for the service," she said. "We'd better go in."

"Let's go in then."

Eliza took Jimmy by the hand, and they prepared to enter the building. Just before they did, Molly said, "Eliza? Maybe ye should talk to Father Michael after the Mass. Tell him about the missionaries and the book. See what he has to say."

Eliza started to object but answered, "Aye. Thank ye, Molly. I will."

They entered, made their obeisance, and settled into a pew just as the service began. Eliza tried to concentrate on the familiar words, keeping her rosary in hand, but she found her mind wandering to the story of Lehi and his four sons, the family wandering in the desert like the Hebrews of old, the broken bow, and the dream of the tree of life. She was also distracted by the small, speculative looks Molly kept throwing her way. She didn't want to share her secret with Father Michael, who was sure to tell her to toss the evil book away, and yet she knew from the way Molly looked at her—from the way James had looked at her too—that speaking with the priest was the first step toward cleansing her mind and heart. It seemed a shame; she had found nothing objectionable in the story, and it had been enjoyable. Still, one could hardly afford to hazard one's soul. She returned her attention to the Mass.

When the service ended, Molly took her elbow and started toward the front of the church. Eliza pulled away. "Ye don't have to lead me, Molly. I'm going," she said. "What did ye think? That I was plannin' to run for it?"

"I don't know what to think," Molly said, but she had the decency to blush. Eliza led out, Molly followed, and moments later the two women stood in front of Father Michael as Eliza stumbled through her story.

When she finished, Father Michael was nodding. "These Mormons are an interesting cult," he said. Eliza noted he said it with the same flat tone as he might have said, "The fruit fly is an interesting insect." She filed that in memory.

"Ye know of them, Father?"

"Aye. We've heard something of their doctrine. In fact, it's said they always wear their hats, even inside buildings, just to cover their devils' horns." Although he kept the same flat tone, Eliza saw his mouth turn up at the corners while his eyes crinkled in mirth.

"Ye're teasing us, Father." Jimmy noticed as well.

"Perhaps a little." He patted Jimmy's head. "Although I doubt these fellows have the horns of devils, ye can't afford to deal lightly with them. Many strange new doctrines have come out of America of late, but this is one of the strangest—all about angels visiting men and bringing golden Bibles. It's meant to lead honest souls astray. I hope ye haven't been spending much time with their book."

"Not much. I found it wasn't what I expected. It's sort of an adventure story about a father with two sons who are faithful and two—"

"No more, please." The priest covered his ears with his hands. Eliza stepped back, startled, and cut off her sentence. Then the priest took her hand in both of his. "I advise ye to burn this evil book, Eliza. Just because it doesn't seem to have evil in it doesn't mean the evil isn't there. The devil is a clever fellow, and well ye know it."

Eliza dropped her gaze. Hadn't Father Michael heard her confession? "Aye, Father."

"He can lead ye along with an interesting story, and then, before ye hardly know it, he's tripping ye up and tossing ye straight into hell."

"Amen," Molly said, making the sign of the cross. Eliza realized the same response was expected of her. Slowly she followed Molly's lead, yet it all seemed an odd overreaction. She wondered how anything she had read could possibly be this bad.

"Promise me ye'll get rid of that book," Father Michael said as she drew Jimmy near.

"Aye, Father. I will."

"Saints be praised," the priest responded and left his blessing upon them.

"Well, I'm glad ye took care of that," Molly said as they left the church. She walked to the church fence and spoke to Smythe, asking him to bring her carriage. "Can I offer ye and Jimmy a ride home?"

"Hm?" Eliza looked up. "Oh, no, thank ye, Molly. Jimmy and I will walk." She turned toward her son, who was trying to climb the fence. "It's a beautiful day, and I have some serious thinkin' to do."

Molly gave her another long look. "Sure ye're all right?"

"Aye." She managed a smile that she hoped looked genuine. As she watched Molly's carriage pull away, she felt like crying. She didn't understand why she suddenly felt so sad, so bereft, and yet she could barely contain her tears.

"Come, son. Let's walk awhile," she said, taking Jimmy's hand.

"Are we gonna walk all the way?" Jimmy asked, his face alight with excitement.

Eliza smiled, her mood lightening. "Aye, son, and ye can count every type of cart and wagon and carriage ye see. I'll help."

"Come on," Jimmy said, tugging on her hand. "Let's go fast, Mum."

"Very well, then," Eliza answered. She let Jimmy set the pace as they started for home.

They had barely gone a block when she heard someone call her name. Looking down the road, she saw Dolly, her former coworker. "Eliza!" Dolly called again.

"Aye, Dolly, I hear ye." Taking her son's hand, Eliza picked up her pace. The women met midblock, and Eliza greeted her friend with a hug. Then she knelt, facing her son. "Jimmy, I've a job for ye. While I'm speaking to Dolly, I want ye to count every cart or wagon that goes by, all right? Then when we walk again, ye can tell me how many have passed. Can ye do that?"

"Aye, Mum." Jimmy turned to his task.

"That's brilliant," Dolly murmured.

"The boy loves anything with wheels." Eliza gave her friend a long look. "Ye're lookin' quite healthy these days, hardly like the half-starved creature I saw in hospital a while ago."

"Aye, I'm feeling myself again. The doctors can do such amazing things. But that's why I want to speak to ye." She sobered. "The diphtheria has come to Sydney. I've heard of several cases, and the most likely to be sick are little ones like your boy."

"The diphtheria . . ." Eliza mumbled, drawing Jimmy against her.

"Ouch, Mum. I can't count when ye do that," he said, pulling away.

Eliza stifled the urge to grab him and run. "It's the diphtheria? Ye're certain."

"Aye. A neighbor of the Karls, the Hudson family, had a little boy just about the size of your Jimmy. How old is he now?"

"Four years," Eliza said, reeling from Dolly's implication.

"Aye, the Hudson boy was also four years old. Last Monday he woke up with a sore throat. Mae Hudson called the doctor immediately, and he confirmed it was the diphtheria, but it was already too late to do much for the child. By Thursday, he was gone."

Eliza swallowed, quietly repeating, "Gone. Oh, the poor mother!" She quickly made the sign of the cross, thinking a prayer toward the poor, bereaved family.

"Amen," Dolly said. "I'm on my way to the church to talk with Father Michael. Mayhap he should close down, at least to the children, until the threat passes."

"Do ye think that will help?" Eliza looked back toward the church.

"Aye, the doctor says the contagion is spread by being around infected people. He says an infected person breathes out humors into the air that can pass the diphtheria on to another even before he knows he is sick. Can ye fathom it?"

"Oh my." Eliza felt herself sway as she thought of the many people who had just surrounded her precious son. "Ye're sure about this?"

"Aye. Mrs. Karl won't let any of her young ones out of the house until the threat has passed. She's only let me come to church today to warn the good father about the spread of contagion. Some churches are closed already."

"I-I hadn't heard." She took Jimmy by the hand.

"Do ye want to hear the count now, Mum?" he asked.

"In a minute, son. When we're walking." She turned back toward Dolly. "Thank ye for the warning," she said. Then she grabbed Jimmy's hand and practically ran down the street.

"I can't keep up with ye, Mum! Are ye all right?" Jimmy asked as he stumbled. Eliza looked down to see her son's eyes wide.

"Aye, Jimmy," she said, forcing herself to slow her steps and give her child a reassuring smile. "Aye, I'm just . . . eager to get home is all. Now why don't ye tell me about the carts and wagons that ye counted?"

"Aye, Mum," Jimmy said and solemnly began his report.

\* \* \* \*

"No, James. We are not going with ye." It was Sunday morning, James was ready for church, and Eliza was making her stand. "It's the diphtheria and it's everywhere. We need to keep Jimmy in, away from crowds, away from anyone who might be infected."

"Ye took him to Mass yesterday."

"Aye, but that was before Dolly told me. I wouldn't have taken him if I'd known." She saw his expression. "They say it's bad all over the world with a spate of deaths in London."

James nodded. "Aye. We heard from the last ship." He hesitated. "All right, but ye'll need to get back to church as soon as ye can. If people hear about the Mormons, they'll wonder."

"Just tell them it's the epidemic," Eliza said. "And by the way, I asked Father Michael about the Mormons' book."

"And what did he say?"

"He said to burn it."

"Aye, that's what we'd agreed on."

"Funny," Eliza said. "It didn't seem to be evil. It was just a story—"

"Eliza, burn it."

She sighed. "Aye, James. I promised Father Michael. And ye."

"Good. Ya can do it while I'm at church this morning."

"I'll see to it," she promised.

When James left for church and she was alone, Eliza went to the outhouse to retrieve the book. She'd bring it into the house, use it for fuel, and then cook their lunch or perhaps their tea. As she carried the book in, she felt drawn to it. She thought of the way the priest had even covered his ears when she started to tell him the story and wondered what could possibly be so evil that it corrupted one's thoughts just from hearing the story. Hadn't the Savior Himself taught in parables, some of which were difficult to bear? She set the book on the woodpile.

Jimmy came in from play to ask why his da had left for church without them. Taking the boy into her lap, Eliza tried to explain about disease and contagion and keeping him away from evil humors. "I just want to keep ye safe, dear one," she said, hugging the boy close.

Minutes later Eliza stood in the kitchen with time on her hands since she usually spent this time at church. She knew she could prepare their midday meal when James returned. Jimmy was playing quietly in the yard, and she had tidied the house the day before. She saw the book sitting on the woodpile and couldn't help wondering. Since she had already agreed to burn it, what would it hurt to read a little more?

With trepidation she picked it up, looked carefully around to be certain no one was watching, and then sat in her favorite rocker. She opened to the place where she had stopped.

She read of Nephi's vision of the colonizing of America and thought, *Of course this Smith fellow could put that in there, since it had already happened.* She read of the loss of many plain and precious parts of the Bible, the resultant state of Gentile apostasy, the Restoration of the gospel, and the coming forth of latter-day scripture, and she realized this was the story the missionaries had been telling them.

Although she couldn't help feeling defensive over the idea that her faith constituted apostasy, she wondered what "plain and precious truths" they felt the Christian Bible was missing. Was it possible some ideas actually had been lost over the centuries? She read that in the last days, there would be only two churches—the church of Satan and the Church of God—and was reminded of the rancor that had come into her own marriage because of their different faiths. Surely the missionaries didn't think she followed the church of Satan?

"That settles it," she said aloud. She carried the book to the stove, used her poker to stir the embers, and prepared to add the book to the fire.

The knock startled her so completely that she gasped and dropped both book and poker. Composing herself, she went to answer and was surprised to see Elders Walton and Yorgasson. "G'day, gents," she said. "I was just . . . um . . . setting a fire."

Elder Walton spied the Book of Mormon atop the woodpile. "Ah, this *is* where we left it." He looked relieved, then suddenly concerned. "It's on the woodpile. You were going to burn it?"

"Aye. I'm sorry. My husband told me I must burn it, and . . . and I promised Father Michael, my priest. I was just putting it into the stove when ye knocked."

"Well then, I'm doubly glad we came," Elder Walton answered. "We didn't know where we'd left this copy, and we don't have the funds to spread them where they won't be used. It was only this morning that we thought of your home. I'm glad we found you."

"I wouldn't have been here, normally." Eliza explained about the diphtheria epidemic and why she had kept Jimmy home.

Elder Walton nodded. "We've heard that too. In the neighborhood near the wharf, there have been reports of several deaths."

Eliza felt the color leave her face as tears came to her eyes. "I stayed home to try to keep my Jimmy safe. I can't imagine what it would be like if—" She stopped, unable to continue.

"We can offer him a blessing," Elder Yorgasson said. "We'd be glad to."

Eliza answered quickly. "No, I don't think so. In fact, given that my husband is not at home, I think it's best ye take yer book and go." When she saw their expressions, she added, "But I thank ye for thinking of Jimmy, and I'd appreciate if ye keep him in yer prayers."

"We will," Elder Walton answered. "Have a blessed Sabbath, Mrs. Martin. Oh, and is it still all right if we return on Thursday?"

"Aye. We'll be expectin' ye."

"Then we'll see you Thursday," Elder Walton answered as they left.

Surprisingly shaken by the encounter, Eliza went to sit in the summer sunshine, watching as her strong, healthy son played with his toys.

Wasn't it odd that the missionaries had come just as she was preparing to burn their book? And they'd come during an hour when she would not normally have been home, yet still they'd found her. It had been kind of them to offer her son a blessing. If James had been here, perhaps she'd have accepted—and even thinking that reminded her of the way Father Michael had reacted when she'd mentioned the missionaries. He was teasing when he talked about their horns, but he hadn't been teasing when he'd covered his ears rather than hearing the story of Father Lehi and his sons.

That memory troubled her. She had read things in the missionaries' book that had given her pause, even some that angered her, but nothing that would hurt her soul. Perhaps the soul-destroying doctrines came later? But wasn't Father Michael studied in world religions? How could it have hurt him to hear the adventure story from that book?

She shook her head, troubled by questions and doubts, and focused on cheering her son in his play.

\* \* \* \*

"Were the Mormons here?" James slammed into the room, his face as dark as a mountain storm.

Eliza answered, "Aye, a while ago."

"And how did ya arrange that, exactly?"

"Pardon?"

"I'm talking about yer staying home from services so ya could see the Mormons behind my back. Are ya listenin' to their doctrine?"

Eliza dropped the glass she was holding. "James! What's gotten into ye? I stayed just as I said, because of the diphtheria, and I didn't plan for the Mormons to drop by. They came here looking for their book they left by accident."

"I thought ya were going to burn that thing."

"I thought so too. I was just putting it in the stove when they knocked. And while we're accusin', who told ye the Mormons were here?"

"I ran into neighbor Jones. He saw them."

"Aye, they were here, and I gave them their book and told them they'd best go. I doubt they stayed all of three minutes." She settled her hands on her hips. "I thought we'd got past this matter of ye distrusting me. Can ye calm down and tell me what's really botherin' ye?"

He fell into a chair. "I'm sorry, Eliza. I just never expected . . ." He sighed. "The minister approached me after services. He wanted to know what we were doing with the 'heathen Mormons from America' and why I'd left my wife and child at home."

Softening, Eliza knelt beside him and laid her hand on his arm. "I'm sorry. What did ye tell him, love?"

"The truth. That we felt it was the Christian thing to feed hungry men, whatever their faith. That we had asked them not to share their strange doctrines, that my wife had found a book they left, and had promised to burn it." He looked up. "Can ye understand why it was so difficult to hear ya were seeing the Mormons while I was away?"

Eliza relented, stroking his hair. "Aye, sure'n I can." She stood. "James, I think ye should know that they offered to give Jimmy a blessing. If ye'd been here, I might have encouraged it. As it was, I thought it best for them to go, and they understood. Truly, I doubt they were here three minutes."

"I believe ya, love." James pulled Eliza into his lap. "These are strange times we're going through, but we can't let them set us against one another."

Eliza released a shaky breath. "No, we can't, and I thank ye for that. Ya and Jimmy come first, always."

"Thank ya, Eliza." James wrapped her in his embrace.

# Chapter 9

FOR THE NEXT THREE DAYS, Eliza watched Jimmy with care, barely letting him out of her sight and never out of their yard. Though the boy complained about not getting to see his friends, he did as his mother asked, and Eliza thought many times of what a good, obedient child he was growing up to be.

Then on Wednesday evening, just as James was arriving home, a nearby scene brought the crisis home. When Eliza greeted James at the door, they heard wailing from the Carlozzi home down the block where eight men emerged carrying a wooden coffin on their shoulders. The priest followed, swinging a censer filled with incense, and the family came behind—all except their son Giancarlo, whose mother, draped in black, followed the coffin crying, "*La difterite cruda! La difterite dura!*"

"What's she saying?" Eliza asked.

"I learned a little of their lingo when I worked with the miners. I think she's wailing about the disease that took—" He paused, visibly paling. "It's the diphtheria," he said. "She's saying the harsh, cruel diphtheria took her son. I think it was Giancarlo."

Eliza gasped. "Not the diphtheria!"

"That's what she's saying."

"But Giancarlo was a man—in his twenties, I'm thinkin'—and healthy as an ox. It couldn't be him."

But Mrs. Carlozzi, staggering with grief, cried out, "*Giancarlo! Il mio figlio!*" and collapsed on the street. Her husband lifted her to her feet and supported her as they followed the coffin toward the cemetery.

"Quick! Get inside." Eliza pulled James in as the procession neared. She shut the door tightly behind him.

James gently took her shoulders. "Eliza, if the diphtheria is here, our front door isn't going to keep it out."

"I've got to try. I've got to do something!"

James saw his wife's terror. He turned her toward Jimmy. "Look at him, sweetheart. He's a strong, healthy boy. He's going to stay strong. He's going to stay well."

"Giancarlo looked perfectly healthy when he left for work on Monday," she reminded. "I saw him *on Monday,* James. It comes so fast."

James had no answers. That evening the family ate a somber meal.

The next morning when Jimmy awoke with a high fever and sore throat, Eliza was near panic. She tried every remedy she could think of: Labarraque's Solution until it was gone, then a homemade mixture of chlorinated soda, and finally even sulfate of zinc mixed with table salt. Nothing seemed to help. The boy's fever continued to rise, and his throat became so raw he refused to swallow unless Eliza spooned the liquid in and forced his mouth shut. Whenever Jimmy slept, Eliza prayed constantly, saying her rosary, never leaving the boy's bedside.

When James returned from work, he went for the doctor and found him too busy to come. Despondent, he took up the vigil beside his wife, the evening meal forgotten. That's where they were, kneeling at Jimmy's bedside, when Ed and Molly arrived for tea.

"Ye'll have to send them away," Eliza said as she heard their friends on the doorstep. "Hurry, please. Molly's with child. She mustn't be near this foul disease, and if Ed were to contract it, we could lose them all."

"I know, love." James was already rising. "I'll tell them."

He had almost reached the front door when Ed burst in. "Hallo the Martins! We've come to eat ye out of house and home!"

"No!" Eliza screamed.

"What in the—I didn't really mean it, ye know—"

"She's right, Ed. Ya have to go. Come on with me to the front porch. I'll tell ya all about it while I walk ya back to yer coach." James closed the door behind him. Moments later Eliza heard Molly's cry of distress as Ed cried out, "Not the diphtheria!"

"I'm afraid it may be," her husband answered. "I've gone for Doc Adams, but so many are sick, he may not be able to come in time."

On the porch, James turned Ed and Molly back toward their coach as he explained the boy's symptoms. Both the Welshes expressed their concern, asking that James stay in touch. They had almost reached the street when they saw the Mormons coming. James met the men as they approached and explained there would be no tea that night.

"They can have this food," Molly said, holding out the two prepared dishes her cook had sent. Ed put his hand on her arm, but she shook him away. "We can have cook prepare more when we get home, but these men are hungry now."

"So am I," Ed grumbled, but with Molly's sharp look, he relented. "Here ye are, gentlemen. Just leave the dishes with the Martins when ye're done. We'll pick 'em up when we come back to check on Jimmy."

"Send Smythe," James counseled. "He's already had the diphtheria."

"That's what he told us," Ed said. He handed the dish he carried toward the Americans.

"Thank you both," Elder Yorgasson said as he accepted it.

"Yes, thank you," Elder Walton added, taking the other from Molly.

"We'll check with ye, James," Ed said. He helped his wife into the coach, and it drove away, Smythe visibly hurrying the horses.

Elder Walton turned to James. "You say the boy shows symptoms of the diphtheria?"

"Aye. High fever and sore throat. He can barely swallow, and he's eaten almost nothing."

"Let us come in," Elder Walton offered. "We'll share this food with you. Then we can give your boy a blessing."

James looked from one man to the other. "Ye'd take that risk?"

"We're here to serve," Elder Walton answered.

"And what if ya get the diphtheria?"

Elder Yorgasson spoke. "The Lord looks out for His servants."

James nodded. "And ya can give my boy a blessing so he recovers?"

Elder Yorgasson looked quickly at his companion. "If the Lord wills it," Walton said. "We merely tell Him what we would hope for and then ask Him to bless His children according to His holy will."

James's eyes narrowed. "That sounds like a fine excuse when yer patient dies."

"Mr. Martin," Elder Walton said, his tone patient. "We bear the holy priesthood. When we offer a blessing, we listen for inspiration. The words we speak are the ones the Lord Himself would use if He were here."

"Some of His children are appointed unto death," Elder Yorgasson continued gently. "Little children go home to Him."

James looked stricken. "Our son was never baptized."

"That's not a worry," Elder Walton answered. "One of the blessings of the restored gospel is the knowledge that little children are without sin. Jimmy doesn't yet need the ordinance of baptism. He is innocent in our Heavenly Father's eyes."

"But what of original sin?" James asked.

Elder Walton smiled gently. "We'll be happy to have this and any other gospel discussion you wish, Mr. Martin. The fact is we don't believe we're responsible for Adam's transgression, or for any sins but our own. But perhaps now is not the best time for this. Let us come in. We'll give your boy the blessing first. We can all eat while the food is still warm. After that, we can talk as long as you wish."

James nodded. "Aye, gentlemen. Please. Give our son yer blessing. It may hurt ya, but it can't hurt him, and I reckon the good Lord hears sincere prayers—even from Mormons."

Elder Yorgasson chuckled drily.

Elder Walton said, "Let's be about it then." They entered the house.

"Are ye here to bless my boy?" Eliza asked as they entered.

James raised his eyebrows.

"Yes, we are," Elder Walton answered.

"I prayed that ye would."

The two men stepped forward. "What's his full name?" Elder Yorgasson asked.

"James William Martin Jr.," Eliza answered. The men nodded in acknowledgment.

James lifted his wife to her feet, and they held each other at the foot of Jimmy's bed while the missionaries stood on either side of the half-conscious child. Taking a small vial from his pocket, Elder Yorgasson began to drip its contents onto the boy's head.

James started forward. "What is this?"

"It's nothing but olive oil," Elder Walton answered. "Except that this oil has been blessed for use in the healing of the sick. It's like when people in Bible times were anointed with oil." He looked to James.

James looked from one to the other then slowly nodded.

Shaking a drop or two of the consecrated oil onto the boy's crown, Elder Yorgasson laid his hands gently upon Jimmy's head, and calling him by his full name, the American cited his priesthood authority and said a short prayer to accompany the anointing.

Elder Walton then stepped forward. Laying his hands on Jimmy's head, he repeated the procedure, using the boy's full name and citing his authority. Then he gave the boy a blessing, saying many things neither James nor Eliza had anticipated. "Jimmy, the disease you are suffering is not diphtheria," he said emphatically. "It is a much milder illness that will pass quickly."

Eliza couldn't help sighing; she wanted so much to believe it.

He went on. "God our Father intends for you to live to serve Him. He will bless you as you follow His commandments, and He means for you to become a man, to marry, and to raise a family in His Church and kingdom. He has sent us to your home in response to your father's repeated prayers that your mother may be able to hear the true gospel and join the true Church. We have come here because the Lord loves your family and wants to answer your father's earnest prayer."

James opened his eyes and stared at the elders. How did they know? Then he realized Eliza was staring at him. He quickly closed his eyes.

Meanwhile, Elder Walton concluded his blessing in the Savior's name. For a moment the adults stood in quiet reverence as a palpable feeling of well-being filled the room.

"I thank ya, gentlemen," James said. He looked around. "Perhaps we can sit down to dinner now." He stepped toward the table.

But he couldn't escape the questions. Eliza caught James by the arm and drew him aside. Then she murmured, "Ye've been praying for me, James? Praying I'd be converted to the truth?"

Looking somewhat shamefaced, James nodded. "Aye, but I didn't mean the Mormon Church." The missionaries overheard and suppressed a chuckle.

Eliza smiled slyly. "Nor did I—when I prayed for ye."

"Ya did?"

"Aye, James."

James touched Eliza's face as he slowly answered her smile. "Seems we've much to discuss, but for now let's eat."

At James's invitation, Elder Walton prayed, asking that the small amount of food, which Molly had intended only as supplement, might serve them all. It surprised both Eliza and James that there were leftovers when all four adults were satisfied. Elder Walton smiled. "He who fed five thousand on a few of loaves and fishes can surely extend a meal to serve four of us."

"I suppose He can," James said in wonder.

As Eliza cleared, the missionaries began discussing the purity of childhood innocence and how the concept of original sin, as taught in orthodoxy, was a false doctrine, introduced by Satan to confuse and confound the Lord's purposes. Though each of them came at it from a different perspective, both James and Eliza were full of questions and ready arguments. Unruffled, the Americans quietly and calmly continued their teaching.

In the midst of a somewhat heated discussion about what really happened in the Garden of Eden, Jimmy's voice interrupted them. "Mum, I'm thirsty."

Looking at the men with mixed surprise and hope in her eyes, Eliza called, "I'm coming, dear one." Then she hurried to the kitchen pump and filled a tall glass. Jimmy drained the whole thing. Eliza took the empty glass and laid her other hand on his forehead. "His fever's broken."

"He could be well by morning," Elder Walton answered.

"Can I have something to eat?" Jimmy asked.

James sighed his relief.

"Sure'n ye can, Jimmy," Eliza answered. She brought him the leftover food.

He ate hungrily, and then, within minutes, he slept peacefully for the first time all day. Checking his pocket watch, Elder Walton rose to leave but assured the Martins he and his companion would return for more gospel discussion whenever the family wished.

"I can't thank ya enough," James said as they saw them to the door.

"We just stood in the way," Elder Yorgasson assured them. "It was the Savior who blessed your son."

"I know that's true," James answered. "I'm not sure about the rest of what ye're teaching, but of that much I'm certain."

"It's *all* true," Elder Walton said with confidence. "We'll teach you more as soon as you're ready."

"Next Thursday perhaps," Eliza said, "when ye come to tea."

"Next Thursday, then," Walton answered as the Mormons took their leave.

James and Eliza began their evening routine, preparing for bed. "I still can't believe that ye prayed for my conversion," she said as she propped open the bedroom door so they could hear Jimmy if he woke in the night.

"I wanted us to worship together," he said simply. "Ya can't blame me, can ya?"

"Not at all. I wanted it too."

They climbed in on either side of their thick feather bed, and James blew out their bedside candle. "What d'ya think of Elder Walton knowing about my prayers?" he asked into the dark.

"I don't know what to think." Eliza snuggled, her head on his shoulder. "But I felt something when the men were blessing Jimmy— something warm and good."

"I felt it too." James stroked her hair.

"I still don't know whether to follow this road, and I worry where it may take us."

"I do too. Sleep now, sweetheart. We'll talk more tomorrow." Exhausted from worry, Eliza slept almost immediately, but James did not. He lay awake praying and asking, Was this an answer to his prayers? If not, how did Elder Walton know what he had prayed for? He realized he had some important questions to answer and that the answers could change his family's life.

\* \* \* \*

Eliza awoke twice in the night for trips to the outhouse. It seemed she'd had to get up much more often in recent weeks. Both times she checked on Jimmy and found him peacefully sleeping. When he woke at his usual time the next morning, the boy seemed more subdued than usual, maybe somewhat listless, but he had no fever and he ate and drank well. James stopped by midmorning and seemed pleased to see their son rallying so fully.

"He looks well already."

"Aye. He's been recovering quickly." Eliza stopped in the midst of kneading fresh bread. "D'ye think it possible that the Mormons' blessing had anything to do with it?"

James sighed. "I've been wondering on it. We felt something when they were saying it, and Elder Walton said some things that were known only to God and me until then."

Eliza smiled, remembering their shared realizations. "Aye. He did that."

"I think we have to say they have power, and power like that comes only from God or the devil himself."

"Aye." Eliza also sighed. "Ye know Father Michael would say it's the devil."

"And so would the minister." They stood watching Jimmy as he played with his pretend wagons. "Did ye feel anything devilish? Anything that felt wrong, I mean?"

"No, love. I felt filled with warmth and light. I felt . . . almost like I couldn't worry about Jimmy anymore because of the words of the blessing, almost as if I knew he would grow up to be a husband and father, just as Elder Walton said."

James nodded. "Aye, I felt it too."

They wrapped their arms around one another. They were still standing there when they heard a coach pull up in front of the cottage.

"I s'pect that'll be Smythe." James started for the door.

Eliza reached the window. "Sure'n it is."

"Ed and Molly will be relieved to hear we don't have the diphtheria."

"Aye, no doubt they'll be very relieved—for themselves as well as us."

James went out to the street and delivered his message. "I'm pleased for ye, sir," Smythe answered. "And Weeks will practically be dancin' in the streets. He hardly knows how to plant a thing without the little un there to dig it up after. We're all so fond of the little un that we've all been prayin' for him."

James reached up and took the driver's hand. "We thank ya for yer prayers, Smythe, and the good Lord has heard them. Please give our thanks to the whole household."

"I'll be pleased to, sir. And while I'm here, the missus asked if ye need to cancel the usual Monday tea at Welsh House."

James shook his head. "Please tell Mrs. Welsh I don't think that will be necessary. We should all be well by Monday, and we'll be happy to come to tea. I'll volunteer Eliza to bring some of her baking."

Smythe nodded in acknowledgment. "Thank ye, sir. I s'pect she'll be sendin' me to fetch ye, so I'll be seein' ye Monday evenin', usual time."

"Monday," James repeated as he stepped back, letting the horses go their way. Pondering with gratitude the power of prayer and the truth that the King of heaven still cared for a small boy, he carried the driver's message inside to his wife.

* * * *

Eliza kept Jimmy home that Sunday, not so much out of fear of the diphtheria but to give him more recovery time. By Monday morning, he seemed himself again.

Eliza wished she could say the same. When had this chronic listlessness begun? The vagueness, the ache in her back? It seemed she'd been craving rest for weeks, and it had only become worse in recent days. Realizing she was likely coming down with the same ailment that had affected her son, she expected that soon she would suffer a severe sore throat and high fever. She resolved to ask Molly if she could spare a servant to watch Jimmy when she became too ill. Wearily, she set herself to baking the favorite bread pudding her husband had requested.

An hour before she expected him home, she took the pudding from the oven and into the pie safe to cool, brought in the wash from the line, changed Jimmy into clean clothes, and straightened her hair. Her reflection in her small, worn mirror concerned her; she looked too pale, too wan. She splashed her face with cool water, carefully dried it, and pinched her cheeks to raise some color. Then, satisfied that it was the best she could do, she sat in her rocker and held her son, telling Jimmy a story while they waited for James.

He arrived minutes later with a cheery "G'day, I'm home," and crossed to Eliza's rocker. He picked up Jimmy and whirled him around the room to the sound of the boy's delighted laughter, then set him down on the floor. "He's looking well," he said as he turned to his wife. "Ya, on the other hand, look a bit bilious. Are ya feeling all right?"

"Aye, mostly." Eliza held out a hand, and James helped her to her feet. "I fear I may be coming down with Jimmy's illness."

His expression darkened. "D'ye think we should tell Ed and Molly we can't make it?"

"No need." She shook her head. "I've no illness yet—no fever, no sore throat. Mostly I'm just tired, like I haven't slept enough."

"Well, ya haven't." James set his hat on the table. "Ye've spent so much time tending Jimmy." He gave her another long look. "Are ya sure ye're well?"

Eliza considered for a moment. She really didn't feel like going out, but they'd all been looking forward to this outing after their days indoors, and she didn't want to cook, either. She summoned a smile. "I'll be all right. Is Smythe here yet?"

He cocked an eyebrow. "Ye're changing the subject."

"Aye." She smiled. "But I hear the coach comin' now." She looked toward the window where they could both see Ed's carriage pulling to a stop at their front gate.

He made one last try. "If ya think ye're well enough . . ."

"I'm just tired is all," she said as she swung her shawl over her shoulders. "I'll walk Jimmy out. Can ye get the bread pudding? It's in the pie safe."

"Ah, bread pudding." James opened the pie safe and took a deep breath. "Smells heavenly!" They shut their door behind them, and James helped first Jimmy, then Eliza into the carriage. The topic was successfully changed and her husband's concern averted, but Eliza didn't feel encouraged. In fact, she felt awful—weak and woozy and mildly nauseated. She turned her gaze to the scenes outside her window.

Ed and Molly greeted the Martins as they arrived, as did several of their staff. Weeks patted Jimmy's head and said how glad he was that the boy seemed so much better, and Jimmy responded with a hug. Jane came around to embrace the boy and told him she had prayed for him. There was much greeting and joy and relief over the child's recovery. Then the guests went inside and the staff to their work.

As they entered the front door, Ed turned to Eliza. "'Liza girl, are ye feelin' all right? Ye're looking white as a convict's—er, as a snow-covered field."

"I noticed that too," Molly said, giving Eliza a hard look. "Are ye well, lass?"

Eliza tried again to summon a smile, but she knew from the expressions of the people around her that she wasn't doing well. Nor was she feeling well. "I'm just tired, is all," she said. "Just a little . . ."

Then she staggered. The scene around her went dark. As she fell, her son's panicked "Mum!" was the last thing she heard.

* * * *

James caught his wife and eased her to the rug. The panic that gripped him reminded him of his worry over his son, and he remembered the warmth and peace he had felt when the missionaries had blessed Jimmy. He looked up at Ed. "Get the Mormons!"

"Wh—what?" Ed looked bewildered.

"Get the Mormon missionaries," James responded.

"I-I don't even know where to find 'em," Ed said as Molly fell to her knees beside Eliza, drawing Jimmy away.

"Bring Smythe. I can tell him where to look," James said. Ed responded with a nod and headed out the door. Then suddenly, inexplicably, James felt the same absorbing peace that had come during the missionaries' last visit. He looked up at Molly and Jimmy. "She's going to be all right," he said with a confidence that surprised him. "We'll get the missionaries here to give her a blessing, but she's going to be all right."

Molly cocked her head to one side. "I think ye've plum lost yer mind," she said, pushing herself to her feet, "but at least Eliza will be safe with you. The boy, well . . . I don't want him to see this. I'm goin' to take him into the kitchen, get him somethin' to eat."

"No!" Jimmy cried. "I want to stay with me mum."

"It'll be all right, Jimmy," his father answered, "and Molly will bring ya back in here when the Mormons come, won't ya, Molly?" Despite her clear hesitation, Molly nodded. "Is that all right with ya, son?"

The boy looked reluctant but took Molly's hand.

"Thank ya, Molly," James said. Moments later, Ed reappeared with Smythe. James explained how to find the park where he had encountered the Mormons before.

"I'll look, sir," Smythe said. "I can't guarantee I'll find 'em, but I'll look."

James felt certain as he answered, "Ye'll find 'em. They'll be there."

"I'm glad I hadn't put the horses away," Smythe said aloud. He hurried toward the carriage muttering under his breath about Mormons and crazy folks.

Ed saw him off and came back to help James. They propped Eliza up, trying to bring her around.

"Let's move her into the front room and up on that big settee. Ye can sit at one end and hold her head in yer lap," Ed offered, and James quickly agreed.

They eased her onto the settee, and Ed went for a cool, damp cloth and some smelling salts while James sat holding his wife, speaking gently to her. Even after Ed returned, it took some time, but they were eventually rewarded when Eliza's eyelids fluttered. Slowly she began to look around.

"What—what happened?"

"Ye fainted," Ed answered.

She carefully lifted a weak hand to her husband's arm. "James, get the Mormons."

Ed gave James an incredulous look and sighed, shaking his head, but James smiled and said, "Smythe has already gone for them, sweetheart. How are ya feeling?"

"Like somebody stuffed my head with cotton," she answered, her speech slurred, "and stole all the bones in my legs as well."

"Just rest," her husband answered. "Ye'll be feeling chipper soon." Over her head he cast Ed a nervous look.

James calculated it would take Smythe roughly a quarter hour to reach the park and another quarter to return. Then there was the matter of looking for the missionaries, who may or may not be easy to find. Ed agreed with this analysis and suggested they find a doctor instead, but James insisted on waiting—at least awhile. They were all surprised when Smythe was back in less than forty minutes, both elders with him. Ida led the group into the sitting room. "How can we help?" Elder Walton asked as they arrived.

"Eliza fainted," James answered. "Can ya do for her what ya did for Little Jimmy?"

"Of course," Walton answered. The two men took their positions near Eliza, and Elder Yorgasson reached into his pocket for his vial of oil.

"I'll step out," Ed said, starting for the door.

"I'd like ya to be here for this," James said, "and I'd like to have Molly and Jimmy here too—that is, if the missionaries don't mind?" He looked up.

"Not at all," Elder Yorgasson assured him.

Ed harrumphed but left to get Molly and Jimmy, looking none too pleased. Alice and Ida came with them, and soon the group had formed in the sitting room with James holding Eliza, the missionaries near her head, and the others gathered nearby. James said, "Just prepare as ya would for a prayer."

Alice and Ida bowed their heads, Jimmy knelt and folded his hands, Ed stood awkwardly, and Molly made something of a show of getting out her rosary.

"Are we ready?" Elder Yorgasson asked. There were a few nods. He anointed Eliza's head and began the ordinance. When he finished, Elder Walton spoke the blessing.

It surprised James that he didn't begin with her health. Instead, the missionary told Eliza that she was a beloved daughter of God, that her Heavenly Father knew her personally and cared about her, and He was pleased with her choices. He said God had given her the opportunity to hear and learn the true gospel of Jesus Christ (Ed snorted loudly), and then he blessed her with peace and the ability to hear and understand truth when she heard it.

Finally he came to what James considered the point: "Sister Martin, you need not be concerned about your health or well-being. Your illness is not serious and should pass quickly. You will be fully well again soon, and the child you carry will be born strong and healthy."

Half a dozen voices gasped, and Eliza spoke aloud. "Child?"

The elder went on. "The Lord has postponed this blessing until you and your husband were ready to receive him. Your child will become a capable man and a leader in Zion. Like his brother, he will marry and have a strong family. He will help to further the work of the Lord."

The missionary closed his blessing in the Lord's name and looked up to see multiple pairs of startled eyes. There was a long moment of silence before everyone spoke at once.

Molly said, "Ye're with child, Eliza? Why didn't ye tell me?"

James said, "Ye're having a baby? When did ya plan to mention that?"

Ed said, "Another little un. I hope ye're pleased."

Eliza looked at Elder Walton. "A baby? Are ye certain?"

Now it was Walton's turn to look shocked. "You didn't know?

"No, I didn't, and I still don't know whether to believe it." She looked from one to another of the faces around her as if she thought one might answer.

"It's true," Elder Yorgasson answered with conviction.

"Surely ye must have had signs," Molly said. "I mean, a woman knows when she's not—well, ye know." Her cheeks colored as she looked away from the men.

"I thought I was goin' through the change. I had an aunt in Ireland who went through it early, and I just—" She paused, remembering how she'd felt when she was first carrying Jimmy, remembering how long it had been since she'd begun to feel certain she was barren, thinking of how bloated and uncomfortable she'd been lately and how her dresses were becoming snug at the waistline. *Am I carrying?* she asked herself inwardly, and the answer came with such force that it brought tears to her eyes, filling her with warmth and light. "I'm with child," she said, her voice full of wonder. "It's true. James, we're havin' another baby."

She looked down at her stomach, gently laying her hand over her womb, and as she did so, she felt the baby quicken. "Oh!" she sat straight up. "He moved! James, I felt him move."

James held her closer. "Sweetheart, are ya sure ye're not imagining this?"

Instead of speaking, Eliza took James's hand and placed it where hers had been. James looked up with an expression that was half surprise and half joy. "I felt him! Aye, there's a baby in there, all right."

A hushed reverence filled the room as James and Eliza held one another and tried to adjust to their miracle.

"I-I don't know what to think," Molly said, breaking the quiet.

"This is too much fer me." Alice made the sign of the cross and quickly left the room.

"Uh, me too," Ida said, mimicking Alice's action.

Ed snorted. "Well I for one think it's poppycock. Ye won't know whether ye're barren or carryin' until ye've seen a doctor. For all ye know, ye're feelin' gas bubbles. And as for it bein' a boy, ye won't know that for months at least, even if the rest is so." He looked at the missionaries. "I'll give ye this, though. Ye've got a fifty-fifty shot at that one. That's better odds than I'd give ye on the preg—uh, on Eliza bein' with child."

Elder Walton smiled. "Mr., uh, Welsh, isn't it?"

"Aye."

"Mr. Welsh, you don't have to believe, although it would bless your family greatly if you did. Either way we thank you for opening your home this evening." He turned to James. "If there's nothing else you need from us"—he nodded toward Ed—"perhaps we'd better go." He started toward the door and his companion followed.

Molly stepped in their way. "Are ye hungry, gentlemen?" Everyone looked at Molly. "I may not know what to think of their preachin', but the good Lord has given me a fine home and kitchen, and I won't be guilty of sendin' these men away empty." She folded her arms across her chest and looked at her husband as if daring him to argue.

He grinned and shrugged his shoulders. "If the lady says she wants t' feed ye, I'm not about to say otherwise."

Molly turned back to the missionaries. "So, are ye hungry or not?"

Elder Yorgasson said, "We'd be grateful of a meal, ma'am."

"Then come with me," Molly said. "In fact, all of ye come. We can always stretch tea to include two more." She swept forward, leading the way to the dining room.

James looked to his wife. "Are ya all right, Eliza? Can ya stand on yer own?"

She touched his cheek. "Aye, love, if ye help me up." He lifted her to her feet, and they followed the others into the dining room. As Molly had predicted—and as James had felt certain would happen—the meal was more than plenty to satisfy them all.

# Chapter 10

ELIZA WORKED AT HER STOVE preparing the usual Thursday evening meal for her family, Ed and Molly, and the Mormons. She looked frequently out the window, eager for her husband's arrival. Soon he was opening their gate, and she met him at the door, greeting him with a hug. "Welcome home, Papa."

"So the missionary was right." James closed the door behind them and removed his hat and coat, his expression sweet. With his empty hand, he stroked his wife's cheek. "Well, love? What did the doctor say?"

Eliza grinned. "He says, Mr. Martin, that yer wife is with child."

James shook his head in wonder. "Well, we knew that, didn't we?"

She chuckled. "No, but Elder Walton did." Still astonished by what had happened, Eliza said, "There's something amazing happening, James."

"We both know it." He hung his things on the hat rack. "So tell me about the doctor."

Eliza settled her hands on her growing waistline. "He says I seem to be over the ailment of last week, the baby also seems healthy, and I'm probably due in mid-October."

"October! Then ye're well along already."

"Nearly halfway," Eliza confirmed.

His face clouded with worry. "Shouldn't ya be showin' more?"

She turned, presenting her profile.

"Ya *are* showing," he said, his voice hushed with amazement. "When did that happen?"

She smiled at him. "It's been happenin' all long. We've just been focused on other things. Also Doc says I'm a little underweight. I was worried about gaining weight, so I've not been eatin' much. If ye feed me up, I'll be big as a house in no time."

"But ye're both healthy?" he asked again. "Even though ye're little, I mean."

"He says the babe is underweight as well, but there's every indication that he—or she—is coming along nicely. In fact, he's so confident we're both fit, he doesn't need to see me again. He's turned me over to the midwife who delivered Jimmy."

"It's amazing." James stepped near, stroking the bump where his baby grew.

"Aye, a miracle."

Then he paused, his brows knit together. "What should we do about the Mormons?"

"About listening to their teaching, ye mean?"

"Aye. That."

"I've been wondering. We've both had experiences unlike any we've known—"

"Good ones," James added. "We both feel they're men of God . . . What if they're teachin' God's own truth? What if it's as Elder Walton said—that they've brought us the restored gospel of Jesus Christ in answer to our prayers?"

Eliza sighed. "I'm not ready to accept that—not at all—but I do feel we need to follow this through, to have their lessons and read their book and pray about their message. If this is the answer we've both prayed for, we have to give it a chance."

He took her hand. "I think ye're right." He paused. The only sounds were the occasional murmurs of Jimmy's voice from their back garden. "Ya know what it could mean if we decided to join with them?" He made it sound like a question.

"Aye. Even before that, I'm fearing. Mr. Hogan has been plain in his feelings."

"But if the Mormons are teaching truth, if we're doing what God wants us to do, can we let Elmer or anyone stand in the way?"

"Sure'n I think not," Eliza answered. "At the same time, we've another little un coming, and we all still have to eat."

"I hear what ye're saying—" A knock at the door interrupted him. He peeked out the window. "The Americans are here," he said, "and I see Ed's carriage comin'."

"Well let them in, James. We'll talk later." Eliza began dishing up food for their tea.

*   *   *

Elder Walton pushed away from the table. "Another excellent meal, Mrs. Martin. We thank you and pray the Lord's blessings upon you and your family."

"Ta, and ye're welcome," Eliza answered. "More pudding, Ed?"

He held up one hand in a 'stop' gesture. "It's one of the most pleasin' puddings I've ever ate, but I haven't room for another bite. Ye've outdone yerself."

Molly smiled. "She always was a good cook. I never saw why Mrs. P. didn't want her in the kitchen."

"It's just as well." Eliza began to clear the table.

"Let us help." Elder Yorgasson began stacking dishes. Everyone pitched in—even Jimmy was getting big enough—and the table was soon cleared.

"We'd like to leave your family with our blessing," Elder Walton offered, "if that's all right with you, Mr. Martin?"

James flashed Eliza a questioning look. She nodded. "If you gentlemen will be kind enough to wait here a moment?" he asked.

"Of course," Elder Walton answered.

James turned to his friends. "Ed? Molly? May we speak with ya on the step?"

Ed and Molly now flashed questioning looks of their own. "O' course, James," Ed answered. He took his wife's hand.

James led the way as the two couples stepped outside and closed the door behind them. A breeze stirred the gum trees, and they heard a night owl call.

Then Ed spoke. "Well?"

James took a deep breath. "We told ya both what happened when Jimmy was so sick, how the missionaries blessed him." He looked from one to the other.

"Aye," Molly said.

"And ye saw what happened with me at yer house," Eliza added.

"Aye." Ed shifted his weight nervously. "What're ye comin' to, James?"

James looked to Eliza. "I saw Doctor Adams this morning," she said. "He confirms I'm with child." She heard the sharp intake of Molly's breath. "He says I'm nearly halfway along."

"That's wonderful!" Molly drew Eliza to her in an exuberant hug. "We'll raise our little uns together."

"It amazes us," James said. "It amazes us more that the Mormons knew."

"Maybe they just noticed what the rest of us have been ignorin'," Ed said. "It's clear when we look at ye now, Eliza, that ye've obviously been thickenin' in the middle—" Then he colored slightly. "Um, that is, if ye don't mind me noticin'." He gave James a sheepish look.

"It's all right, Ed." James smiled. "The point is the missionaries knew it when none of the rest of us did. These men seem to have a godly power—"

"Whoa!" Ed drew back. "Don't tell me ye're takin' 'em serious?"

"Aye, we are," Eliza said. She laid a hand on Molly's arm. "Molly, ye know what our faith has meant to me. I've prayed a great deal these past days. These American missionaries have a power that's—"

"Devilish if it's anything at all." Ed's jaw clenched. "D'ye have any idea what ye're contemplatin'?"

"We've decided to hear their teaching," James said.

"Ye've gone plum loony." Ed drew back. "It's foolishness, James."

"Well, I think ye're doin' the right thing," Molly said. Everyone looked at her.

"Ye do?" Ed's eyes widened.

"Aye, and ye would too, Edmund Welsh, if ye're even half the man I think ye are." Molly braced herself, hands on hips.

"D'ye mean to tell me ye're takin' these Mormons serious too?"

Molly took his hands in hers. "Ed, ye can see what this means to Eliza, to James. If ye're half the friend ye claim to be—"

Ed puffed up. "No one's been a better friend than I—" he began.

"Then let them do what they must," she answered. "Don't stand in their way."

"It's not really that we're askin' yer permission," James said, his tone softening the words. "We don't know yet how we feel about everything they have to say—"

Ed's voice was harsh. "Angels, gold bibles . . . Who could blame ye if ye find it hard to believe?"

"Ed," Molly said, the single word half rebuke and half plea.

"We don't know how we feel about it all," James went on, "but we think we owe it to them to hear it, and we owe to ourselves to find out if it's true."

Ed made a scoffing sound, but Molly turned toward them. "Ye need to do what ye think is right," she said. Then, gently touching her husband's shoulder, she added, "I felt their power too, Ed, and it's occurred to me to wonder if these men may indeed be godly."

"Well, I'm gobsmacked." Ed looked as dazed as if someone had indeed slapped him.

Eliza spoke. "Would ye like to have the lessons with us, Molly?"

Ed started to speak but closed his mouth at Molly's warning look.

"I'd love to," Molly answered, but as Eliza's face filled with elation and Ed's with horror, she added, "but I shan't. Forgive me, but I cannot." Ed's obvious relief joined Eliza's confusion.

"Why not?" James asked.

"I've not told any of ye this," Molly began, "not even ye, Ed, but when my sainted mother was breathin' her last, she called me to her bedside and asked me to kneel beside her. As her dying wish, she bade me promise that no matter what I did or where I went, I'd remain a faithful Catholic so long as I lived. I vowed I would."

Eliza spoke. "Surely, Molly, she'd understand if—"

"No, it's ye who's not understandin'." Molly's voice sobered. "It wasn't just a promise to my mother." She took a deep breath, and her lip trembled. "I promised God as well. I laid my hand on my mother's rosary and swore it as an oath before heaven. It was almost the last thing my mother heard, and God heard it too." She looked from Ed to James and finally to Eliza. "So ye see, I've made my commitment. Even if these Mormons have the Lord's own truth, I'll not be takin' back my oath. Could God forgive me for forswearing myself? I may listen to some of what they teach, and I hope ye'll share it with me, Eliza. I may even come to believe it in my heart, but I can't ever be anything but a faithful Catholic in this life."

Eliza gave her friend a quick hug. "Thank ye for telling us."

"But that doesn't mean ye can't go where yer heart leads ye," Molly said. "I was slow to accept when they came to our home, but I've been ponderin' since, and there's something about these men and the spirit they bring. Follow yer hearts and yer own understanding."

There was a quiet moment as warmth settled over them, and then James asked, "Ed? Would ya like to hear the Mormons?"

"Well, I'm not so hard set against it as I was a few minutes ago." Ed smiled as he pulled Molly closer to him. "God has been good to me," he said, "but for the most part, He and I have gone our separate ways, and I've pretty much left Him alone to take care of His business while I manage mine. I don't suppose He much cares what church I'm in when I'm sayin' my prayers."

"That's a no, then?" James asked, but his grin showed he was teasing.

Molly stepped forward and hugged Eliza. "I think it's time we'd best be goin'. Have a good lesson, and I'll be wantin' to hear about it later."

Eliza nodded. "It's a promise."

The Welshes were soon gone, and the Martins sat down with the missionaries. Elder Yorgasson said a brief prayer, and Elder Walton said, "Let's begin with God's plan for His children's salvation." The teaching had begun.

\* \* \* \*

James was stocking shelves the next morning when Elmer Hogan slammed into the store. There were no preliminaries. "Ye've been seeing the Mer-mans again."

"Yes, sir." James tried to keep his voice both neutral and polite. "I told ya I see it as a Christian duty to feed hungry—"

"But ya didn't just feed 'em, did ya? They stayed after a long time."

*And how exactly do ya know that?* James forced himself to swallow down the defensive response. Did Elmer really think he had the right to control all his time—even during his private evening hours? Or to decide whom he could invite into his own home? He let his breath out slowly. "They stayed awhile, yes."

"Well, what're ya discussing at those late hours?"

*It's none of yer business, Elmer,* James wanted to say, but he knew better than to provoke a fight. "We talked about a lot of things," he answered carefully. "Eliza had some questions about what America is like and—"

"Did ye talk about their faith? About prophets and angels and golden Bibles?"

James did not want to lie; neither did he want to start something that could only end badly. "A little," he answered. "We've heard a lot from others about what their people believe. We thought it might be fair to hear it from them."

"Well, I'll not have it!" Elmer's face had been flushed when he came through the door. Now it was almost purple. "Martin, I warned ya: those cultists will say anything to get ya. I'll not have it, d'ya hear me?"

"Elmer," James said, forcing his own anger aside. "It's not true, the things ye've heard."

"It is so! And don't ya 'Elmer' me, either. I'm Mr. Hogan to ya, James Martin. I'm yer employer, and ye've nothing without me. Ye'd best be rememberin' that!" With a slam of his fist, he turned on his heel and stomped out, leaving James stewing.

He thought about little else that day, stocking the shelves and tending the store with stiff, mechanical gestures. What he'd told Eliza was true: if the Mormons had brought them the word of God, they could not let anyone stand in their way—not even Elmer Hogan, to whom he owed so much. Yet he and Eliza had only had a couple of experiences to persuade them that these men held unusual power. Was that enough they could stake their futures on it, especially with Jimmy and a new child on the way?

When he arrived home that evening, Eliza took one look at his face and sent Jimmy to play in the garden. It took him little time to unravel all that had happened.

"Someone in our neighborhood is spying?" Eliza asked, her tone disbelieving.

"I'd not have thought so," James answered, "and yet, there it is. Elmer knew the Mormons had come and stayed long after dinner."

"And he thinks he can tell ye what to do with yer time away from work."

James shrugged. "Aye, and I suppose he can. If he dismissed me for it, I'd have no recourse save lookin' for something else."

"This isn't a great time to be looking for work," Eliza said, "what with new immigrants willing to work for a song and miners leaving the gold fields. Besides, grocers in the area all know Elmer. They'd not want to be taking up with someone he'd got rid of."

"Eliza, ye're not sayin' . . ."

"I'm not saying anything, love. Just thinking aloud is all." She sighed. "It's a bit of a beehive, isn't it? All the thoughts and what-ifs buzzing around, trying to find some place to land?"

James gave her an admiring look. "I reckon ye're something of a poet, love. That's exactly what it feels like. My brain has been buzzin' all day."

They stood quietly, pondering. Then James said, "We need to pray. Let's ask the Lord about it. If hearin' the Mormons is the right thing, He'll show us a way it can be done without starving us all."

Eliza smiled and gently touched his cheek. "Ye're a good man, James, and a worthy leader for our family. Aye, we'll pray. We'll let the Lord tell us what to do." Then she straightened, retying the bow on her apron. "Now let's get Jimmy in here and have some tea."

James caught her chin in his hand. "That's my Eliza, always the practical one." He gave her a quick kiss and called Jimmy to wash his hands.

*   *   *   *

"So that's how it is." Leaving Saturday morning Mass in Molly's carriage, Eliza had unraveled the whole story. "The Mormons' doctrine still sounds fantastical to us, but there's always this warm feeling when they're talking. We'd like to follow it up—just in case. At the same time, I find it difficult to fathom that I'm actually thinking of giving up my rosary and the Mass and my saints. It almost feels like betraying the memory of my mother, as well as everything I've always believed, but . . . well, ye understand."

Molly patted her hand. "Aye. I understand. So what are ye goin' to do?"

Eliza shrugged. "Pray. Ponder it some more. Ask God for direction and hope it matters enough to Him to solve a minor thing like this for two ordinary people. He has the whole wide world to run, after all." She gave Molly a small, hopeful smile.

Molly took her hand again, firmly this time. "It matters," she said. "God loves ye, Eliza. That I know. He gave ye James and Jimmy, and now this miracle baby . . ." She paused and her eyes filled with tears. "He will give ye answers." The air rang with her conviction. For a moment there was only the sound of the horses' clip-clop on the cobblestones.

Then Molly grinned. "Besides, I'll tell Edmund about the problem with Elmer Hogan. My dear husband works miracles every day in the business world."

"Aye, he does." Eliza smiled. Then she closed her eyes and prayed that maybe Ed—or someone—could help them find their answers.

*    *    *    *

"He said that?" Ed's face reddened. Ed and Molly had joined James and Eliza at Presbyterian services that day—Elmer Hogan had nodded approvingly when James and his family entered the building—and now they were in the carriage, the Welshes giving the Martins a ride home. Jimmy rode on the driver's seat beside Smythe, who always seemed delighted when the boy sought his company.

"It was just as Molly told ya," James responded. "He said he wouldn't have it, that he didn't want me listening to the missionaries or even having 'em at my home. He made it clear I'd be sorry if I did."

"Sorry? Like he'd toss ye out for it?"

"Aye. Like that."

Ed's face darkened. "That's just plain wrong. Ye're doin' the job he's hired ye to do, and ye've been makin' good money for him for years. He hasn't the right to control what ye do in yer own time nor in yer own home, neither. At the same time . . ." He paused.

"Go on," James said.

"Well, it may be partly a business decision. If there's a fair lot of anger against the Mormons amongst his customers, he wouldn't want ye to be joining a church that would make the folks he depends on turn away from him—especially now he has competitors."

"I hadn't thought of that," James responded. "But doesn't a man have a right to his own freedom of conscience? I suppose I could argue that with Elmer, but if he dismissed me for it, what choices would I have? And who would hire me once Hogan had stamped me for a fool?"

The coach rang with silence.

"So what can we do?" Eliza said. "With that spy, whoever it is, in our neighborhood, it would be unwise of us to have the Mormons in our home again."

"At least I've an answer for that one," Ed said.

"Ye do?" Eliza asked.

"Indeed I do. They can teach ye in our library on Mondays, after we all eat together. Just tell 'em to save the teachin' for *after* tea. Religious talk is bad for the digestion." He winked.

Molly glowed with pride. James and Eliza exchanged a grin. "Ye'd do that for us?" Eliza asked. "We know how ye've felt all along about the Mormons' teaching . . ."

"Aye. I still have my doubts, but I'm not afraid of havin' 'em in my home, and heaven help the spy who tries to get me in trouble with anyone."

The power of his statement made Eliza laugh. "Heaven help them indeed."

"Besides," Ed added as they drew near Primrose Cottage, "Molly won't admit it—considerin' her oath and all—but she's itchin' to hear about that gold Bible." He poked his wife in the ribs. "Aren't ye, love?"

She canted her head, giving him a sly look. "And what if I am?"

"If ye want to hear the lessons these blokes from America have to teach, don't ye think it'll be easier if they're teaching right in our own home?"

Molly swallowed. "And ye'd allow that? Seein' how ye feel about them?"

"Dear lady, ask me for the wide Pacific and I swear I'll find a way to get it for ye, though I'm not certain how I'd wrap it up." Ed put his arm around her shoulders. "Surely ye can listen to their lessons. I might pop in now 'n then myself—just out of curiosity, o' course."

"Ye're a blessing." Molly pecked Ed's cheek. "I knew I was gettin' a prince when ye married me, Ed Welsh, and I thank God for ye every day of my life."

Ed gave Molly a long, slow kiss while James and Eliza turned their smiles to one another, allowing their friends a moment's privacy.

"Whoa!" Smythe called to the horses. They could hear him helping Jimmy down from the driver's seat.

Eliza began to gather her things. "Sure'n this is God's own answer," she said. "We can't thank ye enough, Ed. I've only the one regret now."

"And what's that?" Ed asked.

"Just that the Mormons have been able to count on two good meals a week between yer home and ours. Now, if they can't come on Thursdays—"

"They're staying in the back of McClanahan's warehouse near the park," Ed said. "McClanahan lets them put up cots in the back of his building and use his water pump for washing. In exchange, they help with unloading when the big wagons come from the docks and they're there at night to secure the place. Smythe knows how to find 'em, don't ye, Smythe?"

The driver, who had just opened the carriage door, nodded. "Aye, sir."

"So we'll come to tea on Thursday as usual, and we'll bring a couple of extra pie tins. When we eat our meal, we'll fill plates for the Mormons. Then Smythe can drive us by McClanahan's on the way home."

"That's not exactly on the way," Smythe put in.

"It will be now," Ed answered, and Smythe answered with a respectful nod.

Eliza, leaning forward to make her exit, leaned a little farther and kissed Ed's cheek. "Ye're a miracle worker."

Molly beamed and Ed flushed with pleasure. "No, ma'am, but the Lord has been generous with His blessings to Molly and me. It only seems fair to give a little back to good men who're tryin' to do His will—even if I suspect they're wooden headed." He grinned. "Ye have a good evenin' now."

"We will." James offered his hand, and the two men exchanged a warm grip. "Our thanks to ya, Ed, and to ya too, Molly. We'll have a better rest tonight, thanks to ya."

"Our pleasure," Ed answered.

Outside, Jimmy asked, "Mum, are ye comin' or not?"

Eliza chuckled. "Aye, son. I'm comin' right now."

She exited the coach, and James followed. Jimmy ran ahead to the porch while James and Eliza stood at their front gate, waving as the carriage pulled away. "He's a godly man even if he chooses not to know it," James observed quietly.

"Sure'n he is," Eliza answered, "and today he has answered our prayer."

"Aye. I believe he has."

"Then does it follow that the good Lord wants us to hear the Mormons?"

"Aye, my love." James watched the carriage round the corner. "Aye. I believe He does."

*  *  *  *

They had their next lesson at Welsh House the following Monday. After explaining how the Book of Mormon had been translated from plates inscribed with the history of a people called the Nephites, Elder Walton made a gift of the copy Eliza had almost burned. She took it into her hands, grateful to have it back, yet she said, "Our mothers are both gone now. The faiths we practice are among our few remaining links to our dear ones. We can't help feeling we'd be deserting them if we left our churches behind."

Elder Walton smiled. "Families are eternal," he said, and he taught them the doctrine of ordinance work for the dead, explaining that the spirits of departed loved ones live on in paradise and the living can perform proxy ordinances on their behalf. "One day you can be sealed to your mothers and fathers in a house of the Lord," he explained. Eliza thrilled at the thought. When she looked up at her husband, he was beaming back at her.

It was later that evening, when Jimmy was asleep and Eliza was reading aloud to James, that she came upon the prophet Nephi's statement:

*"And it came to pass that I, Nephi, said unto my father: I will go and do the things which the Lord hath commanded, for I know that the Lord giveth no commandments unto the children of men, save he shall prepare a way for them that they may accomplish the thing which he commandeth them."*

She read the words aloud, her face filling with excitement. "James, my darlin', that's just what ye said."

"I did? When? I don't recall sayin' anything like that."

"I admit it's fancier language than ye used, but ye said that if hearing the Mormons was the right thing, the good Lord would find a way to make it possible without starving us all. Remember?"

James nodded. "Aye, I do remember something like that."

"Not just *like* that. Ye said 'without starving us all,' and that's just what the Lord has done. With Ed's help He has given us a way to hear the lessons without Elmer knowin', and because of Ed's plan for Thursday tea, the missionaries won't even go hungry."

"That's true," James said, although he didn't seem impressed.

She stood and placed herself directly in front of him. "Ye're not hearing me, love. I'm telling ye the good Lord has answered our prayer *exactly*—right to the specific meaning of yer words. It's a smaller miracle than announcing the birth of our baby, but it's a miracle nonetheless, and it didn't come through the Mormons. It came through Ed and through ye."

James's eyes widened, and he slowly nodded. "Aye," he said. "Aye, ye're right. A miracle it is. I hadn't thought of it that way, but ye're right."

"And that confirms it—at least for me. We're doin' what God would have us do—at least for now, at least hearing what the Yanks have to say."

James drew his wife into his arms. "Aye, Eliza, I do believe we are."

"What d'ye think about doing ordinances for our loved ones who've passed on?"

"It comforts me. I didn't like believin' that those who lived before the Savior had no chance for salvation, and I like the thought of being with my loved ones when we find our way home again."

*Home again.* The words struck Eliza with force. "Aye, my love." She put down her book and snuggled against him. "So do I. So do I."

# PART FOUR:
## Committing

# Chapter 11

*January 1859*

A GENTLE BREEZE BLEW IN from the harbor, cooling the summer afternoon. While Jimmy followed Weeks around the garden, Molly and Eliza sat on the front porch of Welsh House, each cradling a well-fed baby. Molly looked toward the street. "Our men should be coming soon."

"Aye. It was good of Edmund to give James a ride," said Eliza. "He'd have been late otherwise, what with Hogan demanding he finish inventory today."

"How's Elmer been treatin' James lately? Is he still the crown prince?"

Eliza sighed. "Aye. Of course Hogan hasn't heard any talk of Mormons at our home for some eight months now, and he sees us at services every Sunday. It seems all is forgiven now he thinks we're not talking to the missionaries. I don't know what he'll do if we decide to convert."

Molly made a scoffing sound. "Ye've converted already. Ye just haven't admitted it yet."

"And what makes ye think that?"

"Well," Molly began, "ye quit coming to Mass even before yer little un came. Then too ye've stopped prayin' to Mother Mary and Saint Elizabeth. Ye pray like a Mormon now."

Eliza's brow furrowed. "I didn't realize ye'd noticed."

"Edmund and I both noticed. So have ye given up yer saints after all?"

Eliza dropped her gaze but looked up again, her expression determined. "I think perhaps I have. I remember the first time I reached for my rosary and found it wasn't there. I went looking for it and realized I hadn't picked it up for maybe three or four days, hadn't even thought about it. I'd been reading from the Book of Mormon and praying to know if it was true, but I hadn't even touched my rosary."

"That rather sounds like ye're convertin'." Molly's tone was wry.

"There came a day, maybe a couple of months past, when I realized I hadn't addressed any prayers to Mother Mary or Saint Elizabeth for a while—hadn't even thought of them. Finally I gave up and packed their statues away."

Molly looked surprised. "Ye really did?"

"Aye. I've packed away Mother Mary and Saint Elizabeth as mementos of my childhood and reminders of home, but ye're right that I don't pray to them anymore, not for some time, and I'm not usin' my rosary anymore, either." She sighed. "So. D'ye think less of me?"

Molly chuckled. "Truth is, I've been prayin' more like a Mormon myself. The missionaries make a good point about Christ bein' the intercessor and not needin' others to be intercedin' with Him. And don't look so nervous, Eliza. I'm not goin' to tell on ye."

Eliza relaxed.

"Besides," Molly continued, smiling broadly, "there's always the fact ye named yer son Joseph Smith Martin. I'd call that a clue."

Eliza shifted uneasily. "Most folk here in Sydney don't know what that means," Eliza said. "Sometimes they ask if it's a family name, and we always say 'tis, because of James's uncle Joseph back in Wiltshire County. No one asks about the Smith—it's so common a name."

Molly pursed her lips, giving Eliza a long, assessing look. "So what ye're sayin' is, ye've converted to the Mormon faith. Ye just don't want anyone to know."

Eliza slowly nodded. "Aye, I s'pose 'tis the truth of it. But ye know what we'll be facing if we're baptized. Not only will James lose his job—which we need badly what with two little mouths to feed—but he'll also lose all the progress he's made in Hogan's company. We thought we'd one day buy out Elmer and own the company ourselves."

She sighed again. "Besides, there aren't enough Mormons here for the Church to function the way it does in Deseret, and the missionaries keep talking about how members should gather to Zion." She hesitated. "I can't do it, Molly. I thought the voyage here was going to kill me. I can't abide the thought of some forty or fifty days at sea, crossin' the whole wide Pacific. I just can't abide it."

Molly's scoffing noise was louder this time. "And for that ye'd turn away from what ye consider to be the true word of God?"

Eliza pouted. "It seems like a couple of pretty big reasons to me. Anyway, ye should talk. Ye've been listening to the Mormons just as we have, and ye believe them too."

"Aye, I do. Joseph Smith was a prophet. He reestablished the original Church of Jesus Christ that had lost its authority over time, and he brought back many plain and precious truths that had also been lost. I've even asked the elders for a copy of their book, and I've begun reading it too."

"Ye have?"

"Aye. Yet I continue to attend Mass, and I've had Mary Elizabeth christened."

"And I know why."

"Aye, ye do." Molly paused and rocked. "It's just . . . well . . . Father Michael sees me comin' to Mass without ye for the first time in forever. He sees me havin' Mary christened and ye stayin' away, and . . . well, I didn't want to tell ye this, but he asked me if James was being rough with ye. Ye know, if he's forcin' ye to act like a Presbyterian against yer conscience."

"Oh, my dear heaven! I never thought of that. D'ye think others have the same idea? I can't have folks thinking badly of my James. He's such a gentle man and always so kind. He's never forced me to change my faith before. Why would he do so now? I can't think—"

"Yer problems may be worse'n that. The missionaries have been comin' here faithfully every Monday for months, and ye've made no commitments. I haven't wanted to tell ye this either, but as they were leavin' last week, I overheard Elder Bingham tellin' Elder Walton that they've taught ye too long. He said if ye hadn't come by now to the point where ye're willin' to be baptized, ye likely never will."

"Oh no." Eliza's expression sobered. "With Elder Bingham coming just fresh from Utah to take over for Elder Yorgasson, Elder Walton'll be thinkin' hard about any ideas he's bringing from Church headquarters."

"Aye. It's possible." Molly shaded her eyes as she looked out toward the harbor. "Speakin' of which, I believe that's the missionaries comin' now."

Eliza saw the two men coming toward them. "It seems James and I will need to do some reckoning soon," she said. Then she added, "But ye're right, Molly. If the doctrine these men are teachin' is the true gospel of Jesus Christ, we need to act on it and trust our future to God—no matter the outcome."

"Ye've heard these men tell of what conversion cost them and their families. They will expect ye to do that too, if need be, for the truth."

"At least we know what decision we need to make—either for or against—and what it could cost us."

"There'll be costs either way, ye know."

"Aye." The women stood to greet the missionaries.

\*   \*   \*   \*

Tall Elder Walton and shorter, younger, bespectacled Elder Bingham were still visiting with the women on the porch, admiring the babies and chatting about the weather, when the carriage arrived with both Ed and James. They all went inside for their evening tea. As usual, and in deference to Ed, they left all discussion of religious matters until after their meal.

Then, when the post-tea sweet had been served, the women left Jimmy and the infants in the care of Alice and Ida with instructions to call if problems arose. James led the way, and Molly joined them in the library. Eliza had had no time to warn James, but she felt no surprise when Elder Walton began. "We've been teaching you for several months now, and you have told us that you believe the doctrines we teach. You've been reading the Book of Mormon—"

"We finished it again last week," James cut in.

"Again? So you've read it at least twice?" asked Elder Bingham.

"Three times," Eliza answered. "And no need to look so surprised."

"The point is," Elder Walton said, "you know enough about the Church to know whether you want to join yourself to the Saints. Elder Bingham and I feel that we've been in this area long enough, and we're planning to move on soon. If you wish to be baptized, you will need to make that commitment."

James's face showed concern. "How soon?"

Elder Bingham spoke. "If ye don't commit by the time we see you next Monday, we'll be moving on."

Eliza heard James's sharp gasp. It was matched by another gasp from the hall. They all looked up as Ed joined them in the library. Keeping his mouth tightly closed, he nodded to Eliza. She asked, "If we didn't commit now, could we change our minds and find ye later?"

Elder Walton looked quickly at Elder Bingham. Then he answered, "Of course you can always change your minds, but it may be difficult to find us later, and although there are Latter-day Saints here, at present there's no one with the authority to baptize. We'll probably ordain someone before we leave, but there's no way to be certain, and we've even been talking about moving out of Sydney, perhaps starting the work in another area."

"Ye've given us a great deal to think about," James said.

Elder Walton cleared his throat. "You've been thinking for months now, James—some eight months. The time has come when you need to make a choice." He picked up his copy of the Book of Mormon and turned to a scripture he had marked. "You've read this three times, but maybe it hasn't really sunk in yet. I'm reading from the book of Mosiah. This is the prophet Alma speaking." Then he read aloud:

> And it came to pass that he said unto them: Behold, here are the waters of Mormon (for thus they were called) and now, as ye are desirous to come into the fold of God, and to be called his people, and are willing to bear one another's burdens, that they may be light;
>
> Yea, and are willing to mourn with those that mourn; yea, and comfort those that stand in need of comfort, and to stand as witnesses of God at all times and in all things, and in all places that ye may be in, even until death, that ye may be redeemed of God, and be numbered with those of the first resurrection, that ye may have eternal life—
>
> Now I say unto you, if this be the desire of your hearts, what have you against being baptized in the name of the Lord, as a witness before him that ye have entered into a covenant with him, that ye will serve

him and keep his commandments, that he may pour out his Spirit more abundantly upon you?

Elder Walton closed the book. "So that is our question to you, Brother and Sister Martin, and to Brother and Sister Welsh as well. If you believe what we are teaching, what have you against being baptized?"

James looked at Ed, who still had nothing to say.

Then Eliza spoke. "Since ye asked, let me tell ye what'll happen if and when the word gets 'round that we've joined yer church." Then she laid out for him what Elmer Hogan had said and how James now had a position of trust in Hogan's company but would likely lose both the job and the chance of buying out the business if Hogan learned of the couple's conversion. "It isn't that we don't believe. It's the fear of what we'll have to give up if we accept baptism."

Elder Bingham pushed. "It's a small price to pay for eternal life."

"I've had enough," Ed announced. He quickly left the room, mumbling about people who think they have God's only truth. James flashed the younger missionary a look of sheer exasperation and followed Ed into the hallway.

"Brother Welsh has a point," Elder Walton said, his voice soothing. "We don't believe we have the only truth. Many faiths have portions of the truth, or even much of it. What our faith can offer is the priesthood authority to act in the name of Christ. That authority was given to Adam and passed down through ancient prophets. It was used to ordain the Twelve Apostles of Christ's Church on the earth, and His Apostles ordained others to replace those who died or were martyred. Then, over time, the Apostles could no longer gather to confer the priesthood upon others, and priesthood authority was lost."

"We've heard yer lessons about the Great Apostasy." Eliza's voice was edged with impatience.

"We also have the covenants that God has prepared as saving ordinances for His children," Elder Bingham continued. "We have baptism—"

"I was baptized," Molly cut in, her voice sharp, "and I've had my daughter, Mary, baptized. If baptism shows our commitment to Christ, we've done it."

"But that isn't—" Elder Bingham began.

Elder Walton interrupted. "And ye're prepared to be better people because of it," he said. "But the priests who offer you this covenant belong to that organization that lost the priesthood authority long ago. That could not be reformed; it had to be *restored*. I've no doubt your priests are good men, but they're not authorized to act in the Savior's name, and so the baptism you experienced has no effect in the life beyond."

Molly was less defiant when she answered, "It's the only baptism I'll ever have."

"That need not be the case," Elder Bingham said. "We have the authority to—"

Molly stood. "Stay as long as ye like, Eliza," she said. Then she swept out of the room, pointedly not speaking to the missionaries. Eliza could hear her sniffling as she left.

"She is making a poor choice," Elder Bingham intoned dolefully. "It will have eternal consequences."

Eliza stood. "Elder Bingham, with all due respect, ye know nothing about Molly, nor do ye have any right to judge her. She loves the gospel ye've been teaching her, and she'd be baptized tomorrow if she could, but she cannot. Don't ask her."

"Why not?" Elder Bingham asked. "Is it because of her husband?"

Eliza took a deep, steadying breath before she answered. "Again, with all due respect, that is none of yer business, but no, it's not about her husband. Ed has been gracious enough to feed ye and offer his home for many months now, so I'll thank ye to speak more kindly of him." She tempered the volume of her voice. "Molly has her reasons, and don't ask me to tell ye because they are *hers*. I haven't the right to breach her confidence, but I'm telling ye now and I'm telling ye straight, if ye don't stop pushing so hard, ye're going to do more harm than good."

She turned to Elder Walton. "We'll have a decision for ye next week," she said. Then she too exited the library, leaving the missionaries alone.

As she walked down the hall, she could hear Elder Walton saying, "Hyrum, you may know a great deal about the gospel, but you have a lot to learn about people." She couldn't have said it better herself.

\*   \*   \*   \*

It was late that evening, and both boys were down for the night when James turned to Eliza, the questions he'd been pondering weighing heavily on his heart. "We've a big decision to make," he said slowly, trying to gauge her response. "We both know what we need to do. The only question is whether we've the courage to do it."

"It will change our lives." Eliza sank into her rocker, worry etched in her face. "I want to, James. I want to be baptized, but I'm afraid. And it brings me sorrow too."

"Sorrow?"

"Aye, my love. It's like giving up some of the last memories of my mother. She taught me the rosary, took me to Mass, had me christened as a child. Giving up my Catholic upbringing is like spiting her memory."

He nodded and came closer, taking her hand in sympathy. "Aye, and don't I know it? My mother taught me to be a Presbyterian. In a divided household, she always let me know I was a part of her and she of me because we shared that faith. Now it's as if I'm turning my back on her."

"It's a sorrow, isn't it?" Eliza drew his hand to her cheek, kissed his fingers. "There's so much to think about—all the comfort we'll lose and the trouble we may gain. I don't know how we'll raise our boys without yer income from the store, and well, there's the other part too, the part about gathering."

James began stroking her shoulder. "Ya know it's all a part of the package," he said. "If we join with them, we'll really need to *join* them, selling off what little we have and saving our money until we can afford the passage to travel to Zion."

Eliza shook her head. "I can't do it. I just can't. Ye were there on the dock the day I arrived from Southampton. I must have looked like a half-dead thing, ill as I'd been—"

"Ya looked like an angel to me."

"Ye're a kind man, James Martin, but I know the truth. I thought that voyage would kill me. Once I stepped on that dock in Sydney, I promised I'd never sail again, not even to take the ferry 'cross the harbor."

James adopted a conciliatory tone. "But it wasn't like Molly's promise. Ya didn't swear before God. Surely ya can let go of that—"

"James, don't ask it!" She stared at him, wide-eyed, and he saw the depth of her terror.

He gentled his tone. "Not even so our boys can be raised in the faith we know as truth?"

She took his hand, looking up at him. "Do we know that? Do ye?"

James gave her a long look. "Maybe it's time we asked. Formally, ya know? Like it tells us in the end of the book of Moroni." And he recited:

> And when ye shall receive these things, I would exhort you that ye would ask God, the Eternal Father, in the name of Christ, if these things are not true; and if ye shall ask with a sincere heart, with real intent, having faith in Christ, he will manifest the truth of it unto you, by the power of the Holy Ghost.
>
> And by the power of the Holy Ghost, ye may know the truth of all things.

Eliza raised an eyebrow. "Ye've memorized it."

He nodded. "Aye. It's been much on my mind."

She gave him a long, searching look. "Ye know it's true, don't ye?"

Again he nodded. "Aye, but I think it's time we confirm it with the Lord."

She sighed. "I s'pose I agree." She took his hand in both of hers and looked up again, her eyes imploring. "Let's do it this way: Let's pray and ask the Holy Spirit to confirm to us that this is the true gospel of Jesus Christ. If we get the answer we expect, we'll be baptized and face the consequences of being members here in Sydney. Even Elder Bingham admits the Saints here are strong in the faith. We can become a part of their group—their branch, they call it—and study the gospel with them. But let's not even ask about crossing the sea. At least not yet. I can't bring myself to think of it."

"Ya know ya might have to get used to thinking of it—in time."

"I don't want to think that, either, and I can't do it at all now. Not now."

"It's part of the doctrine they're teaching—the whole 'gathering to Zion' idea. The two times we've met with the Saints here, they've all been studying and worshipping together but planning for the day they can book their passage and leave for Deseret. Ya know—"

"Aye, I know what ye're saying, husband." Eliza came to her feet. "But I can't abide thinking of it, so if ye want me to do this at all, ye're going to have to be willing to take it one step at a time." She pinned him with a stare. "Are ye hearin' me now?"

He smiled. "Aye, lass. I'm hearin' ya. One step at a time, then." He took her into his arms, and she slowly relaxed her defiant posture. He held her, feeling her heart beat against his chest and wondering how any man could love as he loved and not want his wife forever. After a moment, he said, "Shall we pray?"

She gave him a long, searching look, and said, "Aye. I'm fearful and I'm sorrowful and a part of me wants to forget all about it. But I'm thinkin' it's time we ask."

He saw both the fear and the conviction in her eyes. Her faith humbled him, seeing how she came to it through her fear. He gazed at her long and gratefully, inwardly thanking the Father for providing him with such a stalwart companion. "Well then, let's pray," he said finally. As they faced each other, James had the sudden realization that their lives were about to be changed indelibly and forever. He hesitated then helped Eliza to her knees.

* * * *

Eliza stood at Sydney Cove looking down on the calm waters. It was Sunday, the twenty-third day of January. She and James had worshipped that morning in the home of Tom and Sarah Clark. They had sung "Come, Come Ye Saints," partaken of the sacrament, and read together from the Book of Mormon. Then, when the benediction was said, the missionaries had called Brother Clark to lead the small branch and set him apart as the branch president.

Now they were gathered at the cove for the baptism. Eliza stood on the dock with three-month-old Joseph in her arms and five-year-old Jimmy beside her, watching as James and Brother Clark went down into the water. The men were waist deep in the cove and preparing for the ordinance when they heard someone shouting, "Wait! Wait! Ho, there!" Eliza looked up to see Smythe driving his horses hard as he came toward them, the carriage's draft swaying the wattles and banksia shrubs along the quay.

Eliza felt her breath catch in her throat. Was something wrong with Molly? Ed wasn't trying to stop them, was he? "Brethren, wait, please!" she called. Then, as the coach stopped and Smythe got down to open the door, she let out the breath she'd been holding and called, "James, Molly's here!"

Eliza hurried forward to greet her friend, and Molly, handed down from the carriage by her driver, swept out to embrace her.

"I'm so glad ye've come," Eliza said, throwing her arms around Molly.

"Am I too late?" Molly looked around.

"No, ye're just in time." Eliza led Molly to the quay, introducing her to all the people there. James and Brother Clark stayed in the water, but both waved and called to her.

"So sorry to interrupt," Molly called back.

"We're grateful to have ya," James answered, and Brother Clark added, "Aye, we are."

Eliza took her friend's hand. "Thank ye, Molly. Thank ye for comin'."

"I've some idea of what this means to ye," Molly answered.

Eliza smiled and patted Molly's hand. Then she looked around. "Brother Clark, I think we're ready now."

"Then let's begin," he answered.

Eliza listened, her heart full of joy and trepidation, as Elder Bingham instructed Brother Clark in the baptismal prayer. Then she reverently bowed her head as James was baptized, becoming fully immersed in the waters of the cove in a representation of Christ's death and burial, and coming forth as the Savior did in resurrection. Tears filled her eyes when she embraced her soaked husband. She couldn't remember when she'd last seen him so happy, and she prayed they would not regret this choice. She watched as he went through the group, greeting each as "brother" or "sister." Then he returned, taking baby Joseph from her arms.

It was her turn. Giving Elder Walton a nervous smile, she held his arm as she made her way down to the water. "Just take a deep breath," he murmured, reassuring her with a smile. As he recited the baptismal prayer, she prayed as well, asking her mother's forgiveness and begging the Lord to let her know she was making the right choice.

Elder Walton lowered her into the water. She took a deep breath and felt the salt waves close over her. She saw no vision, heard no voice, but despite the chill of the water, she was full of warmth and light, blessed with peace. In that moment, she knew that she and James had many trials ahead but the Lord would be on their side, sustaining them as they worked to honor His plan for them. She also knew this was the answer she had prayed for. She came out of the water brimming with joy and went to greet her husband and their fellow Saints.

\*   \*   \*   \*

James was setting their table that evening, helping Eliza prepare their tea, when a strange thought occurred to him: "Isn't it odd that we're sitting down to tea and we don't have any tea?"

Eliza chuckled. "Aye, I've thought of that too. It's been a challenge to give it up, but we've been tea free for what? Two weeks now?"

"Aye, maybe a day or two longer—ever since that day at Ed and Molly's when the missionaries challenged us to be baptized and we accepted."

Eliza carefully lifted her baked hen from the oven. "It seemed so strange today, celebrating our baptism with the branch, having cakes and lemonade instead of tea, the way we've always done."

"I remember Elder Walton teaching us about it. He said it was given simply as a word to the wise and has only recently become a commandment."

"Aye, just a few years ago." She smiled. "It's just as well the Lord didn't wait until we were members already. Giving it up may have been even harder then."

"It feels so strange. We even had tea to celebrate our wedding."

"The tea is just one of the first changes we notice, and one of the easier, I suspect. I'm grateful ye've never been a drinker nor a user of tobacco. Those would have been harder."

"Aye, it's true. It's a good thing the Presbyterians don't approve of alcohol, either."

Eliza smiled, but it quickly faded. "Little Jimmy asked me today why we never go to church anymore."

"He must mean the Mass. We attended Presbyterian services only two weeks ago."

She shook her head. "I think he means both. Going to study the gospel at the Clarks' home just doesn't feel like church to him, and he doesn't understand what baptism's all about—us getting down in the water in our clothes and coming right back up again. He asked me why we didn't stay to swim."

"We've got some teaching to do." He set a pitcher of water on the table.

"Aye, we do." She called Jimmy to come. "With the Lord's help, Joseph will grow up in the church, but Little Jimmy will need some teaching—just as ye and I do, I s'pose."

"Aye." James watched thoughtfully as five-year-old Jimmy washed his hands at the pump and took his seat. Eliza checked on Baby Joseph, still sleeping peacefully, and joined her men. James offered a blessing, but just as he was saying amen, a loud knock came at the door. He flashed Eliza a look of surprise. "I wonder who—"

"James, are ya home?" The voice came with another loud rap.

James looked at Eliza. "It's Elmer."

"Already?" Her eyes filled with alarm.

"Coming, Elmer!" he called. Then he spoke quietly. "Take the boys into the bedroom."

Her face betrayed her anxiety, but her voice seemed calm as she said, "We'll stay."

He hesitated, torn between fear for his wife and admiration for her courage.

"James Martin, answer this door!" The booming voice came again.

James touched his wife's face. Then he stood straight, pasted a pleasant look on his face, and went to the door. "Elmer! Good to see ya. What brings ya to Primrose Cottage?"

"A rumor," Elmer answered. "One I'm hopin' ain't true."

"Let me take yer hat and coat," James said, reaching out. "Come in, have a seat."

Eliza attempted a smile. "We were just sitting down, but ye're welcome to join us."

Hogan gave her a dismissive look and turned back to James. He took off his hat but kept it in his hand. "I may not be stayin' long enough to sit. Ya weren't at services this morning." It was clearly an accusation.

"No, sir. We weren't."

"And ya didn't come last week, either."

"No, sir, we didn't." James was pleased that his voice sounded steady.

"Will Carter came by the house a while ago. He was walkin' down by the quay, and he saw ye and yer wife and a bunch of other folks going down to Sydney Cove."

James chafed at the idea of his assistant spying on him and tattling to his employer, but that was not the challenge of the moment. He kept his voice even as he said, "We were there."

"He said it looked like ye two was being baptized."

"Aye, sir. Eliza and I were both baptized today."

Elmer's fist shot out, catching James on the chin. He fell against Eliza's rocker, caught himself on its arm, and staggered back to his feet in time to see the second blow coming as Elmer charged into the room. Although it too connected, he was able to dodge to the side enough to keep Hogan from landing it solidly. The blow glanced off his jaw and slid by, throwing Elmer off-balance and into the rocker.

As Elmer straightened, preparing for the third strike, James reached out and caught his arm. Then he quickly turned it behind his employer's back, his other arm around Hogan's throat. It was a move he barely remembered from his days on the Burra-Burra. "Elmer," he said, his voice still calm but heavy with purpose. "I'm both younger and stronger than ya. I don't want to hurt ya, but ya will not be permitted to hit me again. Do ya understand?"

Though he was purple-faced with rage, Elmer growled, "I hear ya."

James slowly let go of the man who had been like a father and stepped around to face him. "I know ye're unhappy, but—"

"Unhappy? *Unhappy,* ya say? I have never felt so betrayed in my life! I took ya in when ya had no place to go. I gave ya work and a decent job, opportunities to grow and improve yer income. I even found ya a place to live when ya wanted to marry. And now ya betray me."

James was startled to realize Elmer had tears in his eyes.

"Forgive me, sir, but I don't understand. I haven't betrayed ya at all. I don't see how decisions about my personal worship have anything to do with—"

"Oh, ya don't?"

"No, sir, I don't. I haven't stopped giving my best every day at the store. I haven't stopped being an honest worker, grateful for the opportunity. I haven't changed—"

"Ye've fallen in with charlatans and scoundrels!" Elmer shouted. "Despite my best advice—and my warnings about what could happen—ye've listened to these cultists from America. Ye've fallen into their traps. Heaven help 'em, man! They're not even Christians!"

"That's not true!"

Elmer stepped forward and caught James by the shirtfront. James had to fight down the impulse to shove him away, trying not to antagonize him any further. "Don't ya know what people here in Sydney think of these Mer-mans?" Elmer asked.

"I can't be too concerned with the ignorant opinions of those who—"

"Well, maybe ya can't, but I must. Those are my customers, and they won't come to me when they find out I've a Mer-man workin' there. Don't come to work tomorrow. Ye're done with Hogan's Mercantile."

James heard Eliza gasp. "I'm sorry ya feel that way, sir, but—"

"Mr. Hogan?" Eliza stepped forward, her baby in her arms. "Will ye please reconsider, sir? We've four mouths to feed, and James has always been a faithful worker—"

"Faithful? Ya can call him faithful after the way he turned my own words against me? Ye've been meeting with the Mer-mans behind my back for months, haven't ya?" He shook his finger at Eliza. "Well, haven't ya?"

She took a step backward, and James saw fear in her eyes.

Then Elmer turned on James again. Pointing at Eliza, he declared, "She's a big part of yer problem, boy. Ya were never foolish nor gullible until ya stepped away from yer faith to marry that Catholic—"

James took a quick step forward, hurt and anger barely contained. "Sir, I respect yer right to speak yer mind, but ya will not criticize my wife, not here in my own home."

A triumphant, ugly smirk split Hogan's face. "It's *my* home, James Martin. Our contract gives me the right t' call in the mortgage the minute ya get as much as two months behind, and ye've been in default fer months now, ever since yer Irish Catholic father-in-law took ill— most likely from the drink. I never saw an Irish who could hold his liquor. I could have called yer loan in clear back then, but I've been carryin' ya all this time because I had hope for yer future with me and mine. I see now how empty that was."

James felt himself weaken at the shock of Hogan's words. "Sir, ye can't put my family out in the street."

"I can and I will! Ye'll learn what it means to defy yer employer, to defy convention and reason and all that's sane. I'm givin' ya to the end of the month to either pay off the mortgage in full or get out. With no job and no home, we'll see how defiant ya are. Unless ya can find an angel willing to give *ya* a stack of gold plates, I s'pect ye'll be havin' second thoughts 'fore long. And don't send that Ed friend o' yers around t' cover fer ya neither. I won't have it."

"Sir, please—"

"Ye've one other option." Hogan's expression softened slightly, and for a moment James could see the expression of his old and trusted friend. "Come back to the faith. Renounce this false doctrine and accept Christ as yer Savior again. Come back to church. Do that and all is forgiven. I'll know ye were duped for a moment, but ye've come in from the fog. I'll put ya right back in charge o' the mercantile. I'll even forgive the mortgage that ye're behind." Then James saw him grit his teeth, and the friend he had known was gone. "If ya don't do that, ye've got only days to get yer wife and yer boys and anything ya want to save out of my home and away from my life. Do ya hear me?"

James swallowed hard, but he couldn't seem to answer.

Elmer stepped forward and caught him by the shirtfront again. "Do ya hear me, James Martin?"

"Aye," James whispered. He cleared his throat. "Aye, sir. I hear ya."

"Then I'm through here, and I'm through with ya." Hogan shoved his hat onto his head and went out, slamming the front door so hard that Eliza's framed picture of her mother dropped to the floor. The glass shattered.

Eliza went to the treasured image and lifted it. With tears in her eyes, she said, "James, yer job, our home—what can we do?"

James went to his wife. For a moment, he felt mired in despair, and then the warm, sweet peace of the Spirit came again. "I'm not sure, sweetheart. But I know what we will *not* do. We will not allow Hogan or anyone else to turn us from the course we've begun. We made a careful, considered choice to join The Church of Jesus Christ. We will not walk away from that choice or from our Savior's will for us just because of one misguided man—or many."

"But—"

"But nothing tonight, my love. Let's eat our meal and calm our frightened boys." He gestured toward Jimmy, who stared fixedly at the portrait in his mother's hand, his face white with shock. "We'll get everything settled down, and we'll put our children to bed. Then we'll pray. We'll ask the Lord's help." He led her back toward the table. "I don't know how we're going to get through this, but we will. Somehow, we will."

Her voice quavered as she said, "Aye, James." He could see her conviction waver in the face of her fear, but he once again felt full of light and warmth and peace. He knew somehow it would all work if they stuck to the truth. He promised he would do exactly that.

## Chapter 12

THE NIGHT WAS FITFUL, BUT James awoke as always that Monday, trained by experience to get up and ready for work. Eliza heard his usual sounds as he went to the outhouse, returned and warmed water, shaved in the half dark of the kitchen, washed, and dressed for the day. Sighing, she rolled out of bed and walked to the bedroom door, only to find her husband in his Sunday best.

"Where're ye going, all fancied up?" she asked as she entered the kitchen.

"I'll need to be about finding work," he said, turning to face her.

She gasped. "Oh, James! Ye can't go out like that!"

He looked down at his shirt, brushing off his trousers. "Why not? They're my best duds."

"Ye look like a prizefighter, love."

"What?"

Eliza stepped forward, gently touching his face. "No shop owner is likely to trust his store to a brawler." She handed him her small mirror. "Ye'd better look."

James took the glass and stepped to the window, examining his reflection. His breath escaped in a long, low whistle as he looked at the blackened chin, the purpling patch below his eye. "Elmer left me some tender reminders, for certain."

"Aye, not that ye're likely to forget."

"No," he said, "not likely." Then his shoulders drooped. "What am I to do? We have only days before we have to pay off the mortgage, and I don't even have work."

"We've a little savings . . ." she began, trying to swallow her own fear.

"Not enough for a month's rent. If I had that much, I'd have paid off Elmer straight away. Then he wouldn't be able to toss us."

Eliza managed a smile. "Ye'll take the day off today. It's too early to go out now, so ye can keep an eye on the boys while I do some of my usual morning errands. It'll be easier without the little fellas along. Then, when I get home, say in midmorning, we can take the boys for a walk and see what's for rent."

He shook his head. "I can't afford to waste a day."

"Be serious, love. Ye saw what ye look like. Ye'll do us no good going out like that. Besides, the day won't be wasted if we find a new place to live."

He searched her eyes, looking for comfort, and she tried to offer it.

"Well then," he said, looking toward the cradle where Joseph was just beginning to stir. "I s'pose ye'd best feed the wee one 'fore ye leave. I've fixed breakfast for Jimmy before, but I can't do that for Joseph."

She smiled back, gently touching his cheek. "No, I don't s'pose." She went to her infant.

Half an hour later, James and Jimmy were seated at the table while Joseph, well fed and happy, lay in his cradle playing with a rattle. Eliza picked up her basket as if she were going shopping and put on her small cottage bonnet. She waved a merry farewell and sauntered down the street. It wasn't until she was well out of sight that she let her shoulders droop and allowed the fear to wash over her. She paused, looked heavenward, and prayed: "Dear Lord, forgive me for sneaking behind my husband's back, and help me with what I must do." Then she took a deep breath, straightened her spine, and turned toward Pembroke House.

\* \* \* \*

"G'day, miss." The girl who opened the door was new to Eliza, even since the last time she'd seen the Pembroke household at Sunday service. Eliza couldn't help wondering how much staff turnover there had been.

"I'm here to see the missus," Eliza said, tilting her head pleasantly as if she were one of the ladies of quality Molly spoke of.

The girl pursed her lips in a gesture of impatience. "May I tell her who is calling?"

Eliza started to answer but thought better of it. "Just an old family friend."

The girl scowled but answered, "Very well, miss," and turned down the hall.

Minutes passed as Eliza waited on the porch, trying to calm her nerves, hoping to compose her expression. Still, despite the rehearsal time, she felt unprepared when Mrs. Pembroke barreled to the door, harrumphed loudly, and said, "What in heaven's name are you doing here?"

The handsome woman she had once known had grown old before her eyes. Eliza's heart swelled with compassion as she said, "G'day, Mrs. Pembroke. Have ye been well?"

"My health is no concern of yours," the woman blustered. "Why are you here?"

Eliza steadied herself and tried to find her smile. "I've need of some work, and I wondered if ye might have a place for me in yer household."

"Work? Work!" Mrs. Pembroke looked her up and down as if she'd escaped from Bedlam. "So the dirty bloke has left you, has he? And you with two little ones. For shame!"

"No, ma'am. Nothing like that. We've just fallen on some hard times, and I heard ye might have need of someone like me—"

"Someone like *you*? It'll be a hot day in heaven before I'll want someone like *you* in my household. You've a gob of nerve coming back here after the way you and your friend stabbed me in the back. I'd been nothing but kind to you, and there you were betraying me, making me look the fool in front of my whole family!"

Eliza blinked then blinked again. "Mrs. Pembroke, I assure ye, it wasn't my idea. I didn't even—"

"Don't you go denying it, either. I heard you laughing with them. All that time you'd been setting up your big joke. Well, where are your rich friends now, huh?"

"I—" Try as she might, Eliza couldn't think of a thing to say. Of course she'd known Mrs. P. was unhappy, but she hadn't expected . . .

Mrs. Pembroke stepped behind the door and came back with a broom. She brandished it at Eliza, handle first. "Get out! Off my porch now, or I'll—" She paused as if considering and then said, "Never mind. I've no need to wait. Ye're unwanted here, an unwelcome trespasser. Go!" She brought the broom down hard on Eliza's shoulder.

"Ahh! Mrs. Pem—"

"I said out!" The older woman struck again, this time landing the broomstick against Eliza's neck, the tip striking her jaw.

Catching her breath in a sob, Eliza broke and ran, fleeing the Pembroke property.

"Stay away from me and mine!" Mrs. Pembroke shouted after her.

Sobbing, Eliza ran as if pursued by all of Satan's armies. In fact, she couldn't help wondering if that was exactly what had happened. How could so much go wrong so very quickly? They'd known they might face difficulties, but this? It hadn't even been twenty-four hours since their baptism! When she could run no farther, she slumped at the side of a public trough not far from the mercantile until she finally caught her breath.

"Oh, dear Lord," she mumbled through tears. "What can I do? What can I do?"

"Hey! Best be gettin' up there, lass! Get movin' now!" came the answer.

She whipped her head around and saw a coach approaching, the driver snapping his crop over the heads of his team as he called to his horses.

"There now, lassie. Ease around that corner now," he said to his lead mare. The coach made a smooth right turn as Eliza settled back against the trough.

It disappeared, taking team and driver with it. Eliza watched until they were of sight before she finally closed her mouth. The coach's appearance had snapped her out of her self-pity and brought her the answer she needed. She looked upward and murmured, "Thank ye, Father. I will get up and moving." She looked down at the moss growing in the base of the trough, but the water above it seemed clean enough. Closing her eyes, she splashed that water across her face and neck until she could pull herself together to face her family. "There's work to be done," she said as she started for home.

* * * *

James stood as he heard Eliza opening their front door, lifting the fussy baby in his arms. "Good thing ye're here," he said as he walked toward her. "Joseph is getting hungry again and—What on earth happened?"

She smiled, a smile he could see right through. Her clothing was disheveled and her shirtwaist was damp, as if she'd had water thrown at her.

"It just took me a little longer than expected, that's all. Here, let me feed our babe." She reached for the child.

James kept hold of the baby but took her shopping basket. "If it took ya so long, why is this thing empty?"

She gave him that false smile again, but he could see the tears puddling in the corners of her eyes. "I, um, I . . ." Joseph gave a small cry, and she reached out. "Here, let me take him."

He gasped; it was the first time she had faced him straight on. "Somebody hit ya!" Putting the baby down, he stepped forward, placing his hands on her shoulders, and turned her so he could look at the left side of her face, where dark bruises were already forming. As he gripped her shoulder, she winced. "Here too?" he asked, touching the shoulder again.

She nodded, and then the tears began. "I'm sorry, James," she said between the tearful blubbering. "Please f-forgive me. I thought I could help."

"Ya didn't go out shopping, did ya?"

She shook her head.

The awful thought struck him. "Ya went to Mrs. Pembroke looking to get yer job back."

"I didn't know what else to do. I thought—"

"And that old bat did *this* to ya?"

She nodded, the tears coming freely so she could no longer speak.

James stepped to the back door. "Jimmy, come here!" The child came running. "Here, son, take yer brother for a bit. He's hungry, so ya may need to distract him while—"

"What's wrong with Mum?" Jimmy held out his arms to the baby, but his wide eyes were fixed on his mother's bruises.

"She's been hurt," James answered. He knelt beside Jimmy, carefully placing the baby into his arms. "I'm going to take her to our room to lie down. Ye're going to have to take good care of Joseph, but ye're getting to be a big boy, so I think ya can handle it. D'ye think ya can?" He gave his son a look that he hoped would inspire confidence.

"Aye, Papa. I can do it."

"Thank ye, son." James embraced both his boys. "Now, why don't ya sit down here in yer mum's rocker. Ya can sing to him if ya'd like."

"James?"

He turned to his wife. "Yes, love?"

"The baby's rattle is in his crib. Why don't ye get that for Joseph? I can get into the bedroom on my own."

"All right, but I'm going to want to see that shoulder." She nodded to him as she started for their room. He found the rattle and gave it to Jimmy, noticing that Joseph was already trying to stuff both chubby fists into his mouth. "I promise ye'll get to eat soon, son," he said. Then he followed his wife, shutting their door behind him.

Eliza sat on the side of the bed, still sniffling, though her tears seemed under control, her dress unbuttoned on her left side. She had taken her arm out of the sleeve, and she was studying her shoulder with the small dresser mirror, the same one he'd used just hours ago to study his own bruises. Even from the doorway, James could see the deep purple-black line forming. Where it crossed her collarbone, the skin was broken and the wound oozed a thin trail of bright red blood.

He stepped toward her, gentle fingers outlining the dark line without touching it. "What did she use on ya?"

"A b-broomstick."

The image of his Eliza being beaten with a broom handle hit James with such an impact that he had to close his eyes. A blinding red haze of anger was sweeping over him, along with an emotion he had never felt and could not name. "A broomstick," he repeated. He was vaguely aware of the hollow sound of his words—and he didn't care.

Eliza nodded. "She said I had betrayed her. She called me an unwelcome trespasser."

Both James's hands were forming fists. He could feel the bile rising in his throat. "I ought to give that old crow a taste of her own medicine," he said. "Let's see how she likes her looks when she's sporting a few bruises of her own." He began to rise.

"James!" Eliza caught his hand. "Ye can't."

"I can," James said. "I'm going to." He could hear the gravel in his voice, feel the rage taking over, almost as if it lived on its own—a thing separate from himself. He saw the fear rising in Eliza's eyes, but he couldn't stop.

She caught his hand. "Please, listen to reason. Ye've never hit a woman."

"No one's ever beaten my wife with a broomstick." He started for the door.

"James! No!"

"Why not?" As he turned back, he could feel the shaking start. It moved throughout his body as the adrenaline ran hot, driving him toward violence, compelling him. "Eliza, I have to do this."

"James, please, no."

He set his jaw. "I've got to do something," he growled, the words low in his throat. "I'm goin' now. Keep a watch on the boys." He turned to the door.

"And what will the boys and I do when we have to move in a week and ye're in jail?"

He paused, one hand on the door. "Jail?"

"If ye go to Mrs. P.'s, she'll be waitin' for ye. She might even have the constable there to set upon ye before ye can touch her. Ye know she has connections." He hesitated.

She reached out, and he closed the distance between them, taking her hands in his. "Please, husband. I need ye now. The boys and me, we all need ye. Don't leave us. Please?"

"She's got to know she can't do things like this to good folk like— Eliza, she beat ya with a broom!"

"I know. Believe me, I know." His wife touched him, gently stroking his shoulder, his face. He pulled away from her, the rage in him demanding violence, not tenderness.

But Eliza went on. "Mrs. P. will have her comeuppance one day, I'm sure of it, but not from ye, my love, and not now. Ye can't afford to give her an excuse to get back at both of us. Our circumstance is desperate enough already. Besides . . ." She paused for emphasis, standing beside him to take his face in both her hands. "Ye're a disciple of the Savior now, a Latter-day Saint. Everything ye do will reflect on the Church and the other Saints."

Her words were beginning to cut through his fog of crimson fury. He rocked forward.

She caught his hands. "Listen to me, love. I know how ye must be feeling, but I need ye now. Maybe more than I've ever needed ye. Please?"

Feeling disconnected from his own steps, he slowly moved away from her and collapsed on the floor as the adrenaline rushed out of him, taking all the starch from his knees. She hurried to him. He took her hand and began to sob over it, his agony palpable. "Oh, Eliza! I knew it would be difficult, but I never imagined this. I never pictured ya being beaten like a stray cur. I can handle anything they do to me, but ya? Oh, my love, forgive me!" He wept like a child as she sat on the bed beside him.

"There is nothing to forgive." She stroked his hair. "We made this choice together, and we're in it together still."

From outside the bedroom door, Joseph began to wail.

"I'll need to feed him," she said, "but then we must kneel and pray together. If we ever needed wisdom and help from heaven, we need it now."

He stood, slowly composing himself. "Ya crawl back into the bed, and we'll prop ya up against the bedstead. I'll bring Joseph to ya."

"Bring Jimmy in too. He's as frightened as ye are. We can all huddle in here together and pretend for a time that we're taking a little holiday, the four of us just enjoying each other."

He started for their door again and then turned back, looking at his lovely wife with her soul-deep bruises. "Will anything ever be all right again?"

"It will," she said, and this time her smile seemed real. "It will, dear one. Ye'll see." And the peace began to seep back around him once again.

\*   \*   \*   \*

Jimmy had long since ceased taking naps, but the emotional tension in the house had exhausted him. He slept soundly on his parents' bed. James stood, taking Joseph from Eliza's arms and offering his hand to help her up. "Thank ye, love," she whispered, grateful for the calm their short family interlude had brought. They stepped out of the bedroom and closed the door.

"Yer bruises are darker now," he said, examining her face. "Are ya hurting much?"

"Aye, some," she admitted. "And I'm feeling such weariness all over, like after ye have a bad cold, y'know?"

"I s'pose that's sensible," James answered. "The past twenty-four hours have taken a toll on all of us."

"Sure'n 'tis true," she said, stretching out some of the stiffness. She tried to swallow her fear.

"I'll put Joseph in his crib," he offered. "Then we can kneel together—that is, if ye're up to kneeling?"

"Oh, aye. I do feel a bit as if I've been beaten with a broomstick"— she paused, underscoring her words with a sly smile—"but nobody hit my knees."

He put the baby in the crib and came back to stand beside her. She gratefully accepted his help as they knelt together beside the small settee that had belonged to Elmer Hogan's late mother-in-law, just another of the worldly goods they were about to lose. "Shall I speak it?" he asked. "Or would ya like to?"

She hoped to reassure him. "Ye say it, James. Ye're the head of this household."

She thought he seemed reluctant as he answered, "All right." He folded his arms and bowed his head, but he seemed unable to go on. "Maybe ya should pray?" he asked.

"I don't mind, love, but why?" Then she looked at his face and knew. "Something's bothering ye, isn't it?"

He seemed unable to meet her eyes as he said, "I can't get past the way I felt this morning. I've never felt such rage, such . . . such a killing fury. I was going to hurt her. I might have even killed her if ya hadn't stopped me. I don't feel worthy to approach the Creator of the universe, not after—" He stopped again, and she saw his tears.

Eliza took his face in her hands and turned him toward her. He quickly dropped his gaze. She lifted his face again, almost forcing him to look at her. "James, that wasn't ye. Ye've never been like that in yer life. Ye're not a violent man, and I'm sure ye'd have stopped before ye hurt anyone. I was just glad ye didn't leave me." She smiled, but he shook his head.

"I was violent this morning. It was almost as if . . . as if something else had taken me over. Like that rage was a thing of its own." His eyes showed his misery.

"Perhaps it was, love. Remember what Elder Walton said about the adversary and the third of the hosts of heaven who fell?"

"Um, mostly."

"He warned us they'd all be trying to distract us just as soon as we took positive steps to join with the Saints. He warned us bad things would happen—even things that we didn't already expect—and that we might have direct confrontation with those fallen spirits."

His mumbled, "Aye. I recall him saying that."

She took his face in her hands and waited until he looked at her. "Darlin' husband, don't let guilt over what ye were feeling paralyze ye. Ye felt fury, ye entertained a few bad thoughts, but when it came right down to it, ye did the right thing—and without too much nagging." She smiled. "Ye're going to be fine," she said. "And now, I think ye should pray."

"Aye, love," he answered, and slowly he began to address their Heavenly Father.

To her surprise, he didn't begin with their desperate situation. The first words that came were thanks—for his dear Eliza, for their beautiful boys, for the opportunity to hear the gospel of Jesus Christ and to be baptized into His kingdom. When he got around to describing their situation, he asked only that they might find the answers the Lord would have them find so that they might serve Him. He closed his prayer and looked at Eliza with some surprise. "I didn't know I was going to say that," he murmured.

"Ye were inspired," she answered. He leaned to kiss her, and she eagerly met his kiss.

*   *   *   *

The knock came at their door just as they finished their midday meal. Eliza turned toward the sound with fear in her heart. "Elmer again?"

"I don't think he'll be back—except to evict us, mayhap." James stood.

From the door, they heard a familiar voice. "Eliza? Are ye home?"

Eliza sighed in relief. She gave Jimmy permission to return to his backyard play as James moved toward the door. "Coming, Ed!" he called.

Ed and Molly were both there, Ed holding Mary in his arms. As James opened the door, Ed said, "What are ye doin' home, James? Has Hogan dismissed ye already?"

"Aye. Please come in." They could hear the kookaburra laughing from its red gum tree as James ushered his friends from the bright light of the porch into the shadowed interior.

Molly saw them first, then gasped and put her hands to her face. Ed took one look and whistled long and low. "Well, fry me up a goanna," he said. "What's happened to ye two? Ye look like ye've been with Her Majesty's troops in the Crimea."

"He's right, ye do," Molly said, "and I only saw ye yesterday. What on earth—?"

Eliza's mouth turned up at the corners. "Well, he hit me with a broomstick, so I punched him." There was startled silence for a moment, and then she and James looked at each other and burst into hysterical giggles.

"They've lost their minds," Ed said.

"Ye'd best sit down," Eliza offered as she composed herself. Over the next several minutes, she and James took turns unraveling the events of the past day.

"There ya have it," James finished. "Neither of us has a position, and Elmer will surely see to it that no one in mercantile will have anything to do with me. In a week, we'll have neither home nor furnishings, and to top it off, we're both beaten and bruised."

Ed shook his head. "Not quite what ye'd hoped for, is it?"

James smiled. "I think it's safe to say that. But that reminds me, Ed, why are ye here? It doesn't surprise me to have Molly visiting in the middle of the day, but shouldn't ya be seeing to banking business?"

Ed looked to his wife. "Molly?"

She flushed. "No, Ed. Ye tell 'em."

"Tell us what?" Eliza prompted.

Ed cleared his throat. "Well . . . Molly had a feelin'—a prompting, she called it—that there was trouble. She had Smythe stop by the bank to get me on her way over." He looked from James to Eliza. "Looks like she was gettin' good information."

Eliza crossed the few steps to hug her friend. "Ye're a saint, Molly. Thanks so much for coming."

"I knew we had to," Molly said. "The question is what d'ye do now?"

James began to outline his plans for approaching store owners as soon as the bruises faded. "I know Elmer will have been there already and it's unlikely any will talk to me, but I have to start somewhere, and I know mercantile better than any other businesses. It seems the best place to start."

"I think ye're right," Ed said. "Listen, I've business I have to take care of, but I'll be back soon. Be ready to go with me when I come back, and I'll take ye all out for tea." He blew a kiss to Molly and rushed out the door.

Molly turned with a startled look. "I wonder what that's all about? He's never been a selfish one," she said. "I never thought I'd see him run out on ye like this, and for business, no less."

"It's all right, Molly," Eliza said. "He has his own interests to look after."

"Still . . ." Molly began. But then she sighed. "What can I do to help?"

An hour passed. James kept an eye on the children while Molly helped Eliza go through the house, making lists of which items had been there when they moved in—and thus would have to be left behind—and which they had purchased. Eliza was surprised to realize that most of her dishes and utensils were hers and even their bed was their own, if they could find a way to move it. They had their clothing and a few personal items, but other than that, their only possession was Eliza's rocking chair. Still, it was better than she had feared.

With Molly's help, she was able to decide how many boxes she would need and how she could pack her things. When Molly volunteered to arrange for boxes and a cart to haul them, another worry vanished.

Both babies cried at the same time, and James went to play with Jimmy while the mothers fed their little ones. As they sat with their infants, Eliza said, "I can't thank ye enough for coming, Molly. It's clear ye were inspired, and ye've helped me face the future again."

"It was nothing, and I know ye'd have done the same for me."

"Well, ye did do it for me and mine, and I'm grateful. We know now what is ours and how we can move it. Now if we only knew where to go—"

"Ed would have some ideas on that score if he hadn't gotten all concerned about his own business. I don't know what's got into that man. He has money. He could do so much more."

"And it's his money which he rightfully earned. He owes us nothing. Let it go, Molly. He's done so much for us."

"Aye, but he's going to hear more about this from me, I can promise ye that."

Moments later, Ed opened the front door, calling to everyone, "I hope ye're all ready."

"Come on in," Eliza said. "Let me call James and Jimmy, and we'll be ready in no time."

They were soon loaded into the carriage and on their way—Jimmy on the driver's seat with Smythe, Molly pouting as she sat opposite her husband. As they clip-clopped along, Eliza asked, "Where are ye taking us? James and I aren't exactly presentable, what with these battle ribbons on our faces."

"I'm takin' ye out to eat. We'll have no problems," Ed answered, "but I'm thinkin' we'll have a late meal tonight." He reached into his pocket. "I picked up a couple of hot cross buns for the little un so he won't starve while we're occupied with other business—"

Molly huffed in disgust. "Not more business. Not now."

He patted her hand. "Don't worry, love. Ye won't mind this." He looked out the window. "Almost there, I should think."

James leaned to have a look. "We're headed down toward the cove, yes? What business d'ya have down here?"

"Ye're about to find out," he said. The coach came to a stop on a busy corner. Smythe got down with Jimmy at his heels and opened the door for the passengers. Ed, with Eliza's blessing, presented the bread he had brought for the boy and spoke to James. "D'ye know this place?"

"Aye. That's the shop Elmer was plannin' to buy for a fourth store."

"Well, I doubt he'll be buying it now," Ed said. "I've bought the big meeting house next door, the three-story on the corner here, and I'm going to turn it into the biggest mercantile in Sydney. Ye're goin' to run it for me."

Three astonished gasps followed his announcement, and then everyone spoke at once. Molly said, "Ye darlin' man! I take back all the awful things I was plannin' to say."

Eliza said, "I can't believe it! It's like a miracle!"

James asked, "Ya did all this in the last two hours?"

Ed answered only James. "'Course not, mate. Been workin' on this for months, but it wasn't quite ready yet. Here, come in and let me show ye around." He took out a skeleton key and unlocked the double doors that opened onto the main floor, a few steps above street level. Then he began to show them around.

The building had been designed to house a gentlemen's club, so its main floor featured a large assembly room surrounded by smaller meeting rooms. The second floor housed offices and more small conference rooms. The third floor was open, as was the full basement except for the furnace, the plumbing, and the janitorial closets. The plan had been for Sydney to enjoy a men's club similar to those in London, complete with both large and small meeting spaces and additional rooms for the occasional game of whist or darts. Upstairs offices would handle not only the organizational needs of the club but rental space for some of the members as well.

The ambitious speculators hadn't counted on the stubbornly non-stuffy, non-London character of the men of Sydney. When their membership had dwindled to the point they could no longer pay their light bill, they had listed the building for sale. Ed had owned it for more than three months already.

"I reckon this large area will be the main sales floor," he said as they concluded the tour.

"These rooms off to the side can be for special items, such as one room just for fabrics and sewing things and another, maybe here, for farm equipment and seeds and such. Hardware might take up another of these side rooms . . . Well, ye can see what I'm going for here."

"Aye," James said, catching the vision, "separate departments for different items, all within the same store. It's brilliant. Since the building has entrances on two sides, we'll need to put the counter and cash register in some central location—"

"Like maybe here?" Ed indicated a place on the windowless back wall.

"That could work. What're ya thinking for all that space upstairs?"

"There may be a need for some specialty shops; I'm thinking things like pretty lamps and other fancy clutter women like, maybe them vases from China and such. Ye'll need an office for keepin' records, and there's no reason we can't rent out other office space, although if my business interests continue to grow the way I hope they might, I could fill that up myself within the next two or three years."

James gave him a speculative look. "Truly?"

"I've got a few tricks up my sleeve. I've been thinkin' about the basement. Ye may have noticed it has its own entrance off the alley in back? Don't ye think we could turn that downstairs space into a store for colored folk?"

James lit up. "Ed, that's bonzer!" He called across the room to where the women were looking at the window curtains. "Did ya hear that, Eliza?"

"Aye, I did," she called back. "It sounds like what ye've always wanted."

Eagerly, James went on. "I've wanted to provide for the native people. They've only a few stores where they can shop, and most are poorly stocked and are underfunded. Because the 'good people' of Sydney feel the way they do about shopping with colored folk, they wouldn't be open to having a mix inside the store, but if we create a separate entrance and stock the downstairs store with all the same goods at the same prices, it should be no time at all before the word spreads and ye'll have that whole business sewn up."

"I thought ye'd feel that way, and the unused third floor can go for extra inventory, so ye never run out of anything."

"That's perfect. One of the problems at Hogan's is people having to wait for a ship to come in before we can fill their order."

"Most of the general stores around here are havin' the same problem," Ed said. "That's why I ordered about three times the inventory I think we'll need."

James stopped walking. "Wait. Ye've already ordered inventory?"

"Aye, some time ago."

"How did ya do that? I mean, I know ye've a fine head for business and all, but how did ya know what to order?"

"I didn't," Ed answered, "but I knew some blokes who did." He explained that around the same time he'd started negotiations on the building, two men had come to him at the bank asking for a loan to start a general store. "They had both worked in mercantile back in England before comin' to mine in the Blues. They were out of work and completely out of cash, but they had a wealth of knowledge. I told 'em I couldn't lend to 'em when they had nothin' to put up front, but I hired 'em both and put 'em to work visiting every mercantile in the city, making lists of all the products available for sale and how many of each the different stores kept in stock. Then I asked 'em what was carried in London that nobody has locally. We combined their lists and came up with what we wanted to order from England."

"But if ya have both of them working for ya, ya don't need me."

"That would be true, except that neither of them is working with me anymore—not retail, anyhow." Ed explained that one of the men had never actually worked in the front part of any store but only as a bookkeeper in the back. "I hired him at the bank," he explained. "And turns out the other fella only wanted to make enough money for passage back to England, so I made him my agent in London. I paid his passage and a little extra, and then I sent him to the wholesalers to represent me with letters of credit and so forth."

"Ya always did know how to help people while making a profit. But how can ya be sure ya can trust the man? He could just take yer money and disappear in London, for all ya know."

"Aye, that could happen," Ed agreed. "But I didn't send any of the money in ready cash, just in letters of credit drawn on my accounts in London and made out to specific manufacturers. And there was one other thing about the man, almost a guarantee."

"And that was?"

Ed grinned. "He's one of yer people, a Mormon. I still think ye're all crazy folk, but at least ye're honest crazy folk. This fella only wanted to get home so he could meet up with his family and head to Deseret. He wanted to 'gather to Zion,' just like the elders keep sayin'."

"One of us," James mused. "Then it must be someone I know or have met at least."

"Andrew Perkins?"

James smiled. "Aye, he's a good man. Ya can trust him with yer life, not just yer funds."

"I always reckon any man I can trust with my money is safe to trust with my life."

James chuckled. "I've never had enough money to look at it that way, but I'm glad ya could put yer trust in someone worthy of it."

"Aye. I got a letter from Perkins on Saturday. He has the things I ordered pretty much put together, and he said they'd be on the next ship out of Southampton, if nothin' goes awry. Assuming good winds, we could be settin' up here within the next week."

James lit up with astonished excitement, but his smile quickly faded. "That's all splendid. Ye've worked it all out in detail, and I give ya credit. I can see only one flaw to yer planning, and it may be a fatal error."

"And that would be?"

"Me. If people would avoid Elmer's store because of me becoming Mormon, they'll be avoidin' yers too. Ya could lose every penny."

"But I shan't." Ed beamed like he'd swallowed the sun. "Ye're right that the good folk here in Sydney like little better than condemnin' others for their skin color, and they're almost as bad when it comes to how people pray, but Elmer exaggerated how suspicious they are of Mormons—probably because of his own hard feelings. Besides, I learned some time ago that one thing matters even more—their pocketbooks.

"Since we're buying in such quantity, and since I'm backed by all the assets of the bank, I'm gettin' the best prices ever. We can undersell Hogan—and ever'body else—by a penny here, two pennies there, a shilling somewhere else. Big ticket items like the ploughs or stoves might go for a pound or more less than at Hogan's. Folks in Sydney will come because the sign over the door says Welsh Mercantile. They'll see ye and remember the stories Elmer's passing 'round and they'll wonder, but then they'll see the prices and buy. Ye'll see."

Then he grinned. "Besides, I'm havin' all my employees spread it about that Elmer dismissed ye out of jealousy 'cause ye were handlin' his affairs so much better than he ever did."

"Ed! Ya can't do that."

"I can and I will, largely because I suspect it's true. I've seen how Hogan ran his business, and he would never've had three stores with a fourth in the works if it hadn't been for yer good business sense." He clapped James on the shoulder. "When I realized that Elmer was havin' a fit about ye hearin' the missionaries, and then I saw how ye kept answerin' the questions those Yanks were asking, I knew the time would likely come when ye'd be needin' a new job. But I'm not doin' this just for ye or Eliza or even because I owe ye my life. I'm a business-man, and I know a great opportunity when I see it. Investin' in yer expertise is an opportunity. I'm only sorry I didn't have this all ready to go when ye needed it."

"It's pretty close," James said. "How soon d'ya think ye'll be needin' a manager?"

"I'd like to put ye on salary starting next Monday, if that's all right. Even if the inventory isn't in by then, we'll be needin' to build the counter and put in shelves, decidin' what goes where in the upstairs and the down, and settin' up the record-keeping system. I'll also want ye to hire a couple of good men who can help around here—delivering large items or helping to fetch and carry, eventually learnin' how to take over at the cash register when business requires ye to be somewhere else, somethin' like Will Carter was doin' at Hogan's."

"All right," James answered. "I can do that."

"And James, if it happens they're also Mormon, just don't mention it to me or bring it up to folks who come into the store. I wouldn't want any of ye to lie about it, o' course, but it might be good if they just didn't mention it until folks start getting used to the idea of doin' business with honest Mormon folk. Once that starts, could be they'll prefer to deal with Mormons. I know I already do." He looked at Eliza and winked.

"Ye're a blessing, Ed." James embraced him. "Thank ya, mate, and by the way, ya didn't owe me anythin' for helpin' ya down on the Burra-Burra, but if ya had, consider it paid in full."

"That's a deal," Ed said, offering his hand and then somberly shaking with James. "This is an investment in my own future income, but I'm not above lettin' ye call us even for that business with the platypus. Now I'll just have to repay ye for settin' me up with my Molly, and that could take a long, long time."

Molly, hearing him from across the room, called out, "Ye don't have to try to get on my good side. I'm already plannin' to make up to ye for the way I doubted ye earlier."

Ed grinned and whispered to James. "I can hardly wait to see how she plans to do that."

James grinned in response but answered, "None of my business, mate." Then he spoke louder. "The only problem Eliza and I are still facin' is where to move our family. D'ya think we can move into the second floor here—at least until we can find somethin' else?"

"Ye could, but the place isn't really set up for livin' quarters. For one thing, there's no place for Jimmy to play." He smiled at the boy, who grinned broadly. "Besides I don't think that's a proper situation for the manager of the newest, best, and biggest mercantile in town."

"I would agree, but—"

"I didn't realize ye were goin' to need a place to live or I'd've had somethin' ready."

"I hadn't realized it, either, but don't concern yerself, Ed. Ye've done more than enough."

"Well, could be I have . . . now, anyway." He grinned broadly. "That was the part I needed to take care of before the close of business."

James raised his eyebrows but didn't get a chance to ask the question before Ed went on.

"I got back to the bank and asked all my loan officers what they knew about available real estate in the area of Elizabeth Street."

"Ed, I can't—"

"I have the addresses of four nice two-bed cottages within a half-mile walk of the store here. Tomorrow morning, Molly and Smythe will come pick up ye and Eliza and the little fellas, and they'll drive ye around, looking at all four of 'em. When ye pick one, come to the bank. I'll pay cash for the purchase. Ye can rent or buy the place from me same way ye was buyin' from Elmer."

"Ed, I can't let ye do that, 'specially since—" He lowered his voice. "'Specially since I'm going to try to talk Eliza into gathering to Zion soon."

"I'd hate like sin to see ye go. But remember real estate is an investment too," Ed said. "I can hardly go wrong purchasin' a pleasant home in this part of town. Since I trust the family that'll be livin' in it, and I know the two of ye will take as good a care of the place whether ye're rentin' or buyin', it makes no difference to me, but I suspect yer wife will feel more secure if she knows ye're buyin' the place."

James pursed his lips, pondering. "I'm not exactly in a position to argue with ya, mate. I think ye've got a renter, at least to begin with. After Eliza and I get a chance to talk, we may decide we'll buy instead."

"And ye'll start workin' for me on Monday?"

"Aye, mate. Ye've got a deal."

They shook solemnly one more time. Then Ed announced, "Come on now, everybody. I'm starvin'. I've got us a private dining room at the Harbour House, and they won't hold tea for us forever."

"Harbour House!" Molly declared. "Ye've never even taken me there."

"I'm takin' ye there now, woman. Hop to it," he said. They left the building in a much different mood than they had brought with them only an hour before.

# Chapter 13

Throughout that autumn, Eliza enjoyed a period of peace unlike any she had known. She was delighted when Ed's predictions about the mercantile proved true. Yes, some customers had grumbled, and a few friends of the Hogans flatly refused to do business with Welsh Mercantile. For a short time, it appeared that Hogan's work of spreading rumors might succeed. Then Matthew Sutton, the royal governor's secretary, who was still supportive of James, came to shop. The following day, the staff from the governor's mansion shopped there as well, and once people saw the carriage with the royal seal parked in front, the customers came—in crowds.

Every three or four weeks, the Martins heard new rumors—almost certainly started by Elmer Hogan—carried by customers into the store, rumors about James that all suggested shady business practices. Still, most folks preferred their pocketbooks to a squabble that was not their own; business was a resounding success. The "second store" in the cellar had been equally popular, and soon James was outselling any general store in town.

Ed was paying him well for his skills, and James was building their savings, preparing for the day when they could buy their home. Eliza knew he'd rather use those funds to take their family to Zion, but she shuddered even to think of the trip. She pointed out they were becoming disciples of Christ and doing fine as Mormons right here in Sydney. And when the news came that Elmer Hogan was shrinking his business back from three stores to two, she noticed the way James chose not to gloat.

Delighted with her new, larger cottage, she began the process of making it a home. By shopping secondhand and doing much of the work herself, she was turning it into a comfortable nest for her family. Then, taking starts or seeds from her neighbors, she planted bottle brush, boronia, and kangaroo paw, lovely flowers to beautify their garden as well.

Her boys were healthy and growing; Jimmy had now passed his sixth birthday. She was also finding increasing joy in her association with the Latter-day Saints, especially two families who had moved in the same week James began managing the store. Simon and Lucy Walker were about the same ages as she and James and had been members of the Church for just about as long. They had two little ones, boys near the ages of her own.

George and Clara Davis were a little older and already the parents of four. They had joined the Church at about the same time as the Walkers, and the two families had moved to central Sydney to have the support of the members there. Both men needed work and both had mercantile experience, so James had hired them on the spot. Soon the three couples had formed a tight friendship which included the Welshes as well. Ed joked that he didn't mind being surrounded by Mormons since it meant he didn't have to watch his pocketbook.

As autumn deepened into winter, Eliza also reveled in her marriage. In joining with the Latter-day Saints, she and James had eliminated their one area of contention, and through the blessing of Ed's rescue, they had even overcome the punishment Elmer Hogan had heaped upon them as a consequence. They both felt greatly blessed.

And now she had new reason to celebrate. One evening in late July, Eliza put the children to bed early and produced an apple pie she had been saving just for her husband.

"What's this about?" he asked, putting down the newspaper as she brought him a slice.

"Enjoy it, Papa," she answered.

He tipped his head. "I don't understand."

"I mean papa of three." She grinned.

"Ya don't mean . . . Ya can't be . . . Joseph is only nine months old!"

"Sure'n I know how old he is. And I can be and I am, according to both the doctor and the midwife. I s'pose the good Lord wanted to make up for lost time."

Shock registered on his face. "We're having another baby?"

She nodded.

"We're having a baby!" He spoke so loudly that Joseph whimpered from the bedroom. Then James jumped from his chair and caught her around the middle, swinging her in a circle and bringing her back for a long kiss. "This will mean some changes. We'll need—"

"We still have a few months to worry about it," she said, stroking his face. "D'ye think ye can put me down now?"

"Oh, of course." He set her feet on the floor. "Months, huh? How long?"

"Around the middle of December, right at the start of summer."

"Wow." He sat again. "By summer we'll be a family of five. D'ye think ye'll have a girl this time?"

"I'd like that, but I love our boys and I wouldn't mind havin' another. Ye'd be all right with having another boy, wouldn't ye?"

"Aye, surely. Another baby. My." He sat heavily. "Have ya told anyone? Besides me?"

"Doc Adams, of course, and Mrs. Johnson, the midwife. Other than that, it's just us."

"Let's keep it that way for a time, all right? For a little while? I mean, just in case—"

"Aye, I understand. We'll keep it to ourselves for a time and hope the pregnancy sticks." Then she paused and gave him a long look. "Ye're not disappointed, are ye?"

"Disappointed? No! Of course not. A little surprised, I s'pose . . . well, shocked, really. I didn't think it was possible again this soon." He looked up at her. "How far apart will they be? Joseph and the new one."

"Just over fourteen months."

"Goodness."

"James, I don't know how I'll feel if ye're not happy about this—"

He looked up to see her eyes filling with tears. "I am happy, sweetheart. Ya know I've always wanted a passel of wee ones. I'm just getting used to the idea." He picked up the huge slice of pie. "Here, sit down and let's celebrate."

"No. Thank ye, anyway. I'll have to watch what I eat so I don't turn into one of those big creatures from Africa they have at the London Zoo. They got it just before I set sail. What was that thing called? A hippy, I think?"

"I think ya mean a hippo. My uncle saw a picture in the *London Times*. And ye'll never look like that. Ye're too pretty." He chucked her under the chin. "Come on now. Ye've cut a huge slice. Let me feed ya some."

"Well, since ye put it that way . . ." She sat on his lap and the two of them shared the pie.

\*　\*　\*　\*

At the end of July, the Davises declared they had saved enough to book passage to San Francisco. "Next Sunday will be our last here," Clara Davis announced. "We want to start the voyage before the hurricane season."

"Hurricanes." Eliza shuddered. "Isn't being at sea horrid enough without storms?"

"I think they've still some room aboard our ship," Clara offered. "Why don't ye talk with James? Maybe yer family can come."

"Ye'll not be getting me to sea again," Eliza declared solemnly.

Clara laid a hand on her arm. "Sister, we need to join the Saints in Deseret to build up Zion. Gathering is a part of what we took on with our baptism."

Eliza brushed her hand away. "Not for me, it isn't." Unwilling to explain further, she walked away, but the incident remained with her.

It didn't help that they were hardly through the door before James said, "They've the right idea, ya know. We should be gathering. Have ya done any more considering?"

Eliza ground her teeth but reined in her temper, embarrassed by the way she'd snapped at Sister Davis. "We can't even think of going while I'm in my present condition, and we're doing well here now. Ye've been so happy with Ed at the new store, and the boys are thriving like weeds in a rose garden. Besides, we still have the Clarks and the Walkers."

"Still I'm thinking we should be preparing, ya know? Saving up the money for the passage, deciding which things to take—"

"Ye promised ye wouldn't push!" The response was so loud it startled little Joseph, who began to cry.

James dropped the subject, but Eliza could not. The idea kept buzzing in her mind, refusing to go away. Was she denying her family blessings because of her fear? She'd hardly thought the question before she realized it didn't matter. Her fear was paralyzing. She would not go. At least now she had the new baby as an excuse, but later?

It occurred to her that she should pray about the decision, but she couldn't bring herself to do that either. If she prayed, she'd get an answer—and she wouldn't like it at all. And so she continued in the peace of the moment, unable to plan beyond the December birth of her third child.

The first Sunday in August was tearful for the small Sydney branch, the sadness made worse when the Clarks announced they had booked passage for mid-September. The other members greeted the news with joy for the Clarks and distress for themselves. With the Davises gone, their small branch was seriously crippled. When the Clarks left, they would lose the home where they had been meeting, their branch president, and the only man in their area with the authority to baptize.

James pointed out all of these problems to Eliza as they walked home. "It's going to be difficult to be members of the Church here soon."

"The Lord will provide," she said with finality. Then she picked up her pace, walking slightly ahead of him so he wouldn't nag her further.

But James was not the only source of nagging. More and more often she felt the whisperings of the still, small voice telling her to prepare for the voyage. By the time both the Davises and the Clarks had gone, she had almost ceased to pray, since praying opened her to the whisperings of the Spirit, and the Spirit kept repeating the same unwelcome message.

"When the baby's born, I'll think about it," she'd said aloud one day. The answer came strongly that she needed to do it sooner, and Eliza stopped praying altogether.

Her one comfort came when the missionaries arrived at the dock to see the Clarks off. Elder Walton and Elder Bingham took the group into a small, unused space in a nearby warehouse and ordained James and Isaac, one of the young single men who'd been meeting with them, giving them both the authority to baptize. They also named James as the temporary leader of the branch. Eliza told herself that as long as her husband was the leader of the local Saints, she needn't worry about being asked to leave.

Besides, they still had Simon and Lucy, who were becoming almost as dear to her as Ed and Molly. Their two families, together with the few single men who had joined them lately, would make a nice group for meetings in their cottage on Sundays.

On the last Sunday in September, the Walkers also announced they had booked passage, due to sail October 2, and Eliza felt like mourning. Privately, she wondered if God had simply abandoned her. The answer came with her own voice speaking in her mind, "Or did ye abandon Him?" Later that day, she retreated into her room, heart full of sorrow, and prayed as she never had, tearfully begging forgiveness but still unable to open her heart to gathering.

The following day, James returned from the mercantile with news. "Send Jimmy out back to play," he said. "Tea can be a little late. Come and sit while I tell ya something Ed and I have been talking about."

With the departure of George Davis and the planned departure of Simon Walker, James had hired and trained two new assistants. Now he told her how well they were both working out. ". . . And especially Herbert Miller. Before he sailed for Sydney, he was a manager at a small mercantile in Hastings, in the south of England. D'ya know it?"

"I've heard of it," she said. "So he's working out well, is he?"

"Aye, very well. None of the Saints were looking for work, and well, with Herbert and Sam, I don't need to worry about them taking off for the Americas just as soon as I get them well trained. Herbert could even take over for me as manager—should we ever need for that to happen." He gave Eliza a sidelong glance.

"It's good to have a plan," she said, ignoring his intention.

He sighed. "There's something else Ed and I have been working on, a way I can build our savings fast." He told her about a man who'd come down from the silver mines in Yerranderie with a large order for groceries and supplies. He had made an offhand comment that he'd happily pay more if he didn't have to make the trip into Sydney. "A lot of the cobbers feel that way," the man had added, and for James, that had sparked an idea.

"So I talked with Ed, and he agreed. I'll try it in early October, right after we see Simon and Lucy off. I'll fill up Ed's store wagon with supplies the miners always need, and I'll borrow the second team of horses. I'll buy everything from Ed before I go, and even though he'll charge a bit above his price, it won't be full retail. Then I'll drive to Yerranderie and sell out of the wagon. If I charge about twenty percent above the store's regular price, the miners should be more than happy to snap it up. By summer we can likely make half the down payment for the house—or whatever other major expense we may have."

"It sounds a little risky," Eliza said. "Ed isn't going to pay ye for days that ye aren't working . . ."

"No, that wouldn't be fair, but I can earn several times what I usually make in a week. Two or three trips like that would be enough."

"But d'ye even know what to take? It's a long time since ye were a miner."

"Now ye're just bein' foolish. I've been selling to miners since I first started working for Elmer, and I know exactly what they want: coffee, sugar, flour, nails for the supports in their tunnels, and a half-dozen other things. If I also take a few pairs of coveralls and plenty of Darjeeling and Earl Grey tea, I should sell out in a flash. Of course, I could make quite a profit if I were willing to carry liquor or chaw, but I wouldn't be comfortable selling those anymore."

"I just don't want ye to go," she admitted. "I don't know why I'm feelin' so edgy, but I am. I just want ye here with the boys and me. We've never been apart that long."

"I won't do it often. We could possibly own the house before the baby comes."

"That would be good," she said, nodding and thinking it would be one more thing to keep them rooted in Sydney. "I s'pose ye'd best go ahead with it then."

"Ya needn't look so happy," he teased. He smiled, trying to ease her worries, but she couldn't put the worry out of her mind.

The second day of October arrived. With a heavy heart, Eliza accompanied her husband to the docks to say good-bye to Simon and Lucy Walker. Jimmy somberly shook the hand of the older Walker boy while Eliza tearfully hugged his mum.

"Write to us when ye get settled in Zion," she said.

Lucy nodded. "I will," she answered. "Simon and I will prepare a place so ye and James can join us."

"Don't be holdin' yer breath," Eliza answered. "Oh, Lucy, I'll miss ye!" She threw her arms around Lucy again.

"There's still room on the ship," Lucy said, her face serious. "Come with us."

Now it was Eliza who shook her head. "Ye know we're not ready. Frankly, I may never be. The sail down here was rough enough to last me a lifetime."

Lucy acted as if she hadn't heard. "We'll let ye know when we find a place. Write back and tell us what ye need, and we'll pave the way."

The "all aboard" call came, and the Walkers said their farewells. As Eliza hugged Lucy once more, she realized she would likely never see this dear friend again, and in that moment she felt nearly overwhelmed by her losses: her parents, her family in Ireland, friends who had left for the Americas on their way to Zion, connections with the Hogans and the Pembrokes, James leaving in days . . . She suddenly couldn't stand another sorrow, even of the smallest kind. While others on the dock still waved, she started for home, leaving her confused husband to grab Jimmy's hand and trail behind her.

She couldn't explain herself, couldn't even fully understand herself, but the morose sadness stayed with her, almost like foreboding. She decided she was simply dreading James's departure for the Blues, now only two days away. It didn't help that while he encouraged her acceptance by talking about a down payment on their home, she knew he hoped to use the added income to buy their journey to Zion. She wished she could share his eagerness and steeled herself for his Saturday morning departure, but she couldn't stop worrying and she couldn't sleep. The bright southern lights she saw every evening now, not usually visible from Sydney, felt like some sort of ominous warning.

Friday, James came home from the mercantile driving a fully loaded wagon. He carried baby Joseph and led Jimmy and Eliza out to show them his purchases. He'd packed carefully, getting in as much product as the wagon could carry and the team could pull. His excitement was palpable, and again she wished she could share it. She kept her own reluctance to herself as she held him in their bed that evening, wondering where her peace had gone and dreading the loneliness until she held him again.

*   *   *   *

James woke frequently in the night, troubled by both his own excitement and Eliza's fretful sleep. The aurora australis made odd, brightly colored patterns on their wall, and the unusual phenomenon created a nervous unease. He felt troubled by the unusual lights, troubled about leaving Eliza, troubled about the tension in their family, and there was another trouble weighing on him that he hadn't mentioned to his wife: Elmer Hogan had been at it again, spreading rumors that James still owed him back rent and other unpaid debts. It had raised a bit of trouble, and although Ed had smoothed everything over easily enough, James felt a great need to be moving on. As long as he was here, near Elmer's influence, there was always a risk things could go bad. Promptings were telling him he needed to take his family to Zion—and the sooner, the better. He had begun to pray for something that would push his wife in the same direction—and when it happened, he would have to be ready.

He was earning well now, and he daily thanked heaven for the opportunities Ed had given him. He had nearly enough saved already to take his family to California in steerage, but buying a cabin for the four—no, five—of them would take more. If this selling trip was as successful as he hoped, he might soon book top accommodations on one of the new English steamers that came bringing cargoes of potatoes, oil, soap, and flour, and then reloaded in Sydney with bales of raw wool and paying passengers. If he could book an attractive cabin, maybe he could persuade Eliza . . .

She snuggled against him in her sleep, and he knew it would take more than a nice cabin to make her sail again. Lying there with Eliza's head on his shoulder, he prayed once more for an answer to their dilemma and for safety on his journey. He left his blessing on his family, asking the Lord to care for them. The first hints of dawn were lighting the east, dimming the brilliant floating lights as he closed his prayer. He tiptoed from their room and began his morning preparations.

By the time he returned from the outhouse and warmed water for a shave, Eliza came dragging out of their bedroom. The growing baby was causing much discomfort, and he knew her rest had been troubled. The dark circles under her eyes gave him pause, but he had just spent much of his family's savings on the load of goods that waited for him in the side yard. He needed to see this through.

"Good morning, sweetheart," he said, trying to sound more cheery than he felt.

"Is it time?"

"I fear so." He set down his shaving basin and took her in his arms. "Ye'll be all right while I'm gone. Ed and Molly will look out for ya, and I'll be home in a week, ten days tops."

"Ten days." She sighed. "It doesn't sound long when ye're looking back on it, but when ye're looking forward?" She shook her head.

He smiled. "Ye're right, but we'll both be looking back on it soon."

"I hope so." She moved uneasily. "Yer new little one doesn't like being up this early," she said, laying his hand over her belly, where he could feel large, rolling motions.

"Boy or girl, this is an active one," he said. Then he kissed her forehead and asked, "D'ya want to wake the boys to see me off?"

"No," she demurred. "Ye said yer good-byes before they went to sleep last night. Jimmy knows ye're leaving, but it might be better if ye're gone when he wakes."

"I won't be long then. I just have to harness the horses, and we'll be away."

"Will ye be safe up there in the Blues?" she asked, although they'd had this discussion already. "Ye'll be there with no shelter and a whole wagonload of valuable goods—"

"I'll have shelter," he said.

"Sleeping under the wagon isn't what I'd call safe."

"Ya know I'll be under the wagon only one night each way. Once I get up there, I can stay with Ed's people at his mine. He gave me letters of introduction—" He cut the sentence off, realizing their talk was only prolonging his departure. "I need yer support," he said simply.

She smiled, although he saw the tears forming in her eyes. "Aye. I hate it, but I'll support ye. Every time I get a minute, I'll be praying for yer safe return."

"And I'll spend my days praying for ya and the boys," he said. Minutes later, he was holding her one last time. A feeling of deep sadness overcame him, and for a moment he wanted nothing more than to stay right there in Eliza's arms with his sons close, but he told himself he was being foolish and pulled away. "I'll be seeing ya soon," he said as he swung onto the seat of the wagon and called to the team.

As they pulled out of the yard, he turned to wave, pretending good cheer, but when they banked right at the end of the block, he could see Eliza still standing in the yard, bringing up her apron to wipe her tears.

* * * *

For Eliza, the rest of that Saturday went slowly. She stayed busy caring for the boys and handling various small chores around the house, including some she'd saved especially for these lonely days when James would be gone.

In late morning, Molly came, riding up in her carriage with Mary. She also brought lunch, including some of Eliza's favorite dishes that Alice and Ida had prepared and packed. "I knew ye'd be feeling lonesome," she announced as she arrived at the door with her arms full.

"Molly, ye're a godsend—as always," Eliza said, welcoming them.

Jimmy was finding both Joseph and Mary to be more enjoyable companions now that they were crawling everywhere and even taking a few steps. He liked playing with them—at least until they crawled into his toys and messed up his plans. Mary, who would celebrate her birthday the following week, was already toddling a little and Joseph was only slightly behind her, so they intruded frequently now. After they had eaten, the mothers moved to the back porch, letting Jimmy keep the little ones entertained while they visited. He didn't mind as long as *he* was playing with *their* toys.

"So how is it with yer husband gone?" Molly asked.

"Not as good as I'd like. Last night was restless for us both, what with this parting coming up—d'ye know it's the first time we'll have been apart overnight since we were married?"

"I think ye mentioned that," Molly said tonelessly, and Eliza had to smile.

"I've bored ye with it, have I?"

Molly grinned.

"It's tough."

Molly touched her hand. "I'm teasin' ye, but it would be a hard thing for me as well, especially if it was several nights in a row. So ye're weary as well as worried?"

"Aye, I s'pose that's exactly it. Then with the southern lights shining so brightly—"

"People everywhere are talkin' about that," Molly answered. "It's a rare thing. Ed says he only saw them twice in all the time he spent in the southern colonies, and they're more common there than here. Some Sydney longtimers have never seen the lights before."

"And now it's night after night, and it seems they're getting brighter, even in the day."

"Aye, I think they are."

"Does anyone know—"

"I've heard a few theories," Molly answered. "Of course some of 'em are silly—like it bein' an aboriginal curse on the white man."

"If the natives had a curse that powerful, they'd have used it some time ago."

"Like I said, it's silly." Molly called to Jimmy to please catch Mary before she toddled into the roses, and the boy quickly complied.

"Have ye heard any other ideas, more believable ones?"

"Some people think it's a sign of the end of everything, the Apocalypse." Molly shook her head. "Some of the folks who work at the bank are sayin' there was a big solar storm that started all this. That sounds peculiar to me. Do they even have clouds and such on the sun?"

"I don't think so," Eliza answered seriously. "But I don't know much about such things. If James were here—" She got just that far before the words caught in her throat.

"Is it that hard to talk about him?"

"It's just . . . I'm worried, Molly—not just about him but about all of us. I can't shake the feeling something awful is about to happen." She looked up. "That's silly too, isn't it?"

"Are ye sure it's not a prompting? Ye know, from the Spirit?"

Eliza gasped, feeling the blood drain from her face. "Oh, Molly! D'ye think it could be?"

Molly leaned to give her a quick hug. "I'm sorry, love. I shouldn't have said that. Forget I said it. Please?"

"Oh, but what if it is? What if it was a warning not to let James go?"

Molly clenched her jaw. "I'm sorry I brought it up. Please just forget it. Ye and I will say lots of prayers—and I'm sure James is praying too. Ed might even be persuaded to say some, though I doubt he'll admit it."

"Aye. He said he would when James asked him to."

Molly nodded. "Sounds like my Ed. Everything's going to be all right. Ye'll see." Molly steered the conversation into other directions then, talking about new draperies she was having made for Welsh House, but she kept giving Eliza cautious, troubled looks.

Eliza couldn't help feeling concerned about her unborn child. Everyone knew this kind of intense worry could cause any number of unpleasant birth defects. It was said that a seriously worried mother would deliver a skittish child who'd spend adult life too shy and frightened to live normally. She forced herself to calm her breathing and think of other things.

Molly turned their talk toward the upcoming birthdays of their little ones, suggesting they should plan a simple dinner for their families to celebrate together. "We can do it at Welsh House," she said. "Alice is a marvel when it comes to fancy pastries. If we schedule it between the birthdays, James should be back."

"That sounds lovely," Eliza said, and she could feel herself rallying as she began to focus on how Joseph would soon be a full year old.

"I'd love to come ever' day while James is gone, but I have appointments next week with the drapery people," Molly said. "If ye don't mind, Ida can come. She can take Jimmy for walks and leave ye some alone time, just ye and little Joseph. Maybe ye can catch a rest. I remember what it's like when ye're this far into yer carryin' and tired all the time." She smiled gently. "'Specially since it's such a short time since ye carried Joseph."

"Aye, I'm tired," Eliza responded. "It already feels like I've been carrying him forever."

Molly smiled. "Did ye realize ye just said him?"

Eliza stroked her belly, light dawning on her face. "Oh! Sure'n I did, didn't I?" Then, "It's a boy," she said. "I'm sure of it now. Another boy. My goodness!"

"Will James be pleased?"

Eliza nodded. "He loves bein' the father of sons. He'll be thrilled." As she felt the little one inside her move, she knew it was true. Excitement about the coming birth filled her heart, replacing some of her anxiety.

Before Molly left, Eliza asked if she would please join them for church tomorrow, even bringing Ed if she could. "With the Walkers gone, the branch is mostly our family and a few single men," she explained. "Now, what with James away, I wouldn't want the neighbors misinterpreting what they see. Ye understand?"

Molly's grin slowly widened. "I think ye've found a good enough excuse to get Ed and me to yer church." Then she nodded. "Aye. We'll come." She hugged Eliza as she left.

After Molly's departure, Eliza thought the day would drag on interminably, but she found more than plenty to do. As evening drew near, she felt certain of a near sleepless night, but exhaustion claimed her almost as soon as she put her head down. Despite the wild display of southern lights still playing in the night sky, she slept hard until the dawn woke her.

Sunday went swiftly too. Ed and Molly came to the simple church services Eliza hosted. Isaac had no one to assist him in blessing the sacrament, but he reverently prepared, blessed, and served to the eight adults who attended. Then Ted, another recently baptized convert among the single men, offered a lesson on the address of King Benjamin in the book of Mosiah. By the time the other members left, Eliza was feeling closer to the Spirit. After eating an early Sunday tea at Ed and Molly's, she was feeling well-nourished in the body as well. With a second good night's sleep in a row, she began to feel she could handle this week after all.

On Monday, Smythe brought Ida, who arrived just in time to take Jimmy walking before Eliza put Joseph down for his nap. "I think we'll walk down by the quay if that's all right with ye," she said, "or do ye fear for him gettin' that close to the water?"

"Jimmy knows not to get in the water unless he has someone with him," Eliza answered. Then just to reassure them both, she asked, "Don't ye, Jimmy?"

"Aye, Mum. No swimmin' without a grown-up."

"And why is that?" she prompted, helping the child to remember his training.

"'Cause I might get drownded," Jimmy answered somberly.

"Drowned," Eliza corrected. "Exactly so." She looked at Ida.

"Sounds safe enough," Ida said with a smile. "Come on, Jimmy. Let's go walkin'."

"'Bye, Mum!" the boy called as he took Ida's hand.

Except for the occasional Sunday when James was home to watch the boys, it was the first restful afternoon nap Eliza had enjoyed since Jimmy had stopped taking them. She and Joseph slept for nearly two hours—long enough that she feared she wouldn't rest at all that evening, especially with the southern lights growing ever brighter. When Ida returned with Jimmy—the boy carrying a bouquet of waratahs and gymea lilies in one grubby hand, Eliza had begun to feel as if she had things under control.

Molly's Tuesday visit was full of talk about the new draperies. "We got so much done yesterday that we've cancelled the appointment for tomorrow," she announced with pride. "I told Ida I'd be comin' to see ye tomorrow myself and she didn't need to come to walk with Jimmy. She acted as if I'd broken her heart, the poor thing." Molly dropped her voice and looked all around as if she and Eliza were not perfectly alone. "She's afraid she won't ever have little uns of her own," she explained. "And she's still two years younger than I was when ye and James matched me up with my sweetheart. I keep assurin' her she has nothin' to worry about, but . . . well, I understand what she's feelin'. I told her she can come tomorrow to walk with Jimmy while we visit. That is, unless ye'd rather I stay away and ye can have another good nap. I know how much extra rest an expectant mama needs when she's getting as close as ye are."

"I've still more than two months to go," Eliza said, patting her growing belly. "And it's been surprising how well I've slept these past few nights. Please come to visit us tomorrow, and bring Ida too, although Jimmy might not want to go walking with both the young ones here." They confirmed their plans before Molly left that afternoon.

The eerie lights in the sky were brighter than ever that evening, but Eliza slept soundly, troubled only slightly by fearful dreams that fled from memory as soon as she awakened.

She got up on Wednesday with a vague sense that something wasn't quite in order, but since she couldn't put her finger on the feeling, she dismissed it and went on about her day. Sometime during the morning, she sat Jimmy down and explained to him that Molly and Mary would be coming for a visit, but Ida was coming too. She gave him the option of playing with the babies or going walking with Ida.

"Down by the quay again?" he asked eagerly.

"I s'pose so," Eliza answered. "Ye enjoyed that last time, didn't ye?"

"Aye, Mum," the boy answered. "And ye liked the flowers I brung ye, right?"

"It's 'brought,' Jimmy, and aye, I liked the flowers ye *brought* me very much."

"Then I'll get ye some more today," Jimmy said. "They've got some pretty ones growin' down by the water."

"Ye know to just pick the wildflowers, right, son? And not from people's yards?"

"Just the ones God planted," Jimmy answered.

Eliza grinned. "Aye, Jimmy, just the ones God planted." And then, overcome by love for her firstborn, she held him close and kissed his forehead. "I love ye, son."

"I love ye too, Mum, and Papa and Joseph." Then Jimmy began to squirm, and she knew it was time to let him go.

# Chapter 14

MOLLY AND IDA ARRIVED AROUND midday with a full picnic basket. The group enjoyed lunch together, and before long the mothers were putting their infants down for naps while Ida prepared to take Jimmy walking.

"Take good care of my Jimmy," Eliza told Ida as she walked them to the gate.

"I will, ma'am," Ida answered.

"And Jimmy, ye take care of Ida."

"Aye, Mum!" he called back.

As she turned, Eliza felt a shiver down her spine but attributed it to the light chill in the air and promised herself she'd stoke the fire. Half an hour later, she sat comfortably with Molly in the warm cottage. As often happened now, they began discussing Molly's reading in the Book of Mormon while Eliza shared insights from recent church meetings. "Ye know," she said, "the time may be coming when ye'll have to recognize ye're a Mormon under the skin."

"Aye, I recognized that some time ago." Molly's smile faded into a sigh. "I can't see any honorable way around my vow, so I'll go to Mass and pray the rosary. I'll take my little uns to be christened and I'll send 'em to study their catechism, but at home, they're going to learn to pray to the Father in the name of the Son, and they'll hear stories from restored scripture. I'm reading to Mary already, though she doesn't understand it yet."

"Ye're a puzzle, Molly. I declare ye are."

"Oh and ye're so much better? How long has it been now since ye joined the Church?"

"It was late January, so nine months or thereabouts. Why're ye asking?"

"Ye knew gathering was a part of it right from the beginning, and still, here ye are—coming up with any excuse ye can think of to avoid setting foot on a ship."

Eliza sighed. "Ye were with me coming down here. Ye saw what it was like—people packed in like cattle, piled up on wobbly bunks, eating from common trays, using the same chamber pots . . ." Eliza shook her head. "I was sick the whole time."

"I know how bad it was." Molly shuddered. "And don't ye go misunderstandin' me. Ye're the best friend I've ever had in all my born life and I don't know how I'll live without ye, but I know it'll be best for ye to go on to Zion. Ye need to gather with the Saints." Then her eyes twinkled as she added, "Besides, how else will I send my young uns to their Aunt Eliza to be taught the gospel?"

Eliza chuckled but quickly sobered. "I can't think of anything I fear more than going to sea again . . . Wait. D'ye hear that?"

"Hear what?"

"Shhh!" Both women paused, alert to any sound. For a few seconds there was nothing, but just when Eliza decided she'd imagined it, the sound came again. "It's like someone yelling from a long way off—a woman's voice, I think. It sounds like she's calling for help."

Molly turned toward the sound. "It sounds like Ida."

Eliza was out of her chair and running before Molly finished speaking, Molly following closely. As they stepped onto the porch, they could see Ida running up Elizabeth Street, stumbling and panting, her face white with shock. When she saw Eliza, she began calling, "They're killin' him, ma'am! They're drownin' him!"

"Drownin' who?" Molly asked, but Eliza was already running.

"Watch the babies!" she called over her shoulder.

Eliza looked at Ida as she ran by, but she didn't slow. Grateful that the road went downhill, she lifted her skirts and ran as fast as she could. As she ran, she prayed. She couldn't think, dared not think, what she might find when she reached the water.

But she didn't reach the water. She'd run only a couple of blocks when she saw Jimmy running toward her. Like Ida he was frantic, stumbling, panting, and white with shock. He was also dripping wet, but he was alive, and her tears ran freely as she thanked God.

She reached her son midblock and caught him in her arms, lifting him, ignoring the strain that the growing pregnancy and the growing six-year-old put on her back. She held and rocked him, murmuring, "Shh, darling, Mummy's here. Shh, dear one, ye're all right now," while her tears mingled with the sea water on his face and in his hair.

After a time, the child's hysteria calmed enough that he was able to tell her about the boys who had seen him skipping ahead of Ida as they neared the quay. They had grabbed his arm and dragged him into the cove.

"They kept yellin' at me, 'Stupid Jimmy. Stupid Mormon Jimmy.' They pushed my head under and held me down. I thought I was gonna get drownded!"

"How did they even know who ye were?"

"One of 'em used to go to church with us back when we went to *real* church," Jimmy said. "He kept askin' me 'Ye're the Mormon boy, ain't ye? I said aye, and he told the other boys that Mormons always get baptized under the water."

"Oh, my sweet son." Eliza dropped her head against him.

Jimmy said, "Mum, I don't wanna be Mormon no more. I wanna go back to real church."

In that moment, Eliza discovered something she feared more than the sea, something that would drive her to Zion after all, and the sooner, the better. "I'm sorry," she said between tearful breaths. "I'm so sorry, Jimmy."

She tried to carry him home, but the pain in her back was crippling. "I'm having trouble, son," she said. "D'ye think ye can walk?"

"Aye, Mum," Jimmy answered soberly.

She put him down and started to walk at his side. That was when the pain hit her, striking in her back and moving with lightning speed down through her abdomen into her pelvis. It was sharp, it was hard, and it felt very much like labor. She groaned and braced her back. "It's too early," she murmured. "Much too early."

"Are ye all right, Mum?"

She tried for a brave smile. "Aye, Jimmy. Oh, but look at ye. Ye're shivering like ye're gonna shake right out of yer shoes." She pulled him against her. They were still several blocks down the street from their cottage, and she wondered whether the cold would reach Jimmy before they reached home or whether the pain would disable her first.

That was when she saw the wagon coming toward them, its driver pushing the horses. The empty wagon looked vaguely familiar, but it was within a block of her before she recognized the driver. "James!"

He barely had time to stop the horses before he was down and running to them, catching them both in his arms. "Ida told me. I was so afraid, so afraid," he murmured as he held and kissed first Eliza, then Jimmy, and Eliza again.

"He's going to be all r—" Eliza began, but the second pain hit her, and she crumpled against him. "It's too soon for this," she murmured.

James swept her up. "Jimmy, ya stand right here, son," he said as he carried Eliza to the wagon. He soon returned with Jimmy, wrapping them both in his blanket and pointing the team toward home.

"I'm so glad to see ye," Eliza said, "but what're ye doing here?"

James kept his eyes forward as he turned the team, but he answered smoothly. "I came drivin' up, and Ida started yelling at me about the quay and some boys drowning Jimmy and ya running to save him. I didn't get the whole story." He flashed a look of concern. "Do ya know what happened?"

"Some of it," she answered. "We can talk later. Right now we need to get Jimmy warm. He's taken a chill."

"And ya?" He looked at her belly. "What's happening with ya?"

"I'm not certain," she said, "but I picked Jimmy up, and I'm thinking my labor has started."

"It's too soon."

"Aye, that it is. I'll need to get Mrs. Johnson. But I didn't mean how did ye get to the quay. I meant what're ye doing back in Sydney already?"

"That's a good story, which I'll be happy to tell ya when we see both ya and Jimmy safe," he answered. When they arrived moments later, James carried first Jimmy and then Eliza into their home and left Molly and Ida to their care while he went for the midwife. "I'll be back soon," he promised as he left.

Eliza went straight to Jimmy and started taking off his wet clothes, but she was unsteady.

"Here, let me do that," Molly said, stepping in to remove Jimmy's jacket and shirt. "Ye don't mind if yer Aunt Molly helps ye, do ye, Jimmy?" she asked.

Shivering, his teeth chattering so hard he couldn't answer, Jimmy shook his head.

"Eliza, ye need to strip down to yer chemise and crawl into bed," Molly said firmly. "We can take care of Jimmy. Take care of yerself and the little un."

"I don't want to leave him," Eliza said. "I was so—" The next pain seized her.

Molly shot her a fearful look. "Ida, get her into bed, and don't let her give ye any trouble." As Ida took Eliza's arm, Molly added, "Eliza, I promise I'll keep ye posted on Jimmy. We may even tuck him in beside ye for a time, once we get him warmed up some."

"Thank ye, Molly. I—"

"Go!" Molly ordered.

Eliza nodded grimly, leaning on Ida as she made her way into the bedroom. Another contraction hit her as she tried to lift her dress over her head and Ida had to wrestle her out of it, but soon Eliza was resting under warm covers, peppering Ida with questions.

"I don't know who the boys were, ma'am," Ida answered. She was getting some color back into her face. "There were five of 'em, the oldest about thirteen or fourteen, the youngest maybe ten. I was bigger and stronger than any of 'em except maybe the oldest; I could have fended 'em off one at a time, but there were five, and they were fast, and Jimmy was skippin' ahead, and oh, missus! I'm so sorry."

Eliza took her hand. "It's not yer fault. I had a feeling I shouldn't let him go, but he likes so much to walk with ye." Eliza recognized the girl's terror. "He thinks of ye as a friend, ye know—not just a grown-up he trusts, but really, truly a friend."

"Truly?" The tension in Ida's face began to ease.

"Truly. He often asks me when we're going to Welsh House to see Molly and Mary and Weeks and Ida."

"He doesn't ask about the others?"

"Well, sometimes he asks when he can drive with Smythe again." She smiled.

Ida smiled back, looking more herself.

"Tell me more about what they were saying—" Eliza began, but that was when James arrived with Mrs. Johnson, who immediately shooed everyone from the room, calling for a full glass of cool water and a cup of hot water for tea. Ida quickly brought them both, and the midwife began steeping tea from a bag in her satchel. She gave Eliza a careful examination, gently stroking her belly and asking many questions. Another contraction came on then, this one harder and longer still.

"It seems to me," she said as she covered Eliza again, "that the early pains have been brought on by yer fear and yer worryin', yer tryin' to lift your boy when ye really shouldn't be liftin' anything heavy, and yer runnin' hard." She pushed her spectacles up on her nose. "None of those things is particular good for a woman in yer condition, but goin' thirsty can bring it early too. I want ye to drink this whole glass of water."

"All right." Eliza picked up the cool water and slowly drained it.

Mrs. Johnson turned and fussed with the hot cup. "Now the tea."

"Mrs. Johnson, I'm sorry, but I don't drink tea—not since I was baptized Mor—"

"I know about yer turnin' Mormon and I know ye don't drink regular tea, but this ain't regular. It's a combination of herbal medicines midwives have been usin' to stop early labor for a long, long time."

Eliza sniffed. "Ooh. It has a pleasing scent. What's in it, exactly?"

"A lot of things," Mrs. Johnson answered. "Lavender, jasmine, sage, chamomile, valerian, skullcap—"

"Something lemony?" Eliza asked, sniffing again.

"Aye, lemon balm and hops and magnolia bark too."

"But no *tea* tea?"

"Not a bit," the midwife answered. "Please drink it now before another pain hits ye."

A contraction hit just as she said it, and Mrs. Johnson held the cup while Eliza outlasted the spasm. "It's not as bad this time," Eliza said as she reached for the tea.

"That's a girl, drink up," Mrs. Johnson encouraged. "It's got all those good herbs that will help to stop yer early labor."

Eliza slowly drained the cup. "I'm already feeling more at ease," she said, "but I don't want to go to sleep until I've seen Jimmy."

"He's at the door now," the midwife said. "I'll have yer husband bring him in. Call out if the pains don't calm soon."

"I will," Eliza promised.

James came in with Jimmy in his arms, the boy wrapped in a thick quilt and no longer shivering. "Looks like ye're decent enough," he said. "Can Molly come in?"

"Aye, sure'n she can. Send her in," Eliza answered, "but first give my Jimmy to me." James placed the boy beside her, and he snuggled. "Are ye all right?" she asked, stroking his damp hair.

"Aye, but I don't wanna get drownded no more, and I don't wanna be Mormon neither."

Over his head her eyes beseeched her husband. "We'll talk, dear one," she told her son. "Rest now and get warm." She pulled him tightly against her.

"Ye're lookin' none the worse for wear." Molly swept into the room. "Ida sent another glass of water for ye." She set the glass beside the bed.

"If I drink any more, I'll spend the afternoon in the outhouse," Eliza teased. "But thanks for bringing it, Molly, and thank ye for being here. It seems ye're always here in a crisis. I can't tell ye how grateful I am."

"Ye know I wouldn't be anywhere else," Molly said. She pulled up a chair. Then she dropped her voice into a whisper. "It seems Jimmy's adventures have left him weary."

Both parents turned to look at Jimmy, who sat resting his head against his mother's shoulder, both eyes closed, his mouth hanging open, his body no longer shuddering.

"Shall I put our boy to bed?" James murmured. "I think he's out of danger now."

Eliza whispered back. "Aye, I think ye should. Ye likely won't be able to get him up the ladder, though. Just put him down on the couch and cover him with a quilt. When ye're out there, ye can thank Mrs. Johnson for me and tell her that her tea seems to be working. I haven't had a contraction in a while, and the last one was milder."

"Sounds like ye're ready to sleep too," James said as he came around to pick up Jimmy.

Eliza yawned. "Aye, I fear I am, but there's still so much more I want to know, like how ye came to be home from the Blues so quickly."

"That story will still be here when ya wake, love," James said, lifting his son.

Molly stood. "I'll see ye later," she promised. She led the way from the room, opening the door for James. Before it had closed again, Eliza was sleeping soundly.

\* \* \* \*

She woke to delicious aromas and muffled voices coming from her kitchen. The fading light told her it was nearing tea time, and she marveled that she had slept away so much of the afternoon. Mrs. Johnson's midwife tea seemed to have done the trick. She hadn't had a single contraction in hours—at least nothing strong enough to wake her.

She opened her bedroom door to find Molly working in her kitchen. Ed sat on the sofa, bouncing Mary while James cradled baby Joseph. Jimmy played at their feet.

"Well, hello there, sleepyhead," Molly said. "Ye're just in time. Tea's almost ready."

"It's good of ye to stay," Eliza said, "but I can help now."

"Ye sit," Molly said firmly, "and put yer feet up. We've had enough scare for one day."

"Really, I can help." Eliza moved toward the stove.

"Don't ye touch it," Molly said sternly, brandishing a wooden spoon. "I don't get to cook much anymore. I gave Alice and Ida the evening off so I could come play in yer kitchen. Now be a good girl and sit. Let me have my fun."

Eliza obediently sat. Minutes later she took her place at the table, and James asked a blessing on their meal. Jimmy ate quickly and excused himself to play with his toys. As the plates were cleared, Eliza asked, "James, what happened to bring ye back so much sooner than ye'd planned?"

Ed said, "Aye, James. I've been curious about that as well. How'd ye get back here so quickly, and with an empty wagon too?"

James shook his head. "Strangest thing," he said. "I got there late Sunday and started selling first thing the next morning. Straightaway I sold enough that I thought I could be done in five days, and most of the fellas said they'd spread the word." He paused to look at Eliza, who moved uncomfortably in her chair. She nodded that she was well, and he went on. "So Tuesday, I got up early, and there were already men lining up to buy. I'd been selling for maybe two hours when I heard a man's voice say, 'Go home, James. Eliza needs ya.' I looked around, but there wasn't anybody close, ya know? I sort of shook my head and went back to selling, and then I heard it again, the same message: 'Go home, James. Eliza needs ya,' only louder this time. I realized it might be a prompting, so I said a little prayer inside, asking if I was hearing a real message and if I needed to leave, and then I heard it again, louder than ever.

"Just then a man rode up with a wagon and said he'd like to purchase my whole load for the men working up the mountain. The fellas still there had bought all they wanted from me, so they helped shift the rest. Thank goodness it's mostly downhill coming back, and I drove the horses hard. So that's how I got back so soon."

Molly and Ed were both staring as Eliza asked, "Ye got this message yesterday morning?"

"Aye, plain and clear: 'Go home. Eliza needs ya.'"

"But I didn't need ye, not then—not until just a little while ago."

James shrugged. "I s'pose the Spirit knows things the rest of us don't. But I'm constantly amazed at the good Lord's love for us."

"Aye, so am I," Ed said, his voice sincere.

"Ed, ye're a blessing," Eliza said. "Thank ye so much for comin' today and for the way ye and Molly always seem to be here when we need ye." She paused. "Honestly, I don't know how we'll handle the problems that come up in our family without ye—when we're on the other side of the world in Zion."

James blinked. "What? Eliza, what'd ya just say?"

Eliza knew it might be better to speak to her husband alone, but she had made her decision. She plunged ahead. "We'll need to talk, of course, but after Jimmy's experience—" Jimmy looked up, and she lowered her voice. "After what happened, I know what we have to do. We need to be goin', and I'm thinking as soon as possible, even before the baby."

James opened his mouth to speak and then closed it again. He finally said, "Woman, I swear I don't understand yer thinking at all, but if ye've come around . . ."

"Just this morning I was telling Molly that I couldn't think of anything that terrified me more than getting on a ship."

"Aye, that part I knew." James sighed.

"That part we *all* knew," Ed said with emphasis.

Eliza let them enjoy a chuckle, then she said, "When I thought those boys had drowned our Jimmy . . ." She sighed. "I suddenly realized there was something I feared even more than the sea. I thought we might lose him to the diphtheria, and it was the worst fear ever—far worse than fearing for myself. This morning when Ida said they were drowning him—" She paused to compose herself. "This morning I knew that getting on a ship would be easier than living through that. Then, when he said he didn't want to be Mormon anymore, that he wanted to go to a real church, I realized that if we don't go soon, our boys may grow up without the gospel. We could lose them forever."

She took her husband's hand. "James, I want to go with ye to the Americas and cross with ye into Zion. I want to go where they're building a temple of the Lord so our family can be sealed. I want our children to be surrounded by others of our faith, where our son won't be mistreated just because of what we believe, and I want to go soon, now, tomorrow if possible."

He stroked her hand. "It's the beginning of storm season, ya know."

"Aye, I know."

"And people at the docks are talking about how this same strange thing that's causing us to see the southern lights is causing big winds and high waves. It could be a rough crossing."

"Aye, sure'n I'm knowin' that too, but the good Lord has finally found a way to get me on a ship, and I'm thinkin' we'd best go now, quickly, before I lose what little nerve I've found."

"Ye're a wonder, Eliza." James stroked her hair as she yawned broadly.

"Sorry," she said, "but I seem to be gettin' quite sleepy again."

"I think I just heard Smythe return with the carriage," Ed said. "We'll check in with ye tomorrow—"

But Eliza said, "Wait, please. Will ye all say a prayer with me before ye go?"

James looked toward Ed and Molly, who both nodded. The friends sat together at the table and held hands as James offered a simple prayer that included asking blessings on Jimmy and Eliza. Then he asked that they might find a ship that would take them safely toward Zion.

As the prayer concluded, Eliza was ready to rest, but before she slept, she said her own private prayer, thanking God for preserving her son's life and for giving her the direction she had avoided hearing for so long.

*   *   *

James felt a swirl of conflicting emotions as he walked Ed and Molly toward their carriage. He was grateful for Jimmy's safety and the end of Eliza's early labor, for the prompting that had brought him home, and for Eliza's willingness to gather with the Saints. At the same time, he was concerned about their voyage. But like Eliza, he knew something he feared even more than the sea, something he hadn't told his wife.

"That was a near escape with Jimmy," Ed said, keeping his voice low as they left Eliza and walked toward the carriage.

"Aye," James answered. "Too near."

"I'm sure the boys were just harassin'," Molly said. "They wouldn't have drowned him."

Ed and James exchanged a somber look.

Molly said, "All right. What is it ye're not sayin'?" She saw James's face and added, "I can keep a secret if I must."

"Well, this one will need keepin'," James said. "Ed, ya tell her."

Ed spoke somberly. "A creamy child was drowned there just last week."

"No!" Molly's eyes went wide. "Then those boys weren't just playin' with Jimmy?"

"It seems likely this was a warnin'," Ed answered. "Maybe they didn't go through with it because Ida had seen them and could identify 'em to the constable, but there's no tellin' they wouldn't do it another time, say if they happened to catch Jimmy alone, or maybe walkin' with a pregnant woman . . ."

"Ye don't have to paint a picture," Molly said. "So what can ye do?"

"Leave," James said. "I was blessed to sell out quickly, so I may have enough—"

"Well come on, then," said Ed. "I can take some time away in the morning. First thing tomorrow we'll get to the docks and see what's sailin'. Let's get yer wife safely to California before the little un comes. I'll see ye in the morning."

"I thank ya, mate," James said as he clasped Ed's shoulder. "Eliza's right, ya know."

"Usually," Ed agreed, "but about what exactly this time?"

"I don't know how we'll manage when we don't have the Welsh family to lift us out of our problems."

"Let's get ye safely to Zion, and we'll all find out," Molly said.

Ed and James both said, "Amen."

*   *   *   *

Ed arrived early the next day. The men drove to the docks and straight to the harbormaster's office. The news wasn't good. Most of the departures in the coming month were cargo only, and they were sailing nearby—to other colonies on the Australian continent or only as far as Auckland. Even then, some of the scheduled ships were delaying their departures given the peculiar lights and weather. Of the three going past New Zealand, only one—a clipper, not one of the new and more reliable steamships—was continuing in the direction they needed, but only as far as the Sandwich Islands. James went to the ship and spoke to the first mate to see if he could afford a cabin. That news was also discouraging.

"We have room in steerage," the man answered to James's query, "but we're carryin' mostly cargo this sail, and we've no cabins available."

"Would it help if I put up cash?" Ed asked.

"It wouldn't matter if ye have solid gold, mate. Our cabins are full. The good news is the steerage hasn't filled. 'Course there's still time 'fore we sail, and we could pick up more in Auckland, but right now we've 120 bunks and only 43 is spoke for."

Ed said, "That won't d—"

James interrupted. "Can we see the steerage?"

"Don't see why not," the man answered. He led the way up the gangplank. The ship was already loading cargo for departure in less than a week. They followed him down the ladder.

It was very like the compartment in which James and Ed had sailed from England, little more than the top six feet of the cargo hold partitioned off to carry living cargo. Two rows of thirty bunks each stretched along either side of the ship's length. Under each of the lower bunks was a space marked off by ropes where the people housed in both upper and lower berths would store their luggage and where it could be roped in during rough weather. The mate explained that passengers could bring only the baggage that fit that space.

Two small rooms had been cobbled together from the same lumber as the berths. These, one marked for men and the other for women, would allow passengers some privacy when using the communal chamber pots—a luxury he hadn't known on his first sail. He found himself releasing a deep breath he hadn't realized he was holding.

"I'll be bringing my wife and two small children," he said. "Can ye tell me about the cabin fare?"

The man answered, "We've a top seaman's cook, and he'll be serving the usual—porridge, oatcake, salt pork, potatoes, biscuits, tea. There may be some fresh foods for the first days out of harbor and the first few out of Auckland. If ye want more than that, ye'll have to bring it yerself. Just make sure it fits in yer space."

"Will there be medical help on board? My wife is with child."

"D'ye expect her to deliver before the Sandwich Islands?"

"We don't expect her to deliver before California. She's not due for two months."

"That still seems short," the mate answered, his scowl deepening, "but I s'pose that's yer choice. And yes, we plan to pick up a doctor in Auckland who'll travel to Honolulu with us."

"I think we'll be sailin' with ya," James said. He got the details on loading and departure times and went to buy their passage.

"I don't like it," Ed said. "Not a bit. I know ye're in a hurry, but couldn't ye just keep a close watch on Jimmy until something better sails? I'll happily buy a cabin for yer family."

"And risk Eliza being too close to her time? I don't think we dare."

"Ye could end up trapped in Honolulu until after the little un is born, and without a job or any way to make money—"

"The harbormaster seemed to think we'd have no trouble meeting up with another ship there," James said. "Ya heard him. The export of sugar and molasses has created regular transport between the islands and San Francisco, and most ships carry passengers. Besides, from what I hear, there are worse places to be stuck than Honolulu." He grinned. "We'll be fine, Ed, and I think this is what we need to do."

"At least let me give ye some money," Ed said, his voice betraying a rare level of distress. "Then ye can book a cabin on the ship to California."

"We can't be dependent on ya forever," James began.

Ed cut him off. "I'm serious when I talk about how much I owe ye—not just yer care during the platypus sting or bringing Molly into my life. James, ye're the best mate I've ever had, closer than my own brothers, and Eliza's like a sister to my Molly. Once ye get on that ship, it's unlikely we'll ever see yer faces again. For heaven's sakes, man! I've got more gold than Midas. Let me use some of it to help ye on yer way."

"And who's going to bail us out once we're in the Americas?" James asked. "We'll have to be independent sometime. It may as well be now."

"Ye're as stubborn as yer wife," Ed said. Then he slapped James's back. "Well, come on, then. Let's go see about gettin' ye on this ship." They entered the harbormaster's office.

*   *   *   *

If James went home to Eliza fearing to tell her that steerage was the best he could do, he need not have worried.

"Ye were able to get two berths?" she said with apparent delight. "I feared we'd be sleeping four to a bunk with the babies in between. Why, that will double our luggage space! And ye tell me they've got some privacy around the chamber pots, and the steerage isn't crowded yet. I'd say this is all good news."

"I'd call it an answer to prayer," Ed said. The rest of the group all looked at him. "Well, just because I'm not the religious sort doesn't mean I can't see a blessing when it's right under my nose." His response brought surprised chuckles.

The realization that they had only six days before sailing set them all into a flurry. Ed began by insisting that he repay their unused rent from mid-October to the end of the month. James reluctantly accepted the money, knowing they were likely to need every bit of it—if not in Honolulu, then surely by the time they reached California.

Eliza began fretting over how best to dispose of the furnishings she had carefully acquired. Molly suggested an auction to be held in three days and promised she'd get the word out. When the hour arrived and the yard was full of people bidding one another up on items that had cost Eliza practically nothing, she realized Molly had orchestrated and probably paid for the whole thing, but she was too grateful for the funds to complain. She thanked Molly wholeheartedly and packed the few items the family would carry onboard. Molly and Ida helped.

She took little from her life in Ireland and less from their years in Australia: clippings about her wedding and Molly's, her mother's rosary, the dresser mirror that was a gift from her father, a teacup that had been her grandmother's, the combs for her hair that James had given her when Jimmy was born. Her statues of Mother Mary and Saint Elizabeth went to Molly. Except for her family's copies of the Book of Mormon and Jimmy's one cup-and-ball toy, most of their luggage was filled with the family's clothing and a few household items.

Eliza had never felt more grateful for Ed and Molly than she did now. Her family spent their last two nights in Sydney as guests in Welsh House, sleeping in beds even after their own had been sold, eating from fine china when they no longer owned dishes, and dining elegantly when they had no way left to prepare food. Although Eliza insisted on helping in the kitchen, she had little else to do but treasure up her last moments with Molly and Mary, letting Jimmy enjoy his time with Ida and Weeks. She even allowed him a ride once or twice with Smythe in the driver's seat, although she never let him go out without either James or Ed.

Their last day in Sydney was little Joseph's first birthday and nearing Mary's. The two families celebrated when both men were home from work, Eliza and Molly getting teary as they watched the children playing, running together in the home and yard, neither knowing they may never be together again. Eliza considered it a mercy of the Lord that Joseph wouldn't be having his birthday at sea. As they put their children to bed, Eliza expressed the feelings of her heart once more, thanking Molly over and over for all her friendship had meant.

Molly answered through tears. "It's I who owe ye, love. I'm here in this elegant home with a wonderful husband and a beautiful little girl. Without ye and James, I could still be serving Mrs. Pembroke, hatin' my life, and losing hope for anything better. Ye saved me from the Pembrokes, and ye gave me Ed and Mary. Ye'll never know how much ye mean to me."

Eliza hugged her close. "Ye're the dearest friend I have, Molly. I'll never forget ye."

"Ye'd best not!" Molly's laughter bubbled through her tears. "If ye know what's good for ye, ye'll write to me regular-like and tell me all that's goin' on."

"And if I don't?" Eliza raised a brow.

"I may just have to come to Zion to straighten ye out." Then Molly pursed her lips. "On second thought, I'd best not tell ye that or ye'll cut out the letters on purpose."

Eliza laughed. "Aye. I might do just that. Oh, Molly, I'll miss ye!"

"And I'll feel like a lost soul without ye." They stayed close throughout the evening.

\* \* \* \*

James shook with a rare kind of nervous excitement. The time had come. Alice, Ida, and Weeks said their tearful good-byes on the porch and then stood watching and waving as both Ed and James loaded their families into the large carriage where Smythe had already stowed their luggage. The two families chatted and visited as they made their final drive through Sydney.

Although James kept up his part of the conversation, much of his attention was directed out the window as he bade a silent farewell to places and things that had been such a part of his life. He had no qualms about moving toward his future, but he certainly had mixed feelings about leaving his past. The emotions were heavy as he passed Hogan's General Store. He saw motion behind the windows and wondered what Elmer might be doing this morning. He whispered a quiet prayer for Elmer's happiness. His mind spun as he thought of all Elmer Hogan had been to him: mentor, second father, tutor, friend, landlord, persecutor, enemy. James had always regretted the way that relationship had ended and wondered whether there was something, anything, he might have done to keep the Hogans' friendship without sacrificing his witness of the gospel. Try as he might, he could think of nothing, but he felt lingering sorrow at the change in the man he had once loved.

The drive passed quickly, and soon they all stood on the deck as the final items were loaded. The boarding call came, and James turned to Ed as their wives said a tearful farewell.

"Come on, Mum." Jimmy tugged at Eliza's hand.

"Soon enough, son," Eliza answered. Then she put her arms around Molly. James could tell the women were offering one another brave faces.

"The *Ocean Monarch*, is it?" Molly said, her voice rough as she swallowed back tears.

"James says the ship seems sound," Eliza answered.

James smiled and turned back to Ed. Then he gasped in surprise. He had not expected to be lifted off his feet.

"Look at Ed," he heard Molly say behind him. "He talks so tough most of the time, ye'd never know he's such a baby."

Ed had failed at fighting back tears. He held James in his arms and shook him like a rag doll, rocking him back and forth, rubbing his back. "I'll miss ye, mate," he said over and over.

James struggled to get his feet to the ground, then gave up and just held on. "Ye've been too good to us, mate. If there's ever anything at all we can do for ya from America, ya just—"

"Don't be silly," Ed said, putting James back on the deck and wiping tears with the backs of both hands. Then he looked toward their women. "Ye know, ye married a fine woman. She's downright terror-struck, but she's goin' nonetheless."

"I've always said it, she's a wonder." He slapped Ed's shoulder. "Ya take care of yer own good woman, ya hear? And maybe come to see us in Zion one day."

"It don't . . . er, doesn't seem likely, mate, what with all my business bein' here. But maybe ye'll return one day."

James tried out his own brave smile. "It doesn't seem likely, mate."

The two families were parting for the final time when a commotion on the dock drew their attention.

"Would ye look at that?" Ed said, watching the coach empty its passengers.

James felt his heart drop to the deck. *After all this time* . . . He straightened and prepared to face whatever came next.

Elmer Hogan strode up, looking prideful and self-important, a uniformed man behind him. Pointing at James, he said, "Constable, arrest that man."

The constable stepped around Elmer and walked purposefully toward him. James stepped forward, sorrow permeating his very soul. "Elmer, what is this?"

"It's Mr. Hogan to ya!" Elmer turned a darkened countenance on the man he'd once treated as a son. "There're laws, ya know, laws that keep debtors, thieves, and ne'er-do-wells from leavin' Sydney without payin' up."

"I owe ya nothing, Mr. Hogan," James said evenly, "and if ya thought I did, why haven't ya mentioned it before?"

The constable said, "No stallin'. I've a complaint against ye and yer under arrest."

James sighed and felt the hope wash out of him. Whatever Elmer was planning, it was going to stop them from joining the Saints. They'd be unable to leave until after the birth and maybe longer than that. He saw Eliza step forward, but Ed stopped her with a gesture and stepped between James and the constable, reaching for his wallet. "How much d'ye think he owes ye, Elmer?"

Hogan's face turned darker. "I'll not have ya interferin'!" he shouted. "Back off, Welsh, before I have ya arrested too. D'ya know what the penalty is fer tryin' to run out on a debt?"

Ed dropped his voice. "And ye, Elmer? D'ye know what the penalty is for bearin' false witness in a court of law?"

Hogan narrowed his eyes, his expression threatening. "What're ya tryin' to do?"

"I'm talkin' about when ye delay the Martin family's departure. Wha'd'ya think will happen when the case goes to court and ye've no evidence to prove James owes ye anything?"

"Evidence? I have evidence!"

"Ye do? Because ye'd better, for a court proceedin'."

Ed's calm argument made sense, and James found himself starting to hope again.

"Abby will testify he owed me money." Hogan looked pleased.

"Yer wife's testimony won't be enough to prove anything. Will it, Constable?"

The constable flushed. "I just handle the arrest. It's up to the judge . . ."

"That's right," Ed went on, speaking smoothly. "The judge won't accept the testimony of ye and yer wife as adequate evidence. Meanwhile, I can go to bank records to show everything that Martin paid ye from the time he first met ye." James looked up, hopeful again. "*That* is what the court will see as evidence. And then we'll start talking about the penalty for perjury."

"Fer what?" James could see Elmer no longer appeared so confident.

"Perjury, Elmer, also known as bearing false witness. I've heard of people deported to the Western Australia prison colonies over less."

Elmer drew in a deep breath while everyone waited. Then the steward called, "All aboard who's comin' aboard!"

James looked up at the steward and back to Ed. Ed's eyes followed the motion, and he gave James a confident wink before he turned back to Elmer. "Well, Elmer? Ye want to risk it?" Then, quietly, he added, "Ye know that it doesn't matter what ye make up to bring in. I'll have better evidence and more of it—and the fact that it comes from the bank will make the court more willin' to accept it." He looked at the steward, at James, and back to Hogan. "Ye might slow this down, but ye won't be able to stop it."

Elmer Hogan growled—a deep, feral sound. Then he turned on his heel and stomped away. The constable, looking flustered, turned first to James and then toward Elmer. He hurried to catch up. "So are ye droppin' the complaint, then?" When he received no answer, he ran to catch the wagon, which lurched toward the road even before the doors closed.

James felt tears of relief. Choked with emotion he reached for Eliza, who rushed into his arms. He turned to Ed. "That was a close one, mate."

"Aye, closer than I like to think."

"It's a blessing ye knew all that," Eliza said. "How do ye know so much, anyway?"

Ed grinned. "I know nothin' about the law, love."

"But . . . Ye mean . . . ?" Eliza let out a surprised giggle.

Molly spoke quietly. "Before he married me, Ed often won at cards," she said. "He's very good at bluffing."

James grinned in admiration. "I should say so. It seems I owe ya once again."

Ed looked in the direction Hogan had taken. "Imagine Elmer thinkin' he could get away with that!"

"He's a bit like the adversary," Molly said.

Eliza gasped. "Satan? Aye, I know he's mean-spirited, but really—"

"I didn't mean he's completely like Satan, only in that one way—that he just couldn't stand to see ye two happy when he's made himself so miserable."

James nodded, remembering the man he had once known. "Aye, I fear that's the case. I feel sorry for him." For a moment they all looked down the shadowy road Hogan had taken.

The steward stepped onto the gangplank. "Are ye comin' with us or no?" he asked, glowering down at them.

"It appears we have to go," James said. "I thank ya again, Ed. I can't thank ya enough."

There was another round of quick hugs while the steward stood at the end of the gangplank, tapping his foot and looking exasperated. "Ye know what they say about time and tides," he urged.

Finally the friends separated, and James led his family up the gangplank onto the deck. There would be time for stowing their gear as the ship made its way slowly out of the harbor, so they stood on the deck, waving and calling as the seamen cast off. James stood with his arms around his dear ones for as long as he could still make out the shapes of Ed, Molly, and Mary waving from the dock.

# PART FIVE:
## Gathering

# Chapter 15

*October 1859–Honolulu*

"I'm almost sorry to say good-bye. It's lovely here," Eliza said as the family sailed out of the harbor the Hawaiians had once called "water of the pearls."

"Aye, but another two weeks—eighteen days at the most—and we should be in San Francisco," James said.

Indeed their time in the islands had been good, Eliza thought as she walked with James toward the hatch. In fact, their trip so far had been blessed, although every step had taken longer than planned. As they prepared to eat their first meal aboard the *Monarch*, James had removed his coat and discovered the reason for the madness of emotion Ed Welsh had displayed on the dock. Every pocket in his coat, both those on the outside and those within, was stuffed with coins. During his flurry of shaking and hugging, Ed had squirreled away stashes into every one of his friend's coat pockets, even some extra into the pants pockets. The total of the added gold and silver came to almost four times what James had been carrying before.

"Ed, ya lovely scoundrel," James had whispered as he and Eliza carefully stuffed their fortune into the folded stockings in their steamer trunks. Their trip to Auckland had been smooth as well, despite some strong headwinds that delayed their arrival. Then, as they arrived at the dock in Auckland, much happened, some of which changed their plans. First, Eliza heard chatter of the August wreck of the *Admella*.

The luxury steamship had been carrying 113 men, women, and children when she struck a submerged reef, driven in by a sudden wind. The ship had capsized and survivors had clung to the wreckage, many taking days to die as they watched the land while one rescue attempt after another failed, driven back by fearsome storms. In the end, eighty-nine were lost. It was the worst sea disaster ever to strike the Australian colonies.

"It's just as well I didn't hear about it before we sailed," Eliza admitted, "but I don't know that I can go on from here, James. I'm afraid."

"We must," James had answered. "But I've learned something that may help." He told her of the *Trieste*, a clipper docked near them that was bound for the Sandwich Islands with a load of wheat and flour. "It's going all the way through to San Francisco. They've plenty of room in steerage, and it looks clean and well-appointed."

"I don't know that I can do it," she had answered tearfully, and they had postponed the discussion while they went into town to purchase their boys some dinner. It was as they returned that they saw a pair of familiar faces. Elder Walton and Elder Bingham had taught a ship's captain and followed him to Auckland to teach his family. The missionaries had offered all of the Martins a blessing, and the comforting words had empowered Eliza and given her the courage to go on. She'd been especially pleased at the promise that her child would be delivered safely and by her sons' blessings that they'd become husbands and fathers in Zion, but one line from James's blessing made her wonder. "What d'ye think Elder Walton meant?" she asked her husband.

"Ya mean about our journey not going as planned but working out for the best? I've no idea, but it seems a good thing."

"Aye," she answered. "It's enough to get me back on board, at least."

"Shall I check out the *Trieste*?" James asked.

"Aye," Eliza agreed.

He returned a little later having sold their berths on the *Monarch* and bought passage to San Francisco. Though they'd had to wait extra days for the *Trieste* to sail, Ed's gold had easily sustained them. Eliza had found the second ship more comfortable than the first and had almost enjoyed the trip to Honolulu.

The native dress in the Sandwich Islands—the women wearing nothing above their grass skirts and the men wearing almost nothing— had certainly shocked her, but she had quickly resolved to enjoy the time ashore with her family. They had walked along the beach together, spotting different trees and flowers, fish and shells. It had been just the break she had needed to face the sea again. Though the *Trieste* had taken on a few more passengers in Honolulu, the steerage was still lightly populated, and Eliza was ready to rebuild her family's nest.

\*   \*   \*   \*

For the next eleven days, the weather held with only an occasional light rain. The new passengers included some who were less than sociable, and Eliza avoided spending much time below decks, preferring not to have grumpy old Mrs. Wax or angry Mr. Beadles snap at her children. She and James spent long stretches in both the morning and afternoon walking the decks with their boys, spotting sails, whales, or dolphins against the endless blue horizon. In the evenings they watched from the deck as the sun set the sky aflame. In their compartment, by lamplight, they read from the scriptures and told the boys Book of Mormon stories. They made friends among the passengers.

Since every day put Eliza closer to her due date, she was pleased to learn that several of the women in the tween deck were experienced midwives. She planned that her third child would be born safely ashore, but she liked feeling prepared—in case.

The storm started on their twelfth day. It was soon clear to everyone that this was no ordinary challenge. Long before the sun set, the sky had darkened to near black. Lightning crashed near them, striking the sea, and the rain beat down in horizontal sheets. Steerage passengers were "hatched down" by the nervous crew, and the nightmare below decks began.

Eliza retreated into an early sleep but soon awoke to the lurching and tossing of the ship and the sound of roaring waters battering the hull, which groaned and creaked under the strain. Some passengers cried out, and she could tell from both the sounds and the smells that several were already sick. She reached for James and found the berth beside her empty.

"James?" she called, parting the sheets of their tent to be nearly overcome by the stench.

"I'm here," he answered. "Just trying to calm the little ones."

"Are they well?"

"They seem all right. At least, neither is ill. Jimmy's sleeping again, but Joseph's scared."

"D'ye want to bring him here? He can snuggle between us."

"That will do for a time. The crew'll be bringing breakfast down before long and—"

"I couldn't. Really."

"Ya haven't just yerself to think of," James reminded. "And besides, ya know they say the sickness is worse for those who don't eat than for those who do."

"No. Is it really?"

"That's what they told us when I sailed to Sydney, and it seemed to be true. Those who ate were often sick, but at least they had something to lose. Those who didn't eat just got weaker and sicker."

"I wish someone had told me that," she said. "Maybe I wouldn't have been so ill on my first trip."

The sheets around her parted. James put Joseph down next to her and then crawled in beside them. For another few hours, they stayed that way—Jimmy sleeping in the boys' berth while Joseph snuggled with his parents. They talked quietly, reassuring their toddler, who settled and slept once he had his mother near. Except for a necessary trip to use the chamber pots, none of them ventured out until a pair of sailors opened the hatch from the upper deck to bring oatcake and fresh water.

By the second day, Eliza was too ill to keep anything in her stomach, although James kept insisting she try. Both boys lay moaning beside her. Although he was also sick at times, James was the only family member who seemed able to keep his feet beneath him. When the steward opened the hatch to bring down rations, James dutifully stumbled out, bringing back food for them all. He insisted they eat it, and when they couldn't keep it down, he did his best to clean up. Many times Eliza thanked him for keeping them going.

Other times she growled at him because he wouldn't let her stay abed and awash in her misery. He insisted that at least twice each day she get up and walk. "Even if ya have to hold on, ye've got to get yer feet under ya for a while," he said. "Come on, Eliza. Get up."

"Stop it. Just let me be," she demanded, but she soon learned he wouldn't be denied even if he had to pull her out bodily and hold her up as she stumbled. Grumbling, she forced herself around the steerage deck. Although she hated it, she could feel the value of moving her muscles and knew James was likely right about it being good for her and her baby. Still, the scenes she witnessed among the other passengers left her feeling even more dispirited. Although she relied on the words of her family's last blessings to assure her they would all reach the land safely, she knew the same could not be said for everyone.

Mary Wallace, an aging widow who had gone to the islands as a missionary some years before, was traveling with them to the new state of California in hopes of finding help for a serious case of consumption—the same illness that had killed Eliza's father. Now, complicated by seasickness and a lack of nourishment, her condition deteriorated rapidly. As Eliza saw her graying complexion, she knew the storm likely could not let up soon enough for Mrs. Wallace.

Old Mr. Weiss, who two days out of Honolulu had bragged about being the oldest person aboard, now looked every day of his seventy-nine years. He lay abed unable even to sit up. Although his two grown sons who were traveling with him tried to keep him clean and fed, everyone knew his hold on life was tenuous.

Eliza's heart ached for poor Mrs. Luddington, who had already lost one of her five-month-old twins. The body lay wrapped in a small bed sheet, awaiting a decent burial at sea. The second baby wasn't well, and Eliza couldn't help fearing the worst. She stopped at the Luddingtons' berth to ask after his welfare and to promise she would keep him in her prayers.

She even felt sorry for Mrs. Wax, whose ill-natured grumbling had given way to almost hysterical screaming. People around her murmured that the storm had taken her mind. Eliza chose to stay away from Mrs. Wax since no one could guess what she might do.

Many others were in little better condition and the rank air below decks, saturated with the odors of illness and death, was doing little to improve their health. Eliza longed for relief, for some air at least. Several times she almost made up her mind to go up the stairs and pound on the hatch until someone opened. Each time she thought it, she heard the rumble of the waves breaking over the deck above them and the shouts of the crew as they labored to stay afloat. Instead of begging for air, she turned her thoughts heavenward, begging God to temper the storm on behalf of them all.

She knew God heard and answered prayers, but apparently He wasn't yet ready to answer this one, or perhaps His answer was no, for the storm only became more serious. For the first two days there had been occasional respites when the wind died down a little, the rain fell more gently, and the ship seemed to right itself. On this dramatic third day, there were no breaks. Lightning crackled constantly, recognized by the tween-decks passengers as near-deafening cracks and resulting rumbles. One older fellow who had been with Her Majesty's troops in the Crimea commented that it sounded like being too near the heavy artillery. Eliza became aware of the seriousness of their situation when the steward who brought down cold cooked potatoes warned them not to touch the walls of the ship since some small amount of water was leaking through and the sea around them was electrified.

Nor was the lightning the worst of it. The increasingly grumpy steward, their only connection to the upper deck, reported winds so heavy the captain had been forced to take down the clipper's sails lest the wind batter them into rags and pull the masts down with them. The rain fell so heavily that the top deck was constantly drenched. The steward had brought extra rations and a mess of dried biscuits in case this was the only time he could open the hatch all day.

His prediction had proven to be prophetic—the hatch had remained tightly battened down as the beleaguered passengers tried to cope with the eerie sounds of the sea pounding against the ship's hull and swamping her decks, keeping her very nearly submerged. It was in this spirit of gloom and fear that a terrifying rumor spread: A boy from the Murphy family had died, some said of cholera. The body lay wrapped in a winding sheet, potentially exposing them all to a painful and ugly death, but there was nothing to be done except wait and worry.

Sometime in that third fearsome night, an even greater threat manifested. Eliza guessed it was near midnight when the steerage passengers were awakened by a man's yells. "Water! There's water below decks!" As one after another rolled out of their berths, each splashed into the ankle-deep water that already covered the steerage deck and deepened as they watched. Several men mounted the stairs and pounded until they got the crew's attention. Meanwhile, panic ensued below decks as people secured their children and old ones in higher berths and searched for personal items now afloat. The curses of some of the less-pleasant passengers echoed through the soggy space.

It surprised Eliza that their crew had prepared for this event. They set up a kind of barrier around the top of the stairwell so they could dare to open it. Within minutes two crewmen joined the passengers with stacks of buckets and organized all of the able-bodied into brigades.

Over James's protests, Eliza took a place near the stairs. "I can see the boys from here," she answered, "and I'll do them more good here, in keeping them from drowning, than I would sitting helplessly on the berth." Still, she was grateful there weren't enough buckets for everyone. The passengers worked in hour-long shifts, turning their buckets over to others as one hour ended and coming back to resume their places when a later hour began. The bailing continued for six shifts. By then the ship's carpenter had found the rupture in the hull and effected an acceptable patch, which he hoped might hold until they reached dry land.

As the steerage was battened down once more, Eliza was pleased to see some gray light in the sky. Still, it was the middle of the storm's fourth day, their fifteenth day at sea, when the winds finally calmed enough that the captain ordered everyone topside. "This storm has hit us hard," he began. "We've sustained serious damage that can only be partially repaired at sea. The worst of it is the mizzen mast." As he spoke he gestured toward the stern of the ship where the mast had once stood. Little remained.

"Lightning struck our mizzen yesternight and shattered it into kindling. I thank God that our crew was able to contain the fire."

"Amen," most of the company responded.

"Additionally, the heavy winds have blown us far off course. We should have been reaching San Francisco sometime in the next few days. Instead, we are far south of our plotted course. With one mast gone and many sails undergoing repair, we've decided to sail for the port of Los Angeles."

"Los Angeles!" The response from the ship's company was immediate as people registered their shock and discontent.

"Once repairs are effected, anyone who wishes to continue to San Francisco will be welcomed aboard," the captain continued. "In the meantime, we need to get things shipshape before our arrival in port." He explained a simple procedure with washing stations on deck for the men and below decks for the women. "The crew will assist you in clean-ing out the steerage deck," he went on. "When we've had a chance to take stock of our situation, I will call you all topside that we may bury our dead."

With that somber announcement, the Martins went below. Eliza welcomed the opportunity to wash and change her clothing and to get both her sons clean again. James came back from his turn on deck looking bright and hopeful, and together they began the task of righting their area. Because James had been vigilant during the worst of the storm, their corner was cleaner than most, and soon James was helping the crew scrub out the lower deck, restoring order and a better smell.

Eliza left that work to others. Her shifts with the buckets had left her weary. Her back ached, and the burden she carried felt heavier than ever. When the crew pronounced the steerage compartment acceptable and the captain called them all topside, it was with grim determination that she dragged herself up the stairs, willing herself to support the families of the lost.

There were eight, their bodies wrapped and lying side by side on the deck: the Luddington baby, whose twin still lived; the Murphy boy; Mrs. Wallace and Mr. Weiss and crazy Mrs. Wax; along with three others she did not know well. One was a boy about the size of her Jimmy, and her heart broke for the grief-stricken mother, who had to be pulled away from the child's body. The captain conducted a simple ceremony, and James volunteered to give a prayer. Then, one by one the bodies were tipped over the side, committed to the deep.

As the captain dismissed them, Eliza turned to her husband. "I want to speak to Mrs. Luddington," she said. "I'm still praying for her other baby."

"Aye, tell her I will pray as well," James answered.

Eliza turned to go—and suddenly found her feet soaked again. She looked up at James with wide eyes. "It's too early!"

James swallowed hard. "Apparently this baby doesn't think so."

A midwife named Mrs. Riggs came up beside them. "Are ye laboring, dear?"

"It appears the bag of waters has broken," Eliza said. "I think—" And then she groaned, bending nearly double as the first contraction hit her.

"My dear," Mrs. Riggs said, taking her other elbow, "I do believe ye're having a baby. Let's see what we can do to make ye more comfortable."

## Chapter 16

"WE'RE COMING INTO THE HARBOR now," James said as he came down from topside, taking Eliza's hand.

"I promised this little one I'd not deliver him aboard ship," Eliza answered with a sigh as she snuggled her baby close. "I wanted him to have a birthplace, unlike his mum." Walton Pacific Martin opened his eyes, gave her a milky, unfocused look, and lapsed into sleep.

"He has a birthplace, just as ya do. We even gave it to him for a middle name." James grinned, and Eliza returned his smile.

"Mum, can I hold the baby?" Jimmy asked, wiggling in beside her.

"Not now, son. He needs to sleep awhile."

"That's all babies ever do is sleep," Jimmy complained. A veteran of Joseph's first year, Jimmy was now an expert.

It had been an easy birth, Eliza realized, even though she was disappointed in the surroundings. Mrs. Riggs immediately took charge. Even the captain and crew gave way to her expertise as she ordered the men to go topside, taking the children with them. Women who could be of help were encouraged to come down. Anyone who would just be in the way was asked to stay on deck. The cook and the grumbling steward served tea to a great many passengers on the deck that evening as the experienced midwives turned steerage into a maternity ward.

They moved a couple of the unused straw-stuffed mattresses onto the floor and set up a makeshift tent around the space. Women who owned sheets or linens not being used piled them nearby while others filled basins with clean water. Then the waiting and watching began in earnest. Eliza's labor progressed quickly, and sometime a little before midnight, the shivering cry of a newborn broke the silence.

James ran to the hatch. "Is she all right?"

"Eliza is fine and healthy," Mrs. Riggs had called up to him. "And you've got yourself another healthy boy."

"A boy," he said now as he held the baby's tiny hand, watching as Walton wrapped his hand around his father's finger. "We're taking three healthy boys to Zion."

"Aye. Now we just have to figure out how to get them there," Eliza said.

James smiled. "We've come most of the way already."

"Sure'n 'tis true," Eliza answered, "but there's still so much to do and we're not even coming ashore where or when we expected. Who knows how long before we get to San Francisco?"

James sighed. "I do believe I married a worrier. Ye're going to need a break before ya start walking across the West anyway," he said, his tone reasonable. "As soon as we're permitted ashore, I'll find a place to stay while the ship is overhauled. Then I'll start making inquiries about the rest of our journey. When we get to San Francisco, we'll have a plan."

"Forgive me for being impatient," Eliza said. "Ye've done well getting us this far. I'll trust ye to manage the rest."

"We've had many blessings," James answered.

Eliza looked at her newborn and thought of Mrs. Luddington and the others who had seen the bodies of their young ones tipped over the side just yesterday. "Aye, we've many blessings indeed," she answered.

*   *   *   *

Two hours later the *Trieste* was safely docked with the captain assessing the damage. He knew the passengers would need time to make accommodations, and he was solicitous of the new mother—her baby not yet twelve hours old—but Captain Rawlins could not begin work until the passengers were ashore. He ordered all decks cleared before tea. James kissed his wife and each of his sons. Then he was first down the gangplank, intent on finding a suitable place to stay until the *Trieste* set sail again.

The responsibility weighed heavily. He knew how vulnerable Eliza was just now, and the precious bundle she held was already dear to him. He needed to find a way to take care of them all without spending too much more of Ed's gold, lest they be unable to get to the Great Salt Lake this year. He set out, eager to find something nearby.

Everything discouraged him. The first public house had a Vacancy sign in the window, but it also had a tinny piano, and the sound of loud laughter rang from its doors. Two men, already drunk at this early hour, came stumbling out as he watched; each leaned on the other for support. He decided to walk farther into town.

There were more Vacancy signs over more saloons. He walked farther. Ahead of him was a place that looked acceptable. His heart lifted—until he drew close enough to see the sign: "Vacancy: No Irish or dogs allowed." Across the street, in an apparent attempt to one-up the competition, the sign read, "No Irish, dogs, nor Mormons." His heart sank still lower as he realized the hatred that had driven them from Sydney was also thriving here.

At the corner of a boardwalk, he stopped in the shade and bowed his head, whispering a prayer that he might find a decent place to shelter his family. And then he had an idea.

*   *   *   *

By midafternoon, Eliza was uneasy. Most of the passengers had gone, and the captain was edgy. The steward had been down several times and used some language she had hoped her sons would never hear. She was greatly relieved when James came into steerage and even more grateful when she heard he'd brought a hired hackney. "It's some distance to where we're going," he said. "I thought it'd be better for ya and the baby to ride."

"That's thoughtful of ye," Eliza said, wearily getting to her feet. "So did ye find a hotel?"

"Nothing I'd let ya stay in," he said as he steadied her.

"Then where are we going?"

"I also found Mrs. Lucy Whitney," he said. "I remembered how people used to stop at the shop to ask about hotels in town, so I stepped into a mercantile nearby. I spoke to the man behind the counter, and Mrs. Whitney overheard. She runs a boardinghouse with an empty room. When I told her ya gave birth aboard ship last night and we also have two other children, she practically insisted we stay with her. She charges more than hotels, but when ya calculate that the meals are all included, it isn't high. If we don't like it, we don't have to stay."

"It sounds perfect," Eliza answered.

"I'm glad ya see it that way since I already paid for tonight." He smiled as he patted her shoulder. "I'll have a couple of the hands help me load our things."

*   *   *   *

Eliza felt an instant kinship with Lucy Whitney, a widow of near the same age as her departed mother. Although it took a little longer for the bond to form—at least partly due to the language barrier—she soon felt sisterly toward the Ortega sisters, Adelita and Irma, who helped Mrs. Whitney keep her large house and feed her many boarders.

Mrs. Whitney took Eliza under her wing immediately, doting on Jimmy and Joseph but giving special attention to the day-old infant. She explained her grown sons had gone back East to reenlist in the army in preparation for the coming war. "I fear I shall be far from my grandchildren, if and when there are any," she explained. "Let me pamper you as I would a daughter-in-law."

"Thank ye, Mrs. Whitney," Eliza answered. "And if ye don't mind, I'd like to think of ye doing for me what my own dear mother would have done—had she lived."

"Please, call me Lucy," her hostess had answered.

Eliza thought of her dear friend Lucy Walker, who had already gone on to Zion. "I'd be pleased, Lucy. I'm Eliza."

"We're of a mind then," Mrs. Whitney answered as she buzzed around the children.

James watched with pleasure as Eliza, not normally accepting of pampering, settled in at Whitney House, appreciating the chance to recover from the birth. In his prayers, he thanked God for bringing them to this secure place where Eliza and Walton could receive such tender care. Once he saw his family safely settled, James set out to learn about repairs aboard the *Trieste*. Once again the news discouraged him.

The mate reported that their assessment and inventory wouldn't be complete before sundown and urged James to return the next day, but he was clear about one thing: The *Trieste* had suffered much more than anyone knew. "We didn't realize it at sea," he said, "but the main mast is cracked through from top to bottom. It wouldn't take much to have it splinter just as our mizzen did, and several of the yards are damaged as well. We expected to replace some sails, but it turns out we'll need to refit everything except for a jib or two.

"Then there's the damage to the hull," he went on. "It was worse than even our carpenter knew. 'Tis a miracle we made it to port and didn't go down with the loss of all hands."

James shivered. "I believe it may well be."

"What's that?"

"I believe it may well be a miracle."

"That's what I said," the mate responded, but he followed it with an oath that showed he was not a religious man and didn't mean *miracle* as James understood it.

"So how long d'ye think before she sails?" James asked.

The mate shook his head as he gave James his best answer.

Back at the Whitney House that evening, after having tea with his family and putting the boys to bed, James shared the news with Eliza, and she too shuddered. Together they thanked God for their safe delivery.

"I will go tomorrow," he said, "and I'll check on the repairs, but it'll be some time before the *Trieste* is seaworthy. The mate was being optimistic when he guessed at least a month."

"A month!" Eliza answered. "Forgive me, but I'm confused on this. Part of me thinks 'twould be a blessing to have a month to recover. Another part thinks a month isn't nearly long enough for me to be ready to walk across the desert. Still another part knows we'll need the money we have to get to Zion. If we spend it here, paying Mrs. Whitney, we won't have it for a wagon or supplies." She sighed. "I don't know what to think."

"Maybe we'd best leave answers to the Lord," James said.

\* \* \* \*

For three more days, the waiting continued. Each day James returned from the docks with more dire predictions for the *Trieste*. When Walton was five days old, James came home midafternoon. "I've news," he said as he swept into Mrs. Whitney's parlor. "Ma'am, would ya and the *hermanas* mind keeping an eye on the boys for a moment? I'd like to talk with my wife."

Adelita looked up from her dusting. "*Ustedes vayan. Miraré a los niños.*"

Mrs. Whitney started to translate, but James said, "*Gracias, amiga,*" and helped Eliza from her chair. Together they walked into their rented room.

"Ye're learning Spanish?" Eliza asked as he closed the door behind them.

"Not much," he confessed, "but I've picked up a bit." Then his eyes sparkled as he added, "I learned quite a lot today." James unraveled the story of how the *Trieste* had been unloaded and hauled up for repairs now estimated to take six weeks. "So I was discouraged and decided I'd best go looking for work. Ya remember that mercantile where I first met Mrs. Whitney?"

"They wanted ye?"

"No, but the owner there knew of a fellow in town who needs extra stockers and clerks. When he learned I'd managed a store in Sydney, he offered me work starting tomorrow. He's not paying much, but it will cover what we pay Mrs. Whitney so we're not depleting our savings, and there may even be a little extra."

"That's wonderful, James! Then we can stay right here until the ship is ready."

"Unless we decide not to sail with the ship."

"I don't understand."

"Turns out there may be better ways to get where we're going than to sail north to San Francisco." He explained his new employer needed extra people to help him stock wagons for a man named Phineas Banning, who ran a regular trade route between Los Angeles and the inland community of San Bernardino.

"I thought I'd heard Elder Bingham mention San Bernardino, so I asked some questions. Although it started around a Catholic mission, there was a Latter-day Saint settlement there until a couple of years ago. No one is exactly certain why President Young recalled the Saints to Utah—the Utah War, mayhap—but they built up a fair-sized community before they left, and others are keeping it going. This Banning fellow takes dry goods from here to trade in San Bernardino for the farm produce they raise there."

Eliza narrowed her gaze. "I still don't see what that has to do with us."

"While the Saints were in San Bernardino, they established a cross-desert trail between their settlement and the Saints in Utah," James said with obvious excitement. "If we were to ride with Banning as far as San Bernardino—say, after the first of the year, we could easily join up with a wagon train to go the rest of the way. Or, if we wanted to make an easier crossing, I could work here . . . or perhaps in San Bernardino until spring, giving ya and the wee one time to prepare for the desert journey."

Eliza's eyes widened. "So that explains it, then."

"Explains what, love?"

"Back in Auckland, when Elder Walton gave ye that blessing. Ye remember? He blessed us with circumstances that would not seem to be blessings at the time but would enable our journey." Her eyes were bright when she looked up at him. "James, I think the Lord may have brought us to Los Angeles a-purpose."

James gaped. "Ya think He brought those storms?"

She touched his arm. "I think those storms were happening anyway, a part of the unusual weather, and we were preserved when the ship might have sunk. And I think He let the winds blow us southward so the *Trieste* could get the help she needs and we could make an easier trip to join the Saints."

James slowly nodded. "Aye. Ya may be right. Heaven blessed us by bringing us here."

Thus James and Eliza began the process of simultaneously settling in at Mrs. Whitney's and deciding how they might leave. James went to work the next morning and quickly made himself an integral part of the shop owner's business, meanwhile learning all he could about the Banning wagon trains. As soon as Eliza could get around, she began helping Mrs. Whitney with the baking and kitchen work, leaving Adelita and Irma free to manage the heavier tasks of laundry and cleaning. Mrs. Whitney reduced the cost of their room and board in compensation for Eliza's work and soon made their stay at the boarding house so appealing that they chose to stay right where they were, at least until it was time to start their journey.

They celebrated Christmas; then the new year, 1860, arrived in the peaceful surroundings of Mrs. Whitney's boarding house, but by mid-January, James was getting itchy feet.

"I don't want to push ya," he said to Eliza one evening. "I know having a baby is an ordeal and all, but I also know the great southwestern desert gets very hot in the summer and may even start to feel like summer by early May. The sooner we can get started, the more likely we can make it this year."

"Is going in the autumn an option?" Eliza asked. "That may be the easier choice for everyone—not just for me, but for the baby as well."

"There's also the threat of war," James said. "If Mr. Lincoln should be reelected, it's possible the Southern states will secede. Travel could be interrupted for some time."

Eliza sighed. "How soon d'ye want to leave?"

"Banning has a train of freight wagons heading for San Bernardino in mid-February, about a month from now."

"A month. And from there?"

"It's possible we may have to stay in San Bernardino for a time, but at least there are still a few Saints there, those who are clearing up some of the business left by the Mormon colony."

"Mrs. Whitney has been good to us."

"Aye, she has. Eliza, if ya don't want to go—"

She sighed. "Find out about wagons and such. If it works, I'll . . . I'll be ready to leave in a month."

He took her hands. "Thank ya, love. I know this is difficult, and I'm not sure why I feel such a push to go, but I'm surely feeling it."

"Maybe it's just that we've come so far already, and now we're this close—"

He refrained from mentioning the signs he'd seen, the talk he'd heard . . . He didn't want her to realize how unwelcome they were in this place. "Aye, maybe that's all. Thank ya, anyway. Ye're a brave woman." He kissed her.

"I'm not near as brave as I try to be," she answered, "but ye help me, James. Ye always give me courage." She paused. "I love ye."

"And I love ya, Eliza," he answered, "more than I ever thought possible."

*   *   *   *

Just after the first of February, James came home from work with a yoke of oxen and a farm wagon. The bed was roughly three-and-a-half feet deep, four feet wide, and maybe eight feet long, covered by staves and canvas. "I've measured the equipment and supplies Banning says we'll need to get to the Salt Lake Valley," he told her. "I reckon it'll fill the wagon to a depth of three feet or so leaving space atop the load to make a bed."

"And what're ye gonna do with yer cattle between now and leavin' day?" Eliza couldn't help looking askance at the two large, lumbering creatures.

"I've found a fellow who'll keep them and the rig for us just outside of town until we're ready to go. He won't grain the oxen, but they'll have plenty of field grass and clean water; he'll have them ready to go for us the day before we need to pack the wagon."

"And he's doing this out of the goodness of his heart?"

"Well, I did catch his horse for him when some boys in town were trying to spook it. He said he owed me a favor."

Eliza shook her head. "That sounds like my James," she said. "And I'm guessing ye already have the full list of recommended supplies."

"Aye. At least I've made the order at the mercantile. Thanks to Ed we can afford it, though we'll have little left. It should arrive some four days before Banning plans to leave."

"Well." Eliza dropped her hands into her lap. "I guess we'll be ready to go then."

James heard the slight catch in his wife's voice and saw the way she blinked. "Ye're frightened, aren't ya?"

"I'm sorry. I can't help it. It's a long trek we're planning across a dry, hostile desert with a babe just a few weeks old and two other little uns. I've heard stories about Indian attacks and diseases and thieves—" Her breath caught in her throat.

"Oh, sweetheart." James took her into his arms. "I can't blame ya for being scared. Can ya try to remember the words of Elder Walton's last blessing? How he promised all of us we'd reach Zion safely?"

She nodded but couldn't seem to stop shivering.

"I know it's frightening, but could it be any worse than taking off across the wide Pacific? The Lord sustained us through that. Few wagons encounter serious Indian attacks or thieves anymore, and it seldom happens with a large wagon train. We'll be going with many others, so we're less vulnerable than small parties, and there haven't been any major outbreaks of cholera or typhoid lately."

He held her away from him, trying to see her eyes, but she turned her face away. "Look at me, sweetheart." She sniffled but looked up. "I promise. Once we get to San Bernardino, if the rest of the crossing looks too dangerous, we'll stop right there until it's better."

"Even if the war begins?"

He swallowed hard. "Even if there's war," he promised.

She nodded. "All right then. I'll try to be brave. And I promise that even if I'm fearful, I'll do my best to look brave for the boys."

"Ye've always been an excellent mother. No one can ever fault ya for that."

They began the process of selecting what they would take.

When Mrs. Whitney heard they were going, she got teary as well. "I've come to love you and your little ones," she said. "But I'm realizing it's more than that. There's a peaceful spirit about you and your family, a sort of quiet calm that I'd like to have in my own life."

James and Eliza exchanged a quick look.

"I see what you're thinking," Mrs. Whitney went on, "and I think you're right. Can you teach me more about being a Mormon?"

"I don't even know if there are missionaries in this area—" Eliza began.

"There are," James said. "As it happens, a pair came into the mercantile last week. I think I know where to find them. Mrs. Whitney, are ya ready to have the missionaries teach ya?"

"I think I am," she answered, "but I want them to come at least the first time while you're still here. Can you arrange it?"

James smiled. "I'm certain I can."

*    *    *    *

On the following Sunday, Eliza and Mrs. Lucy Whitney prepared a special meal for all the boarders at Whitney House complete with a cake in honor of Jimmy's seventh birthday. After the meal they let Adelita and Irma clean while they met in the parlor with Elder Grant and Elder Lowe, both of whom had traveled the Banning route across the desert. After they introduced the restored gospel to Mrs. Whitney and gave her a copy of the Book of Mormon, they answered James and Eliza's questions about the desert crossing. It was both a useful and powerful experience for them all.

Eight days later Eliza and James stood at the door of Whitney House, preparing to say good-bye to more dear friends.

"We've become close in such a short time," Eliza said as she hugged Mrs. Whitney. "I don't know how I can thank ye for the way ye took me in and took care of me when I was needin' a mother's care. Ye were as good to me as my own mother could have been."

"I loved you and your little one from the moment I saw you both," Mrs. Whitney answered. "And you've given me the restored gospel. No one can give more than that."

James grinned. "We know. We were baptized by an Elder Walton."

"Your son, Walton—?"

"Aye," Eliza answered. "I'll write when we get settled. If ye decide to join the Saints, just let us know ye're coming. We'll help ye settle in."

"I doubt that will happen," Mrs. Whitney answered, "but you have a safe trip now, you hear? Take care of those boys."

"We will, ma'am," James answered. "Thank ya for everything." He held up the baby for a final kiss and then led his family to the wagon where he positioned Eliza, Jimmy, and Joseph on the seat and placed baby Walton in Eliza's arms.

Mrs. Whitney stood, her copy of the Book of Mormon in hand, waving on the porch as James led the oxen away.

## Chapter 17

**February 1860**

ELIZA STIRRED THE POT OF beans she'd been soaking. She had set them on to cook as soon as she got a fire going, and they were progressing well. They'd probably be ready in another hour when the camp wanted to eat. She busied herself with preparing some dutch oven biscuits to go alongside the beans.

It was their fourth day on the trail, and she was pleased with the way she'd adapted. Baby Walton didn't seem to know anything had changed. He seemed to like being close to her all the time, slung in a shawl wrapped close against her body. She had found she could feed him while still walking beside the wagon. And she definitely preferred walking to sitting on the hard wagon seat, feeling every bump and ridge in the corrugated wagon ruts.

Her other boys seemed to be thriving too. Joseph couldn't keep up when walking, but his father set him on the back of the lead ox and stayed close, encouraging the little boy to hang on while he led the team. When the child needed to rest, he seemed to have no trouble with the bumps and gyrations that gave Eliza such fits but dropped quickly into sleep inside the wagon. Meanwhile, Jimmy had found other children in the company and seemed eager to run, playing alongside the ponderously slow wagons, covering many more miles than necessary each day.

No sooner had she thought of Jimmy than he appeared at her side. "Mum, Mrs. Raft is going to take a bunch of us out to pick wildflowers. Can I go?"

Eliza looked toward the neighboring wagon and saw Anna Raft with a number of children gathered around her. Mrs. Raft waved, and Eliza returned her greeting. "Very well, Jimmy. Stay with the group and be back before dark."

"Yes, Mum." He took off running. Eliza made a mental note: *We're Americans now. I must remember to say yes, not aye.*

"He seems to be enjoying himself," James said, coming up beside her.

"I'm glad he's found friends." She stood, straightening her apron. "I wish more of them were Latter-day Saints who planned to go through to Salt Lake."

James wrapped his arms around her middle. "It's difficult to let go of our loved ones, isn't it?"

She sighed. "I've missed Molly so much, especially since the baby—" She paused, swallowing the sudden lump in her throat. "And I felt so close to Mrs. Whitney, and we've had to say good-bye to her too."

"And now ye're starting to feel close to Anna and Marilla and some of the other women, but ya know ye'll have to let go of them once we get to San Bernardino."

"Aye." She rested her head against him. "I'm glad I have ye and the boys. The promise of eternal families is one of the blessings of the gospel that means the most to me."

"And to me." He nuzzled her neck. "I want ya with me forever. Our boys too."

She turned to him. "James, promise me that whatever we do, we'll find a way to get to the temple as soon as it's finished. I want our family to be sealed."

"Of course I promise," he answered. "That's part of the reason I'm pushing to get us to Zion. Maybe we can find ways to help the Saints hurry the work on the temple. I want ya to make me a promise too: if the time ever comes when the temple is ready and I'm not ready to take ya there, I want ya to kick me into motion and get me going so we can have the sealing covenants. D'ye promise?"

She smiled. "Aye, James, I promise—though I'm thinking it'll be ye kicking me into motion and not t'other way 'round."

They stood for a moment just holding one another. Then Walton cried from his bed on the wagon seat, and Eliza drew away. "It seems ye've a rival for my attentions."

"He gets first call—at least while he's this little. When he gets a bit older, we'll see." He nipped playfully at her ear.

"I believe ye've some wood to chop?" she asked with a grin as she slipped from his grasp and went to feed their child.

An hour later, the sun was beginning to set, and the camp was ready for the evening. The wagons were drawn into a large circle, the tongue of one resting on the rear step of the wagon before it, the whole making an impromptu corral to keep the oxen, horses, and occasional milk cows from straying. Each family had its own small cooking fire, but the camp's central fire had been established in the middle, and the members of the wagon company had brought their food there, creating a potluck supper. The wagon master made announcements and asked Mr. Raft to offer grace, and then the camp turned to the serious business of eating.

Eliza filled her plate and sat on the ground beside James. Joseph came to sit in her lap and eat from her plate. "Have ye seen Jimmy?" she asked her husband as they began their meal.

"Not since he left with the wildflower party." James waved a biscuit in the direction of the Raft wagon. "He may be eating with Anna and the Raft children."

Eliza put her hand to her forehead, shading her eyes from the sun. She looked in the direction of the Raft wagon. "We've hardly eaten as a family since we started this trip. Jimmy so enjoys eating with the other children. I don't see him, but most of the camp's children are over there together. He's probably in that lot."

"Aye, probably so," James answered.

"Will ye go and find him, James? I don't like eating supper without him."

"Stop fussing, sweetheart. The Raft children ate with us last evening. I'm sure he's fine."

"Aye, if ye say so." Eliza quelled her uneasiness by tending her little ones.

An hour later, when the camp had cleaned up from their dinner and most people were preparing for the night, Eliza still hadn't seen Jimmy. She wrapped Walton into the shawl around her, took Joseph by the hand, and went hunting for James. She found him in a small knot of men, looking at the maps for their route the next day.

"It's a longer day than usual," one of the under-captains was saying. "We'll have to make a quick start in the morning and keep up the pace all along if we're to make it to the water before sundown. We've all got an extra day's ration in our buckets, just in case, but it's best to camp where there's fresh water when we can. Make sure your buckets are full before we leave and tell the folks around you to prepare for an early wake-up."

"Aye, sir," James answered as the group broke up. He turned to join Eliza. "Looks like a big day tomorrow."

"Have ye seen Jimmy?" she asked.

"He's not back yet?"

"He hasn't come to the wagon. I haven't gone looking for him since I've been cleaning up and taking care of the babies. I'm getting worried. He should be back by now."

"Aye, he should." James's face mirrored her concern. "He's probably still with the Raft children. Ya go get the little ones settled. I'll check with the Rafts. If he's not there, I'll speak to the Smiths and some of the other folks with young ones. We'll have to let Jimmy know that he needs to be back at the wagon when the sun sets."

"I reminded him—"

"I'm sure ya did. Go on back now. I'll find him."

Eliza took her babies to her wagon and began the process of putting them to bed, but her worry grew as the light faded. Jimmy had never been away this long. *Something is wrong.* When the thought entered her mind, it immediately took root. Something *was* wrong or Jimmy would have returned. She dropped to her knees beside the wagon and offered a heartfelt prayer: "Dear Heavenly Father, please bless my child. Help us to find him safe and well."

In her mind she heard Elder Walton's words as he promised young James "safety in the wilderness" and success among the Saints. Her growing panic subsided, but minutes later it grew again as James returned alone.

"Anna said she thought Jimmy was with us," he said as he drew near. "The children all picked wildflowers, and Jimmy had a big handful. He wanted to bring them back to ya, so he told her he was coming to camp. She hasn't seen him since."

Eliza felt her back stiffening. "The Smiths? The Wrights? The Landons?"

He shook his head. "No one's seen him."

"James—"

He held her shoulders. "I've talked to the wagon master, and he's sending out word to all the captains. We're making torches and organizing search parties. Anna Raft will show us the direction the children took. We'll find him."

The grim determination on her husband's face only underscored Eliza's fear. "He's so little, and it's going to be a chilly night—"

"We'll find him," James repeated. He let her go and began his own preparations. "Ye've the babies to think of," he said. "Try to get some rest. I'll wake ya when we bring him back."

"I'll lie down with the little ones," she answered, "but ye know I won't sleep." They shared a long, telling look. "My prayers go with ye, James."

"We'll find him," he said again. He drew her against him as if drawing sustenance from her closeness, dropped a kiss on her forehead, and turned to go.

Eliza watched him leave. She could see the other men gathering in the center with their ropes and canteens and torches, organizing into parties and preparing for the search, and she felt encouraged by their numbers and their strength. Then she thought of seven-year-old Jimmy, alone and frightened as the light left the sky, and she struggled to remember the Lord's promises.

\*   \*   \*   \*

James wiped his brow and looked back over his shoulder toward the camp. It was well past midnight, and the search had gone on for hours, so far without success. He hated to admit it, but he knew the longer they went without finding his son, the lower their chances of finding him at all. He hated to think of all the things that could happen to a small boy in country this wild.

"Here, I've found something!" The call came from his right. He ran toward it. He could see other torches bobbing and weaving as other men near them also ran to the place where Arthur Raft was holding his torch near the ground. As James drew near, Raft looked up. "James, was your boy wearing shoes?"

"Not this afternoon," James answered. "We usually don't put them on him unless the weather's bad. Why? What have ya found?"

"It's a human footprint. I suppose it could be from one of the Indians round abouts, but it looks to me more like a boy's."

James leaned down to examine the mark. There were other partial footprints, but this one was clear and distinct. He touched it. "That's Jimmy's footprint. I'm certain."

"The trail goes that way," Raft said. With care, the men who had joined them all followed along, careful to keep the boy's tracks unmarred. The trail went on for several yards until it came to a huge boulder. Arthur Raft, still in the lead, stood. "Maybe you should go back to the wagons," he said, turning to James.

James pushed through to stand beside him. "Why? What have ya found?"

Arthur Raft looked at James with sympathetic eyes. Then he looked down at his feet. Although the soft sand was all around the rock, the boy's footprints ended there and they were covered by huge paw marks.

"Whew, look at that!" One of the younger men came up behind James. "That cat's paw is easy bigger than my head!" James saw the man's face fall as he realized he was talking to the father whose child the huge cat had been stalking. "Oh. Sorry," he murmured.

James felt his heart sink. He swallowed hard. "I can't believe—" he began, but he couldn't make himself say the words.

Raft turned to the other men. "You'd best get back to camp," he said. He called out to a party of men who had searched nearby and were coming their way: "Smith, the search is over. Fire off a shot to let the other parties know."

"Will do!" Smith called back, and James heard the report of the gun.

"We have to make an early start tomorrow," Arthur said, his voice gentle, "and, well, there's nothing more we can do here."

James felt the sorrow well up in his chest. He was glad the search party was breaking up, the other men heading back to camp. Few saw him as his knees gave way and he sank to the earth, and if they heard the heartbroken wail rising up from behind them, they had the decency not to notice. "Jimmy, Jimmy, Jimmy," he moaned as he rocked back and forth, the horror of it overwhelming him. What must it have been like when his son looked up and saw—? He tried to block the images.

Some time passed before he could get his feet beneath him again. Arthur Raft had waited patiently a few yards away, unwilling to leave him alone. Now he walked quietly at James's side. "I . . . I need to get back to the camp," James said unnecessarily. "I have to tell his mother . . ."

"I know," Raft said. He stopped. "I'm sorry, James. I can't tell you how sorry I am."

James couldn't seem to speak, but he nodded his head in acknowledgement. As they neared the camp, he saw Eliza coming. "I'd best go on alone now," he said. Raft grasped his arm, nodded in understanding, and left James alone to tell Eliza.

\* \* \* \*

It had been a nearly sleepless night—the hours broken by the fruitless search for a missing child and the keening sorrow of a grieving mother. Still, the demands of the new day kept anyone from sleeping in. Only the faintest glimmers of dawn touched the eastern sky as the captains walked among the wagons, getting everyone started. The next water source was a long way off, and they had to get moving.

"I won't go." Eliza stood beside her wagon. "My son is alive out there, and I will not leave him."

The wagon master held his hat in his hands. "Ma'am, I appreciate your loss, and I understand you not wanting to recognize what's happened here, but I'm responsible for sixty-two wagons, and sixty-one other families who may also start losing people if we go too long without water. We need to get moving and you need to move with us."

"I won't go," Eliza said again.

James came up beside her. "I'm sorry, Captain Willis. My wife needs more time."

Willis set his jaw. "Then we will simply have to leave without you," he said, "and I won't give much for your chances if the local Indian tribes find a single wagon out here by itself." He seemed to be waiting for Eliza to change her mind.

"Do what ye have to, Captain," Eliza responded. "I will not leave my son."

"Have it your way, ma'am," the captain answered. As he marched away from their wagon, he mumbled, "Stubborn woman's gonna get ya all killed."

James took Eliza into his arms and gently rocked her. "I won't leave ya," he said, "but Eliza, we need to face the facts . . ."

"What facts? Ye didn't see a body," she said, looking up at him with a kind of quiet desperation. "Ye didn't see blood or torn clothing or anything—nothing but tracks. Jimmy is alive and waiting for us to find him, and I will not leave him."

"Eliza—"

"Pray with me, James. Remember Elder Walton's words about safety in the wilderness and how Jimmy would grow to become a fine, strong man and a husband and father in Zion? Remember that? Remember that ye found no clear evidence that Jimmy has been taken, and stay beside me until we find him."

James gave his wife a long look. "All right," he said. "We'll pray again."

A half hour later they were still kneeling beside their wagon, their voices raised in prayer and their little ones perched atop their load. The wagon train was formed up, and the wagon master prepared to issue the order. The disquiet among the others was obvious. Every sympathy was with the grieving parents, and no one wanted to leave them.

"Captain?" It was one of his lieutenants riding up beside him.

"Yes?"

"Would it hurt to give them one more try, to search one more time?"

Captain Willis paused as if making up his mind. Then he cursed under his breath and kicked his horse, cantering toward the Martin wagon. When he approached he spoke loudly enough for the whole company to hear. "Martin, we don't want to leave without you."

"We won't leave without our son," James said, his voice firm.

"I'm willing to offer you a compromise," the captain said.

James looked at Eliza. "We're listening."

"We'll stop for one more search. You tell us which way to go, and we will go in that direction. We will look until we find him or until one hour has passed. If we find . . ." He paused, glancing nervously toward Eliza. "If we find a body or any clear evidence, you go with us. If we find nothing but the hour passes, you go with us anyway. We give you one more clear search, and you leave here with us an hour from now."

James looked to his wife. "Eliza?"

She closed her eyes and swallowed. "All right," she answered. "One search, but ye give it the full hour. Agreed?"

"You have my word, ma'am. Just tell us which direction to start."

Eliza closed her eyes again, listened for inspiration, and then pointed. "That way," she said, turning away from the rising sun.

"You've got it," the captain said. Throughout the camp determined men handed lead ropes to others, picked up their long guns and canteens, and gathered to begin the search again.

* * * *

James felt the time winding down. He could feel Eliza's faith pushing him, but he knew their miracle had to happen soon or not at all. He looked ahead, realizing he was nearing the boulder where they'd found the cat prints atop Jimmy's. He turned to look back over his shoulder. What would it mean to Eliza if they had to leave without finding anything, without ever knowing for certain? She had promised the wagon master, but would she really leave?

He took a deep breath and started toward the boulder. Maybe he could at least find a body; then they'd know. That was when he heard the sound. Looking up, he saw something moving, and then he heard, "Papa!"

"Jimmy? Oh, Jimmy!" He stumbled over his own feet and had to catch himself as he ran toward his child. Moments later he caught Jimmy in his arms, picked him up and whirled him around, holding him close, kissing his tear-stained face and looking for any sign of blood or injury, remarkably finding none. "Where were ya, son? Why didn't ya come back?"

"I tried," Jimmy answered, and he began sniffling. "I told Mrs. Raft I was going back to the camp, and then I saw some other flowers that I wanted. I could hear people getting the dinner and calling for everyone to come eat, but I couldn't find the trail no more, and I didn't know where I got off it, but I wanted to get back . . ." He paused, finally stopping for breath.

"It started getting dark, and I climbed up that big rock to find the wagons, but I couldn't see nothin', and so I just cried until I went to sleep. Then the sun woke me up this morning, but I saw the big cat paw prints and I was scared to get down. Oh, Papa! I was so scared!"

"We were here last night. Didn't ya hear us, son?"

"I woke up one time and heard somebody talking, but I thought it was Indians coming to get me, so I tried to stay real quiet."

The image in James's mind almost broke his heart. He held his son close but remembered he needed to alert the other searchers. "Stand still, Jimmy. I need to fire off a shot so the other men will know I found ya."

"I don't like that sound," Jimmy said.

"Then cover yer ears." James awkwardly cocked the rifle another man had loaned him and fired a shot into the air. "Come on, son. We need to get back to yer mother."

"I have some flowers for her," Jimmy said. He opened his fist. It was filled with wilted wildflowers—desert lilies, lupine, verbena, and primrose. "D'ye think she'll like 'em?"

James had to swallow hard to get past the lump in his throat. "I think these will be her favorite flowers ever," he said. "Come on, Jimmy. Let's take 'em to yer mum."

Some of the other searchers saw James coming with Jimmy on his shoulders. They broke the news to the rest of the camp, and Eliza ran out to meet them. She took her son in her arms, kissing his face and crying into his hair. The whole camp rejoiced with the Martins as they welcomed Jimmy safely back.

"I never thought to see this boy again," Captain Willis said as he rode up beside their wagon, "but we've delayed long enough. Let's get these wagons rolling!"

"Wait, Captain," Eliza said.

"Wait again? Haven't we waited long enough?" Willis turned on Eliza, his face stony.

"There's one more thing we must do, sir," Eliza answered steadily. "Let us give thanks."

Willis, shame-faced, ordered the camp silent while James led them all in a prayer of thanksgiving. Feeling the tension around him, James made the prayer heartfelt but brief.

"Amen!" came the reply from the camp. Then the wagon master shouted, "Now move 'em out! We're late already."

Jimmy slept atop their load, his feet swollen but recovering, while the wagon train rolled forward.

*   *   *

They had stopped for a brief midday meal when the Rafts, Smiths, and a half dozen other couples came to the Martins' wagon. James greeted them eagerly, grasping Arthur's hand and thanking them all for the help they had offered during the search. There was a moment of uneasy silence as the visitors looked expectantly at one another, and then Arthur Raft spoke. "That's what we want to talk with you about, the crisis with Jimmy." He turned to Eliza, "How did you know? How could you be so certain that your boy was still alive? And how did you know which way to look this morning?"

Eliza looked at James, who nodded encouragement. "It was the Spirit," she said simply.

"Spirits!" Maria Gonzalez made the sign of the cross. "I tol' you she is no Christian!" She flounced away, making the sign to ward off the evil eye while murmuring, "Deliver us from evil." Everyone watched her go.

"It was the *Holy* Spirit," Eliza said again, more clearly. "I had been praying, and I felt inspired that Jimmy was alive. When the captain asked which way the searchers should go, I saw an image in my mind of James coming back with Jimmy on his shoulders, and they were coming from the west. I sent the searchers that way."

"You Mormons are really something." Howard Smith brushed his hat against his thigh. "You believe in angels that bring gold Bibles and now in spirits too. I'm going back to my wagon. Come on, Marilla."

Marilla straightened, lifting her chin. "I'd like to stay a little longer, Howard."

Howard opened his mouth to speak but seemed to think better of what he'd planned to say. "Stay if you like. We'll be getting back on the trail soon."

"I'll be there," she said. They all watched as her husband departed.

"If any of ya would like to know more about the restored gospel of Jesus Christ, we will be happy to tell ya what we know," James offered.

"Can we come to your campfire this evening?" Arthur Raft asked.

"We'd be glad of it," James answered.

Nodding, Arthur took his wife by the hand. "Then we'll be back," he said.

"So will we." Joanna and Delbert Wright had been conferring quietly. They nodded pleasantly to Eliza and the children as they left.

The wagons were soon on the trail again, and somehow they arrived at their planned campsite near a spring of fresh water before the light had gone from the sky.

Altogether there were four couples who joined the Martins at their campfire that evening—the Rafts, the Wrights, the Landons, and the Pomeroys, along with Marilla Smith. Working from his copy of the Book of Mormon, James began as the missionaries had taught him, sharing scriptures about the Great Apostasy and how the church had languished in unbelief, false traditions creeping in among truths until much had been lost. He went on to talk about the Restoration—the keys and the organization that had been returned to the earth in modern times. "I invite ya all to pray about what we've read and heard," he said as the meeting broke up. "We can meet again after sunset tomorrow."

*   *   *   *

Three days later, when the wagons reached San Bernardino, they found another wagon train waiting, the one that would carry many of the Martins' new friends to the mining settlements in the Mojave Desert. James and Eliza said good-bye to the Wrights, the Smiths, and a half dozen other families who had traveled with them. They found extra copies of the Book of Mormon among the Saints still in San Bernardino and shared these with the Wrights and Marilla Smith. But they didn't say good-bye to everyone. The Rafts and the Landons had embraced the gospel with open hearts; they were ready to be baptized and to go forward into Zion with James and Eliza instead of joining the desert-bound wagons.

Captain Willis, who was already preparing for his return trip to Los Angeles, shook his head in amazement as he bade them farewell. "You've almost made me think the Almighty might be listening," he said as he saluted them. "Go with God, James, Eliza. May He continue to bless you."

"Go with God, Captain," Eliza answered.

"And if ya ever make it up to the Great Salt Lake, be sure to look us up," James added.

The wagon master made a gruff noise in his throat. "That's not likely," he said. "I don't think I'd do well surrounded by Mormons."

"Ya might be surprised," James answered with a twinkle.

"Ha!" Willis doffed his hat. "I halfway believe you, Martin. I halfway do." He nudged his horse and rode on.

James spoke to Eliza, "I'm going to see what people here can tell me about travel into Zion," he said. He led the oxen to some tall grass growing along a nearby ditch and left them to eat as he walked into the settlement of San Bernardino.

He was back three hours later with news. "There's a wagon train going to Zion next week," he announced. "They're leaving March first, they're going all the way to Salt Lake City, and they'll be happy to have us with them."

"That's wonderful," Eliza answered. "I was worried when we left Mrs. Whitney's, but I have a better sense now of how we handle the trail, and I think I'd rather go before the desert heats up any more."

James grinned. "I thought ya might see it that way."

*  *  *  *

The week passed quickly as some of the families prepared to leave for the Mojave. Their new wagon master demanded they reduce their load to allow for faster travel, so each family began divesting themselves of food they couldn't carry, chickens they could no longer feed, and a variety of other goods that fed the Martins comfortably. When he could, James traded chopped wood or tightly boxed canned goods in exchange, but he eagerly accepted all that was offered when the departing families refused to barter. He didn't know how long it might take them to reach Salt Lake City.

In the evenings, they met with the Saints who remained in the small community, seeking help to teach the Rafts and the Landons to prepare them for baptism. Eliza was pleased at the remarkable progress her new friends were making and commented to James at how much faster these people were to accept the gospel than she had been.

"They were prepared," James answered.

"And we weren't?"

"Best not to question the ways of the Lord."

On the afternoon of Leap Day, February 29, 1860, Eliza and her family gathered with a few dozen Saints at the edge of the river where some of the brethren had dug out a hole deep enough for immersion. The work had been completed earlier, so the stream now ran clear.

Meanwhile the women had created a small tent of bedding hung over ropes stretched between trees. Eliza would be there to assist Anna Raft and Isabella Landon as they came out of the water, helping them change quickly into dry clothing.

As they organized and prepared for the ordinance, she thought of her own baptism and how Molly had come driving up almost at the last instant. The image was so clear in memory that when she saw a wagon tearing at them, its team galloping wildly, she first thought she'd imagined it. Only the motion of the other watchers let her know the wagon was real.

There was an audible gasp from the crowd as Howard Smith jumped down from the wagon seat. "Have ya started without us?" he asked.

The local bishop, who had met the Smiths before they left, spoke for everyone when he asked, "Howard, what are you doing here?"

Howard looked up at his wife, his eyes soft. "Marilla started reading and talking to me about what she read; I'd chime in and tell her what foolishness it all was. Then someone in the camp would see her reading and start attacking the Church and the doctrine, and I'd find myself defending it. After just a couple of days, I realized I was finding it easier to defend than to attack. Marilla suggested we pray about it, and well . . ." He shrugged. "Here we are."

The bishop smiled. "We'll be delighted to have you." He turned to the other members. "If you'll all excuse us for a bit? I need to visit with these folks for a moment."

"Maybe we can sing some hymns while we wait," one of the sisters said, and the group began singing the hymns of the Restoration while the bishop interviewed Howard, Marilla, and their eldest son, Will, who was turning nine.

A few minutes later, there were seven new members of the Church: Arthur and Anna Raft, John and Isabella Landon, Howard and Marilla and William Smith. Eliza helped the women and Will as they came out of the water. When the baptisms and confirmations were completed, the bishop introduced the man who had been called as the priesthood leader for the wagon train and asked for their sustaining vote. Each adult in the group solemnly accepted Captain Hudson. Then Brother Hudson called captains of ten, asking James to serve as one of them, and Eliza happily raised her hand to sustain her husband.

As they drove their team away from the river, Eliza looked back at the red-and-gold sunset reflected in the water. "The last of our preparations are done," she said softly.

"What?" James asked her.

"Baptizing these new friends was a necessary part of our preparation, but the last of our preparations are complete now. We're ready to go, to move on to Zion."

"Aye." James nodded. "I suppose we are."

"I'm proud of ye, husband. Ye'll make a fine leader."

"Well, I can't say about that for certain, but I'm grateful to the Lord for trusting me with this responsibility, and I'll do my best."

"Ye'll be wonderful," Eliza answered. She wrapped her arm through his.

# Chapter 18

*March 1860*

ELIZA STIRRED THE SOUP WHILE Jimmy played with Joseph and cooed at little Walton. The wagon train's progress had been excellent so far. With the Smiths added to their company, they had fifty-four wagons filled with settlers moving into Deseret. Add to that another fifty wagons filled with supplies and accompanied by an armed cavalry escort, and the train was impressive.

Each day they started moving by first light with half the armed men riding in front of the train and half protecting the rear. The supply wagons were interspersed among the settlers' wagons, and the remaining men of the camp walked alongside the moving company with their firearms, if they had one, available at a moment's notice. Although the travelers had sometimes been aware of watchers in the hills, the camp had gone unmolested.

Their first challenge had been fording the Mojave River. Although the crossing had sometimes proven dangerous, even fatal, to a few past travelers, Captain Hudson had sent scouts ahead to find the best places to ford. Since the river was running low this year due to reduced snow-fall in the mountains, the crossing had been little more than a nuisance. Over the past several days, the company had traveled mostly on water they carried, stopping every two or three days to refill at desert streams: first Bitter Creek, then Resting Creek, then Salt Creek. They were camped now beside Mountain Creek in their usual, circle-the-wagons formation with the animals corralled inside. In a few days they'd be at Cottonwood Creek, and then they'd take a rest stop at the Mormon colony founded just five years earlier called "the Vegas," an oasis in the midst of burning sands. Although the trail had been kind, Eliza was ready for a rest stop.

"Hey, neighbor!"

Eliza looked up to see Marilla Smith poking her head around the canvas of her wagon. "Welcome, Marilla." She brushed the last of the flour off her hands and onto her apron.

"I'm baking biscuits and hoping you have some soda to spare."

"Sure'n I'll be happy to lend ye some," Eliza answered, "but ye brought soda, didn't ye? I'm sure I saw some when we helped ye pack yer wagon."

"Yes, we brought soda. I used it yesterday, and I think Minnie must have put it away for me." She nodded toward her wagon where her seven-year-old was stirring a pot. "I thought it might be easier to get a pinch from you than to dig through all our things."

Eliza chuckled. "No problem. Let me just—"

She turned toward the wagon but was stopped in her tracks by a shrill, bone-chilling cry. She knew instantly what it was. "Indians!" she screamed. "Jimmy, get into the wagon. Get down low!" Marilla paled and ran for her own wagon, gathering up her children. Within seconds their wagons were being approached by fifty or more dark-skinned, armed men, riding their horses hard and whooping their intent. Only seconds later, the wagon train bristled with long guns pointed toward the oncoming riders.

The man in the lead rode a brown-and-white paint pony and carried a long gun like those in the camp. As he charged down on the wagons, several of the men trained their rifles on his nose. When he got almost within range, he took an abrupt left turn and led his men, whooping and screaming, all the way around the circle. Eliza crouched low inside her wagon, trying to keep her babies calm.

She peeked out a small hole and watched as the painted warriors formed a circle, the head of the pack following immediately upon the tail, and rode 'round the camp once, twice, three times. Then, as abruptly as they had come, the Indians left, whooping and shouting as if in full attack, their guns raised above their heads even though they were riding away.

"D'ye think it's safe to come out?" Eliza asked as James arrived a few moments later.

"Aye, I think they're gone for now," he said, "but it would be wise to keep the boys close, just in case. I'll go speak with Hudson and the other leaders, see if maybe they know what that was all about."

When he returned, Eliza had the children huddled near, ready to hop back in the wagon box at a moment's notice. "What's happening?" she asked.

"The captain has some guesses," James answered. "He thinks maybe this was a warning—not meant to cause harm, just encouraging us to keep moving and get out of their territory." He warmed his hands at the fire. His voice dropped as he looked toward the children. "Of course, there's also the possibility that they came with every intention of killing us, driving off our animals, and stealing our supplies. They only rode off when they realized they were outmanned and outgunned. At least, that's another theory."

Eliza felt a shiver go down her spine. "Does Captain Hudson think they'll be back?"

"That depends on why they came in the first place," James answered, speaking quietly. "If they were checking out our strength, they may feel we're too powerful to attack. If they're trying to get us out of their territory, who knows?" Then he frowned as he added, "Of course those are just guesses. Maybe it's something we haven't guessed at all. The captain has ordered a double watch for tonight, and he wants us ready to leave at first light—maybe sooner."

"Sooner?"

"Moonrise will be late, and he says there'll be plenty of moonlight."

"He doesn't believe in sleepin', does he?" Eliza let out a frustrated sigh.

"I expect he's more concerned that we all wake up tomorrow," James said. He gave Eliza a supportive hug and went to clean his borrowed rifle.

The camp was edgy that night, and even the men who weren't officially on watch slept little and paced much. Long before the first signs of dawn, the wagons were on the move, and they kept the pace up, not stopping even for a midday meal but eating hard tack and leftover biscuits as they walked, trying to cover as many miles as possible before darkness overtook them. By the time they finally camped near a small spring, the captain figured they'd covered more than twenty miles—a long day for ox-drawn wagons, which rarely made more than two miles an hour.

They made camp as the shadows lengthened. They had little time to build campfires or get their evening meals started. Still, they had scarcely circled their wagons when the war whoops came again, and a party of fifty or sixty warriors came charging at the camp. This time the Martin wagon was not in the direct path of the charging Indians, but Eliza moved just as quickly, getting her boys into the base of the wagon. Then she peered out the small hole in the canvas, watching with mixed terror and fascination as the men charged directly at their camp.

She couldn't know whether it was all the same warriors as before, but she recognized the man on the paint pony, the man who whooped as if he intended murder, whether he really did or not. As before, he led his men directly at the wagons. Then, just when he was nearing rifle range, he made an abrupt turn, circled the camp three times, and led his men back the way they had come, whooping and charging and brandishing their weapons.

"I think they were making a point," Captain Hudson said half an hour later as he stood with James and some of the other men near the Martins' campfire. "They want us out of their territory," he said, "and when they saw us going, they wanted to be certain we kept going. I've no problem obliging them."

"Hear, hear," said one of the men.

"Amen," said another.

"Still, I don't think they meant to harm us, just to keep us moving. That explains why there was not a single shot fired. Nor did they draw our fire but stayed out of range."

"That old codger knows what he's doing," said a man named Booth, his expression admiring. "He's got us on the alert and moving much faster than we would have gone otherwise, but he's done it without harm."

"A good leader is a good leader," Captain Hudson said, "even if he's an Apache. But we can't let our guard down just because we think we've got him figured."

The men talked a little longer, determining to put another double watch on the camp that night and to leave again at first light. "I doubt it's necessary," Captain Hudson said as they concluded, "but we may be misreading their intentions. It's best to be prepared." Eliza listened with mixed fear and admiration.

Despite the double watch, the night was quiet, and by the time they camped the following evening, they were far from where they'd first seen the charging war party. Eliza had served her family their evening meal—which they now called dinner or supper instead of tea—and was busy cleaning up when a murmur ran through camp. People were gathering at one side of the circle, looking out between the wagons. She put Jimmy and Joseph into the back of the wagon, assigning Jimmy to keep an eye on his little brother. Then, with the baby wrapped tightly against her, she went to see what was stirring up the camp.

What she saw made her gasp. Coming out of the trees and crossing the meadow toward them was a dark-skinned man on a paint pony. At first she thought it was the same man, but as he neared, she didn't think so. Two other men rode behind him. Her first instinct was to scream and run for the wagon, but like the others who were watching, she quickly realized this man rode slowly. He came toward their camp with both hands empty, raised at his sides and clearly visible, letting his pony slowly pick its way. Instead of whooping, he rode silently, and he came with two men, not fifty, none of them painted.

She looked around for James. "I'm here," he said as he stepped up behind her.

"What do ye think—?"

"Who knows?" he said. "Captain Hudson has asked some of the men to take defensive positions, but he's waiting to see."

"This certainly doesn't look like the last two times."

"No, but just in case, it's best if ya go back to the wagon and—"

He hadn't finished his sentence before they realized the man on the paint pony had begun speaking. The sounds were not English words and didn't even sound like human speech to Eliza. People in the circle looked at one another, hoping someone could translate, but no one seemed to understand.

Captain Hudson came up behind their group. "Carter, Booth, you two keep your weapons down but at the ready," he said. "Westover and Brown have taken positions inside the Campbell wagon. They'll cover the two outriders. Everybody else stay here and stay calm. No sudden moves." He stepped outside the defensive circle, over the tongue of the closest wagon, and took two steps toward the visitor. Then he slowly motioned for the man to get down.

Keeping his hands visible, the Indian dismounted and stood beside his horse. He repeated the words he had spoken before. When the captain shook his head, the man took a deep breath, pressing in on his stomach. Then he lifted his fingers to his mouth.

"He's hungry," Eliza said. "He's here to find something to eat."

"I do believe you're right," the captain said, still keeping his eye on the visitor.

"Brother Brigham says it's better to feed them than fight them," a man near her said.

"I agree," the captain answered. "Martin, still no quick moves, please, but will you look around the camp? See what we have we can offer these men."

"Aye, sir." James began by escorting Eliza back to their wagon. "See what ya feel ya can part with," he said as he left. For the next few minutes, James went among the other wagons, asking for contributions. Captain Hudson kept the visitor engaged in a conversation of pantomime, and Eliza searched through her dwindling food stores, reminding herself they still had a long way to go to reach Salt Lake. Thanks to the gifts from the settlers headed toward the Mojave, she felt they had enough to share.

"What's happening, Mama?" Jimmy asked. She noticed he no longer called her Mum.

"We're getting some food for the Indians," she answered.

"Can I watch?"

"Aye," she said. "Out that little hole in the canvas right there, but remember to keep an eye on Joseph."

"I want to come where you are."

"No!" she said but quickly softened her tone. "Not this time, son. We can't be certain it's safe. Please promise me ye'll watch Joseph?"

Jimmy hung his head but answered, "Yes, ma'am."

When James returned, she had gathered what was left of a bag of beans—probably two or three quarts of dried pintos—and a chunk of salt pork to go with them. James reached to take them from her, but she murmured, "No, please. I want to come."

He hesitated but apparently decided there was little threat. "Come along, then," he said, "but be prepared to take cover quickly if anything goes awry."

"Of course," she answered and carried her small gifts to where the captain waited. Other travelers brought flour, biscuits, hard tack, three live chickens, and a metal jug full of milk. All of these were handed through, first to the captain and then, when his hands were full, to James and one of the other under-captains. Bearing the food, the three men walked slowly forward. Leading his paint pony, the Indian came to meet them.

An odd sort of procession ensued—the Indian accepting a load of food and carrying it back to one of his followers, returning to accept another load and carrying it to the other follower, and returning a final time to take the third load, the one James carried, putting it on his own horse. When all the food had been offered and accepted, the man made an awkward kind of salute. Then he turned and rode slowly away from the camp. The other men followed.

"That was odd," Eliza said as she and James walked back to the wagon.

"Odd, yes, but understandable. These people never had much to eat. Now, with settlers like us using their resources, they must have even more difficulty feeding their families."

Eliza suppressed a shudder. "We've both heard stories," she said.

"Ya mean about the attacks and murders?"

She nodded.

James blew out a sharp breath. "I suspect these people are much like the Aboriginals we knew in Australia, at least as much sinned against as sinning."

Eliza nodded. "Perhaps so. That's why the prophet keeps encouraging the Saints to feed the Indian tribes and offer them baptism and salvation. I hear that Brother Brigham has been sending people out to build Indian missions throughout the Western territories."

James shrugged. "Well, they are descendants of Lehi. The Book of Mormon is their history, not ours."

"Sure'n it makes sense," Eliza answered, "but I must admit, I felt much better about feeding them than about watching them ride down on us the two nights before."

James sighed. "Aye. I can't help but agree."

The camp settled peacefully into the usual evening chores.

By the time they camped along Cottonwood Creek the following evening, they had not seen another Indian, and the camp scouts reported no watchers in the hills.

\*   \*   \*   \*

"So these are the meadows, I suppose." James stood beside Eliza at the crest of the mountain pass. They looked down upon the valley that the Spanish had named *Las Vegas* for its artesian wells and stretches of green.

"It's too bad the Saints have abandoned the mission," Eliza said. "It would be good if we could meet with other members."

"I guess Brother Brigham recalled them during the Utah War," James said. "It must have been a frightening time for the Saints, what with a whole army marching against them." He grinned. "It's made for some good storytelling, though."

Eliza grinned back. During evenings around the campfire, the Saints had entertained one another with stories of the members' adventures in the Rocky Mountains, including the advance of Johnston's Army from the east, a misadventure now known as the Utah War or, sometimes, as Buchanan's Blunder. People enjoyed telling of the Danites, a militia assigned the task of slowing the army while Brother Brigham organized defenses. Forbidden to harm human life, they stampeded horses, destroyed wagons, and burned grass in front of the advancing men, depriving them of feed so they had to go far out of their way to graze their animals.

In certain notable instances, according to stories shared the night before, the Danites had kidnapped officers and left them tied to trees miles to the rear of the troops, further delaying the army, who had to return to rescue their leaders. By the time the army had reached Fort Bridger, they were becoming desperate, and the Mormon colonies had been called upon to send food to keep the men from starving. It had been a well-engineered miracle that had avoided armed conflict.

"I'm grateful it ended well," James said as they got their wagon moving again.

"Aye, er, yes, so am I," Eliza responded, "but I still think it would be pleasant to meet with other Saints."

"We'll be meeting with them soon—in Zion." He squeezed her shoulder.

"Aye. I mean yes. That we will."

"So ye're working on sounding like an American now, are ya?" He walked beside her.

He thought she looked a bit embarrassed. "Well, we are in the Americas now. It seemed a good idea."

"I agree. Think I'll try it myself."

They made their way into the town's few streets. Though it had grown since the silver strike on the Comstock Lode, Las Vegas was still small, barely more than an assay office—set up to test the purity of the miners' ore—a postal office, a mercantile, and a church or two, as well as a few dozen homes and a batch of saloons. The warmth, even this early in the year, gave James a hint of why he'd heard tales of the hellish summers this desert was forced to endure.

When they'd been camped two days, Captain Hudson announced that the coming Sabbath would be for worship, rest, and preparation; the wagons would resume their journey on Monday. James sighed with relief, glad they'd be moving on. He knew Eliza had been eager for the rest, but when he told her of the captain's decision, she seemed as relieved as he was.

\*   \*   \*   \*

### Late April 1860

The camp had forded the Muddy and now traveled eastward along the banks of the Virgin River. Though there had been a brief scare when the travelers realized they'd all been exposed to smallpox on their last day in Las Vegas, there had been no sign of the disease in the camp, and the wagons had made good progress.

"I never knew God made places like this," Eliza said as they meandered through canyons carved by wind and water. "Are ye sure the captain knows his way?"

James laughed. "He's done this many times."

"I don't see how he'd know. Every canyon looks just like every other."

"The captain has his landmarks—not to mention his compass." He grinned.

"Ah, so ye're knowin' it all now, are ye?"

"Ya sounded so Irish just then." He winked at her.

"Tease if ye like, but I still don't understand how he makes his way through here. 'Twould serve ye right if ye found out we're hopelessly lost." She pouted as she went to check on Jimmy, who was sitting with Walton in the back of the wagon.

That evening as the company began to set up camp beside the Virgin River, Eliza looked at the alien landscape, and an odd thought popped into her mind: "Ye're almost there. Ye're nearly home." She shook her head as if to dislodge the thought, but she was learning to listen when those inner promptings spoke.

An hour later she casually approached one of Captain Hudson's men and asked, "Are we almost to the Salt Lake Valley?"

He laughed. "Oh no, not yet! The fort at the *vegas* is the halfway point. We've still a long way to go, ma'am."

"That's odd," she said aloud, but as she turned away, she heard a soft voice speaking in her mind: "Ye're almost home."

Before she slept that evening, she prayed she would know "home" when she saw it. Then, almost as an afterthought, she prayed that James too would know when they found the home God had prepared for them. She felt peaceful as she slipped into sleep and dreamed.

*She walked beside her wagon as she had almost every day since they'd left Lucy Whitney's home—Walton in his shawl wrap close against her, Jimmy playing along the trail with the other children, James leading the oxen and keeping a watch on Joseph, who sat on the back of the lead ox. The wagons were moving steadily, and the canyons were widening into a valley, a lush-looking, fertile valley with plenty of water and green grass. They made a wide turn and came out to a point where the valley opened. Two rivers converged, and she saw the grass growing rich and green beneath cliff banks of the reddest sandstone she had ever seen. She looked at James and he at her. "We're home," he said simply. "This is it."*

Eliza sat straight up, almost bumping her head against the wagon above her. "That can't be," she said aloud, causing James to stir in his sleep. She knew that wasn't the valley of the Great Salt Lake—there was a lake in that valley, after all—and she knew they were still many days' travel from the center of Zion, yet she couldn't deny the feeling. She had asked to know where "home" was, and this place of red and green had been shown her.

"I'll have to ponder it," she said to herself, deciding she wouldn't mention it to James yet. She almost took back that decision when she had the same dream an hour later, exactly as she'd seen it the first time.

Midmorning the next day, Captain Hudson rode his horse alongside the wagon train, delivering a message: "This afternoon we'll come to the place where the Virgin and Santa Clara Rivers converge. We'll be stopping two nights at Fort Santa Clara, so if you have any exchanges to make, this will be the time."

James thanked him, and Eliza felt a rush of excitement. She thought of the place she'd seen in her dream where two rivers converged. Was it possible her dream was already coming true? She almost approached James but decided against it, uncertain what she might say.

As the day went on, the landscape looked more and more familiar. Her heart raced. Then came the moment when the trail turned in a wide arc and came out into a rich, green valley butted up against amazingly red sandstone. Eliza stood staring.

James poked her arm. "If ya close yer mouth, then the bugs can't get in."

She felt the heat rising in her face. "It's just . . . I saw . . ." She cleared her throat. "Have ye ever seen rocks this red?" Suddenly the dream seemed too sacred to share, even with her husband. And anyway, wasn't *he* supposed to tell *her*?

"I've heard there are rocks this red in Australia," he said, completely missing the words she was thinking at him. "I never saw them 'cause they're way in the outback, but I heard of them from some prospectors."

Eliza shook her head and walked on, marveling at the exactness of her dream-vision and waiting for the confirmation that was sure to come.

Nothing happened. For another three hours, she walked beside the wagon, waiting for the big revelation that would put everything into place. Meanwhile, James led the oxen and chatted with other men about how far they were from the Salt Lake Valley and how many days they still had to go before they arrived at the home of the prophets. "Dear Father," Eliza prayed inwardly, "if this is the place where thou would have us stay, please tell my husband." As the miles and the hours passed, she realized she had been praying for a sign, and knowing what the scriptures said about that, she asked forgiveness. Still, she knew it would take a clear message for James to see "home" this far from the Salt Lake Valley. She prayed that if this was their home, her husband would know it—somehow.

They were setting up camp at the fort when she chose to act. She found James chopping wood. "James," she began, "is there anything about this place that looks like home to ye?"

"No," he answered a bit too quickly. "Ya know we're going through to Salt Lake. Why would ya ask such a thing?"

So she told him—about the impression she'd had in the canyon; about the prayer she had spoken before she slept; about the dream and how he was the one who said they were home; about having the same dream a second time; about the moment when she had seen the green against the red rocks and recognized it all.

"So that's why ya were standing with yer mouth open and that astonished look on yer face." James chucked her under her chin, as if she were a sweet but unruly child.

"James, I'm being serious," she said. "Ye need to hear me and to maybe ask the Lord a few questions of yer own."

"Ye've got yer wires crossed. This is not the place where we're supposed to raise our family. This place is barely civilized—and it's far from the prophets. We are not stopping here."

"James—" she started again, but the look on his face quelled her. She turned away, the words she had been ready to say stinging like ashes on her tongue. "Father," she prayed again, "if this is the place we are meant to stay . . ." She sighed, leaving the prayer unfinished. The Lord knew what she was asking. If this was what He wanted, He would see that the message got through. She went to start their dinner.

*    *    *    *

James chopped wood with uncommon intensity, taking his sudden bout of temper out on the logs. He didn't want to stay here, in this burning desert so far away from the prophets. He shook his head. Clearly Eliza was confused. Surely she wasn't receiving revelation that they should stop here—of all places, not *here*.

"Dear Father," he prayed quietly. "Please help Eliza to receive true revelation to understand where we will make our home. Please help me to have the same experience so I may know it as well." He put down the ax and wiped sweat from his brow. The sense of peace that stole over him was the most calming sensation he had felt in days. He murmured a quiet thank-you and went back to chopping, this time with much less fervor.

More than an hour later, James carried a final armload of firewood into the camp, having worked through the last of his harsh emotions. He stopped by the campfire, where Eliza stirred the pot and leaned down to peck her cheek. "Mmmmm," he said, trying to rebuild some peace between them. "Smells wonderful."

Eliza narrowed her eyes. "It's called Home Stew," she said with emphasis.

He laughed aloud. "Ye've made yer point, love." He put both arms around her and nuzzled her ear. "Perhaps we can find a more private place to sleep tonight—"

"James? Eliza?"

James turned with a start, and a grin split his face. "Simon Walker? Is it really ya?"

"My word, man!" Simon said. "I thought we'd never see ye again. Lucy! Come quick! Ye'll never guess who's here." He crossed the clearing to embrace James. When Eliza saw her dear friend Lucy Walker, she squealed and ran into her arms.

For a few minutes, the two couples caught up with one another's lives, and Simon told of how they'd begun to settle in Salt Lake City when they received the call to come to the Indian mission at Fort Santa Clara. "We prayed and we came. And now ye're here too. I do hope ye plan to stay with us."

James looked pointedly at Eliza then back at Simon. Then he looked thoughtfully into the campfire. "I want to live closer to the prophets."

"It was a prophet who called us to come here," Simon answered.

James remembered standing at the dock in Sydney when Simon Walker joked that he and Lucy would go ahead to prepare a place for them. Was it possible they had done just that? "Father," he prayed silently. "If this is the place where we should build our home, please help me to know it." He quietly closed his prayer but felt nothing to change his mind.

When Eliza introduced the Walkers to their growing family, she asked about the Walker children. Lucy called over her shoulder, and two towheaded youngsters appeared. "Ye remember our boys," she said.

"Neville is nearly seven now, Alec is just turned three, and this . . ." She unwrapped her infant. "This is Eliza. She's eight months old."

James saw the look of wonder on his wife's face.

"Ye call her Eliza?" she said.

"Aye." Lucy grinned. "I named her for the dear friend I left behind in Australia."

"Ah, what a sweet thing she is. May I hold her?"

Lucy settled the little girl in Eliza's arms. As James watched, another warm, peaceful feeling stole over him. Lucy said, "Ye know, we've prayed for ye every day, prayed that yer family would gather to Zion, that we'd see ye again."

"The Lord is kind," Eliza answered, looking at the child in her arms.

\* \* \* \*

Eliza cleaned up after their midday meal and looked toward the sun, already lowering in the sky. This was to be their last day in the red rock country. She still felt a strong confirmation that this was home—the home she had longed for and never quite found since leaving her parents in Ireland. At the same time she couldn't deny her conviction that, as the head of the family, it was James's job—and right—to make that decision. Once again she prayed that, if this was the place, James would come to know it and quickly. The wagons were pulling out early tomorrow.

Meanwhile, James sat in the makeshift circle of logs and settlers' chairs. The local leaders had conducted a short meeting and had turned the time over for the singing of hymns. James sang along, barely mindful of the words. His thoughts were on the wagon train and how they would leave in the morning. He'd prayed to know whether this might be his family's future home and had received no answer. He now looked forward to moving on toward the Salt Lake Valley as planned and forgetting Eliza's foolish notions. He knew his family was meant to live close to the prophets. He was ready for the wagons to roll, ready to move on to the city by the Great Salt Lake.

Eliza took his hand, bringing him out of his reverie. She leaned near and whispered in his ear, "Ye should hear what Jimmy just said to me." Whatever it was had clearly pleased her.

"What was that?" James whispered back.

Eliza practically purred. "He says it's great to go to 'real church' again."

"Oh. My." James's throat thickened as he thought of all Jimmy had gone through in recent months, but he managed to whisper, "That's good." He realized they were singing "Come, Come Ye Saints," and he tuned in to the third verse:

*We'll find the place which God for us prepared,*
*Far away in the West,*
*Where none shall come to hurt or make afraid;*
*There the Saints will be blessed.*

He looked at Eliza, who smiled with knowing eyes. Then he knew. Just like that, he *knew*. The confirmation poured through him like warm, flowing water. This was the place which God had prepared for him, for Eliza, for their family. He thought of the thousands of miles they had traveled to come to this place "far away in the West," and he thought of Simon and Lucy preparing the way. In his mind's eye, he could almost see his children growing up here, and he also knew there would be a prophet nearby and a temple and all the blessings of heaven.

He turned to Eliza and whispered, "We're not going with the wagon train tomorrow. We're staying here."

She gave a little squeal, covered her mouth with both her hands, and squeezed his arm, leaning her head against him, happy tears soon dampening his sleeve.

"We'll be happy here," he said.

"Yes," she answered. "We've come home."

The wagon train rolled out the next morning as scheduled. James and Eliza stood by the wayside, waving as their friends moved on toward the Great Salt Lake. Arthur and Anna Raft stood beside James and Eliza, having made the same decision to stay. Simon and Lucy Walker also stood with them. As the last of the wagons disappeared around the bend, Eliza turned to her loved ones and welcomed them home at last.

# Epilogue

IN THE SPRING OF 1861, Brigham Young came to the confluence of the Virgin and Santa Clara to meet with local leaders. With the coming of war to the Eastern states, he wanted a new colony in Zion's Dixie where cotton, grapes, and other warm-weather crops could grow in abundance, increasing the Saints' self-sufficiency. He declared the beginnings of a new city where he would build his winter home, thus fulfilling James's inspiration that they would live near the prophet. Soon, James was one of the foremost shopkeepers in the new city of St. George. It wasn't long before Eliza was invited to learn to play the tabernacle's beautiful grand piano, which had been carried by sea from New York.

In 1871, Brigham Young conducted the groundbreaking for the St. George Temple. By then Eliza had borne the rest of their family: first another boy, Edmund Simon, and then three daughters—Molly, Lucy, and Anna. When the temple was completed some six years later, it was the first to be finished after the Saints were forced to abandon their beloved temple in Illinois. A week following its April 1877 dedication, James and Eliza Martin were sealed as an eternal family together with their seven children. They went on to do proxy ordinance work for their parents and other departed loved ones and were sealed to their birth families as well.

Although they never saw Ed or Molly again, they stayed in regular correspondence. When Mary turned sixteen, her father offered her either a London season or a trip to Utah to visit her Auntie Eliza and Uncle James. She quickly chose the latter, traveled to St. George, and joined the LDS Church. On the day following the Martin family's temple sealing, James William Martin Jr. took Mary Elizabeth Welsh as his wife.

# Notes

PEOPLE HAVE ASKED ME HOW much of this is true. These events all happened to real people even if they didn't all happen to my family, but the tale is based loosely on the lives of my great-great-grandparents, Henry Gale and Sarah Wills. Henry, like James, was born in Box, Wiltshire County, England, on October 18, 1818. He was sixteen when he traveled to Australia in search of work. Sarah Wills was the daughter of Martin Wills and Elizabeth McAudra, born February 2, 1822. Henry and Sarah met in Sydney and were married April 18, 1844. At the time of their wedding, Henry worked as a shopkeeper. They did not experience the marital stresses of different faiths as both were Protestants from childhood.

*Q: Why did you change the names?*

A: Eliza(beth) and James were the first two children born to Henry and Sarah. Their firstborn child, Elizabeth Gale, was my grandmother's mother. She was eight when her family joined the Church and emigrated to America. Her younger brother, James, was six, and it is through his history that we know so much about them.

*Q: Why did you change the dates?*

A: I wanted to fictionalize the two missionaries who taught James and Eliza, rather than sticking to the history of John Murdock and Charles W. Wandell, the first missionaries to Australia in 1852. By making the time a little later, I was able to imagine the missionaries I needed to teach James and Eliza. I also wanted to add the gold strike as an element, making Ed Welsh, who is purely fictional, an integral part of the tale. By putting the story at the time of the Australian gold rush, I was able to conjure up a wealthy friend to help James and Eliza through the rough spots.

*Q: What other parts of the story are true to your family's history?*

A: It's often said that truth is stranger than fiction. In this story, I've kept the stranger elements that are true and taken directly from my family's history. For example, Sarah Wills really was born on a ship in Mayo harbor, and she really did give birth to her third child, Wandell Pacific, during their sea crossing. Also, the story about Little Jimmy being lost in the desert comes directly from James Gale's personal history and can be found at http://gale.surnames.com/history/galehistory.htm.

*Q: Are other parts of the story true?*

A: Bits and pieces are true to history. Some examples: (a) The Australian gold rush, complete with strikes on the Burra-Burra and in the Blue Mountains and a battle at the Eureka Stockade, is well documented; (b) The Carrington Event of 1859 was the largest solar storm in recorded history with elaborate displays of northern and southern lights; (c) The wreck of the *Admella* happened just as mentioned and is still the worst sea disaster in Australian history; (d) the *Trieste* sailed with a load of wheat but at a different time. The events of this sea voyage are borrowed from other adventures on other ships; (e) the founding of Fort Santa Clara is not exactly as mentioned here. In fact, Santa Clara predated St. George by only a short time, but the mission was there as early as 1854. St. George was founded in 1861 as Brigham Young's winter home and as a place for the Latter-day Saints to grow cotton, grapes, and silkworms, making them less dependent on outside trade; (f) references to LDS colonies in San Bernardino and Las Vegas, the Utah War, the Danites, and other history from the period are as recorded; Elder Lowe, who teaches Lucy Whitney in chapter 16, is a quick reference to my late mother-in-law's father, who served a mission in Southern California in the early 1920s.

*Q: What did you learn from writing this history?*

A: I developed an even deeper appreciation for my ancestors, who didn't do things in the usual manner. There were many Latter-day Saints who didn't cross the Atlantic, take wagons along the Platte River, or cross the Rocky Mountains into the new state of Deseret. Mine were among those who had to travel east to get to the place which God had prepared "far away in the West." I'm grateful to them all, however they came. If they hadn't built up the kingdom, there would be no place in it for any of us who have come along since.

## A FINAL NOTE

When my great-grandmother, Elizabeth Gale Kartchner, was a grown and married woman, she received her patriarchal blessing. In it was a promise that her sons would one day return to the land of her birth to teach the gospel. My husband and I saw that prophecy fulfilled in December 1992 when our son Adam began his service in the Australia Melbourne Mission.

# Discussion Questions

How does the Martins' story differ from typical stories of English and Irish immigrants to America? Which elements differ and which are the same? How did your family come to be in the place of your birth, and what events have brought you to where you are now?

1. Historians speak of immigration being driven by both "push" and "pull." Some of each are present in the story of the Martins. Consider both the forces that pushed them out of Australia and those that pulled them to America and finally to Southern Utah. What push-and-pull forces have driven you and those around you?

2. Belief systems both unite and divide the characters in this book. In what ways do religious differences still unite and divide? When people hurt others in the name of religion, is the religious belief responsible or does the fault lie with the individual?

3. Friendship is an important theme of this story. James and Eliza feel upheld and sustained by some of their friendships but damaged and betrayed by others. What place does friendship have in your life? What do you see as the obligations of friendship? Family ties are also important. Which of James and Eliza's decisions are influenced by family love and connection? What ties bind you to your family?

4. In the century and a half since this story took place, much has changed in human life and technology. Consider how long it takes for James's and Eliza to cross from Sydney to Southern Utah. How long would it take to make the same journey today?

What are some other obvious differences? As you look ahead, what projections can you imagine for the coming century? What might happen to accelerate or impede those changes?

5. The Martins are motivated not just by push and pull or connections to friends and family but also by their belief in personal revelation; they believe in a personal God who hears and answers their prayers. Think of times when you have felt prompted. How did you interpret the experience? In what ways has your life been influenced by these "spiritual" experiences—large or small, amazing or mundane?

6. Bigotry, prejudice, and misconception are important themes in this story, including ethnic, cultural, and religious bigotry in various forms. Point out some instances of each. How are these similar to what you have seen or experienced? Why do you think such incidents occur? What can be done to limit such incidents and their effects?

# About the Author

SUSAN AYLWORTH STARTED HER FIRST book when she was nine. "It was called *Buff, The Proud Stallion*, a rip-off of *Black Beauty*. I wrote eight whole pages." For her fifth-grade career day, she stated her ambition to become "a rich and famous author." Decades later, she is pleased to have achieved the *author* part of that goal. A former university professor, she enjoys researching backgrounds and careers for her novels. "It's one way to live many lives at once."

Servant to two spoiled cats, she lives in Northern California with Roger, her husband of forty-four years, who is also a writer. She loves hanging out with her seven children, their perfect-for-them spouses, and twenty-three grandchildren. When she can't be with her blood family, she hangs with her fictional characters, the children of her mind. *Eastward to Zion* is her lucky thirteenth published novel.

"I love travel, great music, and perfect raspberry jam," she says, "and every author loves good reviews." She points out that four- and five-star reviews are highly valued in the publishing industry. "You can do every good book a favor by giving it a strong Goodreads review."

"I always love hearing from readers, especially those who relate to the characters in my stories." Reach her at www.susanaylworth.com or at susan.aylworth.author@gmail.com, follow her @SusanAylworth, or